COUNT ME IN

AN UGLY DUCKLING RETELLING

SAMANTHA GAIL

STAR PUBLISHING

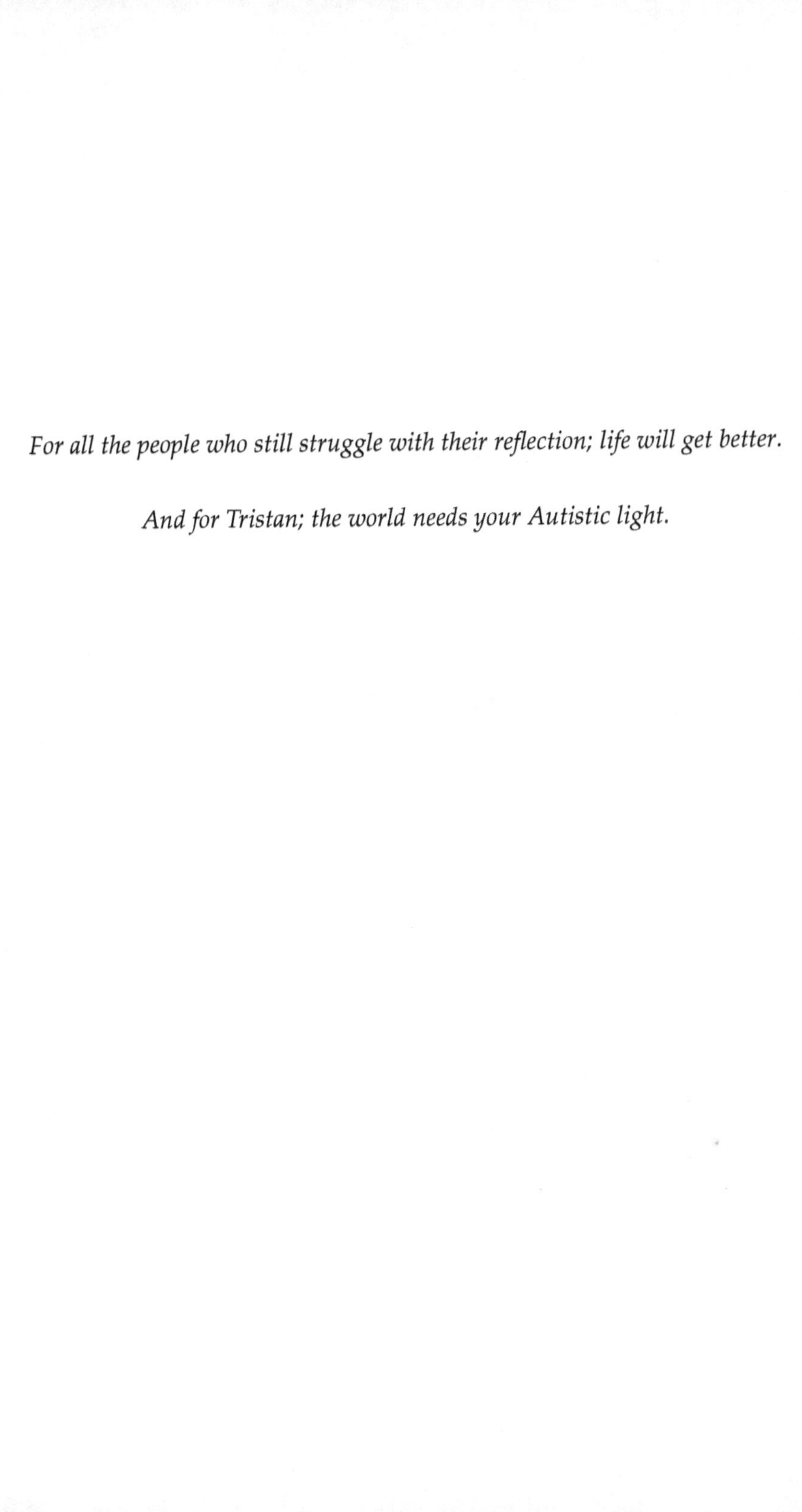

For all the people who still struggle with their reflection; life will get better.

And for Tristan; the world needs your Autistic light.

CONTENTS

TRIGGER WARNINGS

Please proceed with caution as the following book contains graphic scenes and content that may be troubling for some readers. Always read with your mental health in mind.

Triggers include:

-Suicidal thoughts and ideation

-Thoughts, actions, and obsessions associated with an eating disorder, including but not limited to: purging, counting calories, body dysmorphia, self-loathing, and mirror avoidance

-Emotional abuse and manipulation

-Psychological abuse

-Physical abuse

-References to past child abuse

-Depression

-Anxiety

-Violent rage

-Drug use

-Gun violence

-Stalking

-Sexual shaming

If you or someone you love suffers from disordered eating and/or body dysmorphia, help is available. Please visit the website below for more information on symptoms, resources, and treatment options.

And always remember: your weight does not define your worth.

www.nationaleatingdisorders.org

PROLOGUE
MAGGIE

PEOPLE SAY that beauty is only skin deep. And that's probably true. I'd never call myself a scholar by any means, so it's not like I have the facts and figures to back it up, but for placing such little value in the concept, people sure chase beauty around until their bank accounts run dry and their bodies break. My whole life circled around the idea that I needed to be beautiful. I had to look a certain way and attract a certain kind of attention. My mother drilled it into my head from the moment I could speak. And beauty of any kind wasn't worth it unless others noticed. You had to have a man validate your beauty or it just didn't count.

But no matter what I did, their validation never made me *feel* beautiful.

From beauty pageants to makeup tutorials, I tried it all. It didn't matter what I had to do to get a boy's attention. My life depended on it the way an addict's depended on their next fix. Girls with reputations like the one I developed in high school didn't get any respect in a small town like River's Run, Georgia. People looked at me differently. They called me everything from "boy crazy" to "slut." Names that hurt from people I cared about, which only fueled the need to have someone validate my worth. But no teenage boy alive could've done that, no matter how quickly and easily he charmed me out of my panties. I was a wreck on the inside and that bled into my outward appearance quickly.

By the time I realized the damage I had done to my mind, heart, and body, I was too far gone. I lost myself until the person staring back in the mirror was no longer my own reflection. It took a long time for me to recognize the darkness surrounding me, and when I finally clawed my way out, I felt like I finally breathed air for the first time. I wouldn't wish that feeling on my worst enemy.

I changed. And it saved my life. But all changes come with a price.

I'm not sure exactly when the sting of disappointing my mother ebbed away, but I know it only happened because of Zeke Hayes. He was the first person in my life to see me—the real me—hiding underneath all the layers of makeup, hair color, and insecurity. Somehow, without even really trying, he salvaged what was left of my fractured soul and gave me the courage I needed to love the pieces back together.

Beauty might only be skin deep. But love? In its purest, unfiltered form? That shit seeps into your bones, right down into your very being.

And finding that kind of love with a man like Ezekiel Hayes? Well, you could count me in.

CHAPTER 1
THE DECISION
MAGGIE

No matter how many times I packed my stuff, most of it wound up in garbage bags. I learned at a young age to never form an attachment to anything because there was a good chance it would be long gone by the next move. And I had moved a *lot* so far in my nineteen years of life. River's Run was by far the only place I could call home because it was the only town I lived in for more than a year. Once we moved here and I made instant friends with Celeste Hendricks and her boyfriend-but-she-wouldn't-call-him-that-friend Wesley Madden, I drew a line in the sand and told my mother that my days of packing up and moving were gone. We were staying put, whether she liked it or not.

That may have been a blessing or a curse because it resulted in a lot of nights at home by myself. My mom kept our tiny apartment, but dipped out, sometimes for weeks at a time, to go stay at her latest boyfriend's place. And there was always a new boyfriend. River's Run's close proximity to an Army base meant there was a revolving door of men at Diana Eaton's disposal.

It was what led to my parents' divorce. Monogamy, conceptually, sounded like a great idea to my mom, but it in practice…well, let's just say my dad was better off. He found someone else as committed to the idea of marriage as him, and they lived happily in southern Florida with their kids. I became an afterthought, someone he conveniently forgot about after my half-siblings arrived.

Not that I could begrudge him. Wasn't finding a life partner the sole reason of life? Nobody wanted to weather the storm alone.

Which was why I found myself currently shoving all of my belongings back in garbage bags while my best and only friend, Celeste Hendricks, sat on my bed with her toddler, Iris, in her lap. Poor Celeste became a mom at only sixteen, and although I did everything I could to help her, she made motherhood look terrifying. Celeste hadn't slept a full night in years and constantly teetered on the edge of a nervous breakdown. Iris was a good kid, too, so I couldn't imagine being a mother to a little monster like some of our classmates now were.

"I don't understand," Celeste said again, cradling her forehead in her hand. "Where exactly are you going to go?"

"I'm not sure yet," I admitted. "But anywhere has to be better than here."

"Maggie, that's insane. You *just* passed your boards!"

I nodded. "And that will make it easier for me to find a job so I can land on my feet."

The results from the Georgia Cosmetology Board sat open on my dresser. I passed with flying colors and would receive my official cosmetology license in the mail within the next few days. Celeste had become the test subject of many attempts to master the art of hair color, haircuts, and extensions.

"All I'm saying is, maybe find the job first so you can save up a little money and then get a place of your own. Don't just run away." Celeste fixed me with what I now called her Mom Glare, much to her dismay.

"Hey, that might work on my honorary daughter here, but that's not gonna work on me." To break her scrutiny, I plucked Iris off her lap and tossed the giggling toddler into the air before catching her around the waist. Iris' laughter served to soften Celeste's expression. A rarity, these days.

"I can't stay here, Celeste, you know that," I reminded her quietly. "Diana's gotten worse."

Once I started high school, I ceased to call my mother by anything other than her real name. She actually preferred it that way, saying it made us seem more like sisters, thereby making her feel younger. It was hard to call someone you couldn't respect a title that held so much weight to it. I saw firsthand how much Celeste still missed her mom, even seven years after her death. Diana didn't deserve that kind of reverence from me.

"Why can't you just tell me what happened?" my best friend prompted, sending an involuntary shudder down my spine.

The memory of the night before when I left my room to refill my glass of water only to find Diana and her latest flavor of the month making out on the couch made my heart race. She straddled him, their gyrations clearly indicating what was to come, but the man broke away from her long enough to flirtatiously peruse my body.

"You're legal now, right?" he growled at me. "Care to join? I've never had a mother and daughter at once."

Then the humiliation washed over me as my mother looked up at me with interest, as though the idea intrigued her rather than repulsed her. I had never scurried back into my room so fast, locking the door and dragging my dresser in front of it just for good measure. Thankfully both of them were gone by the time I got up this morning.

Celeste had enough on her plate. Ever since we graduated high school, her evil stepmother made her work from sun up to sun down at their family's diner. She worked herself to the point of exhaustion, never spending more than a few minutes a day with Iris. The only reason Celeste could stop by now was due to the restaurant's annual pest treatment that closed it down for the day. I couldn't burden her with the knowledge of just how low my mother stooped.

"You trust me, right? So when I tell you that it's past the point of no return, I need you to believe it." Hopefully that satisfied her because I had no intent of airing last night's events out loud.

She sighed, taking Iris from my arms to cuddle her. Although I knew Celeste would never admit it, Iris' resemblance to her dad, Wesley, acted like a phantom. Even I missed Wes, and I didn't have a baby with him.

Celeste never told me exactly what happened or why he left, only that she never wanted to see him again. Those words sounded a lot like they came from Desiree's mouth, but it was no secret that I didn't like her stepmother. Nobody in River's Run did.

"Did I tell you that Desiree fired Marla? Said she didn't need Marla's two cents' worth on all the restaurant's business." Tears welled in her eyes and Celeste pulled her daughter closer. Marla was like a mother to Celeste, being her real mom's best friend and all. Once her mom died and Celeste's dad was left to run the restaurant by himself, Marla stepped in, giving up her job at the canning factory to fill in the gaps Rachel Hendricks left. For Desiree to fire Marla…that wouldn't sit well with any of the folks in River's Run.

"I guess Desiree better be ready for all the hate coming her way," I added thoughtfully. I didn't know how The Comfy Cushion, their restaurant, could survive without Marla.

"Marla said something about the business space underneath her apartment being available. I think she might open a bakery or something. You know how good her sweets are," Celeste commented. "Maybe she would let you stay with her if you were willing to help out with the rent. That would at least give you some time to get things straightened out."

It certainly wasn't a bad idea. Marla should go down in history as the prime example of tough love, but she always made me feel welcomed and cared for. Certainly more than Diana Eaton ever did.

"I'll consider it," I hedged. "But the bottom line is, I have to get out of this place. I can't live here anymore."

Celeste plopped Iris down on the floor and handed the girl a doll. "Then I better help you pack or you're gonna be here all day."

I grinned at her. "And this is why I love you."

She gave me a flash of her signature soft smile. "Hand me a garbage bag. I'm gonna try to tackle your desk."

I grimaced. "Don't judge me for all the yearbook photos with hearts drawn in."

Celeste rolled her eyes. "Boy crazy Maggie. I know!"

My heart felt hollow to hear her call me that, but I kept the grin plastered to my face. Being "boy crazy," as she called it, never led to anything more than heartache. And that organ can only be broken so many times before it gives up altogether.

CHAPTER 2
THE LONER

ZEKE

"Maxwell! Bledsoe! Get in formation!" The commander's eyes pierced through the two Privates who raced to their places in line. I frowned, recognizing the last names of the two newest arrivals in my unit. Their behavior just ensured I would get an ass chewing at the end of formation, meaning I would have to give *them* an ass chewing. Not the best way to start my morning.

"Alright, I realize this is a four day weekend," Captain Durham bellowed. "Don't do anything stupid! One wrong move can have permanent consequences! Check in with your chain of command for reporting instructions. HOOAH!"

We all screamed HOOAH in response and stayed at attention until we returned the captain's salute and the squad leaders dismissed everyone. Even though I was only a sergeant, I had been plucked into a squad leader position, and I hated every second of it. Bearing the responsibility of ten soldiers felt wrong, like a shoe that didn't quite fit. But that was what happened when your mentor became a general in the United States Army. General James Leggett tended to make things happen his way, whether you wanted them to or not.

"Maxwell! Bledsoe!" I barked. "Can you give me a good reason why you were late to formation this morning?"

Both Privates, so new they hadn't even earned an insignia for their uniforms, hung their heads. They had only arrived from training school a few days prior.

"We got lost," Bledsoe offered. "We're still learning where everything is on post."

I figured as much, but I couldn't let them off the hook. Any whiff of leniency and Leggett would call me into his office before I drew my next breath. "Then you need to leave early enough to look. It's basically land navigation. I assume you passed that course in basic training or else you wouldn't be here."

Both men looked ashamed of themselves, and I internally cringed. This was the worst part of my job. "You'll both have an added staff duty this month. Don't be late again."

I spun on my heel to escape the looks of despair and incredulity I knew the members of my squad wore. My reputation as a hard ass meant I had to remain firm, keeping everyone in my unit an arm's length away. That had never been hard for me. I could no sooner conversate with an alien lifeform than I could my peers.

But it gets awfully lonely spending an entire life by yourself. When I turned twenty-one on my last birthday, I spent the day alone in my barracks room without a single text or phone call. Even Leggett, as my mentor, didn't bother. "Sentimentality breeds ineptitude," he always said. Birthdays weren't meant to be acknowledged.

And most days, I learned to live with being alone. I accepted it the same way I accepted that my freedom was no longer my own the day I enlisted in the Army. It was only difficult during moments like this where I recognized that I was being too harsh, but I didn't know any other way to handle it.

Captain Durham approached me and I saluted him as I brought myself to attention. "At ease, Sergeant," he snapped. "What kind of a shitty squad are you running if you can't get your guys into formation on time?"

"I'm sorry, sir," I replied, taking great pain to keep my voice even and my expression blank. "I've already addressed the issue and both men will serve extra staff duty this month. It won't happen again."

"Be sure that it doesn't!" Durham snapped. "You're a good soldier, Hayes, but that doesn't make you a good leader. Don't disappoint me again!"

"Yes, sir!" I nodded once, which satisfied Durham enough to leave. That was probably the quickest I'd ever gotten out of an ass chewing before.

My phone buzzed in my pocket.

> CONTROL YOUR MEN BEFORE THEY CONTROL YOU.

Of course Leggett already knew about my guys' fuck up. The man had eyes and ears everywhere, especially wherever I was concerned.

Sighing, I pocketed the phone again and headed into the office to grab my gear. Today consisted of marksman training at the gun range, a task at which I not only excelled, but allowed my mind the freedom to wander. It was exactly what I needed.

Except, when I arrived at the range and saw the motley assortment of soldiers assembled, the prospect of enjoyment disappeared. Part of my job as an Army Ranger included training at marksmanship because all Army Rangers were required to achieve expert level. New recruits had to hit a certain percentage of targets, and I had to help them get there. Soldiers from outside our battalion had been sent over, likely the work of General Leggett, who liked to posit my abilities as if they were a direct reflection of him.

With just a single glance, I could already tell these soldiers weren't up to snuff.

I sighed wearily. It was going to be a long day.

* * *

By the time the sun scaled the Western horizon, I wanted to yank my hair out by the roots. Either this was the biggest group of incompetent idiots to ever enlist or my reputation proved to be impossible to work against.

One soldier visibly shook in her boots if I so much as looked at her. None of them would achieve expert marksman qualification without a *lot* of help.

Needless to say, everyone in the group walked out to the parking lot with slumped shoulders and frown lines at the end of the day. Five of them clustered together around a battered SUV, likely a carpool where everyone lived in the same barracks. They parked just one car away from my pickup truck and although I knew it wouldn't help my mood to hear them complain about me, I slowed my steps and fumbled with my keys to eavesdrop.

"Yeah, man, Cremshaw's hooking up with this girl off post and she's throwing a party this weekend. It's gonna be lit!" one soldier said. He knocked back a Redbull like it was water.

"And she doesn't care who shows up?" asked the woman who shook from the sight of me. Anderczak, if I remembered her uniform correctly. "We can all seriously go?"

The first soldier nodded. "I swear. Cremshaw said anything goes and this chick has a lot of friends. Got me hopin' to find my own little Georgia peach!" He thrust his hips suggestively, indicating what kind of peach he meant. His friends all laughed.

"Okay, then I guess we'll be there." The female soldier next to Anderczak gestured to her companion. "You said it's that white house at the end of Bowers Road?"

Just as the air humping soldier nodded, one of his companions slapped his chest and pointed towards me. All of them stood up straighter and looked at me expectantly.

"Sorry, sir," one of them said. "We didn't see you standing there."

"It's fine. You're going to a party?" I had no idea why I asked. Parties were never my scene.

They all exchanged a look, clearly battling over how much to tell me. Rambunctious parties were exactly the kind of thing that got young soldiers in trouble. They were the reason we needed to have quarterly safety briefs and trainings against sexual harassment, drug use, and alcohol poisoning. Admitting they planned to go to one that could then lead to someone's arrest, drunk driving, or any other number of punishable offenses wasn't wise, especially to a non-commissioned officer like myself.

"One of the guys in the barracks is dating a local," a soldier named Kreugla stated. "We were just discussing whether or not we were gonna go. You're welcome to stop by, sir. It won't get wild."

Reading body language usually stumped me, but I was nearly certain that the looks of horror they flashed him meant the rest of the group didn't want to extend an invitation to me.

"Thanks," I replied. "I may just do that. To make sure it doesn't get out of hand for any of you," I added.

The panic stricken looks that crossed their faces told me the thinly veiled threat worked. Hopefully it meant they thought twice before doing something stupid. I hated filling out the paperwork, and even if they weren't my soldiers, I would still spare their chain of command if I could.

Once I settled in my truck, I rolled down the windows just enough to hear their argumentative whispers above the roar of the truck's engine.

"Yo, why would you invite him, man?!"

"That's *the* Sergeant Hayes—are you nuts?" the dark haired female demanded. "Everyone knows he's a freak!"

Kreugla shrugged. "I didn't want to act like we had something to hide. He could run back to Leggett and then we'd all be fucked!"

Anderczak tilted her head thoughtfully. "Why do all the hot ones have to be so weird? I'd bend like a pretzel for him."

The group broke out in laughter, which served as my cue to pull out of the parking spot.

I frowned as their words cut me deep. But they were right. I never belonged. And I likely never would.

CHAPTER 3
THE ULTIMATUM
MAGGIE

PACKING up my room served as a great excuse to throw away all the excess clutter I'd accumulated over the past few years. Once Iris started getting fussy for her afternoon nap, Celeste left and I took bags upon bags out to the dumpster behind the building. Our apartment complex was the only one in River's Run, two buildings that sat perpendicular to one another, with a shared parking lot in the middle. Most of the residents worked at the canning factory, the biggest employer in Smithson County. The building supervisor hadn't done much to maintain the units, and over half of them sat empty to disrepair.

When I compared it to the comfortable home that Celeste had, or even Wesley's great aunt Shirley's house back when we were younger, I couldn't help but sigh. My lot in life seemed to be that of the poor outcast. I never quite fit in and the places I lived in tended to demonstrate that I operated in the gray areas of society. The roughnecks, the pariahs, the people who created the base of the societal foundation that everyone refused to see. I longed for beauty, for recognition. Just once I wanted someone to notice me in a way that didn't make my insides squirm. But that wasn't how life worked for people like me.

Just as I reached the open hallway for my building, Spencer Church hopped out of a parked vehicle to my left. He was two classes ahead of mine in high school with a terrible reputation, especially with young girls. Smoke wafted out behind him, and I could just make out the face of Max Daniels, one of my first crushes in River's Run, in the driver's seat.

"Hey there, Mags," Spencer called, his voice oily in a way that made my skin break out in goosebumps. "You want in on this action?"

"No, thanks." Knowing Spencer, his weed came from an unreliable dealer who laced it with something else just for the fun of it.

"Aw, c'mon. You don't think we forgot all those times we had fun before." Spencer looked at me expectantly, as if the very memory of that "fun" would make me change my mind.

It had been anything but.

I stumbled to the door in stiletto pumps I borrowed from Diana. This was my first high school party, and from what I overheard Hilary Stanbrooke say in the girls' bathroom, freshman almost never got invited to Lola Mae Kravitz's house. She was easily the most popular senior at Smithson High. I had no idea how I managed to get an invite, but with Celeste and Wesley gone every weekend up to Atlanta, I needed the reason to get out of the house.

"You're wearing that?" Diana asked from the kitchen. She had the food scale out to measure the ingredients of her salad. No more than 400 calories per meal, that was her rule.

Confused, I looked down at the jean mini-skirt and plain pink polo shirt I had on. "What's wrong with it?"

Diana shrugged innocently. "I guess I just admire your confidence. That color makes you look so red in the face. I wouldn't be caught dead in it if I had your complexion." She flashed me a quick smile. "But that's what's so great about you, Maggie. You never care about things like that."

Was my complexion really that bad? I didn't want to wear a color that made me look ugly.

"I'll go change," I replied.

My mom nodded. "Put on something black. It's so slimming!"

After changing quickly into a ruched black top that Diana insisted hid my belly fat, I tottered down the two flights of stairs to the ground floor of our apartment. A group of teens from our apartment complex had also been invited to Lola Mae's and they offered to let me ride along.

Except, when I reached the red Pontiac, I counted far too many bodies for the five available seats.

"Don't worry, Mags," Spencer Church, a junior with the most chiseled jaw I'd ever seen, winked at me conspiratorially. "There's plenty of room on my lap."

Oh my god, SPENCER FRICKIN CHURCH was flirting with me!

Dopamine flooded my system, and I almost wished Diana had come down, too, so she could see the sexiest guy in the group paying attention to me. She could eat her heart out.

"Okay," I replied with a breathy giggle.

Spencer slapped his buddy in the chest, wiggling his eyebrows in a way that communicated something in guy code. I followed him around to the driver's side where the car's owner, Andy Figgs, held the seat forward so we could climb in. Spencer folded himself in first before pulling me in to sit on his lap. There wasn't enough room to maneuver myself up and pull down my mini skirt that had ridden just a little too high for comfort. Spencer didn't seem to mind and instead wrapped his large hand around my thigh, his long fingers tracing lightly along the sensitive skin near my hemline. Something hard wedged itself between my ass cheeks, but it wasn't until Spencer shifted to lean against the window that I realized what it was. The knowledge that Spencer Church had a hard on underneath me was as terrifying as it was exhilarating.

"You're so sexy," he breathed in my ear, pulling the hair away from my neck. "You wore this skirt just to tease me, didn't you? I think it's only fair that I do the same."

His other hand came up between my thighs, a single finger grazing the front of my cotton panties. I jumped in surprise, making everyone in the car turn my way.

"Don't say a word, Mags," Spencer whispered in my ear. "They don't need to know what a dirty, little slut you are for me."

Spencer's words made my blood run cold. I remembered my father hurtling that term at my mom when he found proof of yet another affair. The cycle was always the same; she'd beg and plead with him to stay, swearing that if they moved to a new place where she didn't know anybody, the cheating would stop. Only it never did.

"Hiccups," I mumbled to everyone, my cheeks flushing pink. Spencer's

friend from earlier, someone I knew on sight but not by name, smirked at him over my shoulder.

This time his finger pressed harder against my panties, parting the lips of my pussy under the cotton.

"Please don't." I turned to him, my eyes pleading with him to stop. No matter how good looking Spencer was, I didn't want our first experience together to be in a car full of teenagers. Fear made my breath hitch, which he noticed right away.

A sly grin crossed his face. "Oh, you're gonna have to pay a rider's tax somehow, Mags," he promised. "You didn't think we'd let you ride along for free, did you?"

Once we got to the party that night, I had my first experience giving a guy a blow job. Spencer swore his friends wouldn't take me home until I did it. The only mercy he granted was allowing me to fumble my way through it in a darkened room without an audience. I never used him for a ride to a party again after that.

And somehow even four years later he managed to make me feel as dirty now as he did then.

I glared at him. "Hard pass."

Diana's car pulled into the lot, parking on the other side of the walkway, and saved me from having to continue the conversation.

"Hi, there!" She smiled suggestively at Spencer as she got out of the car, batting her eyelashes in a way that made me want to gag. One half of his mouth turned up as if he enjoyed getting the attention of woman twice his age. As soon as Diana's gaze turned to me, all of her charm disappeared.

"Lord alive, Maggie, you're wearing that in public?" If my mom owned a set of pearls, she would've been clutching them at that moment. She scanned my body from head to toe, shaking her head in disapproval.

I glanced down at the simple tank top and dark gray sweatpants I wore. Since I had been cleaning and packing all morning, it wasn't like I wanted to put on good clothes. My hair, that Diana always insisted I keep long despite my requests to cut it, had been shoved under one of my dad's ratty baseball caps that he left behind.

Diana sighed. "I guess if I could get away without wearing a bra like you, I wouldn't bother dressing up either. C'mon, we've got stuff to talk about."

From the corner of my eye, I could see Spencer trying to hold back his laughter as I tried not to burst in flames from embarrassment. I stomped up the stairs behind her and secretly hoped that she noticed. I'd love a reason to pick a fight with her at the moment.

Once I shut the door behind me, Diana headed straight for the fridge and grabbed the bottle of Tylenol we kept in the cabinet on top. She guzzled a water bottle as she swallowed down the pills and I sank onto one of the kitchen chairs across the room. The apartment was small, but it had an open concept that allowed her to see me from all angles. That was why I kept to my room any time Diana came home.

"We need to talk about last night," she said.

A faint flicker of hope swelled in my chest. My plan had been to leave the apartment by the time she came back, but maybe this would be better.

"Yeah. We do," I agreed after she didn't say anything else.

Diana chewed on her bottom lip, eyes darting everywhere but my face. The flicker of hope snuffed out as I recognized her guilty ticks for what they were. Whatever was about to come out of her mouth wouldn't be pretty.

"You know I wouldn't have let Tyson say any of that stuff to you if I wasn't drunk, right? I swear, that's all it was, Maggie!"

Swallowing thickly, I nodded. My mom didn't drink very often, which made her a total lightweight when it came to alcohol. One daiquiri was enough to send her to bed for the night. If they had any drinks last night, she was likely pretty wasted during our encounter.

"But when we woke up and went to breakfast this morning, Tyson brought it up again. Like, he genuinely thinks I'm gonna have a three way with my boyfriend and my daughter!" Diana huffed, blowing her bangs off her forehead and folding her arms over her chest.

I repressed a shiver at the image. I didn't want to think about it.

"Anyways, it just got me thinking," continued Diana, "you're nineteen now, so it's probably time for you to start thinking about moving out. I let a lot of things slide after you graduated because you were doing that hair school stuff. But you haven't given me a free cut or nothing! You tried everything out on Celeste, and she doesn't even care about what she looks like. It's not like she has a man to impress!" Diana paused for several seconds as though steeling herself to deliver her next sentence. "I just can't share my apartment with a woman who's more like my competition than my friend."

A torrent of anger, disbelief, and shame circled in my brain as I tried to form a response. Anything I could think of to say got caught on my tongue. Diana wanted me to leave because her sleazeball boyfriend hit on me? Like I would ever let a guy like that touch me!

"I haven't said anything to Tyrell—" I started.

"Tyson!" she corrected me with a snap.

I rolled my eyes. "Whatever! I would never, *ever* do anything with him. I don't want him."

Diana sighed wearily, like the entire world's problems rested on her shoulders. "If it's not him, it'll be someone else. Let's face it, Maggie, you're grown now! It's only a matter of time before we want the same guy! Do you wanna let *a man* come between us? Is that the kind of relationship we're gonna have?"

Grinding my back teeth, I felt like I was on the verge of murder. "A man already did."

CHAPTER 4
THE ORDER

As the post commander, General Leggett had the authority to control my schedule as he saw fit. From the moment you sign your name on that enlistment contract, the U.S. government owns you. They tell you where to eat, sleep, and shit as well as everything you're required to do in between. Many people thought having Leggett as my mentor gave me special privileges that other soldiers could only dream of.

They were wrong.

Leggett dictated every aspect of my career, right down to the position I accepted in the recruiter's office, the command I served under, and which barracks I lived in. When I graduated from training school after basic, it was no surprise that my orders sent me to Hunter Army Airfield in Georgia, where General Leggett had recently been appointed post commander. Nor did I question the strings he undoubtedly pulled to get me into Army Ranger school far earlier than any other candidate. A fast track in rank followed, which he viewed as a direct reflection of the wisdom he had instilled in me, not the blood, sweat, and tears I put my body through to achieve such a thing.

In all three years of service, I had been required to report to his office every Friday morning. Four day weekends like this one didn't matter. At eight a.m. on the dot I walked into his office. I was never late. I knew better than to risk it.

After a gruff "Come in!" followed my knock at the door, I entered his office. He sat behind a desk covered in papers and maps and did not so much as glance in my direction. I took a few steps away from the door and waited. Patience was the first test.

"Explain to me why I vouched for you to become a squad leader if you cannot even get your soldiers to morning formation on time," Leggett barked without looking up. He notated something on the map in front of him before pulling another stack of papers in front.

Leggett always liked it better when I let him get the anger out of his system, then answered. He didn't actually want me to speak yet.

"If you act weak, your men will walk all over you. Is that what you want? To be weak?" He finally looked up, a sneer darkening his face. Ruthless black eyes stared coldly at me.

I remained as still as a statue, keeping my focus just above his right ear. My hands remained firmly clasped behind my back, which was the only reason he couldn't see the way they clenched at his insult.

An Army Ranger was never weak. My body had been broken to the limit and beyond, and I never once showed an ounce of weakness.

"You disappoint me," Leggett continued. "I've given you everything, and yet you have no ambition! No drive! How do you plan on making this a career if your soldiers don't respect you, hmm?"

It took all my willpower not to clench my jaw. He wanted me to break down. That was why he said things that would rattle me. I just had to maintain my composure.

"So much potential. So much promise. And for what? For you to settle in as nothing more than a sergeant and a piss poor one at that?" The general leaned back in his chair to assess me. "Speak, soldier!"

That was the magic signal. "I have already addressed the issue. My men won't be late again." My voice sounded like flint, bitter and harsh, in the echo of the room.

My mentor nodded. "And what are your plans this weekend?"

"Preparing, sir," I replied instantly. It was the only answer he would ever accept. To be a good soldier meant you had to be in a constant state of preparation, for war or catastrophe. We lived on the brink of disaster at all times, according to Leggett.

Leggett nodded again. "As you should. I received word that there may be some illegal drugs working their way on post through the locals. I need your eyes and ears everywhere to help me get to the bottom of it."

"Yes, sir." For some reason, I added, "There's a party at a local woman's house tomorrow night. I overheard some of the soldiers talking about it at the range yesterday."

Leggett stood up to put the map from his desk onto a cork board on the wall to his right. Aerial shots and scaled drawings littered the board. "Then I expect you to go, too. See what you can find. I'll not have my base or my reputation ruined." He sat back down, dragging the next stack of papers in front of him. "That will be all, Hayes."

Air filled my lungs when Leggett's office door clicked shut behind me. No matter how many times we had the same meeting with the same discussions, anxiety sent my heart rate sky high. Leggett wasn't the kind of man to exchange pleasantries or engage in any topic unrelated to Army business. He had been that way for as long as I could remember.

I had to take several deep breaths before my regular heart rate resumed. Internally, I berated myself for bringing up the party. As much as I wanted the soldiers from yesterday to stay safe and spare everyone headaches, I didn't want to rain on their parade. And I definitely didn't want to go to a party.

I went to one once on my first weekend off after I completed AIT, or Advanced Individual Training, as the Army called it. Everyone in my barracks planned to go and after being sequestered in drills and training labs for so long; they all wanted to blow off some steam. One of the guys hammered on my door until I answered. He insisted on dragging me along for the ride, then promptly abandoned me when he met a girl he wanted to talk to instead. I spent the majority of the night sitting in a chair by myself with only the homeowner's cat for company.

Finally, one of the guys noticed that I sat off in a corner, alone, and sent a girl over. She had already drunk too much and slurred her words.

Davies, the soldier who brought me, laughed as he clapped me on the shoulder.

"She's a sure thing!" he insisted in my ear.

The lighting was far too dim for me to see much of the girl's face. Stringy blonde hair trailed down her back as she came to straddle me in the recliner. My back went ramrod straight. I had never been so physically close to a woman like that and found it jarring. She danced on my lap, one arm holding a red Solo cup filled with cheap beer while the other arm rested on the head of the recliner for balance.

"Don't you like what you see?" the girl had yelled over the music, shoving her large tits in my face.

My skin felt hot despite the fact that my palms were slick with sweat. Tension rippled up my spine as my back arched straighter. I wanted nothing more than to put some space between us. I didn't want her touching me. All of it was wrong—the music too loud and her movements too jerky.

"Come on, big boy," she had whisper shouted. "I'm gonna show you a great time!"

The girl proceeded to dismount, only to grab my hand and yank me upward. All of the guys shouted and wolf whistled as she led me from the room. But it sounded like it came from the bottom of a well because my ears roared too loudly for me to hear properly.

I wasn't stupid. I knew about sex, and I definitely heard and saw enough raunchy, stolen hookups during boot camp. It simply never looked or sounded appealing to me. I couldn't imagine letting someone's skin touch mine. That kind of intimacy made me want to throw up.

But all the guys from my barracks watched us go down the hallway to the girl's room. They expected us to hook up, and wasn't I supposed to fit in? Would that make me one of them like all the brochures from the recruiter promised? I might wear the uniform, but I didn't feel like a soldier any more than I felt like a racecar driver.

Even now, three years after the fact, I still cringed when I remembered the way her rough skin slid across mine. The girl had been far too drunk to care about the lack of enthusiasm in my performance. I let her take the lead the whole time, laying down stiffly while she rode my cock, somewhat shocked when it actually worked the way it was supposed to.

Leggett caught me masturbating in the bathroom one time and damn near beat the shit out of me. "Soldiers never chase pleasure!" he had screamed. "They chase honor!"

I had been too afraid to touch myself again after that.

Everything about sex stood out as wrong to me. While I technically got off, there was no enjoyment in it. There were no feelings involved. Rather, it made me recognize my own emptiness far more than I had before I went to the party.

The whole thing concerned me so much that the following weekend I had gone by myself to a club in Savannah, the closest major city to Hunter Army Airfield. It didn't take long for me to find a man who winked at me after wickedly perusing my body. I went back to his house afterwards and tried again, thinking sex with a man might crack through the emptiness and let some light in. But there was nothing. He rolled over and went straight to sleep, and I drove myself back to the barracks without even asking him his name. It was totally meaningless.

That was why the prospect of attending another party didn't sit well. Usually I spent the weekends in my room, reading. There was an excellent post library not far from my room. I typically stopped there on Thursday or Friday night, depending on when the weekend started, and checked out 15 to 20 books. They kept me company until Monday morning.

Just thinking about being packed in with all the dancing bodies and loud music made me want to vomit. And I would need to visit the mall because other than my uniforms and an array of workout clothing, I had nothing appropriate to wear to a party in town. Now that Leggett ordered me to go, however, he would no doubt send someone to my room to check.

Resigning myself, I climbed into my truck and headed towards Savannah.

CHAPTER 5
THE RITUAL
MAGGIE

My body moved in slow motion for the rest of the afternoon. Diana had judiciously granted me the rest of the weekend to find some place to go, swearing to stay at Ty-something's place in the meantime so that I didn't "interrupt" them. She also informed me that I couldn't take anything other than my clothes. All of the furniture in the room was hers, so not only did I need to find a place to live in two days, I had to furnish it.

All with the whopping $122.85 I had left in my bank account. The accelerated cosmetology program had definitely been worth it since I earned my license faster, however it prevented me from working for the past year. The money I had was all that remained from my financial aid, and therefore would not be replenished.

It was fine. I could get through this. I just needed to panic for a minute first.

Calling Celeste didn't seem fair. Her life was so rough as it was, and ultimately, Celeste was a fixer. She liked to fix problems, not just listen to me vent. I equally hated and loved her for the loyalty she always gave me.

If her news about Marla had been true, crashing with her was probably my only choice.

Since Marla also lived in town, it made more sense for me to walk rather than waste the little bit of gas I had to drive over to her place. Plus, I didn't exactly know where Diana's new boyfriend lived and I didn't want either of them knowing where I was going. As I walked, I planned a pitch in my head so good that Marla wouldn't be able to say no. She was tough, there was no doubt about it, but Marla was also realistic and practical. I just had to present the right set of facts that would make her see how we could help one another.

Marla herself stood on the sidewalk, one hand shielding the sun from her eyes as she stared up at the front of her building. I nearly walked into her because I was so focused on nailing my reasons for letting me stay with her.

"Oh, good," she greeted me. "I been wonderin' when you was gonna show up."

I momentarily panicked. If I promised to help her and forgot about it, Marla would never let me live it down. "Um…what?"

She lowered her hand, the intense gaze landing on my face instead. Every word of the speech I prepared disappeared from my brain.

"I heard you're in need of a place to stay," Marla informed me.

Frowning, I deflated like a balloon. "Did Celeste tell you?"

Marla shook her head. "Nope. Heard your mama prattlin' on about it to Desiree this morning down at the Cushion. I had to turn in my keys," she added when confusion danced across my face.

"Diana's telling people about it?" That was a new low, even for her.

"She's telling *Desiree*," Marla corrected me. "Like attracts like. So get to it! Where's all your stuff?"

I blinked several times before hitching a thumb over my shoulder. "Back at my place. I was just coming over to ask you."

With a roll of her eyes, Marla went to open the door that led up to her apartment. "Because I was likely to say no? C'mon now, Maggie, you're a right side smarter than that!"

I followed her upstairs where she led me straight into her second bedroom. Celeste stayed there sometimes whenever she was too tired to go home after a long day at the diner. The room had been gutted of all

Celeste's belongings and it smelled like a mixture of fabric softener and bleach.

"I took the liberty of scrubbing everything. You never know what Iris has dropped around here. All of Celeste's things will stay in the hall closet. You're welcome to use the dressers and the closet. I don't have anything in here anyway, so I hope you'll consider it well and truly yours." Marla fixed me with a hard stare, the kind only she could give. It went along with her tough love thing. She could probably see straight through to people's souls. "You gonna be alright?"

This wasn't a conversation I was ready to have. I choked back on the sobs that threatened to escape, Marla's eyes too astute not to notice. "I can't thank you enough." Examining my nails and the chipped polish they sported, I avoided seeing her reaction. "I'm not sure how I can pay you yet."

Marla snorted. "Families don't charge one another rent, Maggie. You can help me get things ready downstairs and we'll call it even."

She marched back downstairs with me trailing behind to wipe my eyes. Her kindness was like a balm, soothing frazzled nerves that prevented me from sleeping the night before. It was also exactly like Marla and for whatever reason, I really needed that.

"So what do you think?" Marla gestured towards the shop front beneath her apartment. The windows were covered in grime and the inside looked dark. What was once an appliance store, had sat vacant for years, longer than I lived in River's Run.

"About what?"

"My new shop!" There was a hint of pride to her voice that I hadn't heard before.

I broke out into a wide smile. "So you're really doing it? You're gonna open a bakery?"

"Marla's Sweets," she confirmed, the pride now evident. "Just got the keys this morning!"

"Dang, Marla, I'm so happy for you!" I threw my arms around her neck in delight.

She laughed as she hugged me back. "Alright, alright! No use in carryin' on when we've got loads of work to do. I need you to take our girl out tonight and celebrate, y'hear?"

Celeste? Go out? That would never happen.

"Marla, you know she can't. What about the diner? What about Iris?"

"I'm going to keep Iris for the night. How else am I supposed to celebrate? And The Comfy Cushion is closing down early anyway. Desiree didn't pay the food vendor on time, so they're out of too much stuff." Marla looked like a force to be reckoned with over that last bit of news, but it lined up with every awful thing I knew about Celeste's stepmother. What had once been the best restaurant in southern Georgia had slowly become a ghost town.

Still doubtful, chewed on my thumb nail. "Are you sure? You don't mind?"

Marla moved to play-slap me. "Girl, if you don't git on over there and git your clothes!"

I knew better than to ignore Marla's instructions. The woman had no qualms about swatting people upside their heads.

By the time I got all of my suitcases and garbage bags into my car and reached Marla's, Celeste and Iris had arrived. She helped me lug everything upstairs, with Iris laughing her head off while jumping headfirst into the pile of bags.

"You have…way…too many…clothes," Celeste panted, depositing the final suitcase in the corner.

"I know. Because I never know what's going to fit!" The math supported this. Women's bodies fluctuated a lot throughout the month depending on their cycle and hormones. It was just science.

Celeste shook her head and wiped the sweat from her brow. "Maggie, you lost all that weight our sophomore year and you've never gained an ounce of it back!" She plopped down on the bed, smiling when Iris climbed up next to her.

Thankfully that distraction prevented her from seeing the guilty look that crossed my face. We never talked about my rapid weight loss, and after nearly four years of avoiding the subject, I had no desire to start now.

"I'm gonna have to find something if we're going out tonight." I rummaged through one of the bags half-heartedly.

My bestie leaned up on her elbows to give me a look that said *really?*

"Hey, no, you don't get to back out of this! You NEVER have a babysitter and you DESERVE to be a normal nineteen year old!"

Celeste turned her head away from me, but not before I saw the tears pooling in the corners of her eyes. Neither of us ever said his name and yet I knew Wesley hung in the air between us. She didn't want to let him go but she didn't want to move on either. The never ending circle.

"Okay, fine. Where did you have in mind?"

I smiled and pulled up my phone. "Let's see if anyone on Facebook knows about a party tonight!"

Several hours later, I styled both of our hair to perfection. I even curled Iris' hair, which made her giggle. We both called her our little princess and she twirled delightedly in her nightgown. I went into the bathroom under the guise that I was doing my makeup after Celeste claimed she didn't want me to do hers. Makeup had never really mattered to her, but she had the kind of natural beauty that didn't need it.

Locking the door for good measure, I turned on the faucet so that the running water could obscure any noise. I pulled my toothbrush from my bag of toiletries, along with a worn eyeliner pencil, and moved to stand in front of the mirror, shedding the sparkly dress I had carefully selected. My bra and panties came off next so that I stood as naked as the day I was born.

This was my dirty little secret. Nobody could know, especially Marla and Celeste, because they would flip out. And while I loved how much they cared about me, I *needed* to do this. I couldn't function without it.

The ritual always started with my feet. I circled my toes in the mirror with the eyeliner, cursing how long they were, too long to be considered dainty. They made my feet look manly, or so Diana always told me, which then made my ankles look disproportionately small for my body.

The eyeliner highlighted their width and I cursed yet again over the fact that I couldn't send fat to the right parts of my body. Strawberry skin screamed at me as my gaze travelled upward, and I popped dots of their pattern along my reflection. Despite all the weight I lost, my thighs still touched. I would never achieve a thigh gap, something Diana always insisted men looked for on a woman. No number of skirts or dresses could hide the fact that my thighs stretched wider than the palms of my hands. Angrily, I slashed a line across my thighs in the mirror.

This was usually when the tears started. Salty and hot, they coated my cheeks and dribbled down my chest. I couldn't focus on them when my hips jutted out at odd, noticeable angles. Ab routines did nothing to flatten the small, fleshy bump that hung over my pussy. At least it was waxed. The entire process was painful and expensive, not to mention a little humiliating, but bikini waxes were something I strictly maintained. I never missed an appointment.

I continued upward, noting the hideous shape of my belly button on the mirror, and cringing at the small stretch marks along the bottom of my breasts. I imitated their lines on the mirror. My ribs were no longer visible at that moment, probably due to the cheeseburger I ate with Marla and Celeste earlier. As if recognizing the time, my stomach groaned loudly in protest.

Next it was onto the breasts themselves, the offensive things that started it all. They snuck up on me, virtually overnight, and within a single day at school, my round globes were all anyone could talk about. Dozens of boys tried to grope me—in the hallways, on the bus, as I stood at my locker. I saw the envious ways my female classmates stared, their jealousy so tangible that it nearly gagged me. I started hunching over in hopes that it lessened the impact of the large rack I then sported. Gratitude overwhelmed me when the weight loss meant they deflated, no longer the objects of everyone's attention. The only downside was that now I realized how much boys appreciated a good set of tits and I had nothing to offer them.

Bony shoulders served as arrows to even bonier clavicles, all of which I drew on my reflected self, followed by a neck far too long for my height. My entire torso was distinctly too square and short for my frame. I resembled one of the characters on *South Park* with the asymmetrical way my body aligned itself.

And my face? God, my fucking face. The thing that was the most excruciating to look at. By now it was marred with the tears that poured from my eyes. A dull, lifeless hazel that married far too many hues to be anything distinct or mesmerizing. Large and wideset, they stretched out my face in a way that I hated. My nose was far too pointed while my lips were far too thin. I longed to get fillers for the bags under my eyes. And although my teeth were white, thanks to the teeth whitening tool I picked up in a bargain bin at Madden Markets, nothing short of orthodonture could fix the crooked nature of my front teeth. Thankfully that served as a focal point to take away from the monstrosities that were my ears. If they stuck out any farther, I'd be forced to take flight like Dumbo.

All in all, the sight made me sick. I was a mutant, an ugly duckling unworthy of anyone's love or attention. Celeste and Marla had no right to care about someone as disgusting as me. Like Diana always told me, beautiful people get what they deserve in life. And I was no one's definition of beautiful.

Soft sobs trickled out as I slowly turned to the toilet and kneeled. This was my penance. The only way I could cleanse for all the ugliness my natural state unleashed on the world. Yes, I could dye my hair or even fix my complexion with the right contour. But in the end, when the makeup washed off and the hair grew out, I was ugly, plain and simple.

The toothbrush handle tickled the back of my throat as I did my best to stifle the retching sounds that came with it. Nobody could know how I purged my soul in the bathroom. I would do it as many times as it took to sink in. I needed to be pretty. To be loved. Then, and only then, would Diana become the mother I wanted her to be.

Once my stomach felt empty and hollow, the only reassurance I could accept, I quickly brushed my teeth and used the cleaner under the sink to wipe off the mirror. Marla was far too sharp not to notice my ritual, so while I appreciated her offer to stay for as long as I needed, there was definitely an expiration date. I couldn't *not* do this…my ritual was all I had.

In just a few minutes I had an entirely new face, thanks to hundreds of hours practicing makeup techniques. Makeup helped me morph into the person I wanted to be. The kind of woman who was alluring. Mysterious. A woman powerful and beautiful enough to have men falling at her feet.

Iris cooed in excitement when I walked out to the living room. Gone were the days where I struggled to walk in a pair of stilettos. Put a runway in front of me and I could rock Paris Fashion Week. Tonight's pair sported a five inch heel, making me close to six feet tall. Large rhinestones made them glitter, matching the holographic purple dress I wore. If only I still had the jumbo boobs to fill it out. I would look so much sexier.

As soon as I had my living situation settled and my finances in order, I was getting implants. Even Diana agreed that was the smart thing to do.

Celeste's body had changed, too, filling out in a way that only a mother's could. She still looked beautiful to me, even more so now that she let me style her hair into plush curls that framed her face. One of my old shirts from freshman year fit her—a little too tightly, according to Celeste—but the red color suited her perfectly. She refused to wear anything more than a frilly top and shorts, and even that didn't deter me. We were going to have so much fun tonight!

"Now, don't worry about what time you're getting home." Marla held up a hand to stop her as soon as Celeste opened her mouth. "This baby and I are gonna do some puddin' paintin' and then we're gonna have a bubble bath, and then I think a Disney princess is in order."

I smirked as Celeste looked at her in horror. "It's already eight-thirty!" she cried. "Iris normally goes to bed at nine!"

Marla scowled at her. "Shoo!" she said, waving her hands in the direction of the door.

Before we entered into a battle of wills, the likes of which River's Run had never seen, I grabbed Celeste's hand and pulled her after me down the stairs. According to someone we went to high school with, there was supposed to be a rager at Skylar Perkins' house. She inherited a small house just down the road from the Army base after her grandmother died. It was tucked back far enough from the road that neighbors didn't really call the cops if things got too rowdy.

It was the perfect place to go and blow off some steam. And I needed that after the past couple days I'd had.

CHAPTER 6
THE PARTY

ZEKE

EVERY SINGLE ROOM in this house had a speaker. The back porch had three. Even the fire pit in the back of the yard had a speaker. Bass pounded so hard in my ears that it rattled my teeth, and I quickly developed a migraine from how hard I clenched my jaw shut.

There were people everywhere. Without anyone in uniform, it was hard to tell who lived in town versus who lived on post, but some of the men could be distinguished by their military haircut. I had gotten one myself just that afternoon once I bought an outfit to wear.

I checked my watch again for the time, resolving myself to spend one hour there. One hour had to be enough. Any more than that and I would probably wind up taking a sledgehammer to those stupid speakers. It kind of defeated the purpose of watching over the soldiers if I became the reckless one whose actions created a safety brief on Tuesday morning.

Leggett wanted me to find out about any drugs that might be working their way on post, but he hadn't said anything about watching out for the people using them *at* the party. The acidic smell of bad weed made my nose crinkle, and I noticed more than one person throw back a pill with a tequila chaser. Quite frankly, anyone's drug usage was none of my business. As far as I was concerned, they knew the risks, especially soldiers. You play stupid games and you win stupid prizes.

I wandered from room to room, trying to find somewhere noncommittal to sit or stand where I wouldn't be noticed but could also keep my eyes and ears open. Each time I thought I found a spot, I caught the eye of a flirtatious woman or dodged a couple vying for the spot at the same time. I settled for circling the layout. A reasonable person would have noticed, but everyone I saw looked to be about three sheets to the wind.

After three quarters of an hour with nothing but discomfort, sweat, and a pounding headache, I grabbed a soda from the kitchen and headed outside. A detached garage sat at the end of the gravel driveway, more than thirty feet away from the house. I noticed a small bench along the side not facing the yard. It seemed quieter there without a subwoofer to thrum the bass and I sat down to wait out my last fifteen minutes. This entire endeavor was a waste of time and money. I avoided spending money at all costs, so dropping anything on a pair of jeans and a button up shirt I'd never wear again felt stupid.

A new car pulled into the drive, the headlights briefly illuminating me with bright white light. Instincts kicked in and I sat up straighter, immediately on high alert at someone new. Two women climbed out of a dark sedan. One had on a simple red shirt and jean shorts while the other had on some kind of shimmery dress that barely reached mid-thigh. Light from the firepit in the backyard danced along the girl's sparkly high heels as they rounded the house to use the back deck to enter the party.

There was something about the shiny girl's appearance that drew my attention. She reminded me of a peacock, strutting about with beautiful feathers wide open. For some reason, the girl called to me like a siren to a sailor, and I stood up to watch as both women greeted people on the back deck. They must be locals; the girl in the red shirt wouldn't have passed military fitness standards and the shiny girl would know better than to wear such dangerous footwear on the soft ground outside.

For a brief moment, Shiny Girl looked over in my direction, and I would've sworn her eyes caught mine. But her gaze didn't linger. She surveyed her surroundings with the tiniest trace of a smile that I could only just make out in the weak porch light. The song changed and Shiny

Girl hopped up and down like a bunny, clapping her hands and whooping with delight. A real smile broke through, and she grabbed her companion's hand to lead her inside the house.

Something beckoned me to follow. I was drawn to this girl in a way I had never felt before. I needed to at least see her up close. Maybe then my visceral reaction would go away and I could return to my room.

Back inside, I didn't see them right away. They weren't in the kitchen or the dining room. I came around the corner and noticed the girl in the red shirt standing near the front door, deep in conversation with someone. Shiny Girl was nowhere to be seen. I followed the hallway through a laundry room that opened up into what had likely once been an attached garage, but instead had been converted into a rec room. There was an air hockey table and an old Galaga arcade game along with a bunch of neon beer signs hanging along the walls. A large tv sat on cement cinderblocks in front of a rather moth-eaten couch. I tried not to crinkle my nose at the smell of stale beer and body odor.

And there was my Shiny Girl in the middle of the room. A cluster of guys stood in a semi-circle around her, and judging from the tension I could see in her spine, she wasn't happy about it. A couple of the men, the ones centered directly in front of her, sneered at her in a way that made my hackles rise.

I made my way over, not bothering to excuse myself when I pushed past people, and right as I was ready to tap her on the shoulder, Shiny Girl turned on her heel and walked into me. There wasn't time to react. I instinctually wrapped my arms around her waist to steady her, and the sweetest pair of doe eyes looked up at me. There was fear in them, a quiver to her bottom lip that she was trying to hide.

An animalistic rage burned through me. Nobody *ever* had the right to make this girl scared. Anyone who did could answer to me and make their peace with their god.

What I found equally as startling were the way her arms wound around my neck. "Please just go with it," the girl murmured in a breathy plea before drawing my mouth to hers.

A bomb detonated when her lips touched mine. I no longer cared about her name, my name, or anyone else in the world. New purpose grounded me in that moment. From there on out, my only singular goal in life was to make the woman in my arms happy. I would protect her, defend her, and honor her with every fiber of my being.

And I felt ravenous to continue the kiss. My body wanted to possess her.

Intimately.

Spiritually.

Permanently.

I didn't even realize I could experience those kinds of feelings. The very shock of it sent me stumbling backward, pulling away from her just as quickly as she had kissed me.

"See, boys?" Shiny Girl turned back to the men watching us, several of them now with angry scowls. "I'm taken."

One of the guys started to step forward, his ire more pronounced in the way his fists clenched at his sides. The animal in me roared again and I found myself stepping up to wrap a possessive arm around the girl's waist, holding her tightly against my side.

"Yo, man, that's Sergeant Hayes!" Another guy, obviously a soldier, though I didn't recognize him, slapped his hand onto the angry man's chest. It brought the guy up short.

Shiny Girl didn't waste any time, turning towards the door, lacing her fingers through mine to have me follow. And I didn't mind. I would follow her anywhere she asked.

"I won't forget about this, Mags!" the one guy called. "Once a whore, always a whore."

Whore? Had I just kissed a sex worker? Not that there was anything wrong with that kind of profession. But did they hand out kisses like free samples, or was I expected to pay her for that?

The girl didn't stop until we were back outside and sitting on the bench where I first saw her. By that time she was panting, likely from an adrenaline crash, and I squatted down in front of where she sat.

"I don't have a paper bag or anything, so you'll need to lean your head down between your legs and take a few deep breaths," I advised her. I could barely make out her face in the darkness.

"I'm so sorry I kissed you!" she whimpered. The sound made some part of me feel guilty, though I wasn't sure what I had done wrong.

Even though she couldn't see me, I shrugged. "It's okay. Glad I could help."

A weak, watery laugh escaped. "Yeah, you definitely helped. Although you might have a target on your back now." Her accent sounded distinctly southern, with a lilt to it that reminded me of music.

"I've had targets on my back before."

The girl took a couple shaky breaths before saying, "I'm Maggie Eaton, by the way."

I smiled. I liked the name Maggie.

"My name is Ezekiel Hayes. But you can call me Zeke." No one ever called me anything other than "sir", "sergeant", or "Hayes". I liked that Maggie might be the first and only one to call me by a nickname. It made her special. And if that kiss had been any indication, there was definitely something very special about Maggie.

"Well, Zeke, I need to go inside and find my friend. Will you go with me? In case I run into any of them again?"

One of her hands slid through the darkness to find mine. And the feel of her skin didn't repel me like it usually did. I liked it, which was yet another first for me.

I gripped her hand tightly and pulled her upright with me as I stood. "Count me in," I assured her.

CHAPTER 7
THE INTRODUCTION
MAGGIE

OF COURSE SPENCER and his stupid band of friends came to the party. There was never much else to do unless you wanted to drive all the way out to Savannah, and that could get real expensive real quick. I should've assumed I'd run into him. And in true Spencer-like fashion, he had to be dick. Who only thought with his dick.

I wasn't proud of the reputation I'd garnered back in high school. Boys like Spencer Church made it hard to forget. But despite the way I played fast and loose with the boys at Smithson County High, I would certainly never agree to the gangbang situation Spencer propositioned me for! The whole point was to get a guy to like me!

That hadn't exactly happened yet, but still.

The way they all started to circle around me made me panic a bit, I admit. I also didn't want Celeste to find us and then have to explain how I knew any of them. That was a part of my life that I never wanted her to see and I didn't know why. Maybe because she still seemed so innocent and hopeful. She had a chance at living a happily ever after whereas I had resigned myself to merely chasing the endorphin rush that came from getting a man's attention.

It was pure, dumb luck that set Zeke up behind me. I had been refusing Spencer's advances, making up a boyfriend out of convenience in the hopes that it made him back down. Instead, it made Spencer call my bluff, pompously asking Chase Hubbard and Grant Dupree if I had ever had a boyfriend before. They had both been part of my rotation of hook ups in high school and knew better. I didn't even recognize the rest of the guys in the group, and I shivered at the thought of what Spencer, Chase, and Grant might have promised them.

When I turned and walked into what felt like a solid wall, I didn't think, just reacted. Zeke's tall frame, rigid with muscle from what I could tell upon wrapping my arms around him, towered over everyone and a sense of security washed over me as soon as his grip steadied me. He was handsome, closely cropped hair in the military style, and although he looked downright alarmed, he didn't question my actions.

And that kiss? Holy hell, that kiss could change my religion. His lips were strong. Firm. I wanted to get so lost in them that I never had to come back up for air. Most of the time I didn't bother kissing the guys I hooked up with. That wasn't what they wanted from me, and it seemed easier to cut to the chase and get us both off. But I craved a thousand more kisses from Zeke Hayes—a million, if he'd let me.

But then he jumped away from me like a terrified little bird. His facial expression told me he wanted to bolt even if he went through the motions with me. Perhaps Zeke wasn't used to girls coming on as strongly as I did. Or maybe he just felt the power behind that kiss like I did. Either way, a voice in the back of my mind warned me not to push him much more. Zeke's fight or flight instinct had been activated. It may have settled somewhat while we were outside and he helped me prevent a full blown panic attack, but I got the sense that Zeke didn't know what to make of me.

Once we got back inside the house, I made a beeline for the living room. Celeste still stood in the same spot I left her in, a Solo cup full of what I knew to be water in hand. She refused to drink in case Iris had an emergency while we were out.

"Hey!" she greeted me. "Where have you been?"

"Just...around," I replied noncommittally.

I couldn't remember exactly when I started leading a double life as far as Celeste was concerned. Our friendship changed my life, and I wouldn't trade a second of it for anything, but Celeste *always* had something going on. I didn't begrudge her for any of it because I knew she didn't intentionally try to monopolize our time. But at the end of the day, I often wound up alone. Even when we first met and clicked, Celeste had a lot on her plate, and she came as a packaged deal with Wesley Madden. Their love gave me goosebumps. It was the kind of thing that made even the coldest of hearts thaw.

That was the kind of love I wanted and could never have.

"This is Ezekiel Hayes!" I told her, drawing up beside me. Her eyes instantly zeroed in on the way Zeke's hand remained firmly clasped in mine, and there was a sparkle in them that I hadn't seen since Wesley left.

"It's excellent to meet you, Ezekiel!" My best friend beamed at him.

Nearly a foot taller than her, Zeke had to lean down even just to shout above the music. "You can call me Hayes. Everybody does."

For some reason, I liked the fact that he gave her a different, generic name to call him. It was like it somehow gave me a claim over him that I hadn't realized I wanted.

And yet, the fact that I wanted it frightened me.

"I'm gonna go get a drink!" I announced, my voice just a pitch too high, even over the music. "Wait right here!"

Zeke frowned. "I think I should go with you. What if you run into those guys again?"

Celeste's eyebrows went up. "What guys?"

Never mind, Zeke had to come with me. "Oh, nothing. We'll be right back!"

I looped my arm through his and steered us back into the kitchen. Rather than take a Solo cup of whatever cheap beer lined the kitchen island, I headed over to the far counter where all the hard liquor waited. That was the only way I saw myself making it through tonight without the shame of Spencer's proposition eating me alive.

Downing half a cup of the first bottle I touched made my throat burn and my chest wheeze. I thumped a fist on my chest, forcing myself to cough, before grabbing another bottle and refilling it.

"Take it easy, okay?" Zeke patted firmly between my shoulder blades. "Are you even old enough to drink?"

The question made me laugh as it was laced with worry. Did he seriously care about me drinking at a party filled with uncontrolled booze and drugs? Half the people I'd seen so far were underage, some of them still in high school.

"You're one of those do-gooder types, aren't you?" I asked as I gulped down another drink. This one tasted fruitier and went down a lot smoother.

Better lighting in the kitchen meant I had a chance to give Zeke more than a cursory glance under faint neon lights. There was a little bit of length to the hair on top of his head that would have looked much better if he styled it. I could tell from the way it fell on his forehead that he hadn't done anything to make his hair appear more presentable. Soft blue eyes stared at me above high, sharp cheekbones that should've graced the cover of a magazine. The light blue of his shirt only enhanced the brilliance of his eyes and I couldn't help but wonder if he picked it out himself or if it was a gift from a previous girlfriend. She certainly knew how to dress him.

Except, when I continued my perusal down his body, I noticed a tag hanging out of the bottom of his shirt. With a quick, forceful tug, I yanked it off and handed it to him.

"New shirt?" I bit back a grin.

He flushed. "Yeah. But don't change the subject. Are you old enough to be drinking that?"

I rolled my eyes and angled my body so that I leaned against the countertop for support. "I'm not old enough to buy it on my own. I think that's more what you meant, right?"

Zeke's lips flattened into a thin line, a sight so comical that I burst out laughing. He brightened at the sight of my laughter, looking pleased with himself, and he stepped closer to me so that we were nearly chest to chest.

The temperature rose by several degrees as the storm clouds in his eyes drew me in. I was mesmerized by the way they focused on me. My breath hitched and I didn't dare move. As much as I wanted to kiss him again, I wanted him to be the one to do it this time. To prove that he felt attracted to me the same way I did to him.

"I just want to keep you safe, Trouble." So gently that I almost didn't register it at first, Zeke tucked the hair behind my ear, tracing the shell of my earlobe down to my jaw. His fingers continued their light descent, spreading fire in their wake, until they stopped under my jaw. He tipped my chin up just enough to make me look at him directly.

"I-I'm...I'm not t-trouble," I stuttered. I swallowed thickly, overwhelmed by his presence and the way his scent tickled my nose. A hint of vanilla amongst a rich pine.

Zeke smiled. And that smile sealed the deal for me. He was breathtakingly beautiful and someone as ugly and awful as me would never land a guy like him.

"Why do I get the feeling that's not true?" he asked.

With the spell broken as my brain reminded me of all the ways this perfect specimen of a human would never condescend to be with someone like me, I sidestepped him and grabbed the entire bottle of the fruity liquor off the counter.

"C'mon. Celeste is waiting for us," I called over my shoulder.

CHAPTER 8
THE AFTERPARTY

ZEKE

I APPRECIATED the way the lights in the kitchen granted me the opportunity to look at Maggie outright. There was a craftsmanship to the way her sparkly eye makeup highlighted her best feature. Huge curls bounced down her back with every movement, a cascading array of dark colors, and I had to physically restrain myself to keep from touching them. I didn't know how hair could be so long and thick. Her cheeks were rosy, and part of me hoped that it was because of the effect I had on her, but I was too chicken to ask.

Just like the peacock I pegged her for, everything about Maggie drew me in. But something seemed off about her appearance, almost like trying to note tiny details while an image started to blur. I didn't know a thing about the stuff women used on their bodies, only what Army regulations said. And I was too afraid of a sexual harassment claim to ever tell a female soldier that their hair, makeup, or nails weren't compliant. I wanted to see what Maggie looked like beneath the big curls and sparkles.

I caught a glimpse of it when she laughed. God, I needed to keep giving her a reason to make that sound. It could be the soundtrack of my life. And that smile...she could probably get me to agree to just about anything by sending that smile in my direction. It was raw and real. Exactly how I wanted to get to know Maggie.

Something definitely changed after I called her Trouble. I meant it more for myself, as in getting to know Maggie Eaton would cause me a lot of trouble, but I think she took it the wrong way. Her entire body language changed, and she rushed off with a full bottle of alcohol in hand.

Reasonably, I knew there were plenty of underage people drinking tonight. Maggie couldn't be the only one, especially with a party so jampacked full of people. But she was the only one I cared about and that meant I didn't want her to be in any kind of danger, even if it was only the danger of getting caught by the police. She didn't seem ready or willing to give up the bottle just yet though, so I planned to stay close to her just in case. If a cop came along, I would take the bottle out of her hand and push her behind me. Hopefully that would be enough, but I didn't know how cops broke up a party. I'd never been to one before.

As I followed Maggie back out to the living room, where most of the furniture had been pushed along the walls to create a pseudo-dance floor, I realized just how much I didn't know about social interactions. The glaringly obvious thing at the moment? How to dance.

Maggie was easily the most captivating girl in the room. The way her hips swayed to the beat of the music mocked the way my heart raced at the sight. I wanted to rip off the head of every man in the room for even breathing the same air, which was entirely irrational. Who honestly felt that way over someone they just met?

And while I accepted that it was wholly illogical to want to keep her all to myself, I was also thrilled to feel anything at all. Some people simply lived their lives alone. That was a fact of life. I never minded that I might be one of them until now.

Celeste, Maggie's friend, siddled up to me after more than an hour of watching Maggie dance. In that time she had managed to polish off what remained in the bottle she snagged from the kitchen as well as several cups of beer that Celeste brought her. I noted the way Celeste's frown grew deeper each time, as though she procured the drink against her better judgement.

"She's had too much," Celeste yelled. Worry lines etched across her forehead. "I can't get her to stop, though. And I need to be leaving soon to get back to my daughter."

Ah, so she was a mother. That explained why she appeared so anxious over Maggie's well-being. I liked her even more than before.

"I can take her home," I offered. "Your kid has to come first."

Uncertainty flashed across her face as she chewed on her bottom lip. "I can't ask that of you…"

"You didn't ask. I insisted," I replied with the same level, firm tone that typically made my soldiers pay more attention. "Let's go tell Maggie."

Weaving through the gyrating bodies, I made my way over to Maggie, who stood in the center like a glittery disco ball. Sweat ran down her face, smearing her makeup, but she threw her hands up in the air in time with the music.

"Maggie, I've really gotta go!" Celeste shouted next to me. "It's getting late. Hayes said he could take you home."

Maggie's eyes darted to me and for a split second I saw surprise there before the same distant look as before settled back in place. A mask she wore for me? Why?

"But I wanted us to have fun!" Maggie protested. She grabbed her friend's hand and tried to get her to shimmy along, but Celeste wouldn't budge.

"I have to go!"

Some of the steam seemed to come out of her because Maggie slumped forward to give Celeste a brief hug. "I'll call you tomorrow!"

Meanwhile, Celeste turned back to me, her index finger pointing straight between my eyes and pinned me with all the sternness I'd expect from a mom. "You harm one hair on this girl's head and I will have the entire Smithson County Sheriff's Department come after you! She's important to me. Keep her safe."

I fought back the urge to salute. "I swear on your kid's life that Maggie will be safe with me."

If the vow upset her, Celeste didn't let on. Jerking her finger one last time in my face as if she needed to drive the point across, she waved goodbye to Maggie and slipped out through the writhing bodies towards the dining room where the back door was located.

Maggie turned to me with a lazy smile, the sway to her step more to do with the alcohol pumping through her system than rhythm. "Dance with me, Ezekiel Hayes?"

Every fiber of my being screamed in protest. Dancing would never be a skill I mastered. I didn't really want my first time to be in a crowded room of sweaty strangers. But it wasn't like I could deny such a simple request from her. And oddly enough, the thought of touching her again was exhilarating.

My throat felt too tight to swallow as I took another step towards her. There was no room between us, and she hiked a thigh up so that her long leg wrapped around my hips. Her hands snaked their way up my neck and into my hair. Suddenly Maggie's scent was everywhere, like a balmy coconut and sunshine that made me long for a home I'd never known. Her breasts pressed against my chest when she arched her back, the ripple of her movement traveling the length of her body so that she thrust her hips against mine.

The sharp sting of arousal had me stumbling backward. Maggie must've thought I was trying to dance along because she returned her leg to the ground and began shaking her hips in a figure eight along my groin. Thankfully the loud music covered my moan. The hard on I now sported felt strong enough to cut glass.

While I knew nobody in the room paid any attention to us, Leggett's face burst into my mind and my hands dropped from Maggie's waist as if hit with acid. This time Maggie noticed and stopped dancing, too. Something in my face sobered her enough to ask, "Zeke, are you okay?"

All I could think of were fists slamming into my side. Bare skin on bare flesh. And pain. So much pain. It left me gasping for air until the beating ended.

Now the room darkened as all the oxygen escaped. Just like then. Just like the beating. I wasn't gonna make it this time. I couldn't make it. I didn't want it to end like this—

"ZEKE!" Both of Maggie's hands cupped my face, forcing me to look at her. My chest hurt like I had just completed a twenty mile ruck march at a ten minute pace. A bead of sweat trickled down the side of my forehead and onto Maggie's fingers, but she didn't seem to care. "Just focus on me, okay? Can you do that for me? I need you to focus, Zeke!"

She held my face too tightly for me to nod, but I still couldn't speak. I settled for mimicking her breathing, taking deep inhales through my nose and exhaling through my mouth. We completed five rounds before I managed to gasp, "Thank you."

"I think you were having a panic attack," she replied.

"Okay." I didn't know what to say. Army Rangers didn't get panic attacks. I had already gone on a year long deployment shortly after completing my training. My sergeant rank came from my honorable service in Afghanistan. There was no way I just had a panic attack.

"I think it's our sign to leave," she said, gesturing towards the dining room.

She didn't need to tell me twice. I couldn't wait to get out of this place.

Rather than going out the back, I grabbed her hand and led her through the front door. My truck was parked further up the road to ensure nobody hit it, or worse, blocked me in. After several seconds of Maggie wobbling beside me, I realized her stiletto heels and the dark street made it impossible for her to walk.

Once again, I didn't think. Her siren's call just directed me on what to do. Swinging her legs out from under her, I pulled her up into a bride's hold and continued down to the end of the driveway.

"Zeke, put me down!" she objected instantly. "I'm too heavy."

That made me laugh. "Trouble, you probably don't even weigh a hundred and ten pounds. I can bench press more than twice your body weight."

She huffed, a disgruntled sound that didn't match the way her head rested against my shoulder. "Fine, but only because I don't want to break an ankle."

"Why are you wearing such ridiculous shoes anyway?" I asked.

"Because they complete the look!" Maggie sounded like the point was obvious. Maybe it was. I didn't know a thing about women's fashion.

"Don't they hurt? It can't be natural for your feet to go up like that."

After a moment, she sighed. "Yes, but that's not the point. They completed the look, so I wore them."

"Even though you can't walk safely in them and now your feet hurt?" I repeated.

"Yes!"

We reached my truck, which I unlocked before placing her in the passenger seat. I rounded the front and climbed in next to her, grateful that we were far enough up the road that a streetlight permeated some of the darkness. "Where to?" I asked quietly. I hated that our night had to end when I still didn't know enough about her.

Maggie sighed again and leaned her head back. "Nowhere, really." Her voice was so low I almost didn't hear her.

Wait—was she homeless? A sinking feeling started in my gut. There was no way I had it in me to drop this girl off at a shelter.

I put the car in drive and headed back towards post.

"Where are you going?" she asked in annoyance.

I didn't trust myself to answer, just continued on my way to the Fairfield Inn close to post. It was probably the nicest hotel in the area and would be the safest option for her.

Maggie didn't say a word as I pulled into the lot and parked in front of the front door. Worried that her feet might still hurt, I walked around to the passenger door so I could carry her inside. She held up a hand and slowly shook her head.

"Listen…I'm not sure what you think is going to happen here, but…" Her voice trailed off, uncertain and small.

Oh god, she thinks I'm propositioning her!

"I think you're going to get a good night's sleep in a safe place and a warm breakfast in the morning. I'll pay for it and give you the cash for an Uber tomorrow. Or I can take you wherever you need to go," I tacked on, trying to buoy the hope that rose at the thought of seeing her again tomorrow. "I don't even have to go up to the room with you, if you don't want. I just need to know you're safe."

At that, Maggie shot me a quizzical look. Whatever future our relationship had stood on the precipice of that look.

"You don't want to come up?" she questioned cautiously.

"Not unless you want me to, and certainly not for any reason other than to talk to you." I would let her tell me every detail of her entire life's story without complaint if it meant I could stay in her presence.

The longest twelve seconds of my life stretched between us as I waited for her answer.

"Okay. I'd like that, too," she finally whispered. A small smile played at her lips as I scooped her up once more.

CHAPTER 9
THE HOTEL
MAGGIE

Maybe I lost my touch. It had been so long since there was a guy genuinely interested in me that I forgot what signs looked like. That was the only explanation I could come up with as I followed Zeke into the elevator. He requested a room on the top floor, closest to the emergency exit that was farthest from the elevators. That was the safest room in the hotel, he assured me.

I appreciated his forethought and concern. I couldn't remember a time when either of my parents showed that kind of consideration for me.

When we arrived on the top floor, I stopped long enough to peel off my rhinestone pumps and carried them in my hand. Zeke was absolutely correct. They hurt like a bitch. A fact that I tried to hide as I hobbled down the hall, me on one side, Zeke on the other. Even the small distance between us gave me pause. He held my hand so easily before, and carried me like I weighed less than a sack of potatoes. Was he just trying to be polite or had I truly misunderstood his interest?

Zeke, being the one who checked me into the room, unlocked the door with the key card, then stood back so I could open it. The room was clean and comfortable, with two queen beds and a large white bathroom. A tv sat on top of a cabinet with a mini fridge, and there was a table with two chairs positioned in front of the window.

I immediately darted to the air conditioning unit under the window, cranking it up so that the cold air blasted into the room. Flopping down on the bed, I tried not to purr from the lush mattress underneath. This was way better than the one I had at Diana's place!

My eyes shot open a moment later when strong hands pulled my left foot upward. Zeke sat down on the chair closest to me and had taken it upon himself to start massaging my battered feet. His deft fingers worked at the kinks in the ball of my foot, and this time I didn't stop myself from moaning aloud. It felt simply divine.

"You shouldn't wear torture devices and call them shoes," Zeke said after a minute. He continued to massage the foot, never going above the ankle.

I nodded in agreement, a spoiled alley cat basking in my pampered dream.

After a few more miraculous minutes, by which time my left foot had turned to putty, Zeke pulled up the other one and repeated the exercise. If he wasn't careful, I might just take him back to River's Run with me.

"Do you really not have anywhere to live?" he asked me suddenly, breaking the silence.

Immediately, my blissful, trance-like state evaporated. "I never said that," I hedged.

"But do you?"

I glanced up, which was a big mistake. Zeke's blue eyes were thoughtful, concerned. Guilt pooled in my conscience for making him believe such a thing.

"The woman who gave birth to me just made me move out," I admitted through clenched teeth. It was mortifying to say such a thing to a stranger, let alone one as kind as Zeke. If there were any chance of him liking me, that probably went out the window the second he heard what a horrible family he'd be exposed to.

"Wouldn't that make her your mom?" he asked again after a long pause.

"No." Even to my ears, it sounded hollow and jaded. "That woman is *not* my mother."

"Okay." Zeke seemed to sense that I didn't want to talk about it because he poked his tongue into his cheek before saying, "But you found a place? I can pay for another night in the room if you need me to."

As kind as the gesture was, his charity irked me. I pulled my foot from his lap and rolled over, getting up to head towards the bathroom. "You think this place has a robe I can wear tonight?"

"They should," Zeke replied. "I'm kind of hungry. Would you like me to order a pizza?"

Eating in front of anyone had become a source of tension for me ever since I started my purging ritual all those years ago. Most nights, since Diana wasn't home, I didn't have to worry about it, and I could avoid eating altogether if I wanted. But in moments like this, I never knew what to do. Would Zeke find it strange for me to refuse? Could I stomach something like pizza?

"Um, maybe just a side salad for me?" I suggested. Lettuce I could do. The few calories it might add would've been more than cancelled out from all the dancing I did earlier.

But what about all the calories from the alcohol?

The lurking voice in the back of my mind, the one that sounded like a suspiciously high, pixelated version of Diana's, interrupted me once more. All those empty calories just to get drunk for no reason! I needed to purge. Immediately. I didn't want it all sitting in my stomach, going straight to my thighs. Or worse—that small bump of my lower abdomen.

"I'm just gonna take a shower real quick," I told Zeke. "Hope you don't mind!" I didn't give him a chance to answer before I scampered into the bathroom and slammed the door shut behind me.

I didn't have the eyeliner pencil with me, so I had to settle for mentally scavenging my body. Every flaw stuck out to me like it had a neon sign announcing its presence. My bony knees, red and blotchy in the harsh lighting. The rat's nest that had become my hair. All of the makeup running down from my eyes, spots of the foundation peeling off. I had to use the cheap stuff. I couldn't afford the good shit that lasted through a night of dancing and sweating my ass off.

The areola of one nipple looked larger than another.

A new array of freckles lined my chest.

Hair on my forearm dark enough to notice that I hadn't remembered to shave off during my last shower.

Ugly. All I could see was ugliness.

I didn't even need the toothbrush to make the contents of my stomach come up. The alcohol burned far more on the ascent, but it was worth it to know the toxins were leaving my body. I never should have consumed something without checking the nutrition label anyway. Who knew how many calories I actually swallowed? Purging wasn't fool proof, so there was bound to still be something in my system.

That was my penance. I could be ugly *and* fat. There was no one to blame but that horrendous girl in the mirror.

Hot water beat down on me in the shower a moment later, stifling my sobs. No wonder Zeke wasn't attracted to me. Who could like such a hot mess of a girl? I wouldn't be surprised if he had left the room altogether by the time I got out of the shower. He probably ran screaming down the hall.

I stayed in the shower until the water ran cold, washing myself three times with the small bar of hotel soap. The cheap shampoo and conditioner would undoubtedly ruin my hair color, but I had grown bored with the color anyway, so if I needed to change it, I would. I double checked my reflection once I climbed out to make sure all of the makeup washed off. My skin looked a little red from how hard I scrubbed, but it was otherwise free of glitter and eyeshadow.

Only then it dawned on me. I didn't have any other makeup with me to put on before joining Zeke in the room. I couldn't let him see me like this! Forget about running away, he would be flying to the closest news station to report a fresh sighting of Bigfoot. Very few people, outside of my inner circle with Celeste and Marla, actually knew what I looked like without makeup on.

I cracked open the door a tiny fraction of an inch. "Zeke?" I called out.

I heard the sounds of his soft footsteps approaching, and ducked my head behind the door so he couldn't see any part of my face.

"Is everything okay? You were in there a long time," he said.

The worry in his voice softened me, and I wished I had the strength to let him see the real me. That could never happen if I had any hope of him ever developing feelings for me. And I wasn't ready to accept defeat in that regard. Kisses like that didn't come along very often.

"No, I'm actually not feeling very well." Which was actually the truth, if I were being honest. He didn't need to know that the nausea came from my own self-loathing. "I think it would be better if you went home. I'm so sorry. Thank you so, so much for everything tonight!"

"Oh. Okay." The words fell flat and I wanted to kick myself for not remembering to bring a purse with my emergency face essentials. Since the plan was to go out with Celeste, I never considered I had a chance of needing it.

"For what it's worth, Maggie, meeting you was the best part of my night," Zeke confessed. His voice sounded louder, like he leaned into the door just to guarantee I heard him.

And I couldn't help but grin. It was the corniest line in the book, but Zeke Hayes didn't seem like the kind of guy who used it that way.

I waited until I heard the front door to the room close with a snap before whispering back, "It was mine, too, Zeke."

CHAPTER 10
THE PLAN

ZEKE

My HEART SANK along with the elevator as I rode it down to the ground floor. There was something off about Maggie's sudden change of heart. While I knew that drinking too much led to stomach issues, she hadn't acted that intoxicated since I had my panic attack. And I didn't want to entertain the alternative, that she blew me off because she wasn't interested in seeing me again.

I *had* to see her again. It was just that simple.

By the time I reached my car, a tentative idea took root. There was a huge risk of it backfiring because it probably crossed a boundary of some kind, but since I hadn't even gotten her phone number, I owed it to myself to try it anyway. Just having a plan energized me enough that I headed to the battalion gym rather than the barracks. I kept a spare change of workout clothes in a lockbox in the bed of my truck for the dumb soldiers who showed up in something that violated dress code, which I grabbed now to use for myself.

By now the clock on the dash read 0200, but I had the security clearance to enter the building at all hours. I changed quickly and jumped onto a treadmill, choosing a light run to wake up my dormant muscles.

For the next several hours, I worked myself to failure on the various machines. As soon as the sun kissed the horizon, I finally called it a night and headed back to my room to shower and change. Even the heavy workout did little to subdue the optimistic energy coursing through my system. I discovered I was smiling as I looked in the mirror to shave. And I kind of liked it.

After a quick stop at Walmart, the only place available to shop that close to base, I returned to Maggie's hotel room. According to my watch, it was half past seven, and I had already seen other patrons downstairs eating the continental breakfast.

I only hesitated when I got to the door. The room key was still in my wallet, having placed it there before I left, but I didn't want to violate Maggie's privacy. What if she slept naked?

But on the other hand, if she really had been sick last night, she might need the help now. I'd found my share of passed out soldiers in puddles of their own vomit and urine after a night of heavy partying. The animalistic need to care for her, possessively and intimately, roared inside me again.

I settled for knocking on the door. It took several minutes of pounding before I heard the latch on the door slide. The chain was still in place, and the small sliver beyond was pitch black. Cold air filtered through.

"Um, can I *help* you?!" Maggie screeched from behind the door.

Shit, abort mission! ABORT MISSION!

"Sorry. It's—a...it's just me, Zeke," I supplied lamely. "I wanted to invite you to breakfast. My bad. I shouldn't have come." My face burned with embarrassment.

I heard Maggie groan. "As sweet as that offer is, I don't really want to do a walk of shame in last night's dress."

Eagerly, I pushed the bags from Walmart into the gap in the door. "That's what I figured!"

A light flipped on, but only Maggie's hand came into view. We had to wedge them a bit, but we managed to get all three bags through. The plastic bags rustled for a minute before I heard Maggie's sharp intake of breath.

"Did you buy me clothes and makeup?"

The way her voice caught at the end made me second guess my decision. Since she had on makeup at the party last night, I assumed she was the kind of woman who liked it. I bought her one of everything in the CoverGirl line because I remembered seeing their ads on one of the shuttles I took to pick up toiletries during basic training. The clothing I wouldn't exactly call a big deal. Without knowing her size or preference, I simply grabbed a plain black t-shirt and blue shorts. We weren't talking designer couture or anything.

"I just didn't want you to go home in the dress from last night if you didn't want to. I'm not saying you need makeup! Not at all! I think you're perfect!"

A very pregnant pause followed my confession. Right as I was about to start cursing myself, Maggie whispered, "Just give me a couple minutes."

Victory!

When Maggie emerged, I couldn't help swelling with pride at how well I guessed her size. The shirt looked roomy enough that she could be comfortable without swallowing her like a dress. Her tiny frame looked even smaller in the shorts, but that only brought out the fierce protector in me.

Although the makeup was far more subtle than what she wore last night, I liked this version of Maggie better. The timid smile she graced me with damn near made my heart forget to beat.

"Wow," I breathed. My cheeks, one of my rarely used muscle groups, began to ache from smiling so much.

A delightful blush crept up her neck. "Thank you for doing this. And for the room. For everything, really. You didn't have to."

"But I wanted to."

The next smile was even better. We headed down in comfortable silence, both of us grinning like idiots and sneaking looks at one another when we thought the other wasn't looking. The way Maggie Eaton looked at me made me want to be a better man.

"Do you want to eat here at the hotel or go somewhere?"

Maggie paused for a moment, watching the hotel guests gather food at the buffet style set up before shaking her head. "I know the perfect place."

We drove for nearly half an hour until we reached a small town with one flashing traffic light. A decorative wooden sign proclaimed it as River's Run, Georgia.

"This is where I live," Maggie said quietly as we passed the sign. "This has been home to me since my parents' divorce."

I nodded, tucking that information away for later. Parents would be a sensitive subject for me, too, and I wasn't ready to dive into that just yet.

She pointed up the road to what she described as the best restaurant in all of Georgia. A quaint shop front lined with windows and cheerful blue paint sat across from a park that Maggie said served as the town square. The paint on the door labeled the place as The Comfy Cushion.

The place certainly had plenty of patrons when we walked in. To my surprise, Celeste stood behind the counter, slapping an order slip in the grill line window. "Order up!" she hollered.

Maggie bounded forward, drumming out a beat on the counter in front of her best friend. "Hey, girl, hey! I survived!"

Celeste laughed, though her smile widened when she saw me behind Maggie. "And I see you brought Hayes with you! Welcome to The Comfy Cushion!"

Maggie flashed a grin my way over her shoulder and slid into one of the counter barstools. "I told him this was the best place to have break-fast! I'll take my usual! C'mon, Zeke. You'll love it here!"

I took the seat next to her. "Then I'll have whatever Maggie's having."

It almost looked like a hint of apprehension flashed in her eyes, but it was gone just as quickly as it came. My brain probably wanted to read far more into Maggie's body language since I had become so obsessed with her in the past twelve hours.

Celeste, however, did look outright panic stricken. "Are you sure about that? Do you have any idea what Maggie's usual is?"

"No. But I trust her."

Her friend didn't look convinced. "Our Maggie here is gonna put herself into a diabetic coma by the time she's twenty-five."

Maggie rolled her eyes, but laughed at the same time. "I like what I like!"

Only I barely heard her over that animalistic roar again that Celeste already labeled Maggie as mine. I was glad other people already noticed.

"That bad, huh?" I tried not to laugh at Maggie's expense so that she didn't think me rude. "I don't care. I want the Maggie Special."

Celeste smirked. "Okay, but just remember, you asked for it!"

Twenty minutes later I stared at the monstrosity before us in abject horror. "You actually put this in your body?!" I asked.

Maggie and Celeste laughed. Even the cook in the kitchen watched in amusement.

The Maggie Special apparently consisted of a stack of three chocolate chip pancakes with a layer of vanilla ice cream slathered in caramel. A top layer of whipped cream with even more chocolate chips finished it off, complete with a maraschino cherry. I actually wondered why Celeste assumed Maggie would reach a sugar coma by twenty-five when I was pretty certain she'd be in one by the end of the meal.

"I should probably exchange phone numbers with you now before we're both rushed to the hospital after this." Nobody ever found me as funny as Celeste and Maggie seemed to be, both of them throwing their heads back in laughter again.

"Speaking of, that reminds me!" Celeste disappeared through the swinging door to the kitchen and reappeared a moment later with a cell phone in hand. "I found this in my car last night! I'm so glad you showed up here or I would have had to go beat down Marla's door after the breakfast rush."

The adorable flush crept up Maggie's neck again, and she refused to meet my eye. "I...um...didn't stay at Marla's last night."

Her friend blinked at her in surprise, casting an incredulous glance my way. "Oh. Well, that's..."

"Trust me, it's nothing like that," I assured her. "Maggie didn't feel well and didn't want to disturb Marla, so I got her a hotel room and left. I've been in the gym all night."

"You went to the gym? Why didn't you go back to your room on base?" Maggie asked.

I shrugged in nonchalance. "Just wasn't tired. I don't sleep much anyway. Occupational hazard."

Somehow, I caught Maggie's gaze at that moment and couldn't look away. I needed to figure out a way to ask her out again, or at least convince her to let this day continue, but the words died on the tip of my tongue. She looked so wistful, her eyes in their wild mirage of colors, and my gaze inadvertently dropped to her lips. I wondered if kissing her again would pack as much of a punch as it did last night.

As if she were thinking the same thing, Maggie licked her lips. This was communication in its most intrinsic form. Just being near her made me feel closer to her than I had with anyone else before. Even Leggett.

Celeste clapped her hand in between us, causing Maggie and me to jump in our seats.

"Good gravy, you two, get a room!" She shook her head incredulously before walking out to greet a newly arrived family at the door.

Maggie smirked at me as she leaned closer. "Pretty sure we already did that," she whispered conspiratorially.

I laughed so hard that the partially melted whipped cream on the plate in front of me sprayed everywhere.

CHAPTER 11
THE AFTERGLOW
MAGGIE

I WASN'T sure if breakfast at The Comfy Cushion counted as a date, but I'd like to say that it did. A real one, not like the pathetic parking lot "hangouts" and random bonfires I'd gone to with boys in high school. All I knew is that I didn't want it to end. The only reason I needed to go back to Marla's was to go through the motions of my ritual. I could barely tolerate eating anything this morning after all the wasted calories last night, but I had concocted the pancake/ice cream creation after I realized how much easier it was to purge my stomach with ice cream. By the time it reached your stomach, the warmth of the human body turned it back to a liquid, and it hurt less to come back up. I added the ridiculous pancakes so that I could call it a breakfast food.

It killed me every time Celeste described me as a sugar-ridden junkie. In actuality, I hated the guilt that came with eating anything sugary or sweet. Guilt could cripple you just as badly as a poor diet. And when you obsess over calorie deficits and macronutrients, guilt becomes a part of the routine. I knew what I was doing was wrong enough that I didn't feel comfortable telling my best friend about what I did each day, but I didn't want to stop either.

I settled for trying to swirl the food around on my plate. Whenever I took a bite, I tried to make them small and dainty, focusing more on the vanilla ice cream so that I knew I had an easier shot at getting it back up.

Zeke, though, seemed to notice. Every time I lifted my fork, I caught his furtive glance to my face, followed by an infinitesimal frown whenever I didn't raise the fork to my mouth. After a few moments of his scrutiny, I couldn't take it anymore.

"What is it?" I snapped.

Rudeness was so uncalled for, especially when Zeke had already shown me nothing but patience and kindness, but I hated the way he watched me. I was *not* that interesting.

"You've only had six bites of food," he replied evenly. Like my frustration didn't faze him. "Do you still feel sick?"

Why was he counting how many bites of food I ate? Did he obsess over calories and macros, too?

Still, he gave me an out, and I would be a fool not to take it.

"Yeah. I thought I was ready to eat, but the food isn't sitting well in my stomach. I think I'm done."

A look of concern crossed his face. "Of course. How can I help make it better?"

It was such a simple request. Something polite that anyone would say upon hearing another person didn't feel well. Yet when Zeke said it to me, it sounded authentic, like he genuinely wanted an exact list of all the ways in which he could make me feel better. His attentiveness wasn't something I was used to, and I caught myself on the same loop of wondering if I misread the signs. Did Zeke like me or not? Guys weren't usually this polite and helpful in River's Run.

"Nothing. I think I'm just done eating this for now," I replied.

"Okay. Let me get the check from Celeste and I can take you wherever you'd like to go."

I noticed that he didn't say he would take me home. My heart leapt at the possibility of it being an intentional word choice because Zeke didn't want our time together to end any more than I did.

"Who is Marla? Is that your not-mother?" Zeke looked at me so curiously that I laughed.

"Um, it's kind of hard to explain. Marla used to work here at The Comfy Cushion with Celeste and now she's opening her own bakery in the shop underneath her apartment building. She's letting me stay with her in exchange for helping to get the shop set up."

"I'm happy to help, too," Zeke offered. "I know how to do some things."

God, he was so sweet! My heart wouldn't be able to crush on a man properly after this.

"You really don't have to do that," I insisted. "But it's real kind of you to offer. Besides, I have nothing but time on my hands right now, so I should be able to get a lot of the work done."

He frowned. "You don't work?"

I grinned, trying not to sound too boastful when I said, "Actually, I just graduated with my cosmetology license. I'm going to try and find work at a salon now."

Zeke nodded and turned back to his food. "Oh. That makes sense."

While I knew cosmetology wasn't exactly brain surgery, I was still disappointed that my chosen profession didn't impress him. "What makes sense?" I ground out through clenched teeth.

"If you're a cosmetologist, I understand why you made yourself look like that last night and like this right now." He continued to eat his breakfast as if he didn't care how much that statement just hurt.

"Wow." I tried to keep my voice level so that I didn't disturb all of Celeste's customers. "Why don't you use a knife next time? You'll kill me faster!"

In a huff, I abruptly sprung up from the breakfast bar and stomped out of the restaurant. The door might've slammed a bit behind me, but I would apologize to Celeste for that later. For right now, I just needed to get someplace where I could nurse my tears in private.

Did I really look that ugly now? Zeke brought me makeup this morning, which I thought was born out of kindness, but what if he meant it as an intentional jab? Like I needed makeup in order to be seen with him. Was I really that ugly? He was far more attractive than any guy I'd seen in River's Run. Maybe that made him out of my league.

Even Quasimodo wouldn't touch you, the critical voice in my head reminded me.

A gentle hand circled my elbow, pulling me to a stop. I hadn't even realized where I was going, and somehow wound up in the alleyway behind all the businesses along Main Street. Sniffling, I turned around slowly, keeping my head down so I didn't have to look Zeke in the eye. The truth would hurt too much.

"Trouble, you're gonna have to help me with this one because I don't understand how I upset you. I didn't mean anything bad."

Even Zeke's shoes were perfect, a pristinely white pair of sneakers.

Traitorous tears continued to run down my cheeks. Every time I cried in front of Diana, her criticism increased tenfold. Sometimes I almost suspected my tears made her feel powerful, but I couldn't believe that hurting me was a deliberate action. Crying now in front of Zeke felt even worse.

"Then what did you mean?" I whispered.

He squatted down to try and catch my eye. "You're the only girl I've met who knows how to use makeup. I just logically concluded you would be interested in doing hair, too."

Quietly wiping my nose on the back of my hand, I scoffed. "You must not know many women."

Zeke grinned. "Nope. And you're the only one I want to know, so you're all that matters."

You're all that matters.

It was hard to keep the smile off my face at hearing those words. I might've been glowing from the inside out.

"I find that kinda hard to believe," I admitted. A handsome soldier like Zeke wouldn't have any trouble finding a girlfriend, or even just someone to go home with. Although none of his behavior so far indicated he was that kind of person, I couldn't wrap my head around the idea that he struggled to pick up women. Certainly a smile like his would simply make them all line up at his door.

"Guess there's a lot for you to learn about me." He shrugged, nonplussed at the idea. "Maybe we should spend the day together and rectify that."

The glowing thing was definitely happening now. There was no way for me to misread an invitation like that. Guys didn't ask to spend time with you if they weren't interested.

"Oh yeah? What d'you have in mind?" I asked coyly.

Zeke paused for a moment, staring off into the distance as he considered it. "I've never been to the ocean. Apparently, Tybee Island is within driving distance. Wanna go?" He held out his hand, just like last night when he saved me from the panic attack Spencer and his gang of misfits instigated.

I liked that he always made it sound like an invitation, not an expectation. I had the freedom to choose either way.

There was zero hesitation on my part as I slipped my hand into his. "Count me in."

CHAPTER 12
THE BEACH

ZEKE

I had never once had any kind of inclination to go to the beach. The prospect of getting sand into uncomfortable places and submerging any part of my body into water that contained urine, feces, and the remains of dead organisms—among other things—never held any appeal. I would never consider myself that kind of adventurous person.

But the lure of spending an entire day with Maggie was too great to ignore. And going to Tybee Island would be an outing; from here in River's Run, it would take approximately an hour and a half to get there. On a gorgeous summer day, and a military four day weekend at that, it was sure to be packed, but I didn't care. Crowds no longer scared me if it meant I could stay with Maggie.

Besides, she seemed genuinely excited by the idea, and that was enough for me. A long drive would give me the perfect opportunity to get her talking. I wanted to know everything about her. Even that probably wouldn't be enough.

In less than a single day, Maggie Eaton had enough of a hold on me that I could never let her go.

"Can we swing by Marla's place so I can get ready?" Maggie asked. "Then we can stop by your place for you to change on the way out there."

I glanced down at the simple t-shirt and shorts I had on. "Um... change into what?"

She laughed, a rich, throaty sound that I hoped to haunt my dreams. When I didn't join in, the laugh died out abruptly. "Oh, you're serious! Don't you want a bathing suit?"

"I don't own a bathing suit."

"Of course you do, silly!" Maggie swatted me playfully on the arm. "Everybody owns a bathing suit!"

I shook my head, which made her laugh again.

"Why, Zeke Hayes. You continue to surprise me!"

I wasn't entirely sure if that was a good thing or a bad thing, but she grabbed my hand to lead me out of the alleyway before I could ask.

Even though Marla's apartment was only a few blocks away, according to Maggie, she said it would be easier for us to drive so that we could leave right from her place.

"Plus, you can meet Marla and get her approval!" Maggie winked like it was a joke, yet my stomach plummeted. Marla was clearly important to Maggie, which already made her important to me, and I needed to make a good first impression.

"Marla, I'm home! And I brought a new friend!" she called as soon as we crossed the threshold. The apartment had a loft-like feel, with one wall of exposed brick and high ceilings that featured exposed duct work.

A woman around Leggett's age stood at the kitchen island, stirring something in a large bowl that she held against her hip. Her brown hair had wisps of gray in it, piled into a lumpy bun on her head, and her eyes narrowed as she took me in. Instinctually, I stood taller, fully prepared to stand at attention like Marla was an Army officer if it got me in her good graces.

"And who might this be?" Marla asked in a thick Southern accent.

"I'm Sergeant Ezekiel Hayes, ma'am," I said. I approached the island to hold out a hand in greeting.

She didn't take it. Marla's shrewd eyes scanned me from head to toe. Apprehension made me break out in a cold sweat under her scrutiny.

"Thank you for your service to our country," Marla finally said.

It was a sentiment that most civilians expressed whenever they learned my profession. Leggett always told me from a young age that the polite thing to do was thank them, even if it didn't feel right to accept their gratitude. *"It's an honor and a privilege to serve in the United States Army, Hayes. That's why only the best get to do it."*

"Thank you, ma'am. I appreciate you saying so."

"What are you making?" Maggie asked her, taking the heat off me. I had a sneaking suspicion that I wasn't yet in the clear with Marla.

Marla frowned. "Nothing if I can't get this batter to thicken like I need. What are y'all up to?"

"Zeke here has never been to the ocean before, so we're gonna head out to the beach for the day." Maggie winked at me. The act made my heart skip a beat.

A quizzical brow rose as Marla directed her attention back on me. "Is that so? I'll have you know, Mr. Hayes, that I have friends on law enforcement out that way. You get outta line with Maggie here and I'll make sure it's the last thing you ever do, Army or no Army!"

My cheeks burned in shame. "I swear on my life that I won't let any harm come to her, ma'am. I'm not that kind of person."

"Yeah, well be sure that you don't turn into one!" Marla slammed the bowl down hard on the counter to emphasize her point. Eyebrows shooting up in alarm, I turned to Maggie for help.

She just smiled and rolled her eyes, waving off Marla's threat. "Zeke's not like that, Marla. I think I found a good one this time. I want to shower real quick before we go, so make yourself at home." The last line was directed at me, but Maggie had to know there was no way I could do that under Marla's watchful eye.

Racking my brain for a book that had a similar situation so I knew how to act, my tongue suddenly felt like it stuck to the roof of my mouth. I could tell Marla reserved her judgment. A scowl slowly worked its way onto her face as I continued to stand there like a mute.

"So…Maggie tells me you're gonna open a bakery," I finally settled on. "That sounds like quite an undertaking."

She harumphed, though I didn't know what I said that could've been funny. "You don't know the half of it! Neither do I, truth be told. And the shop needs a whole lot of work."

"I'm happy to help, ma'am," I offered. "I'm good with my hands and I've done some things at my mentor's house."

Marla fixed me with an indiscernible stare. After several long seconds, she nodded. "I could use all the help I can get. Come by tomorrow morning and I'll set you to work."

And if I'm here, that only increases my chances of seeing Maggie again! I loved that idea.

"Yes, ma'am. I'll be here."

A gaze almost akin to pity softened her features. She turned around and grabbed a muffin off the counter behind her to hand to me. "Here. Eat this. It'll help with your nerves."

My cheeks felt like they were on fire again. "Oh, I'm not nervous, ma'am, I'm just—"

"You're just standing there like a lost calf ready to follow the truck to the slaughter house," Marla finished for me. "I know a bit about men who get swept up in the antics of my girls."

"Oh, I'm sorry. Maggie said you're not her mom…" I didn't know how to end that statement without it sounding even more awkward, and I cringed slightly at the tension that hung in the air.

Marla snorted again. "I ain't her mama, but I'm a right side better than that she-devil. You just stay on my good side, young man. Be respectful to Maggie and Celeste, too, 'cause you can't have one without the other. We clear on that?"

I nodded, swallowing thickly.

She gestured towards the kitchen table. "Have a seat. I'll get you a cup o' coffee."

Caffeine would probably be beneficial at the moment because adrenaline could only take me so far. I thanked her as she set it down in front of me, breaking off a small piece of the muffin Marla gave me so I didn't appear rude. Mercifully, Marla returned to her batter and didn't continue with the conversation after that. I caught her shrewd glances periodically, but I kept my eyes trained on the tree line I could see from the window.

Intrusive thoughts began to pepper me with worst-case scenarios. I had absolutely zero experience with socializing. I'd never even had someone close enough that I would consider them a friend. And while I wasn't exactly sure what romantic feelings felt like, the way I felt about Maggie didn't seem normal. What if I said the wrong thing and she never spoke to me again? What if I couldn't recognize a social cue? Like that one time in high school when I tried to have a conversation with an upperclassman holding the same book I was reading. He apparently had been trying to end the conversation, but I didn't know it, so I followed him all the way into the bathroom to keep asking him questions about whether or not he enjoyed the book as much as I did. The principal ended up calling Leggett in and I received three days of in school suspension for disrespecting personal boundaries.

The memory of it still seared through my brain from time to time. I never tried to engage someone in conversation willingly after that. At least, not until Maggie.

Just then, Maggie breezed into the room, her hair piled into a messy bun. She had on a bright orange string bikini top and Daisy Dukes. I could just detect the orange string of the bikini bottoms poking out at her waist. Huge sunglasses concealed most of her face, but she grinned at me in a way that made my heart start dancing again. If I spent much more time with her, I might need to get on heart medicine.

"Be sure to pack plenty of sunblock," Marla advised her. "It's gonna be a scorcher today, and a sunburn won't save you from working tomorrow!"

"Yes, ma'am," Maggie and I said in unison. Her grin widened as I blushed again, embarrassed to believe Marla might've been speaking to me. Nobody ever spoke to me. Just Leggett, and he barely counted.

"We have to stop at Madden Markets and get this clown a bathing suit anyway, so I'll be sure to load up!" Maggie assured her. Grabbing my hand, she led us out the front door, barely giving me a moment to call out a thank you to Marla on our descent.

There wasn't a cloud in the sky as we walked towards my truck, which I hoped was a good sign of the day to come. Maggie turned quiet beside me, putting up a wall that nearly felt tangible, and I didn't know why. I was also too shy to ask. People didn't like it when you pry, I'd learned.

We had almost reached my truck, parked along the street a few spaces down from Marla's building, when a woman exited the laundromat to our left and stopped Maggie in her tracks.

"Well, I'll be, Maggie," the woman said, balancing a small hamper on her hip. "You leave my house and forget to wear clothes?"

The way Maggie's back went rigid alerted me to the fact that she was upset. Yet she didn't say a word to the woman, merely glowered at her, a scowl that I never wanted to see on her face again.

"Excuse me, ma'am, but I think you're making Maggie uncomfortable." I glared at the woman, instantly willing to hate anyone who made Maggie look like that.

But instead of apologizing, the woman smiled at me, taking a step closer to peruse the length of my body in a way that made my skin crawl. If she noticed the way I recoiled at her leering, the woman didn't show it.

"And who might this fine specimen be?" she crooned. Only it reminded me of one of those evil witches in kids' movies.

After a glance at Maggie indicated her lips would remain firmly shut, I held out my hand, too trained to be polite. "Sergeant Ezekiel Hayes, ma'am."

Rather than shake it, the woman grabbed my hand and pulled me even closer, letting go only so that her fingers could graze up my arm. She seemed particularly interested in my biceps, but the attention made me want to gag.

"And how did my daughter here land such a handsome man, Sergeant?"

This was Maggie's mother?! She had all of the charm and appeal of a rattlesnake.

"Shouldn't you be running along to Tyrese, *Diana*." Maggie added the name pointedly, as if it was an expletive meant to insult the woman.

"Tyson," her mother snapped back immediately. The oily charisma she showed me disappeared in an instant. "And no, we broke up. I suppose that means you could come back home for a little while." Except her tone implied it wasn't a real invitation.

"I'm good. Have a nice life," Maggie replied with a sneer. She sidestepped her mother, literally leaning away from her as if Diana had barbed wire around her.

Diana sighed dramatically, her blue eyes flicking to me again with piqued interest. "Be careful with that one, soldier. No sense in ruining your life over Maggie's attitude. She's nothing special."

I frowned, my temper beginning to boil over. "We'll have to agree to disagree on that one, ma'am. Excuse me." I brushed past her and caught up to Maggie in two strides, who now bridged the last few feet to my truck like her feet were on fire.

Although she ducked her head and tried to turn away from me, I squatted down so that I was eye level with her and tucked my hand under her chin to stop her. "Maggie, what is it?" I asked gently. My thumb rubbed what I hoped were soothing circles along her cheek.

A solitary tear rolled onto my thumb and I wanted to die. "I'm sorry," whimpered Maggie, her voice small. "Diana just…she just gets under my skin, and I hate it."

"Don't *ever* apologize for the way you feel," I ordered her. I recognized the squad leader voice coming out, but I couldn't help myself. I needed her to heed this. "Not with me. I'm your safe space, okay? I want to see all the parts of you that you hide from everybody else. Do you understand, Maggie Eaton?"

Another tear slid down from under her sunglasses, but Maggie hastily wiped it away. She nodded quickly.

"No, I need to hear it. Do you understand?"

"I understand, Zeke."

Satisfied, I took a step back, and offered her my hand. "So will you go to the beach with me?"

Her grin wasn't quite as wide as before, but she shoved the sunglasses up onto her head, casting me under a spell with her gorgeous, tear-soaked eyes. Maggie's head bobbed as she nodded, clasping her hand in mine.

CHAPTER 13
THE CALM
MAGGIE

Zeke couldn't possibly know what his words did to me outside his truck. Any encounter with Diana usually soured my mood for the next twenty-four hours, but when it came unexpectedly like that, it tended to be even worse. No one had ever focused on me like he did in the heat of the moment. Poor Celeste always tried to help me whenever I shared with her, but sometimes it was easier to keep Diana's ugliness close to the chest.

And yet Zeke immediately stepped in to calm me. His words lifted my spirit, getting me out of the downward self-hatred spiral I'd started, and kept me grounded. If only Zeke's promise to be my safe space could be true. There was no way someone as good as him would accept my dark side. I never wanted him to see that down at my core, I inherited every bit of Diana's ugliness and then some.

Thankfully he stayed quiet on the drive. I got the sense that Zeke wasn't the type to fill long silences. With the way he kept stealing glances my way, it almost seemed like he couldn't believe I was real. But I knew that couldn't be true. He had only ever seen me as a walking disaster; he should have been running away, screaming, in the opposite direction.

The further we got from River's Run, the more my bad mood lifted. It was amazing how much distance could alleviate your problems. Bright sun paved the way out to Tybee Island, traffic relatively light for the season. When Zeke offered to pull off the highway to stop at a Madden Market, as I promised Marla we would, fear suddenly gripped me that I would freak out again over seeing Wesley's name—or worse, one of his advertisements. It was hard enough to shield the fact that Wesley was now the face of Madden Markets from Celeste, but losing Wes hurt much like I'd imagined it would hurt to lose a sibling. I didn't need that when I already felt vulnerable.

Instead, we kept going, stopping at one of those little beach hut pop ups close to the ocean where they sold cheap swimsuits, towels, and kitschy tourist gifts. The bathing suit I picked out for him would prob-ably disintegrate if Zeke chose to wear it a second time, but he went behind one of the changing curtains all the same. He told me to pick out anything I wanted or thought we might need, so I was happily filling a cart with extra beach towels, tanning lotion, sunglasses, and any other random thing I could find.

I stopped dead in my tracks when Zeke stepped out from behind the curtain. The lime green suit was supposed to look ridiculous, something to make us both laugh, yet the way the shorts gripped his muscular thighs made me bite back a moan. Abs with actual rivulets between them, making each tight muscle distinct and eye-catching, drew my attention. A well cut V angled down underneath the waistband, and I had never wanted to follow a physical feature more. Zeke's biceps were huge and defined. One flex and he could choke the life out of me, but oddly, that thought only aroused me all the more. I wanted to lick every inch of him. Then plaster a painted sign on both sides that labeled him as mine.

Where that possessiveness came from, I had no idea.

Slowly, with my mouth outright hanging open, I raised the sunglasses up to the top of my head, drinking in Zeke's powerful form like it was the eighth wonder of the world. Which, it at least deserved a nomination for.

Zeke merely looked around self-consciously as if he were afraid someone might laugh at him.

"You are so fucking hot," I breathed. My hands moved on auto-pilot, lightly tracing along his torso up to pecs hard enough to break glass. I couldn't fathom how many hours Zeke must've spent in the gym to earn a physique like this. No wonder he could barely stomach the pancakes Celeste served this morning. Men like this had to eat some kind of special protein diet, right?

At my words, Zeke flushed, his eyes darting to the ground in embarrassment. "Um…thanks. If you say so."

I hated that he seemed so unsure of himself. Had no one ever told him that he qualified as the sexiest man alive? Seriously?

Words failed me as I continued to drink him in.

"Did you get everything you wanted?" Zeke nodded toward the shopping cart I had piled high with stuff.

I crinkled my nose apologetically. "Yeah, I usually just dump everything that catches my eye into the basket and then I sort through it at check out to decided what I can actually afford. Not the best shopping method, actually. Sorry."

He shrugged. "You don't have to 'afford' anything today. I'll take care of it. Pick out whatever you want."

A laugh escaped, only for me to realize a beat later that he didn't join me. "Oh-you're serious?"

"Of course. Why would I invite you out for the day if I wasn't going to pay for everything?"

All of the soldiers Diana brought home were as broke as a joke. I didn't want to out him, but I didn't exactly believe the United States Army paid him what he deserved.

"I mean, I don't want to spend all your money…" I let the sentence filter off, suddenly too awkward and shy to call him out on being poor. It wasn't a foreign concept to me. We barely had two nickels to rub together my entire life.

Even Zeke's frowns were sexy. As the wrinkles formed between his brows, the urge to kiss them away overwhelmed me.

"Maggie, I will never offer something that I can't readily give." Zeke took a few steps towards me so that he towered over me. Without my heels on, I had to crane my neck to look at him. One big breath would send my boobs into his chest, and as much as I wanted to know how sensational that would feel, Zeke's presence was also overpowering. His eyes lasered me with a soulful gaze that had to reveal my deepest, darkest secrets to him.

I shivered, unable to back away without hitting the cart behind me. Not that anyone could want to back away from Zeke Hayes. Planets would rather orbit him than the sun.

My voice sounded small, even to my ears, as I explained, "I don't want to be a burden to anybody." When he didn't respond after a moment, I glanced up at him through my lashes, an unreadable expression on his face.

"You're not a burden, you're a gift," Zeke finally said. His tone indicated he would not hear another word on the subject.

My skin warmed at his praise. I wanted to bask in his opinion like a cat in the sun. He made me feel beautiful, and cherished, in a way that I hadn't thought possible. If I wasn't careful, I could fall for a guy like him. There's only so much sex appeal and romance a girl can take.

Since I didn't trust myself to speak over the lump forming in my throat, I simply nodded and turned back to the cart. "Well, I have everything I want. Is there anything else you'd like to get?"

"Nope. Let's pay and get our toes in the sand." He moved to stand beside me, gently throwing an arm in front of me so that he could commandeer the cart up to the register. The total came close to two hundred dollars, but Zeke didn't bat an eye.

Finding parking with beach access proved to be difficult. We had to drive around for a while, and the whole time I chewed on my thumbnail, waiting for Zeke to admit defeat, that taking me to the beach wasn't worth the hassle of parking three miles away from the ocean. He still wore the unreadable expression from the beach hut, but I was too scared of bursting the perfect bubble we were in to ask what was wrong.

You're not a burden, you're a gift.

I needed him to record it as a voice memo so I could play it on repeat forever. His words were a lifeline in the storm, hooking me in and guiding me towards a warm light that offered safety. The possibility of anyone seeing something good in me, something Diana never could, made me feel hopefully anxious. I so desperately wanted to believe in their truth, even though the voice in my head insisted they couldn't be. Optimism took root in my heart.

Once we found a spot, Zeke refused to let me carry anything. "What kind of guy do you take me for?" he argued, pulling a large tote from my shoulder. He lugged all of it, including two small beach chairs, all the way to the beach by himself. I noticed the way Zeke naturally drifted away from large groups of people, so I pointed out a spot farther away from the water to set up. He immediately plopped a chair down and ordered me to sit in it.

"You're not to lift a finger, do you understand?"

"But I—"

"I said, do you understand?" He fixed me with a stern look that probably frightened the wits out of his soldiers.

"Yes, I understand." I also understood the aching need building in my core from being with a man so authoritative. While I always thought that would be an unattractive quality in a man—especially the losers I typically saw Diana submitting to—when Zeke did it, his firm demeanor made me want to jump to his bidding.

I wonder if he would be like that with other activities…

Besides, Zeke's manner of command made me feel cared for and appreciated, not disrespected. It was entirely different, and surprisingly, enjoyable.

I settled back in my chair, lounging contentedly as Zeke laid out the towels and set up an umbrella along with a second beach chair next to me. Waves crashing along the shore sounded like a lullaby ready to sing me to sleep. It was peaceful, I realized, a feeling I hadn't experienced in a long time. He made me feel so comfortable in his presence that it set my mind at ease, allowing me to enjoy the moment without a mental breakdown over what parts of my body were visible.

Zeke cleared his throat loudly, shooting me a sheepish expression. "Um, can you put this sunscreen on my back? Please?"

Could I rub his rippling back muscles with a lotion that smelled like sweet jasmine and citrus because Zeke sprang for the good stuff? Absolutely. Could I do so without soaking through my bikini bottoms? Unlikely.

Still, I wasn't going to admit that to him. Zeke kneeled in front of me so that his back was within easy reach and I bit down hard enough on my bottom lip that I tasted blood. Even from this angle, his body looked like a work of art. His skin was silky smooth to the touch, and although I noted the way he initially tensed when my hand applied the lotion, he quickly relaxed. It was then I noticed the scars lacing across his back.

My hand stilled as my mouth dropped open in horror. There were *dozens* of scars, like Zeke had been whipped. Some of them were clearly older and more deeply embedded in his skin.

"Zeke, what happened to you?" Tears clogged my throat now for an entirely different reason.

Rather than answer, Zeke stood up and sat in the chair beside me. "Thanks," he said curtly.

Zeke so far had shown me nothing but respect in regard to my boundaries. He never pried or forced me to open up, and while I knew I should reply in kind, word vomit came out instead. "Seriously? What happened? Those look bad."

"I learned things the hard way a lot as a kid," he finally said. Tension lined his jaw and he shoved a new pair of aviators on his nose to block his expression.

My heart softened at the prospect of a young Zeke receiving such a harsh punishment. Unless he set fire to nursing homes and drowned puppies, I couldn't see how he could have done anything bad enough to warrant marks like those. Even at Diana's worst she would never lay a hand on me. I couldn't even remember a single time my father disciplined me for anything.

"You know, you can talk about it with me and I'll listen," I offered. "No strings attached. Sometimes saying things out loud makes you feel better. At least, that's what Marla always says. And she's pretty much never wrong."

A ghost of a smile darted across his face, there and gone in an instant. "I'll keep that in mind."

Silence descended on us again. This time I didn't fill it as shyness suddenly rendered me speechless. I wanted to comfort him, but didn't know how. To show him that he wasn't really alone.

So I did what I did best. I flirted.

Rolling forward so that I lay chest down on the towel in front of me, I kept my hips arched up so that I could push my shorts off. This particular bikini, while also a bold color that caught people's attention, featured a hiked style bottom that exposed a lot more of my ass. I chose it specifically in hopes that Zeke might finally make a move. A move I was even more desperate for now that I knew how unnaturally hot his body was. Settling myself back down, I tugged at the string holding the back of the bikini top, then let the string around my neck fall loose.

Coyly, I looked over my shoulder at him and said, "Guess that means it's my turn."

Zeke was not immune to my wiles. His eyes had widened to the point where I could see the whites all the way around the irises, and his jaw clenched down hard enough that I could hear his teeth grinding. He cast furtive glances around us as if daring someone else to look at me.

A smug grin lined my face. Men were so predictable. The sand gave a little as Zeke kneeled down beside me, lathering in lotion with the kind of gentle caress I expected from him. On the exterior, especially in a swimsuit with rippling muscles on display, Zeke looked like someone you should be fearful of, but the more time I spent around him, the more I realized he was actually a very considerate, compassionate soul. How he managed to fight in combat was a mystery I could never solve.

"Is…is this okay?" Zeke asked, his voice a tight whisper.

"Yep! This is perfect." I tried and failed to keep myself from shuddering underneath his touch. Zeke's fingers moved deftly between my shoulder blades and down my spine, massaging the lotion into the clefts at my lower back. But he didn't linger, only touching me long enough to put the lotion on and then returning to his chair.

I peered at him over my shoulder.

"Should you really have your top undone like that?" Zeke refused to meet my gaze, focusing on something off in the distance. "What if you need to jump up suddenly and then you're half naked?"

I couldn't help but laugh. "Well, that's never happened to me before, so when it does, I'll let you know. I just don't want to get tan lines. They're so unattractive."

Zeke snorted. "Like anything is ever unattractive on you."

Now I was the one unnerved. I shuffled my hips as the blush burned across my face. Compliments sounded so sincere when they came from Zeke Hayes' lips. He didn't say them as a way to get in my pants, he said them because he truly felt that way. It was high praise, and I drank it in.

"So where are you from?" I needed to change the subject before I threw myself at him, topless and all, in front of all the families trying to enjoy their day at the beach.

"Michigan," he supplied. "Sort of."

Okay, laying down wasn't the right way to have this conversation. Zeke needed answers pulled out of him, like a dentist yanking teeth. I hastily tied the bikini strings around my neck, then sat up while holding the back strings. Turning so that I kneeled in front of him, I tied a knot behind my back as I pressed further, "What does that mean?"

Zeke tried to keep his eyes poised on my face, but I caught them darting down to my chest as I adjusted the bikini cups. "Um...I just moved around a lot."

"Oh. Was your dad in the military, too?"

"Something like that." His eyes fell to my chest again, then back up to my face, his cheeks turning beet red.

I grinned. "Is there something wrong with my bikini top?"

His face reddened even more. "Of course not!"

"Because you seem really concerned with it."

"I just want you to be comfortable, Maggie." Sincerity layered his words, and I fell back on my heels. Most guys I know would have turned that into a disgusting innuendo. The sweet talkers like Spencer would have found a way to flip the conversation into something flirtatious that gave me the hit of adrenaline and serotonin my mind craved from run ins with meaningless flings. But of course Zeke didn't do that. Zeke genuinely concerned himself with my well-being.

"I don't understand you," I burst out in irritation. "Do you like me or not?"

A puzzled expression replaced the crimson shame on his face as Zeke stared me down. "I like you a lot, Trouble. That's why I'm here."

An answer that didn't really answer anything. "But *how* do you like me?" I whined. "In what way?"

He chewed on the inside of his cheek as he considered the question. "I don't know," Zeke finally admitted. "But I'm determined to find out."

I didn't want to become an overly emotional woman who scared him away. Diana always told me that men didn't like that. Getting teary-eyed would only make them clam up and start to look for a better partner. At the same time, though, I was afraid of Zeke slipping through my fingers. Just because he claimed he didn't have any other girls vying for his attention didn't mean it would stay that way. I needed to stake my ground now before it became a bloody war.

"Well, I'm not going anywhere," I replied.

Zeke smiled, displaying gleaming white teeth. "Then I have about a million questions for you."

CHAPTER 14
THE INFORMATION
ZEKE

I SPENT the rest of the day peppering Maggie with questions. She probably thought I was grilling her for information like some kind of CIA interrogator, but I couldn't help myself. I found everything about her fascinating. Any given answer would sprout another hundred questions in my mind until I wanted to give her a notebook and order her to write down her entire life's journey for me to read and understand her. Maybe she had a diary she'd allow me to look at?

Maggie was an obsession of which I could never grow bored. Her mannerisms completely changed when I tried to bring up her family again, so I steered clear of that subject. After how badly I screwed up when she mentioned the scars on my back, it only seemed fair, but I was dying to know what her mother had done that hurt Maggie so deeply. The woman certainly made the hairs on the back of my neck stand up when I met her in River's Run. Yet I sensed what Maggie felt somehow ran deeper; there was an underlying pain there that fermented under the surface. I wanted to take it all away.

Without even realizing it, Maggie and I walked nearly four miles up the beach and back again. Although I wanted to scrub my skin with the strongest disinfectant the human body could handle after walking through the ocean surf, I also didn't want to break away from her long enough to do that. Somehow as we walked, her hand slipped into mine, our fingers laced together, and I loved how complete and whole it looked for us to be joined together that way. Taking her hand was as natural as breathing.

The sun started to set, sending long shadows dancing along the sand, which created a picturesque backdrop. Most of the people on the beach had long since packed up to go to one of the many restaurants dotting the boardwalk. Music called out to us from the open doors of all the bars while the crashing waves drowned out the lyrics. She stopped short as we arrived back where our belongings waited, simply standing in the wet sand as the tide ebbed around our feet. Our hands remained clasped between us as Maggie turned to face me, her eyes round with longing.

The rose gold hue of sunlight illuminated every feature on her face that I wanted to commit to memory. Truly, I'd never seen anyone so gorgeous. The wind threatened to pull her hair from the bun piled on her head all day, and despite the wide-brimmed hat Maggie wore when the sun sat directly overhead, I could already count the new freckles dotting her nose and cheeks. We would both be sunburned, but I didn't care.

An urge to release her hair and let it cascade around her became too much, and I tugged at the hairband. Disheveled waves of dark hair whipped around us and my heart leapt in my throat. I found myself staring at Maggie's lips. I would give anything to know if the powerful kiss we shared last night could be repeated, but I didn't know how to ask.

"Zeke," she whispered. My name sounded like a prayer from her mouth. "Will you kiss me again?"

I gulped. Had she read my mind or did she want to repeat the experience as much as I did? It wouldn't surprise me that Maggie could read my thoughts; everything about her bewitched me anyway.

"I'm not very good at it," I confessed quietly.

She shook her head, rejecting the idea. "Yes, you are. You're perfect."

Before I could answer her, Maggie leaned up on her tip toes. I found myself bending down to meet her. As soon as our lips touched, that same explosion rocketed through me as the night before. Her mouth molded to mine, soft and pliable, yet I'd never been so grounded. Her body was an anchor, the only thing preventing me from levitating into the clouds. All the sounds around us faded away to the kind of silence I'd only managed to find in dreams.

What started off as a tentative kiss grew hot and desperate. The angry animal inside roared in delight, and I possessively wrapped an arm around her waist so that there was no longer any space between us. Her body fit perfectly against mine as though we were two pieces cut from the same cloth. Both of her arms snaked around the back of my neck to hold me in place. As if I ever planned on leaving.

The muffled sound of a child laughing broke through the fog and I pulled away just enough to rest my forehead on hers. There were still a few stray people on the beach. I didn't need an audience for the passion that grew between us.

"Wow," Maggie muttered in a daze. Her fingers lazily rubbed the cropped hair on the back of my head, sending tiny shivers of pleasure down my spine. "Who the hell told you that you're not good at this?"

I chuckled. "You're my first kiss."

Maggie stumbled backwards, blinking rapidly. Her alarmed state put me on edge. *Had I said the wrong thing?*

"You've never been kissed before?" she asked incredulously.

I shook my head.

Her eyes narrowed in suspicion. "How old are you, Zeke?"

"I turned twenty-one a few months ago. Is that okay?"

Maggie ignored my question, staring at me for several beats longer than was comfortable. I stood there awkwardly, fisted hands drumming on my hips.

"Are you..." Her voice trailed off as she glanced back towards the beach. The few people that remained weren't paying us any attention. "Are you a virgin?" Maggie asked.

Maybe a giant whale would leap out of the ocean and swallow me whole. Her opinion of me would probably change with my answer. "No, I'm not a virgin." Leggett always told me to keep my pants on, and although I didn't read a lot of fiction, the classics I'd read seemed to place a lot of importance on saving oneself. It never occurred to me that it mattered until now. I couldn't bear her rejection over my worthless experiences.

She sighed in obvious relief. "Thank god," Maggie cried. "You had me worried there for a second!"

I frowned. "You don't mind that I'm not a virgin?"

One of her golden laughs followed. "Of course not! I just don't understand how you don't have women falling at your feet," she admitted.

Shrugging, I told her the truth. "Most people think I'm a freak."

Maggie shook her head sadly, stepping closer so she could hold my face in her hands. The forced eye contact made my heart rate spike, but I didn't pull away. "Most people are idiots," she corrected me gently. "But luckily for you, I'm not. Let's get out of here, okay? This is enough of the beach for one day."

If she meant to lift my spirits, Maggie more than succeeded. I no longer cared about all the names I'd been called or the way soldiers and classmates made me feel about myself. Maggie liked me, and that was enough.

Our drive back to River's Run was quiet, but that was mostly because she kept her hand laced in mine on the center console between us. Even with the nasty ocean water and the sting of my newly formed sunburn, this was the perfect day. Probably my favorite day ever, if I were being honest.

I pulled into an open space in front of Marla's apartment and killed the engine. Maggie shifted in her seat so that her body faced more towards me, but made no move to get out of the car.

"I'm not really ready for the day with you to end," I admitted quietly, laughing at how ridiculous I sounded.

She smiled. "I don't really want it to either. Do you want to come up? You must be starving. You haven't eaten anything since breakfast."

"Are you sure Marla would be okay with it?"

Maggie rolled her eyes. "I'm positive Marla will be okay with force-feeding you. It's kind of her thing."

Up in the apartment, we once again found Marla in the kitchen pulling a pie from the oven. Five more already sat on the kitchen island.

"Whoa," Maggie commented. "What's going on? What's with all the baking?"

"When I get worked up, the only thing I can do is take it out on pie crust. You know that!" Marla sounded irritated to me, but Maggie didn't flinch. Maybe this was just how Marla operated.

Maggie slipped onto one of the island barstools, gesturing for me to join her. "Anything we can do to help?"

"There's just so much that needs to be done downstairs!" Marla snapped. "Rachel was the one who could organize projects and start a business! I don't know why I thought I could. I don't even know where to start!"

Maggie glanced at me, her eyebrows raised. I had to look just as bewildered.

"Well, you already got the location sorted out," I offered. "That seems like a pretty good start to me."

"Yeah! That's a great start! And I can spend the whole day tomorrow helping you get it cleaned out. Then we can decide what you want the inside to look like." Maggie shot me a grateful smile, rubbing a hand on my thigh.

My dick chose this inopportune time to respond to her touch. I leaned forward, acting as if I were smelling one of the pies before me. "You're definitely gonna sell a lot of these!" Inhaling deeply, I tried to imagine ice baths and a documentary on eye surgeries I once watched, but my erection would not go down.

Marla huffed out a laugh. "Clearly you're new in town."

Maggie giggled, too. "People go out of their way for a slice of Marla's pie. It's legendary. And she has this crazy gift for guessing people's favorite."

"Oh yeah?" I inquired. "What's mine?"

If Marla's shrewd assessment didn't make my dick behave, nothing would. She surveyed me carefully for so long that my eyes began to water. I didn't want to blink and somehow break the spell.

"You're a coconut cream pie man," she finally announced. Turning, she pulled a pie out of the refrigerator and found a knife to slice into it.

Setting a slice on a plate in front of me, she nodded to it. "Go ahead—try it. Your life's about to change," Marla goaded me.

Like they had a mind of their own, my eyes flicked in Maggie's direction. She watched me eagerly, Marla's skill exciting her. "Yes, it is," I breathed without thinking.

Maggie blushed and I grabbed a fork to shovel a large piece of pie into my mouth to prevent any other stupid phrase from popping out. At least the embarrassment made my dick deflate enough for me to sit comfortably.

I moaned as the flavor hit my tongue. Marla could bake me anything she liked if it tasted this good. I wasn't one to eat a lot of desserts, but she might just convert me.

Out of the corner of my eye, I noticed Maggie chew on her bottom lip as she stared at my mouth. The heat of her gaze made my dick stand at attention again. I paused so that I could drink her in. She was so fucking beautiful it hurt.

"I'm happy to help too, ma'am," I finally said to Marla. She watched us both with those shrewd brown eyes of hers.

"That's so sweet of you!" Maggie cried. "Isn't that nice, Marla? We could use the extra set of hands!"

Marla snorted. "I suppose it would make more sense for you to stay the night than to go back to your place."

I shook my head, waving my hand in protest. "No, you don't need to put me up anywhere. I can be here at whatever time you tell me."

"And what if I tell you to be here as soon as the sun comes up?" she challenged, hands on her hips. "There's a lot to do down there, young man."

"Then you'll see me with the sunrise." Early mornings were nothing new, thanks to the Army. I shot Maggie a small smile. "I should probably be going."

Wishing Marla a good night, I took a chance and grabbed Maggie's hand for a quick squeeze. Kissing her would have been better, but I didn't want to do something that might make Marla think less of me. I thought I caught a glimpse of disappointment line Maggie's face, but the door shut on me before I could be certain.

The drive back to base passed in a blur. I might have been driving on air. Although I went through the motions of showering and settling into bed, I was afraid to go to sleep, lest it all have been a dream. My mind felt like it was on high alert like a deployment. I couldn't stop reliving all the moments of the day with Maggie.

For the first time in my life, I couldn't wait for the morning.

CHAPTER 15
THE MISTAKE
MAGGIE

THE DOOR HAD BARELY SHUT behind Zeke before Marla laid into me.

"Girl, do you have the slightest idea what the hell you're doin?"

I turned to her, surprised at her outburst. A dopey grin still tugged at the corners of my mouth, and I found myself struggling to keep it from my face. While I had hoped that Zeke would give me a goodbye kiss, nothing could erase the memories from Tybee Island. The day had been nothing short of perfect. I couldn't remember the last time I spent that much time with a guy. At least not without feeling bad about myself afterwards.

Zeke didn't make me hate myself, though. He made me feel amazing. Like I was something special.

You're not a burden, you're a gift.

"What do you mean, Marla? I haven't done anything!" I protested.

She shook her head and started slamming dishes into the sink. "That boy is greener than a cow pasture. He might be a soldier, but the poor thing is scared of his own dang shadow. You can't fool around with a man like that."

Why did everyone assume I only wanted to fool around with guys? Why couldn't I want more? Even Marla didn't think it possible.

"I like him," I whispered. Tears caught in my throat, but I tried to hold them back. Marla didn't much tolerate crying.

"I like him, too," she agreed. "That's why I'm telling you to be careful. He ain't the kind to break hearts and add notches to his belt. He's a good one."

As much as her words stung, deep down I knew she was right. Zeke would be as good a man as Mr. Hendricks, Celeste's dad. The kind of guy who took care of his loved ones and made you believe that kindness still existed. Someone who would never go for a girl with a reputation like mine.

I crept into the bathroom, letting the tears fall once I had the door locked. Turning on the shower, I stripped naked to stand in front of the mirror. Since I didn't have any makeup with me to mark my imperfections I settled for listing them in my head. It wasn't hard as Marla's warning rattled through.

Ugly.

Boy-crazy.

Slut.

Like mother, like daughter. Maybe I wasn't any better than Diana. I was always going to be the girl you had fun with before you found the girl to take home for Sunday dinner. Marla was absolutely right; Zeke deserved better.

Snot trickled out of my nose, but I did nothing to wipe it off. I could barely hold myself together. Wrapping my arms around my waist to fortify myself, it was all I could do to keep my sobs from breaking free. This wasn't something I could explain to Marla.

I sank onto the ground and stuffed my fist in my mouth to stifle the tears. Would I ever get to be something more than Maggie Eaton, the girl who slept her way through high school? Did reputations ever change? Nobody in River's Run seemed willing to let that happen.

Besides, what if they were all right? What if I followed in Diana's footsteps and couldn't handle a serious relationship? Maybe that was my lot in life and I simply needed to learn how to be okay with it. There was nothing wrong with having many sexual partners if I owned up to it, right?

My thoughts continued to swirl. Without giving it a second thought, I pulled my cell from my shorts pocket and texted Spencer Church.

YOU BUSY?

His response came a few seconds later.

FREE IF YOU NEED ME. I GOT SOME GOOD SHIT.

More tears threatened to spill over, but what did I really have to lose? The damage had already been done.

ON MY WAY

By the time I crept into my room and changed into a simple sundress, then touched up my makeup, Marla had already cleaned up the kitchen and gone to bed. I slipped out as quietly as I could.

Spencer lived in a ramshackle trailer on the edge of town. He shared it with a few other guys who also peaked in high school. I'd been there a few times for different hook ups. That was all Spencer was good for, along with his roommates…two of whom I'd also slept with.

The door swung open as soon as I pulled up in front of his place. Spencer held it open, shirtless, with his black jeans already unbuttoned. A blunt hung from his mouth and he blew smoke in my face as I swept past him.

"I knew you couldn't stay away from me, Mags," he drawled, coming up behind me and pinning my body to his.

His cockiness irritated me. I chose to focus on that rather than my rising disappointment for coming here. The air hung with stale cigarette and weed smoke mixed with the undeniable stench of body odor that only teenage boys could create. I felt dirty just from stepping inside.

Jabbing my elbow into his side, I whirled on him with a scowl. "Are your roommates here?"

Spencer shook his head. "Just you and me. Pretty sure I know how to satisfy you by now." His laughter barked out through the room.

I settled down on the ratty futon, the only piece of real furniture to sit on in the living room, and hiked up my skirt to reveal more of my thighs. "Then shut up and do it."

He smirked before plopping down beside me. Taking another long drag on the blunt, Spencer offered me a hit while also sliding a hand between my legs. The smirk widened when he discovered I didn't have any panties on. In our past hookups they were often left behind or shoved into couch cushions, so I knew better than to wear any at this point. I tried to focus more on the pot than on the way his fingers pawing at my slit made my skin crawl. The calluses on his fingers weren't as gentle as Zeke's, nor did they move in a caress as though I was meant to be treasured. It was all wrong, and somewhere in the back of my mind an alarm screamed in protest.

"Damn, Mags, you're normally a lot wetter for me than this," Spencer commented. "Are we doing this or not?"

I rolled my eyes. "Just shut up and take your pants off."

Spencer grinned and did as I ordered. He pulled a condom out from his back pocket, sliding it on, then moved to hover over me. I turned my face away so that he couldn't see the shame in my eyes. The blunt fell from my mouth to the floor as I bit down on my tongue hard enough to taste blood. Spencer spat on my pussy and thrust his way inside.

Just like every other time we'd hooked up, Spencer only cared for his own pleasure. He rutted inside me for a few quick thrusts before coming loudly with a growl in my ear. The weight of his body turned oppressive when he slumped down on top of me, pinning me to the futon.

Out of all the random times Spencer and I had fooled around over the years, I'd never before felt so cheap. Zeke's sweet face burst into my mind as clearly as if he kneeled beside me.

You're not a burden, you're a gift.

I shoved Spencer hard enough that he landed hard on his ass on the floor. Neither of us had even bothered to remove our clothes; his jeans were still bunched at his ankles.

"What the fuck was that for?" he yelled.

Hot tears streamed down my face. "I've gotta go," I mumbled. My knee caught a stack of old pizza boxes that served as a side table, dumping the ashtray, cigarettes, a grinder, and a baggie with a white substance everywhere. To my horror, the baggie was already open, and the powder sprayed into the shaggy carpet.

"YOU DUMB FUCKING BITCH!" Spencer screamed.

I didn't want to spend another second in that trailer with him. I ran out to my car as fast as I could, not even bothering to put on a seatbelt or turn on my headlights until I got closer to town. Fear paralyzed me so much that I didn't dare look in the rearview mirror, too terrified that Spencer in his violent rage might be following me. It didn't take a genius to know that I'd probably just cost him a lot of money by wasting the contents of that bag.

Even when I arrived back at Marla's, her door locks didn't feel like enough, and I found myself barricading the door to my room once more. Spencer wouldn't hesitate to break his way in. He and his stupid group of friends used to laugh about all the places they snuck in during high school and the things they pilfered while doing it. Sheriff Hillsborough hated them for it, but never managed to catch them in the act.

There really wasn't any difference moving from Diana's apartment to this one. Nothing ever changed for me. The only consistent thing about me was that I continued to make stupid decisions involving idiots like Spencer Church. No wonder Zeke barely made a move on me.

Rather than crawl into bed, I sat on the floor with my back against the bed frame, drawing my knees up to my chest. From this spot I had a clear view of both the door and the window.

I was in for another long night.

CHAPTER 16
THE DAY AFTER

ZEKE

My mind turned off long enough for me to catch a few hours of sleep, but I wanted to be back at Marla's bright and early to get started. Maggie and Marla both made it sound like there was a lot to do in the bakery, and while I never steered away from hard work, I also wanted to be the one doing the most of it so that they both could focus on getting whatever they needed for the design.

It wasn't a gender thing. Women were oftentimes far more capable than men, at least with most of the soldiers I'd met, but after the way I saw Maggie break down when we ran into her mother, I hoped that taking more of the stress off her plate would make her feel better. Since Marla was so important to Maggie, that meant I had to do the same for her.

A hazy blue filter settled over River's Run as I pulled into the parking space outside the bakery. The sun barely peaked over the horizon. Main Street was a ghost town, although I had the impression that River's Run was normally like that.

None of the lights were on upstairs in Marla's apartment yet, so I tried the door handle of what would be Marla's bakery. It stuck a little but opened when I added some brute force. The interior was fairly barren; I think the space mostly needed a good scrub. She would need to add a kitchen area because it all looked to be one giant room. A folding partition separated an area in the corner that had an old desk, and a small door led to one of the tiniest bathrooms I'd ever seen, even by Army standards.

I decided to start with cleaning the windows to at least let in more natural light. I planned ahead enough to bring my own set of cleaning supplies along with several tools I borrowed from the supply closet of my unit's office. A soldier was always prepared, even if that meant power drills and hammers.

Judging by the brightness of the sun, quite some time passed before Marla joined me. By that time I had already managed to scrub both sides of the windows, sweep the floor, move the desk outside, and wash three of the walls. I kept a notebook in the middle of the floor where I jotted down things that needed to be done or items that Marla should purchase as I thought of them. She came inside clutching a travel mug of coffee with her jaw hanging open.

"Did you do all of this?" she asked in surprise.

I peered around, hoping it was enough. "I wasn't sure what all you wanted done, so I figured cleaning was best. We're gonna need to pick up a power washer for the brick outside, and you definitely need some new air filters, although I'd recommend getting a full flush of the system. Has an inspector been by yet to check the HVAC system?"

Marla's eyes looked ready to pop out of their sockets. "You've already determined all of that? How long have you been here?"

"Around two hours," I replied with a quick glance at my watch. "Where's Maggie?"

She pursed her lips. "That girl wouldn't wake up if the Devil himself knocked. I'm sure she's still in bed."

I frowned. "Should I go get her? Do you want her to help?"

"Better you than me. She'll probably be a right side nicer to you first thing in the morning."

Rousing soldiers was nothing new to me. While I always seemed to operate best on a few hours of sleep, there were lots of other guys on my floor who needed a whole marching band in their ear to get up on time. I didn't want to set a foghorn beside Maggie, but I had the feeling that

Marla wouldn't hesitate to douse her with ice water if I didn't get her downstairs to help.

Marla's apartment was eerily silent when I entered. I had no idea which bedroom Maggie used, but I also couldn't resist the allure of seeing her while she slept. Maggie always had her guard up; sleep might be the only time where she found a bit of peace.

The first door yielded a coat closet. I opened the second door on my left just enough to peek inside and saw sparkly clothing thrown across the bed…the empty bed. Opening it wider confirmed, Maggie's makeup and the wide-brimmed hat I bought her yesterday at the beach laid across the top of a dresser. But where was she?

A door opened behind me, triggering my defensive instinct, and I whipped around with my fists ready. Adrenaline surged through my system, but for an entirely different reason than an intruder.

CHAPTER 17
THE LOOK
MAGGIE

WHAT THE FUCK *was he doing here?!*

My heart sputtered to a stop at the sight of Zeke in front of me, fists up and brows furrowed. He looked ready to attack. But he looked like a dream doing it. His hair was disheveled in a way that suggested sex, and the tattered sleeveless shirt he wore revealed his rippling biceps. I wanted to use them to keep me steady as I rode his cock.

Except…*oh my god I don't have makeup on or my hair done!*

I froze worse than a deer in headlights as I realized I left the bathroom after my hasty shower in nothing but a towel. My wet hair hung in stringy waves around my face and my face was as bare as the day I was born. At least Marla's towels were the good kind, thick and long to ensure all of the important parts were covered.

Although not very well, I realized as I hastily pulled the towel up higher so that I didn't accidentally reveal a nipple. Not that I didn't want Zeke to see a nipple. I wanted him to be so familiar with them that he could draw them with his eyes closed, but now that he was the first man to ever see me without my makeup and hair done, any small shot I had that Zeke would be interested disintegrated before my eyes.

I couldn't look away, too caught up in the horror of the moment. Zeke immediately relaxed and flashed me a smile that made my knees shake.

He was so damn good-looking. How had nobody noticed it before? And how was he not running away from me in terror right now? That smile couldn't possibly be for me, could it?

My mouth opened and closed several times in rapid succession like a goldfish. I didn't know what to do. My feet didn't want to listen to the flight reflex that kicked in, possibly because Zeke's eyes held mine hostage. He wasn't looking at me as if he were disgusted. If anything, Zeke looked downright captivated.

Flames erupted low in my belly as a hungry gleam crossed his face. It was a look that made me feel beautiful, a look that promised more.

Zeke took a step closer so that there was barely any room between us. I had to crane my head back to see him, glancing up through my lashes as my body trembled—from need or from fear, I couldn't be certain. His breath hitched as I looked up, and his hands gripped both of my elbows tightly as though he might prevent me from disappearing.

"I didn't mean to scare you," he whispered.

I swallowed thickly, my tongue suddenly too heavy for my mouth. "You don't scare me, Zeke Hayes," I murmured back.

His gaze dropped to my lips, and I nervously bit down on my bottom one, both awestruck and terrified that he might actually kiss me. A kiss from a man like Zeke Hayes could change your religion, but for him to kiss me when I was as raw and vulnerable as I was right now would change my entire genetic makeup.

"When you bite on your lip like that it distracts me," Zeke said. His voice was low and gravelly, and I longed for him to whisper dirty words in my ear.

"Distracts you from what?" My eyebrow rose in challenge, intentionally biting down on the lip again so that I could push him further. What could I say? I welcomed the change of our kiss.

Just as he angled his head down to meet mine, Marla's shrill cry came from downstairs. "Y'all have work to do down here! Hurry it up!"

Zeke fell back like he had been shocked. Gone was the spellbound man who I wanted to climb like a tree. Instead, Zeke nervously averted his eyes and held his hands up as if he had surrendered. He backed away slowly towards the door, keeping his face downcast.

"I'm so sorry, Maggie! I'll—I'll just m-meet you down there." He bolted down the stairs like his feet were on fire.

The horror of it all came crashing down in a tidal wave of shame. How could I even let Zeke kiss me again after what I did last night? Despite scrubbing my body raw, I could still feel Spencer's putrid breath on my skin. He lingered around me like a ghost, a reminder of the kind of man I deserved. I was my mother's daughter, after all. Wasn't sleeping with one guy while having feelings for another kind of her thing?

I slipped inside my bedroom, scrambling into spandex shorts and a sports bra. There wouldn't be any air conditioning downstairs, so it was bound to be hotter than hell. A small part of me that I chose to steadfastly ignore couldn't help but wonder if Zeke would appreciate the view of me in tight clothes. I threw on a loose tank top to appease Marla's sense of decency before shoving on some Crocs and joining them downstairs.

Neither of them noticed as I came in behind them where Marla and Zeke discussed the best place to put display cases and how much counter space she might need. I hastily braided my hair over one shoulder, trying—and failing—to keep my eyes from drinking in Zeke's round backside. Normally people only wanted women to have lush, thick asses, but I begged to differ. Zeke's looked strong and curvy, and drool pooled in my mouth as I imagined sinking my teeth into it.

"So where do you want me?" I finally interjected.

Marla and Zeke both spun to meet me. Marla's jaw dropped while Zeke gave me a smile that quite literally stole my ability to breathe. I found myself swaying from lack of oxygen, enough so that he reached a steadying hand for my elbow again.

"Maggie Eaton!" Marla said in alarm. "You don't—"

"Have to do anything you don't want to do today," Zeke finished for her firmly. He shot Marla a look laced with warning. "Let me handle all the hard stuff."

To my surprise, Marla obeyed, her lips pursing into a thin line before she nodded. "I'm gonna run out to the hardware store and get the stuff we mentioned. Y'all just keep cleaning. Harry is gonna stop by to look at that HVAC, Ezekiel. I'll be back."

Her behavior gave me goosebumps, but I couldn't figure out why. Was there something wrong with my outfit? I brushed my teeth and hadn't eaten anything, so I know there wasn't something stuck in them. I even spritzed on some body spray. Maybe smelling fruity would catch Zeke's attention again so we could finish what we started upstairs.

Zeke turned to me with a smile. "Why don't you just sit and tell me more about yourself while I clean?"

I rolled my eyes. "I didn't wake up early just to sit on my ass. Let me do something!"

Laughing, Zeke handed me a mop and gestured to the suds-filled bucket. "Be my guest."

Time passed quickly as I cleaned the floors and the baseboards while Zeke used a different kind of mop to clean the walls. They were really grimy, making us pour out the mop bucket to refill it several times. Parts of the drywall had cracks, but Zeke brought tools with him to fix some things. He made marks with pink chalk on places that needed filled in so that they didn't miss them when Marla returned with the spackle and paint. According to Zeke, the plan was to prime all the walls today and paint them a base color while Marla decided on what kind of layout she wanted.

Afterwards, Zeke and I used the chalk to mark on the floor where we thought it made the most sense for things to go. He said she would need to add a wall to divide the shop front from the kitchen, and we had fun designing the best way to utilize the space. Chalk handprints kept "accidentally" appearing on both of us since we couldn't seem to keep our hands off one another. It was like the best kind of junior high flirting ever.

A loud knock came from the front when Harry Stevens, the local handyman and jack of all trades, arrived. He worked out in Savannah mostly, but lived here in River's Run, and always had a soft spot for Marla. I remembered many times at The Comfy Cushion when even Mr.

Hendricks couldn't get Harry to come out, but one word from Marla had Harry arriving within the hour. Even now, he appeared to have a freshly ironed shirt that looked a little out of place for a repairman.

"This may take a while," Harry advised us after Zeke explained Marla hadn't returned yet. "Why don't y'all grab a bite while I get to work. Have to get the job done right!"

I coughed to cover my snicker. Of course Harry had to get Marla's job done right.

Zeke could sense the laughter threatening to burst out of me and grabbed my hand to yank me behind him as he thanked Harry for being so thorough. He pulled me out onto the street just as the laugh bubbled over, flashing another swoon-worthy smile at me when the door closed behind us. I only realized belatedly that my hand was still clasped in his. They fit perfectly together.

As if sensing that, too, Zeke glanced down at our joined hands before bringing his free one up to brush a stray lock of hair from my face. The passionate gleam from Marla's apartment was back on his face. Rather than letting the hand drop, he continued to softly rub my earlobe, sending shivers down my spine.

"Well, isn't this a picture!"

Oh my god, not again…

I turned in dismay to face Diana, who wore a sundress at least two sizes too small that pushed her breasts up near her chin. A new man I didn't recognize stood just behind her with oily hair slicked back and a leer that made the hairs on the back of my neck stand up.

Diana gasped. "Margaret Elizabeth Eaton, don't you own a mirror?! Haven't I taught you better than to run around town without your face on?"

This had to be what people called an out of body experience. I was paralyzed in place, equal parts fear, guilt, and shame. How had I gone all morning without makeup on? And worse, how had I let *Zeke* continue to see me without makeup?

A cross between a whimper and a scream left my throat. I tore my hand from Zeke's and raced up to my bedroom, turning and locking the door behind me. The ugly truth glared back at me from the mirror: my real face had been borne to the world. This time I didn't even need a toothbrush to vomit. It came up all on its own.

I didn't make it to the bathroom in time. Puke coated my front, making my shirt cling to my stomach. I collapsed in a heap in front of the toilet. Shaking so hard my teeth chattered, I huddled down in the fetal position. Tears coated my face and I could no longer breathe. More vomit rose up in my throat again, but panic prevented it from coming out. The dizzying sense of my downward spiral only made me cry harder.

"Trouble, baby, what's wrong?" Zeke came into the bathroom, crouching down beside me.

Pushing him away was a lesson in futility. He pulled me into his arms, vomit and all, squeezing me to his chest while sobs wracked my body.

"I've got you, Maggie. Let it all out," he murmured into my hair, which only served to make me cry harder.

Hideous.

Disgusting.

Ugly.

Worthless.

My mother's words scratched at the forefront of my mind like talons on a chalkboard. The repulsed look that crossed her face down there without makeup on…The way her new boyfriend recoiled from me…all of her words were true.

I *am* ugly.

Sobs wracked through my body, hard enough that my kneecaps kept cracking together. Zeke held me through it all. He murmured words of comfort into my hair as I cried into his shirt, my hand twisting the front in knots. It was a true testament as to how far gone I was in my misery that it was the first time my hands could have traced the hard lines of Zeke's stomach and I didn't even care.

A lot of time passed before the tears dried up. Shuddering, gasping breaths echoed throughout the bathroom as I tried to dry heave while simultaneously put enough air in my lungs.

"Maggie," Zeke said, his voice low and concerned, "please tell me what's going on. I can't fix it if you don't tell me. I don't understand."

Cold air and a sense of dread washed over me as I pushed away from him. The more the distance grew between us, the icier it became. I sank onto the edge of the bathtub, keeping my eyes pinned to the floor so that I didn't have to look at him. Zeke had already seen more of my shame than I could stomach.

"You don't need to understand, Zeke. Hell, you never could, looking the way you do." A watery chuckle, composed more of sarcasm than amusement, leaked out as I aimlessly gestured towards him. "Who could have low self esteem when they look like you?"

I closed my eyes and winced as I felt him kneel down in front of me and gently take my hands in his. If I looked at him and saw pity, I would break beyond repair.

"Trouble, you're the only friend I've ever had. I've spoken more to you in the past forty-eight hours than I have to everyone else I've ever met, combined. You're gorgeous in my eyes. Not sure how that relates to your self-esteem, but it doesn't make it any less true."

Hardly daring to breathe, I slowly opened my eyes to find Zeke staring at me. Concern etched across his face, and I wanted to smooth away the wrinkles marring his brow. The vulnerability it took to admit such a heartbreaking truth made me want to be equally frank with Zeke. "Ever since I turned twelve, I've never gone a single day without makeup. Nobody has ever seen me bare faced other than my mom, Celeste, and Marla—once. Having Diana call me out like that in front of you made me panic."

Rather than laugh or scoff, as I anticipated him to do, Zeke merely nodded. "Is it really that important to you that you wear makeup in front of everyone?"

I nodded, too. "I feel ugly without it. Like everyone is judging me."

Zeke sighed as he reflected on my answer. The seconds passed like the agonizing wait for the final buzzer of a basketball game. "Then go ahead and take some time to put on whatever makes you feel comfortable. I'll go tell Marla you aren't feeling well and need some time up here."

He stood up and crossed to the door, pausing to look back at me. Blue eyes wary with candor found mine as he added, "I'm honored that I got to be one of the people who saw you in your natural form. I still think you're gorgeous either way."

CHAPTER 18
THE WINDOW

THE NEXT TWO days passed by in a blur. Maggie and I never discussed her revelation from the bathroom, and even I knew enough about women to realize that it wasn't a subject to broach unless Maggie herself brought it up. She continued to wear makeup as we worked in the shop and kept her hair perfectly curled in a ponytail. Sadness clawed at me every time I thought of how Maggie saw herself. I truly couldn't imagine a more perfect woman, so I hadn't the foggiest idea how she pictured herself as any less than that. I vowed that even if it took the rest of my life, I would convince her to see herself the way I saw her—the most exquisite woman on the planet.

I only returned to the barracks to sleep for a few hours and shower before going back to River's Run. Thanks to Marla's formidable list of contacts—and probably her terrifying demeanor, if we're being honest—things were moving pretty quickly at her bakery. I knew how to lay flooring thanks to one of the remodels I'd done with Leggett on his lake house in Michigan, so Marla went to one of the big box stores out in Savannah and picked out a black and white tile pattern that could be delivered right away. Maggie wanted me to teach her, but we both grew frustrated when I couldn't find the right words to express what I meant in a way that she understood, so she quickly settled on sitting next to me and handing me tools as I went.

Harry came back and we built out the frame for the new walls that needed to be added to separate the kitchen space. Marla set Maggie to work on demolishing the bathroom so that a bigger one could take its place. Oddly enough, the task seemed to really suit Maggie as she had a huge smile on her face after she saw the wreckage at her feet.

I found myself constantly smiling to the point where my cheeks hurt. Nothing in the Army ever left me with a feeling as fulfilled as it did to see something emerge from my own two hands. I certainly never received praise from a commanding officer like I did from Marla, Maggie, and even Harry, who seemed impressed with my knowledge of tools and basic craftsmanship. He offered me a business card and said if I ever wanted to help him out with handyman work on the weekends, he would gladly accept the support.

When Monday night rolled around and I faced the prospect of going back to the barracks to start another dreary week of drills and training, the same monotonous routine as always, I found myself digging in my heels. I didn't want to go back to it. Not when I could share a cup of coffee with Maggie every morning, who, so far, joined me first thing in the kitchen every day still fresh faced and glowing from her morning shower. Only after we finished a cup of coffee and a light breakfast would she go and put on makeup. To my unknowledgeable eye, it almost looked like she wore less makeup than before, too. Her face appeared softer...although it might have simply been the smile that never left her face either.

Being in Maggie's presence had to be comparable to Icarus' flight to the sun. A warm glow that spread from the inside out until the very thought of turning away crusted you with ice. I loved being around her. Especially when I managed to make her laugh. Every time the high pitched squeal rang out through the shop Marla's whole face lit up, and she flashed me a look of gratitude. I didn't quite know what to make of it, but I was also too chicken shit to ask.

Late Monday night, long after Marla had gone up to bed and I should have been on my way back to the barracks, Maggie and I sat on the floor, our backs to the wall and legs stretched out between us. Once Marla's stern supervision left us, we abandoned cleaning up in favor of swapping stories of our childhoods. It turned out that Maggie moved around a lot as a child, too, and knew what it meant to not have a lot of friends.

"Yeah, none of the kids in my neighborhood ever really wanted to play with me. They were too scared of Leggett. He can be a bit of an asshole," I offered. I drew a line around the edge of the tile with my finger, hardly daring to look up lest I see Maggie's wild eyes fill with sadness at my pathetic backstory.

"I still don't understand," she replied, crossing one leg over the other and flexing her toes. "Is Leggett your dad? Why do you call him by his last name?"

I shrugged. "That's a military thing. Everybody calls everybody by their last name because that's what's on all of our gear and uniforms."

"Okay, but it sounds like you grew up with him," challenged Maggie. "I don't understand how you're related."

This was a part of my past I never had to explain. Everyone in the Army simply accepted that Leggett was my mentor and took a vested interest in my future. It wasn't uncommon.

But I wanted Maggie to know the real me. Even the sad parts of my past that I never got to share with anyone else.

"A very sweet woman and her husband adopted me when I was six. She died unexpectedly shortly after the adoption was finalized. Leggett was there, after that." It wasn't the entire truth and I held my breath as I waited for Maggie to fill in the gaps.

A thoughtful expression crossed her face, but she didn't press. Instead, her hand found its way in mine again, and she began examining the scarred knuckles. "You look like you've been in a lot of fights," Maggie commented playfully.

I shook my head. "Nope. I just work out a lot. Sometimes it helps."

"Helps what?"

"Keep all the fear at bay."

Maggie nodded. "You've been deployed already, right?"

"Yep. And Leggett will probably send me back to Afghanistan if I don't get back to the barracks soon. We have a ruck march at 0500 tomorrow morning." A heavy sigh escaped as I gloomily prepared myself for leaving Maggie's sun.

To my surprise, she leaned over and placed a feather-light kiss on my cheek. "I can't wait to see you again." Her breathy voice matched the flush in her cheeks. My dick stood at attention.

Gently, I brushed a stray curl behind her ear, getting lost in her eyes. I could drown in them. This had to be crazy, right? For two people to be so drawn to one another the way I seemed to be to Maggie. Did these kind of connections exist in real life?

Only half an inch, at most, separated my mouth from hers. One good exhale was all it would take to bridge the gap. Rather than let myself overthink it, I leaned down, my lips barely dusting hers when the sound of shattering glass reverberated through the room.

I jumped to my feet in a flash as the loud rev of an engine echoed from outside. Someone had thrown a large rock through one of the windows. The street was far too dark to see who was behind the wheel or make out anything distinguishable as the car sped away.

Maggie remained seated, but had turned a sickly shade of green. Her gaze zeroed in on the rock that narrowly avoided hitting her outstretched feet.

"I can't believe someone just did that!" I yelled. River's Run seemed like a quiet town from everything I'd seen. Everyone I'd met had a lot of respect for Marla, too, which made the vandalism all the more unsettling. "You better go up and let Marla know what happened."

"What about you?" Maggie's eyes finally darted up to my face, anxiety and something akin to guilt crossing her features. She stood up and I noticed a slight tremble to her movements.

"I'm gonna use some of the cardboard from all the flooring boxes to cover up the window," I explained. "If Marla already has insurance on the place, it should be covered. We should probably call the police, too, so we can make a report."

"NO!" Maggie's shout held an inch of hysteria to it. "Sheriff Hillsborough won't be able to do anything about it anyway. We didn't see who did it."

Was she serious? Some asshole just broke one of Marla's windows on the shop we'd spent the better part of the weekend working on. Maggie wanted to let it go?

"I guess we'll leave it up to Marla," I suggested. "It's her place, after all."

Maggie nodded slowly, eyes fixating on the rock again. "I'll go wake her up…" Her voice trailed off in uncertainty as she hastily left through the front door.

* * *

Her behavior continued to make my anxiety run on high alert as we relayed everything to Marla, then again to Sheriff Hillsborough, a burly curmudgeon, if such a person existed outside of a Dickens novel. He kept shooting skeptical glances Maggie's way, questioning her over and over again about whether or not she had any idea who might've thrown a rock through the window. The sheriff's attitude towards me was that of a total dismissal until Marla identified me as a sergeant in the Army. I recognized the look he gave as he sized me up…a man in uniform judging me as competition rather than an ally. Like we both didn't live to serve and protect.

"Sir, it was too dark to see anything," I ground out again through clenched teeth. Why was he grilling Maggie so hard on this?

Sheriff Hillsborough merely adjusted the toothpick stuck between his teeth in reply.

"Can I stop by first thing tomorrow morning and pick up that report?" Marla asked. "I'm sure the insurance company will want it."

He nodded, his cunning eyes softening. "That'll be just fine, Miss Marla. Have a good evening, y'all." Snapping another photo of the damaged window again, he sauntered off towards his vehicle.

"Well isn't this just like a fly in the ice cream!" Marla sputtered. "I can't believe someone in River's Run would break my window!"

Indeed, in the short time I'd spent in town, everyone seemed to revere Marla. Nearly everyone we had encountered on the street made it a point to tell her how much they were looking forward to her grand opening. She certainly wasn't someone I would turn into an enemy. Marla's words had venom in them.

"Why don't the two of you get up to bed? I'll clean up down here," I offered.

A jolt of pride shot through me when I noticed how Marla's shoulders sagged with relief.

"That would be a huge help. Thank you, Hayes." Marla clapped me on the elbow with as much fondness as I'd ever seen. "I don't know what we'd do without you these past few days."

Maggie's arms hugged her waist as she flashed a tight smile to both of us. "You go on up, Marla," she said, "I'll be right behind in a minute."

Our friend's rigid finger pointed in both our faces in warning. "No sex in the shop. That's the very first rule!"

My face flamed. I would never be so disrespectful!

Judging by the bright red blooms spreading across Maggie's cheeks, she felt the same. "Marla!"

The woman simply shook her head, mumbling something about "wild hormones" as she waved. Maggie bit her bottom lip to repress a laugh.

Seeing that tooth burrow into her soft mouth made me hyper aware of how much I wanted to do the same thing. All I could do was fixate on that very spot, imagining the ways in which Maggie's whole body would press against mine. The way she felt in my arms. I suddenly needed that more than anything.

"Are you alright?" I asked in low voice.

Maggie's eyes darted to mine, then dropped to the ground again, the same skittish behavior she showed the sheriff. "I'm fine. Do you need me down here to clean up?"

"Of course not. I want you upstairs, where it's safe. But I need to know you're good first."

Like my hand had a mind of its own, I found it circling around her waist, drawing her hips against mine. A faint buzzing sensation in the back of my head that I hadn't noticed until then disappeared as soon as her body made contact. I gently rubbed both of her arms and tried not to preen at the goosebumps that rose along her skin. Knowing that I could have an effect on her the way she did on me sent a thrill down my spine.

"It's gonna be hard not to see you tomorrow," I admitted quietly.

Slowly her eyes found mine, shining with uncertainty and a faint trace of hope. "Really?" Her voice was a husky whisper that went straight to my dick.

I didn't even trust myself to respond. My body resumed autopilot, leaning down to place a gentle kiss on her lips.

At first Maggie resisted, as if too scared to believe I initiated something. Even I was startled by my own lead. But as my fingers trailed upward to tangle themselves in her hair, Maggie's body yielded to me, her mouth opening so that her tongue could sweep through mine. I let her take control. I never wanted her to doubt that she was in charge; that we could go at any pace she felt comfortable. Hell, whatever she wanted, Maggie Eaton could count me in. I never wanted whatever this was to end.

She broke away abruptly, this time with stars in her eyes and the sweetest smile on her face. "You could break my heart, you know," Maggie whispered.

"I would lay down my life for you before I ever let that happen," I promised.

CHAPTER 19
THE FALLOUT

ZEKE

As soon as I got back to my room in the barracks, my stomach immediately filled with dread. The buzzing sound in the back of my head grew louder as if my brain protested the distance between us, especially not knowing when I would see Maggie next. Longing settled in my chest like pneumonia—making it nearly impossible to breathe.

Cold sweats continued to slick my skin as I tossed and turned all night long. The red analog numbers on the digital clock across the room mocked me as time passed but sleep remained evasive. Fear of losing her, of never seeing Maggie again drove me nearly crazy.

I knew it was rude as fuck, but I couldn't help pulling out my cell to text her. Maybe that would at least keep the fear from swallowing me whole.

HEY, TROUBLE.

Although the clock read 0304, three dots appeared on the screen right away.

WHATCHA DOIN UP?

CAN'T SLEEP. KEEP THINKING ABOUT YOU.

I MISS YOU TOO.

I HAVE TO SEE YOU TOMORROW. OR TODAY, I
GUESS.

GOOD THING YOU KNOW WHERE TO FIND ME 😊

I smiled like a lovestruck idiot down at my phone. Is this what it felt like? To love someone? Was it too soon to feel that way?

Never once had I considered what I missed out on by not pursuing a romantic relationship with someone. While the novels I read made love sound passionate and lifechanging, I was perfectly content with what I had. The Army took up most of my time and that was enough for me.

But what if it was no longer enough?

What if I wanted something more? Someone to share it with?

What if Maggie Eaton changed my life?

* * *

The sound of my alarm broke my daydream of a picturesque future filled with Maggie. We would travel the world, or settle down in River's Run, or go wherever the Army sent us. Whatever she wanted to do. I didn't care if that meant me finishing out my contract and becoming a civilian or if that meant staying in the Army for rest of my life. Maggie was the only thing that mattered.

The revelation of it all, how right and happy it felt, came to a crashing halt when I realized I needed to report for physical training. After a four day weekend, the commander was sure to crush us with a workout. And since I ignored any text that hadn't come from Maggie or Marla all weekend, I could very well walk into a shitshow if any other soldiers got in trouble. Just the thought of going through the motions of training rather than greeting Maggie with a cup of coffee as she joined me down in the bakery made me want to vomit.

Oh, god, no—I was actually going to puke…

I barely made it to the toilet in time to hurl up my guts. What if I reported and there was another fuck up that required me to stay all day? What if the person who threw the rock through the window came back and threatened Maggie or Marla again?

The anxiety of it all made me throw up all over again. I had a physical *need* to see her. There would be no functioning today unless I had some sort of guarantee that Maggie would be a part of my day.

Whipping out my phone, I texted Staff Sergeant Bridges, the next person in my chain of command, that I was too sick to report.

GO TO SICK CALL.

I had never resorted to using sick call, a system the Army offered for soldiers to seek immediate medical care for sickness and injuries that would in turn notify their chain of command. Through the years I'd seen plenty of other soldiers in my unit use it as a means to get out of work for a day or two simply because they were too hung over or tired from partying the night before.

However, if the very thought of not seeing Maggie made me throw up, there was definitely something wrong with me.

Thankfully the line when I arrived at the clinic was blessedly short. A nurse called me back right away, noting how flushed my face was. I clung to her observation like a lifeline.

"Yeah," I agreed. "I really don't feel well."

Guilt briefly flared in my chest, but it wasn't an outright lie. I *didn't* feel well…I just knew it had nothing to do with me actually being sick.

Dr. Sudemyer, an Army captain with a ruddy complexion and brisk demeanor, checked my ears, nose, and throat in swift movements before stating, "There's a flu going around post. If you're vomiting, you probably have that."

Yet another bone Fate threw me. "Uh, yes, sir. I must definitely have the flu. I was around a lot of people this weekend."

Technically also not a lie.

The doctor nodded. "I'll give you quarters for the next 72 hours. Stay hydrated. I'll send your scripts to the pharmacy."

"Thank you, sir." I saluted him and accepted the slip of paper he offered with the quartering instructions for my chain of command.

I hadn't even hit the parking lot before a text came in from Leggett.

GOOD SOLDIERS DON'T GET SICK. PUSH THROUGH IT.

Anger flared. My jaw clenched so tightly that I heard my teeth clack against one another.

CAN'T. TOO SICK

REPORT TO MY OFFICE IMMEDIATELY.

In all my years of service—hell, even during all of high school, if I really thought about it—I had never stayed home sick. Leggett viewed all illnesses as a mental issue. One simply had to strengthen mind over matter and the symptoms would go away. The fact that I had gone to sick call in the first place wasn't just a red flag to him. It might as well have been a flashing neon sign with pyrotechnics.

I gritted my teeth in irritation, weighing my options if I told him no. Years' worth of habit and training had me automatically driving to his office, however. I didn't know how to refuse Leggett on anything.

Playing up the sickness card, I grabbed a face mask that I continued to carry in my truck after Covid-19 and headed inside.

Like always, Leggett ignored me when I entered and stood at attention at the door. A laptop was opened on his desk and bifocals sat on the end of his nose as he read something on the screen.

"'It is exercise alone that supports the spirits,'" quoted Leggett. "You should be at PT, not gallivanting around post like a Private on leave."

Shame washed over me at his accusations. Quoting an ancient Roman scholar like Marcus Tullius Cicero would only appeal to my intellect and innate drive to excellence. I had always been the best because I simply couldn't accept anything less. No decent soldier could.

But Maggie's beautiful face came to mind, mouth quirking up when I attempted to flirt and spectacularly failed. How she had already grown more comfortable around me with less makeup on. The way the sweat from a hard day's work glistened on her skin in those spandex shorts she wore to drive me crazy. I didn't want to miss that.

"I'm sorry, sir. I don't feel well. I need rest." How I managed to maintain the cool, detached tone, I would never know.

Leggett grunted in response. "You go to one party and suddenly you can't obey orders? Is this the kind of shitty soldier you're going to become?"

I was grateful the mask covered most of my face so that he couldn't see how thin my lips flattened from his allegations. I allowed the silence to grow, determined to wait him out. He would not make me budge on this. Already the contents of my stomach churned, anxiety rising over not seeing Maggie today if Leggett forced my hand.

"I still control your career, boy. I could have you on a plane to no man's land today if I want."

My blood ran cold at the threat. He had never gone so far before. Then again, the general had never had to. I always complied.

After several long, agonizing minutes of my continued silence, Leggett grunted again. "Get out of my sight!"

He didn't need to repeat himself. I slid into the driver's seat before the door had even fully closed in his office. Now I had another nagging fear in the back of my mind, though. General Leggett could drum up orders to another duty station and I would have no way to fight them. Once a person enlisted, the Army owned them and could dictate their location like any other property.

As soon as I drove through Fort Stewart's gates, I whipped out my phone to text Maggie.

ON MY WAY TO YOU, TROUBLE.

CHAPTER 20
THE DILEMMA
MAGGIE

Sheriff Hillsborough knew I was lying to him, that much was obvious. It certainly wouldn't be the first time, and given how much the old bastard hated me because of my friendship with Wesley and Celeste back in the day, I doubted it would be the last. That rock came through the window because of Spencer, I'd bet my life on it. I recognized the sounds of his suped up Camaro that he used for illegal races down on the Florida state line.

Spencer would continue to torment me until I either paid up or gave him what he wanted—only I doubted what he wanted was anything I would be willing to give. I still hadn't told Zeke the truth about sleeping with Spencer. I couldn't bring myself to say the words, letting the betrayal fester in my gut like an ulcer. Whatever this thing was between Zeke and me…I wanted it to grow.

I couldn't sleep after I went upstairs. Marla fretted to herself about the window, how soon it could be repaired, and what insurance would say to her filing a claim less than a week after leasing the space. Her pacing footsteps echoed into my room for hours before she finally went to bed herself. Guilt, nasty and bitter, twisted its way through my heart. *I* had done this to her. Spencer only threw that rock through the window because of *me*. Marla deserved better than that.

WHAT DO YOU WANT?

I finally texted Spencer. Until I knew how to get rid of him, he would only up the ante. Hillsborough didn't scare him.

WHAT I'M OWED

came Spencer's terse response.
Wincing, I typed back,

WHICH IS WHAT?

$5000 AND YOU AT MY BECK AND CALL

came his sleazy reply.

An involuntary shudder worked down my spine. I would rather chug gasoline than give Spencer Church a hold over me. There was no way the little bit of powder I spilled was worth five grand, but it wasn't like Spencer would give up an opportunity to make a quick buck.

There was no way for me to come up with five thousand dollars. I didn't even have a job to cover my own living expenses. Spencer knew that, though, which probably contributed to the high amount. Anything to make me squirm.

My lungs started to seize when I considered what Spencer might do to Zeke if he found out how important Zeke had become to me. Obviously, that was why he targeted Marla's place; everyone in River's Run knew she was basically family to me. Blood drained from my face as I considered whether or not he would target Celeste next. What if he went after Iris?

Different scenarios played through my mind, each one more devastating than the last. Paranoia spiraled out of control as I imagined the worst possible outcomes for all the people I cared about. Spencer could do whatever he wanted to me, and he knew that. But I would be damned if anyone I loved paid for my mistakes.

Right as the panic started to set in while I considered different ways to come up with his goddamn money, another text came through.

> HEY, TROUBLE.

It was Zeke. A warm, fuzzy feeling spread through my chest. His presence, even through messages, soothed the stress coursing through my veins. Like even my body recognized that he would have some kind of solution.

Not that I wanted to admit anything about Spencer to him. I was too chicken shit to face the heartbroken look in Zeke's eyes when I told him not only had I slept with Spencer after our romantic day at the beach, but Spencer was now extorting me into paying an obscene amount of money for the drugs I spilled at his house. Given how much Zeke scolded me when he caught me drinking alcohol underage, I very much doubted he would be understanding to paying back a drug dealer's wasted cocaine.

> WHATCHA DOIN UP?

The warm, fuzzy feeling skyrocketed when I read his response.

> CAN'T SLEEP. KEEP THINKING ABOUT YOU.

God, I didn't deserve this man! It used to annoy the piss out of me to hear and see how loving and doting Wesley acted around Celeste. If he could move the sun to make her happy, Wes would have found a way to make it happen. Zeke reminded me so much of him, of that sweet ache in my chest as a young teenager desperate to know what true love felt like.

Not that I believed Zeke loved me. How could he? Underneath all the makeup, eyelashes, and hair extensions, I was a train wreck. And now I had Spencer frickin' Church as baggage.

But I couldn't help replying,

> I MISS YOU TOO.

Zeke made me feel special, probably for the first time in my life, in a way that I fiercely wanted to keep.

> I HAVE TO SEE YOU TOMORROW. OR TODAY, I GUESS.

His awkward wording only made my smile grow. Over the past few days I'd picked up on how stilted Zeke's social interactions could be. He often looked like his brain flipped through a rolodex of responses before settling on one and opening his mouth to speak. I noticed, too, that he didn't know what to do when Harry clapped him on the shoulder and complimented his work. Any kind of flattery made Zeke visibly uncomfortable.

Maybe it would be better for both of us if I cut things off now. Zeke and I couldn't have a future—even if he hadn't caught on yet to how hunky and gorgeous he was, soon enough some simpering goddess with a body to die for would catch his eye, and he would leave me in the dust. Hell, if Spencer continued terrorizing me, Zeke might even leave before then. It was better to end things on my terms, with some of my dignity still intact. Remain aloof. Mysterious, even. Didn't Diana swear by that rule when first meeting men?

Yet the thought of turning Zeke away, of never feeling the way his gaze burned into me from anywhere in the room, never hearing his rough laugh at my corny jokes...I couldn't do it. I guess I really was a chicken shit.

> GOOD THING YOU KNOW WHERE TO FIND ME ☺

I sent back.

Scientists needed to study how it was physiologically possible for me to be so damn giddy, yet so damn sad at the same time.

CHAPTER 21

THE DRIVE

Hitting the River's Run city limits brought air back into my lungs. A huge weight lifted off my shoulders at the relief of being so close to Maggie. Love really did make people act crazy, I realized.

I found Marla already inside the bakery. Two men I didn't recognize were also there, taking measurements through the middle of the room. Marla's posture didn't give anything away, but I hated seeing her alone with two men. My protective instincts kicked in as I stood to my full height, letting my shoulders spread out.

"What's going on here?" I asked loudly, making both men jump.

Marla tried to hide a smirk. "These boys are here from a glass company out near Savannah. They're gonna replace the window and get me set up with a couple of custom display cases. I figure I might as well get something fancy if I'm gonna do this right."

"I'm Sergeant Ezekiel Hayes," I said to both men, holding out my hand to the one closest. "And who might you be?"

Both men shook my hand, identifying themselves as Rhett and Wyatt.

"Miss Marla here is important to me, which means she needs to be important to you. Take good care of her," I cautioned them. I used my sternest leadership voice, the one that intimidated soldiers when barking orders.

"Zeke!" came a breathy cry behind me.

I spun on my heel to find Maggie in the doorway. A soft glow from the early morning sun framed her like a beacon, accentuating her brown curls and the soft curves of her body. She wore a white floral dress that fluttered to mid-thigh with white sneakers—basically, she never looked lovelier.

"Did ya miss me?" I grinned.

She gave a little squeal before running into my arms. All of the anxiety melted away, my stomach finally settling, the buzzing in my head long gone. Maggie was exactly where she needed to be—with me.

"Can I talk to you for a bit before we get started here?" I asked.

"Actually, I was just heading out to Savannah. There's a salon out there that called me up for a job interview this morning!"

I smiled. "Hop in the truck. We can talk on the way."

A blush crept across her cheeks. "You don't need to drive me. Shouldn't you be at work?"

"Nope. I'm yours for the next seventy-two hours," I countered.

"Okay." Confusion flashed on her face before she looked over my shoulder at Marla. "Wish me luck!"

"You don't need luck. They're the lucky ones to have you," Marla replied.

Maggie didn't hesitate to climb into my truck and prop her feet up on the dash. I loved seeing how comfortable she already felt with my stuff. We hit the highway before she finally asked, "So what's going on? You're makin' me feel some type of way."

"Don't laugh at me, but I sort of threw up this morning when I realized I might not get to see you today." I cringed at how silly it sounded when said out loud.

Maggie's jaw fell open as she sat upright to stare at me. "You're serious," she said flatly.

"As a heart attack." I glanced at her for a moment before focusing on the road again. Her scrutiny suddenly made me feel ridiculous.

"So then why the oddly specific number of hours?" asked Maggie.

"That's how long I was given quarters."

"What does that mean?"

"That's what the Army calls it when you're given sick leave," I explained. "The doctor told me this morning that I must have the flu if I threw up. But I know the truth."

"And the truth is?"

I shrugged. "Going without you makes me sick. I'm just gonna have to keep you." I let out a dramatic sigh as if it was a hardship.

Maggie's mouth closed with a snap.

"Is that okay?" I pressed.

Her mouth opened and closed several times like a goldfish before she straightened in her seat to watch the highway ahead of us. Tension filled the space, creating a chasm I didn't understand or know how to close.

"Talk to me, Trouble. What's going on in that pretty head of yours?" I finally asked.

"You became physically ill just because we spent a night apart, Zeke," Maggie replied, her voice thick with an emotion I couldn't name. "I'm not sure how I'm supposed to respond to that. We have to spend time apart."

"I know that," I scoffed. "But I'd like it if we could plan more time together so that I don't have worry about the time apart. Let me just lay it out there for you—I like you. More than I thought I could like anybody. Don't you feel whatever this is between us? Or am I just crazy?"

Either my imagination was in overdrive or I saw Maggie stiffen.

"Zeke, you don't wanna be with a girl like me," she said softly. I hated hearing how small her voice sounded, the sadness laced through it.

Chuckling, I asked, "Oh? And why not?"

"Because you deserve someone better than me." This time there was no mistaking how she hugged herself, her long arms almost entirely circling her waiflike waist.

Frustration like I'd never known gave me tunnel vision. "There isn't anybody better than you!"

She shot me another incredulous look before repeating, "You're serious."

"Of course I am, damn it! When have I ever lied to you?"

Throwing up her hands in defeat, Maggie snarled, "I can't talk about this right now! I need to focus on this interview!"

Without meaning to, my voice rose to match hers. "You're gonna rock it, but fine! We'll finish this conversation over brunch afterwards!"

Both of us sat there huffing for a few seconds before bursting into laughter.

"I really hope I get this job," Maggie commented. "I need the money."

"What made you decide to go to beauty school?" I asked.

Maggie shrugged. "I like having control over what I look like. Hair and makeup are fun to play around with, and if you know what you're doing, you can truly transform yourself."

"On the outside," I amended.

She shot a questioning look my way before nodding in agreement. "Yeah. You can transform yourself on the outside."

"But it's what's on the inside that counts, right? Isn't that what people say?"

"That's what ugly people say!" Maggie rolled her eyes and laughed. "Kidding! But I think when people look good, they feel good, and that's really something you can't put a price on."

"Not quite sure how you can charge for your services then."

We both burst into laughter again, even harder than before. It was the kind of moment you wanted to capture on film so you could replay it over and over again. Now there wasn't a single doubt in my mind—I was head over heels in love with Maggie Eaton. And I didn't have a damn clue what to do about it.

CHAPTER 22
THE PANIC
MAGGIE

It's actually impossible to focus on a job interview when you're too busy overanalyzing everything a sexy soldier said to you on the car ride there. I could tell Rochelle, the salon manager, became more and more annoyed as the interview went on because I had to keep asking her to repeat herself. In my haste to jump into Zeke's truck and be alone with him, I completely forgot my portfolio and instead had to whip out my cell phone to show pictures of the hair I'd done. Seeing everything through a cracked, out-of-date iPhone doesn't have quite the same impact, however.

Truthfully, Zeke's revelation scared the bejeesus out of me. In less than a week we had taken a nosedive into something more serious and tangible than I could admit. My brain kept screaming at me to shut it down, that it was all in my head and he'd drop me like a hot potato any second. But my heart raised its hackles and insisted that these feelings were real. I didn't know which to believe.

Spending time with Zeke, even something as simple as going for a drive, made my heart race and my skin flush. Butterflies invaded my gut in his proximity, but they were addictive. I loved his smile. Being on the receiving end made you feel like you won the lottery. And it already seemed like I got to see it more than anyone else. Like he settled into being around me enough to be comfortable. Just in the little he'd shared with me about his childhood and his life until now, I recognized that was no small thing. I didn't want to take it for granted.

But what happened when it didn't work out? Because even my heart couldn't convince me that this had any chance of lasting. We might make it work for the here and now, but at some point, he would see the ugly truth of me and leave. Did I want to turn into Diana and just have meaningless, superficial relationships?

Isn't that what you already have?

Damn you, Heart, be on my side!

Exiting the salon and seeing Zeke standing there, his broad shoulders and strong chest filling out his Army fatigues in a way that made angel's weep, I instantly forgot about the interview. Rochelle told me she'd "follow up" with me—which I knew was code for "I'm not interested." Zeke's bright grin and gleaming eyes meant it didn't matter. But then the fact that he held a small bouquet of flowers in his hand to congratulate me lifted my spirits in a way that I no longer cared about the botched interview. Zeke believed in me, so that was enough.

I nervously twisted a curl around my finger on the way to Denny's, insecurity creeping in like poison. So far I'd managed to avoid eating in front of him because he focused so much on the work in Marla's shop, but I didn't have a good excuse handy at the moment. Maybe I could just get something simple like egg whites. That wouldn't be too suspicious, right? Zeke preferred eating healthy and working out. He might admire me for joining him.

Except when we slid into the booth and the hostess suggested upgrading to the cookies and crème pancakes with the Grand Slam breakfast, Zeke's eyes lit up. "That's my favorite ice cream flavor!" he whispered conspiratorially across the table.

A ball of dread grew in my stomach. Would he expect me to eat them, too? What if he wanted to share? I wouldn't have access to a bathroom to purge for at least an hour because it took that long to drive back to River's Run.

The words on the menu blurred as I tried to come up with a feasible excuse. Zeke had a habit of seeing right through me. He questioned things that Celeste and Marla had always let slip by. I wouldn't be able to put him off the same way.

"So," he began. "Can we talk about what happened in the truck?"

Oh god! No!

"Um…sure." My cheeks flamed under his scrutiny. How could a man have such clear, vivid eyes like that? They conveyed every emotion, every thought, if you only knew how to read them.

To my shock, I realized that I did.

"Maggie Eaton, I want us to be in a relationship," Zeke declared. Right as the hostess came back with our requested waters.

"Oh my god, that is the *sweetest* thing!" the woman gushed. I could see the hearts forming in her eyes like an emoji.

I blinked rapidly as my heart rate spiked. *Ezekiel "Too Hot to Handle" Hayes wants a relationship with* me?!

"But…why?" I asked lamely.

The hostess gasped. "Sugar, don't question the man, just say yes!" She playfully slapped me on the shoulder. I cringed, which Zeke instantly noted.

"Could we maybe talk without an audience?" he inquired pointedly. He used what I had come to call his Army voice.

It definitely caught her attention. "Oh of course! I'm so sorry!" She hightailed it back to the hostess stand, keeping her eyes fixed on her feet in shame.

Zeke offered me a small, tight smile. His back had gone rigid and I recognized one of his anxious ticks as he started running the edge of the menu under his fingernails. He would do it repeatedly until something calmed him. "I'm not sure how to explain why other than I really, really like you. Do people normally say more?"

I flushed from my hairline to my neckline. "I wouldn't know. I've never been in a relationship before," I admitted quietly.

"Then let's figure it out together." He reached across the table, holding up a hand in offering.

The innocence and sweetness of the gesture blocked out all the arguments my brain continued to make. For whatever reason, Zeke genuinely liked me. Only a fool would walk away from that.

Gently, I slid my hand over until it joined his. "I'm probably gonna be bad at the whole girlfriend thing."

"I won't know it any other way," Zeke joked with a shrug.

Hope buoyed in my chest and I laughed. "Zeke Hayes...my boyfriend," I stated to test the words out loud. It made them real. And I really liked how they sounded.

His returning smile lit up the room. Even his eyes sparkled.

Our waitress arrived, a harried older woman who looked like she could give Marla a run for her money. "What'll it be, folks?"

Zeke's proud grin might have given the poor woman heart failure. She did a double take, looking between the two of us in awe. "Whatever my girlfriend wants!"

Oh, I definitely liked that. My thighs clenched together at the sudden need building in my core. There was nothing sexier than being claimed.

"Um, I'll have two scrambled egg whites, please," I requested. Folding my menu closed, I handed it to her and looked at Zeke expectantly.

His brow furrowed. "And...?"

Shit!

"Nothing," I replied firmly, averting my eyes to the placemat that advertised other specials. From the corner of my eye I could see Zeke continue to watch me in confusion.

"Um, I'll have the Grand Slam with the cookies and crème pancakes. Turkey bacon, scrambled egg whites, and a fruit platter. Please," Zeke added.

The waitress scratched everything down on a pad and mumbled something about being right back. Zeke waited until she rounded the corner into the kitchen before asking me, "Why are you only getting a couple eggs?"

I shrugged, hoping to appear casual enough that he dropped it. "I don't need to eat much."

"Two egg whites isn't even enough to feed a child. You need more calories than that."

Shaking my head, I stared at the placemat again. "Trust me, I don't need anymore calories. I have plenty."

He blew out a huff of air in frustration. "Maggie, the human body needs a minimum of twelve hundred calories just to sustain basic functions. If we're gonna go back and work at Marla's, you're going to burn off a lot of calories. Your body literally can't sustain itself on just a couple egg whites."

I met his explanation with hard silence and zero eye contact. Shame and guilt were putting a damper on what should have been a happy moment.

"Is this a money thing?" Zeke finally asked.

That he would jump to that conclusion created a lump in my throat. I didn't want his pity, nor did I want to be seen as a charity case. Obviously, my current financial situation wasn't great, but as soon as I got a job, that could change. It wasn't like I wanted to have someone else pay my way.

"You don't have to pay for my lunch. I can get it myself." Embarrassment flamed my cheeks.

"Oh my god, no!" barked Zeke. "You will never pay for a single thing while we're together. That's not what I meant at all!" He scrubbed a hand down his face. "I just don't understand why you're not eating."

"It sounds like you're picking a fight," I volunteered. It was a cheap shot, one that I instantly regretted when I saw the hurt in his eyes, but the fear of someone discovering my secret was too great to take it back.

"Consider the subject closed. I won't say another word about it." Zeke lifted my hand to his mouth, dusting a featherlight kiss across the back of it in a way that would have made Mr. Darcy proud.

But I saw the way his face fell when I slowly chewed on my eggs after they arrived. Everything had to be chewed fifty times before I could swallow it or my throat literally wouldn't work. That was just how I operated. It was a force of habit so strong that I couldn't stop it, even if I wanted to.

He was quiet on the walk out to the truck, taking my hand and lacing his fingers through mine as soon as we stood up. He seemed reluctant to let me go so that I could climb in.

"You know, I don't have to go back to the barracks," Zeke suddenly offered as we zipped along the highway. "I could stay out in River's Run for the next few days."

I considered his suggestion carefully before responding. Marla wasn't the kind of woman who would tolerate us sleeping in the same bed, but I knew she wouldn't turn him away. Zeke hadn't done or said anything that made me think this was an attempt at seduction anyway. That was probably something we were going to have to talk about because a girl has needs. And when she's now in a committed relationship with a man who looks like Zeke Hayes, she has a *lot* of needs.

"I'd like that, but you'd probably have to sleep on the couch. Marla is old school."

Zeke blanched. "I would never disrespect her home like that. I'll sleep in the bed of my truck if it makes her feel better. Or I can get a room at a motel. I just figured why make the drive back to post every night if I could spend more time with you."

Now, how is a girl not supposed to turn into a puddle of mush when her new boyfriend says things like that?

"I'd love that. I can show you more of River's Run. It's not much, but it's definitely home."

He grinned, pleased that I agreed. "I'll need to pick up a few things then, so let's make a quick stop."

Before I knew it, we pulled into the parking lot of a Madden Market. A new lump formed in my throat, this time for an entirely different reason. Marla and Celeste's Nana used to love taking us out here for a little "retail therapy," as they called it, especially on the weekends when the store slashed all the prices in their bargain bins. But ever since Wesley left and broke Celeste's heart, I tried to avoid shopping there when I could. The last time I visited one, large banners and posters featuring Wes modeling different clothing or products were plastered on nearly every surface.

Indeed, the moment we stepped inside, Wes's bright smile greeted us on the interior welcome sign. Only I knew him well enough to know that the smile was staged; it didn't reach his eyes the way it did when that smile turned on Celeste. I paused at the sign as memories surged forward. Wes had been like a brother to me, someone who always had my back and stepped in when I needed help. He never treated me like any of the other boys at school. While I understood why Celeste had to let him go, I couldn't help but miss him and wish things had played out differently for them. They seemed like the epitome of a perfect couple. What true love actually looked like in real time. It was what I hoped would develop between Zeke and me.

"Do you know him or something?" Zeke inquired, glancing between the poster and me in surprise.

"I thought I did. At one point." It was hard to keep the sadness from my voice as I remembered that despite how much I envied their relationship, the Wes I remembered never would have stayed away from Celeste. It had been three years now and we hadn't heard a peep from him. People changed, but Wes was the first person whose changes let me down. And they broke my best friend's heart, which I couldn't forgive.

Zeke wrapped an arm around my shoulder, pulling me into his side, and soothingly rubbing along my arm. He steered us inside and into the men's clothing section where I had to keep my eyes pinned on him or else Wesley's face would continue to smirk at me from all angles. Zeke made it easier to forget, though, when he handed me a credit card and said, "Okay. Dress me."

"Wh-what?" I stuttered. Dumbfounded, I took the card from him and held it up as if I couldn't understand what it was.

"I want you to give me a makeover," Zeke explained. "Pick out whatever clothes and shoes you think I need for the next few days in River's Run. You're the one with all the style, right?"

An unbidden squeal burst out of me. There was nothing I loved more than a makeover.

"Can I do your hair, too?" I asked, practically bouncing on the balls of my feet.

Shrugging, he said, "As long as it's within Army regs, I don't care. Whatever you want, Trouble."

If only Zeke knew how much he might come to regret that freedom. I proceeded to go through every single rack in the men's clothing section over the next two hours, giving him stack after stack of things to try on. Some of them were completely impractical, like a rich black suit, but the way he filled it out made my panties wet. That would definitely go in my spank bank arsenal because *damn*. Zeke could wear the hell out of a suit.

After I filled the cart with more clothes than he would need in two weeks at River's Run, we meandered over to the hair and makeup section. Zeke didn't hesitate when I paused to look at a line of hair care products I'd seen online, sweeping the entire row into the cart. He let me pick out different gels to style his hair, and even agreed to trying a little guyliner. That act alone made me want to pull him into a dressing room for a blow job.

It was a desire that I couldn't resist. I grabbed him by the hand and dragged him into the back where the fitting rooms remained open and unguarded, as I knew they would be. Madden Markets were notoriously understaffed due to the low pay.

Shoving him into the largest one, I closed the door behind me and turned the lock, looking up at Zeke through hooded lashes. There was an excitement in his gaze that I hadn't seen before, like maybe some part of him finally became aroused at the sight of me.

Knowing I finally got a rise out of him made my pussy clench with longing. I wanted his dick in my mouth more than I wanted my next breath.

Sliding down to my knees, I started to unbuckle his belt when both his hands wrapped around my wrists.

"Maggie, what are you doing?" he whispered.

An eyebrow arched as I gazed up at him. "Rocking your world."

Slowly, I licked along his fingers until he let go of my wrists, drawing one of the digits into my mouth. My tongue swirled around his finger, and Zeke rewarded me by growing a noticeable bulge in his pants. And boy, was it *noticeable*. I felt a momentary trace of fear that I was about to unleash an anaconda.

His eyes glazed over as I continued to suck on his finger, using both of my hands to finish unbuckling his belt. Zeke helped me with all the buttons on his uniform and I realized that I was basically playing with government property. It made the whole thing more wicked and erotic. Almost like I should have gotten permission to undress him but did it anyway. He laced his fingers through my hair to hold me in place.

"Is this what you want to do, or what you think *I* want you to do?" Zeke murmured. "Because I only want this if *you* want this. You're in charge."

The fact that he was so concerned with my pleasure rather than his own made my heart soar and my pussy throb. He wasn't like the other guys I'd hooked up with. This wasn't about him, it was about me, and somehow he knew I needed the reminder.

"If you don't get your cock in my mouth in the next five seconds, I'm going to walk home!" I growled.

A cocky grin worked his way out, making Zeke impossibly sexier. He leaned his hips off the wall enough to push his pants and boxers down and unfurled himself. Forget an anaconda—that would cower in fear of this thing. I pretty much tuned out through all of high school biology and physics, but I might've paid more attention if one of the teachers ever mentioned I'd need to know how to get a dick like this inside me. Rigid and veiny, it was a damn work of art.

Saliva pooled in my mouth, which I spit onto the base of his shaft. I let my tongue swirl around the head as both hands worked him. A deep rumble purred from his chest as Zeke tried to stifle his moan. I couldn't help myself. As I took him farther into my mouth, letting my tongue flatten out to take more of him in, I reached a hand down into my own panties and began circling my clit.

Zeke's hands were fists at his sides. He threw his head back in ecstasy, still trying to keep the moans at bay. I didn't want him to fight it. I wanted the entire store to know how much pleasure I brought him. Me

—ugly, little Maggie Eaton could make an Adonis like Zeke Hayes cry out in the throws of passion.

The sounds he made gave me more confidence and I boldly took more of him down my throat. It hurt to try and unhinge my jaw to accommodate the girth of him, but I didn't want to stop. I loved the way he tasted on my tongue. A steady drip of precum already coated my throat.

My own orgasm built, climbing higher and higher like I was on the precipice of a cliff. All it would take was Zeke's release and I would come hard enough to black out. Assuming his enormous cock didn't do that for me. Perhaps all my years of training my gag reflex had paid off.

Tears streamed down my cheeks as I tried to trace my tongue along the vein at the bottom of his shaft, but Zeke wouldn't let me. He slowly started to thrust, picking up speed when I whimpered in response. Tenderly, Zeke's hands framed my face to wipe away the tears. Meanwhile, the electricity sparking from the intensity of his eyes on mine would cause a power outage.

"I'm gonna come, Maggie. Holy shit, I'm gonna come!" he cried out. Either he no longer cared that someone might hear or he didn't remember where we were, but the thrill of the announcement, of hearing the sensuality in his voice tipped me over the edge. An orgasm exploded through me just as his cum filled my mouth.

Having nowhere to dispose of it, I swallowed it all. His eyes lit up as though Zeke had received a present. The look on his face made me want to give him a blow job all over again. Normally I found a paper towel or garbage can to spit out the guy's cum. I hated the salty flavor of it and none of my previous partners ever mattered enough to me to bother. But Zeke's reaction made it worth it

He hauled me up by the biceps and crushed his lips to mine. There was no hesitation to yield my mouth to his, where he swept his tongue through and dominated me. My knees quaked; I still hadn't caught my breath or come down from the high.

"I love the taste of me in your mouth," Zeke murmured against my lips, breaking out into a grin. "That was seriously the sexiest thing ever."

Suddenly shy, I gave him a small smile. "Good, I'm glad." This was normally the part where a guy would dismiss me. He got what he wanted out of me, so I could be carelessly tossed aside. I didn't know how to act with someone who stayed.

What if he doesn't stay?

I ignored the thought, fighting to stay present in the moment myself. Zeke wasn't like Spencer or any of the other assholes from Smithson County High.

Spencer...

Zeke, for once, remained oblivious to my discomfort. He gently kissed my forehead and wrapped his arms around my waist to pull me in flush with his body. "You're amazing, you know that?"

All the guilt from the hookup with Spencer came crashing down on me. How could I be someone's girlfriend if they didn't even know the truth about what I'd done? Zeke deserved that much from me, at least. I just hoped he didn't break up with me afterwards.

I tried to hide the tears in my eyes as I turned away from him and straightened out the skirt of my dress. The sounds of him fixing his own appearance bought me some time. Steeling myself, I took the coward's way out and kept my back to him.

"Don't sing my praises just yet," I began. "There's something I need to tell you."

"Okay. Tell me." Zeke turned me towards him, lightly tilting my chin up so that I would look at him.

I hated myself more in that moment than I had ever hated myself before. To break the heart of someone as trusting and loving and good as Zeke Hayes had to make me the worst kind of person.

"You remember that day we went to Tybee Island? The first day we spent together?" I whispered. At his nod, I took a deep breath to steady myself. "That night I met up with someone. A guy from my past. And we...we...I slept with him."

His mouth parted in an exhale of surprise.

Lord, if Nana's Jesus is real, may he smite me where I stand.

"It didn't mean anything, I swear. I absolutely swear it. Everything about you just confused me…all my thoughts and feelings got tangled up and…I'm sorry."

Lame. Such a pathetic way to end the explanation that wasn't even really an explanation. But there was no way to accurately say it.

I trembled and closed my eyes, waiting for the names and swearing that were sure to come. Although Zeke was such a classy, stand up guy, he probably wouldn't go that route. He would simply leave and I'd never see him again. Only it wasn't until that moment that I realized just how much it would devastate me if that were true.

"Who is he?" Zeke's voice was quiet. Even. Giving nothing away.

"Just—someone that I know. He's nothing to me. Never has been." Tears clogged my throat, but I choked them down. I had no right to cry in the bed *I* made.

"So it's not gonna happen again?" he asked, a tinge of sorrow lacing his tone. "Now that we're really doing this, it's just you and me?"

My eyes flew open as the last remaining piece of my heart shattered. Now Zeke would always feel insecure about us—about me—and it was entirely my fault. There wasn't a single thing about Spencer Church that made my actions worth the remorse I felt.

"Of course it's just you and me! That was before I realized how much you mean to me. Before I knew what was happening between us. I promise, I swear on Marla's bakery, I don't want anybody else, Zeke. Just us."

His fingers were softer than I deserved as they carefully brushed the curls away from my face. "Then you can count me in." Zeke's deep blue eyes held mine until my tears blurred and finally fell.

CHAPTER 23
THE CHOICE

ZEKE

Maggie suffered silently the entire drive back to River's Run, that much was obvious, but I didn't know how to snap her out of it. Not everyone existed the way I did; I couldn't exactly fault her for having a past. She already told me that she had multiple partners before and that sex was something important to her. Until she sucked my cock like it was a damn Olympic sport and she was the reigning gold medalist, it hadn't occurred to me that sex would be important to me, too. But now that I knew what sex with *Maggie* entailed, sign me up. I itched to return the favor and use my tongue on her. Every inch of her body needed to be embedded and permanently imprinted to my brain.

I just wanted to guarantee that I could be enough for her. A girl like Maggie must have expectations and I didn't want to disappoint her with a subpar performance. What if I couldn't do that? What if she preferred this other dude over me?

"Marla texted me that Harry is there and wants to start working on the bathroom. Are you going to help him?"

"Definitely. I told them both I would help."

Maggie smiled and gave my arm a grateful squeeze. "I'll let her know we're almost there. And I'll ask about you staying for a few days."

"I don't mind getting a hotel room," I reminded her. Maybe then we could pick up where we left off in the fitting room.

She grimaced. "There aren't any decent hotels in River's Run. And traveling to the closest one would be the same as going back to Fort Stewart, so that would be a waste. I'm sure it'll be fine if you stay with us."

"Whatever you want, Trouble. As long as I get to see you."

Marla downright refused to let me stay at a hotel when I offered after returning to River's Run. She insisted I would stay with them and sleep in her room, while she slept on the couch.

"No disrespect, ma'am, but like hell am I taking your bed from you." I frowned, which made Maggie snort. She quickly covered her mouth to stifle the giggle when Marla shot her a look of annoyance.

"We can decide the sleeping arrangements later. But there'll be no funny business under my roof, now, y'hear? Y'all are just starting out and I know everything's coming in hot, but keep your hands and mouths to yourselves!"

Now Maggie had to step a few feet away after Marla swatted at her for the giggles that burst forth. I couldn't look either of them in the eye, too horrified by Marla's accusations…that were completely spot on.

"I'll be on my best behavior," I agreed. I grabbed Maggie at the waist with both hands, tickling her enough to make her outright laugh. "Let me go up and change, and I'll get started with Harry."

Eavesdropping was rude, but as I walked out of the shop, I couldn't help but overhear Marla as she declared, "Y'know what, Maggie? Happiness looks real good on you. Better keep this one."

She better, indeed.

* * *

Working on the bathroom kept my hands busy and my mind idle. I continued to fixate on Maggie's revelation, wondering if I could be enough for her. I wanted to always be the reason for the smile on her face, whether that came from teasing her, supporting her, or whatever happened behind closed doors.

Harry and I were nearing supper time when I decided that what I felt wasn't jealousy. Maggie agreed to be *my* girlfriend—which I proudly told Marla the moment we arrived back—and I knew I was her first relationship. We got to grow and learn how to do this together. But what bothered me now was the uncertainty of it all. I didn't want to lose a competition I hadn't meant to enter.

Maggie had gone upstairs to continue sending out resumes rather than staying down with us to work. Being apart wasn't nearly so bad when I knew how soon I would get to see her.

When Harry said he needed to leave in order to make it to his bowling league, I offered to finish with the drywall. There wasn't much left to do anyway. A text from Maggie told me she would head down to The Comfy Cushion to grab us something to eat, making me grin like a fool, so I planned to keep working until she told me to stop. Silence enveloped me as I carefully applied a joint compound to all the seams to smooth out the wall surface. It would dry overnight so that we could paint and apply the beadboard trim tomorrow that Marla picked out.

I didn't notice anyone joined me until someone cleared their throat gruffly behind me.

"Ah, the boyfriend," he said when I turned around.

I knew instantly that this was the guy Maggie had slept with. Dark hair rolled in greasy waves down his forehead and several skull earrings lined both ears. He had on a grungy black t-shirt and baggy black pants, and I could tell he thought the effect made him look dangerous. While he might've been slightly taller than me, I easily had a good thirty pounds on him in muscle. The faintly acrid smell of stale cigarettes and weeds roiled off him.

"You don't have any business here," I stated firmly. For good measure, I folded my arms across my chest, flexing my biceps to remind him who had the real advantage here.

He smirked at me. "Wherever I can find Mags *is* my business. She here?"

Fury ripped through me, that same animalistic level of protection and claim needing to put him in his place. I stayed silent instead, not trusting myself to say anything.

A knowing grin spread across his face. He shuffled towards the open door, hiking a finger over his shoulder. "Just let her know that Spencer Church stopped by. Trust me, she knows where to find me.

"Oh, and Boyfriend?" Spencer paused to ensure he still held my full attention. "The money has to come from her, not you. Make sure she knows the rules." He spun on his heels and disappeared down the street.

What money? Why would Maggie owe him anything?

Anxiety burned through my gut because I knew that no matter what Spencer meant, it wouldn't be good.

CHAPTER 24
THE JOY
MAGGIE

"Celeste, I am *telling* you," I swore, "I've never felt like this before!"

I sat at the counter of The Comfy Cushion, waiting for the salads and sandwiches I ordered for Zeke and me. Marla flat out refused to eat at the diner ever again after the way Desiree fired her. Celeste never once charged us for anything we ate, so it wasn't like we were lining Desiree's pockets, but I wasn't going to argue with her. I wasn't going to turn down free food either.

My bestie rolled her eyes as she wiped down the counter behind the dining ledge. "Maybe if I hadn't heard you say the same thing about every single guy since the day I met you," she teased.

"No, this is *different*!" I huffed in frustration. There wasn't really a solid explanation for why things were different with Zeke. I could simply feel it. "Even Marla said so!"

That made her pause in cleaning. "Really?" she asked skeptically.

I nodded. "Yep. Told me that I better keep him because happiness looks good on me."

"Happiness looks good on everybody!" Celeste said with a laugh. "But you definitely deserve to be happy, so if Hayes does that for you, then I'm all for it."

The smile hadn't left my face since Marla pointed it out to me. Zeke hadn't thrown in the towel after I made my ugly confession. He still wanted to be with me, and made it a point to tell Marla, then Harry, as soon as we got back from Savannah. All of my insecurities disappeared the moment I heard him claim me like that. Now I just wanted to give into the bubbly joy that filtered out through my broken cracks.

"Just…make sure you take the time to get to know him," Celeste cautioned. The sadness in her voice reminded me of the pain from seeing all Wesley's modeling shots earlier at Madden Markets. Celeste and I *had* known Wes…and he still wound up breaking her heart.

But the happiness and hope blooming in my heart wouldn't hear it. A smile tugged at the corners of my mouth knowing I was grabbing food to take home to him.

Home…maybe being with Zeke Hayes is what a home is supposed to feel like.

"I'll be fine," I promised her. "I really think this is different, Cee. He's not like anyone I've ever met before."

Celeste gave me one of her rare smiles. "Then I'm happy for you. Certainly doesn't hurt that he's damn good looking!"

"Right?!" I laughed.

She reached across the counter to squeeze my hand. "Whatever you do, don't let your mother ruin this for you, okay?"

And like a storm cloud covering the sun, there went all the giddiness boiling up inside of me. If Diana saw that I had a hot, young soldier on my arm, she would turn into a jealous snake, and try to ruin it for me. Hadn't she already said that she now saw me more as "competition" than "child"? In the past few days of staying with Marla, my guards had gone down enough that any time I saw Diana, I experienced the shame and guilt all over again.

"I won't let her," I assured Celeste, while deep down I knew that wasn't something I had in me to promise.

Celeste handed over the takeout bags with a hug and a promise to stop by soon with Iris, and I walked slowly back to Marla's shop. Doubt crept back in along the way. Maybe things with Zeke weren't as special and wonderful as I believed. I always had a flair for the dramatics; it wouldn't be out of character for me to overinflate feelings for a guy—

hell, I once thought Spencer was the hottest dude around! If I followed in Diana's footsteps, I would only end up hurting Zeke. We might turn into my parents. He might go off and find a whole new family after I broke his heart.

The very thought of him meeting someone new hit me like a blow to the head. I stopped and tipped against the brick siding of an empty shop, leaning my hands down on my knees to catch my breath.

A few minutes went by before I sensed Zeke, like I had somehow sent a telepathic message directing him right to me. He didn't say anything, just squatted down so that he could look up into my eyes.

"Whose ass do I need to kick, Trouble?" he asked gently.

It eased the tension along my spine enough to make me laugh and stand upright. "I thought men only said shit like that in romance books?"

"Guess we're writing our own love story." He grinned, wrapping an arm around my waist to draw me closer. I immediately yielded to him, twining both arms around his neck and inhaling deeply. The faint smell of cedarwood and vanilla hit my nose. It was comforting, as were the feel of his arms around my back. Zeke hugged like he truly meant it.

He drew back enough to place a light kiss on my forehead and brush the stray curls from my face. "You were taking a while, so I came to find you. Figured you and Celeste got so caught up with girl talk that you'd still be at The Comfy Cushion."

I mean, he wasn't that far off. Celeste just didn't have time for that kind of gab fest anymore.

"Sort of. She just said somethings that got me thinking. I guess I got lost in my own head."

Zeke nodded. "I get that. I do that, too. Anything you wanna share so you can find your way out?" He reached down and picked up both of the takeout bags, moving them both to the right, and pulling me to his left. We strolled at a leisurely pace, our hands clasped, as I contemplated how much I wanted to tell him. Was nine hours of dating too soon to reveal how fucked up my family made me?

"I don't want to be like my parents," I finally said. "You and me—I wanna do this right. I'm afraid I'll hurt you."

We were almost to Marla's door before Zeke answered. "The thing is, you probably will. And I'll hurt your feelings, too, at some point. I don't really know what I'm doing either. I think the important part is that we figure it out together, right?"

He turned to face me fully and my breath caught in my throat. In the fading sunset, with orange and pink and a haze of blue crisscrossing the sky, Zeke had never looked so handsome. The light gave his tan skin a glow and a day's worth of stubble already lined his jaw. His earnest blue eyes held mine as he waited for my answer.

"We'll probably get more things wrong than right," I hedged. The fear still whispered in my ear, wondering where the similarities between myself and Diana ended.

Zeke agreed, "Of course we will, but I've got all the time in the world. I'm not going anywhere. Just promise me that if I do something wrong or you're upset, that you'll tell me. The rest we can make up as we go along."

I wanted to be as sure of myself as Zeke someday. So far, he always knew what to say to make me feel better.

"C'mon, let's go eat. I'm sure Marla's on the phone with the sheriff to look for us at this point."

CHAPTER 25
THE BACKLASH

Despite Marla's insistence, I slept on the couch rather than her room. It wouldn't feel right to take the bed of a woman kind enough to host me.

Not that I really got much sleeping done. A current of awareness ran through me like a livewire all night knowing that Maggie, my girlfriend, slept only a room away. While I had been horrified when Marla warned us off from any physical activity, I couldn't stop the raging hormones that screamed at me to have Maggie do that thing with her tongue again on my cock.

Her anxiety that evening before dinner destroyed any chance I had of mentioning Spencer's visit. I didn't want to burden her with something else when she opened up to me about her fears of us repeating her parents' mistakes. My girl didn't need anymore on her plate. But I desperately wanted to know why she owed Spencer money and what I needed to do to make the douchebag go away. The last thing I wanted was for her to have a reason to keep talking to him.

As soon as my watch showed 0500 the next morning, I called it and went downstairs to start working on the bakery again. Keeping my hands busy helped distract me enough that all the swirling thoughts stopped.

Until my phone lit up with a text from General Leggett.

I KNOW YOU DIDN'T STAY IN THE BARRACKS LAST NIGHT. I WILL NOT TOLERATE YOUR INSOLENCE.

I clenched my phone so tight that I almost cracked the case. The Army had a right to tell me geographically where I had to live. Technically, as long as I wasn't in some kind of trouble, they didn't have the right to tell me I couldn't sleep at my girlfriend's house.

The swoop of joy and pride at referring to this as my "girlfriend's house" was the only thing that made me calm enough to answer him.

I HAVEN'T DISOBEYED AN ORDER, SIR.

Leggett would make me pay for that statement in some fashion, but I hardly cared at the moment. I would tackle whatever extra duties or trainings he sent my way.

Barely ten minutes had gone by before I received another text, this time from Staff Sergeant Bridges.

WHY AM I RECEIVING AN ORDER FROM GENERAL LEGGETT FOR YOU TO PCS TO HUMPHREYS?

"Shit," I muttered. I couldn't stop staring at my phone, willing the words to disappear. A permanent change of station, or PCS, meant Leggett intended to send me away. In this case, I would be reassigned to Camp Humphreys…in South Korea.

"Hey! I wondered where you went!" Maggie breezed inside, her hair already curled and partially pinned up to reveal more of her face, a simple white shirt and jean shorts on. She held out a travel mug of coffee to me. "Just a dash of creamer, like you said you liked it."

After several seconds of me not taking the mug or responding, her face fell. "What's the matter? You look like someone just kicked a puppy right in front of you."

It was my turn to open and close my mouth like a goldfish, like she had done in the truck yesterday. God, had it really only been one day of bliss with her?

"I have to go," I mumbled. "I have to get to post and get something straightened out."

Her brows furrowed in concern, but she nodded. "Okay. Just call me later? Or come back when you can?"

I hated how lost and uncertain she sounded. How everything between us was still too fresh and new for her to know I'd come back. Even if I had to fight my way through every soldier in my unit, I'd always find a way to come back to her.

Kissing her wasn't optional, it was my life force. Despite her surprise, Maggie's mouth instantly yielded to mine, her soft curves pressing into my chest. A chill went through me that I might not get to experience this every day.

"I'll be back soon," I promised. "It's just a quick thing I've gotta take care of. Don't worry."

The drive to base wasn't enough to calm my racing heart. Soldiers from my unit glanced at me in alarm, having never seen me outside my uniform, as I stormed into Staff Sergeant Bridges' office. Though he sat there with two other non-commissioned officers from our unit, one look at my face and Bridges asked them to give us a moment.

"Please, sir, do not send me to South Korea." Camp Humphreys was the largest military installation not on U.S. soil. I always knew chances were high that I'd wind up stationed there at some point, but that was B.M.—before Maggie. Now I needed to at least remain in the United States. She would never be able to visit me overseas.

"Hayes, what do you want me to do? Refuse an order from the base general? No offense, but I don't know you well enough to stick my neck out for you." Bridges held up his hands in a placating gesture.

If I pushed back at Leggett myself, it would only make things worse. He could force me to stay in Korea until I fell back in line. I never stood up to him, not even as a kid.

"How soon am I to report?" I asked grimly. There was no point in fighting it. I knew when I enlisted that the Army owned me. I just never had a reason to care until now.

Bridges grimaced. "These are immediate orders. Once they're pushed through, you have to be on a plane within twenty-four hours."

Of course they were. Leggett meant this to be a punishment, not a warning.

How am I going to tell Maggie?

Picturing her angelic face this morning, full of hope and delight at something as simple as bringing me a cup of coffee, made my chest ache. Just last night I promised her that we would keep trying because I wasn't going anywhere, and now I was headed to the other side of the world.

"Can...can you just buy me some time? A couple days, at least?" I asked.

The staff sergeant leaned back in his chair, considering. I had never asked for anything and up until I went to sick call yesterday, I never missed anything. I was the soldier everyone went to for help, to step up when everyone else stepped out. My work ethic had saved Bridges' ass more than once from getting chewed out from the higher ups.

"I'll do what I can, Hayes, but you know I can't hold onto this paperwork for long. Leggett is insisting that you leave immediately."

"Any time you can give me will help, man. Thank you," I said and offered my hand for him to shake.

Bridges leveled me with a firm look. "Whatever your issue is, you better go take care of it now, Hayes. The orders are coming, one way or another."

I nodded in confirmation before sweeping out the door.

Even in the short time I'd spent there, River's Run brought me more good memories than any other place I'd been. I wasn't ready to leave. Marla was counting on my help to get the bakery up and running. The food at The Comfy Cushion really did taste best, and since I knew how important Celeste was to Maggie, I wanted to get to know her better, too. River's Run gave me a chance at belonging and I didn't want to give that up.

I found Marla and Harry in the bakery when I pulled in. Neither one of them questioned what had to be a pained look on my face, but I noted how Marla's eyes narrowed in suspicion. She told me to go up to the apartment to find Maggie.

Maggie stood at the kitchen table, a mannequin head on a stand in front of her and her laptop open to an instructional video. She had some sort of hair tool in her hand as she tried to replicate the hairstyle on the video to the mannequin. All of it was forgotten when she spotted me.

"Zeke, you're home!" she squealed. Dropping the hair tool with a clunk, Maggie rounded the table and launched herself into my arms. I laughed as I scooped her up so that her tiny legs could wrap around my waist.

God, the way my heart wanted to burst at hearing my girl call this home…

"Listen, we need to talk. It's really important," I told her.

She peeled away from me, concern marring her face, and sat down on the couch, tugging on my hand so that I sat down next to her.

"Okay, you're scaring me, Zeke. What is it?"

"I received orders to PCS," I said.

She interrupted before I could continue. "I don't speak Army-ese. What does that mean?"

I rolled my eyes, but grinned at her. "Some Army girlfriend you are, not even knowing the acronyms. A PCS is a 'permanent change of station' in the military. It basically means I have to move."

Tears pooled in the corners of her eyes. "Okay," Maggie said slowly. "Is it far?"

A lump formed in my throat. "Yeah. It's about as far away as I could go. They're sending me to South Korea."

"Oh my god!" Maggie sat up straighter. "You won't even be in this country! How is that possible?!"

"The Army still has bases all over the world. I have to go wherever they send me."

"So there's nothing you can do?" she cried. "You don't get a say?"

I shook my head.

"How come I don't get a say? I'm a tax payer, right? Why can't I say you get to stay here?" Maggie sounded frantic. Even filled with tears, her hazel eyes were so beautiful, darting around and yet seeing nothing as she scrambled for a solution.

Her logic made me chuckle. As much as I hated to leave her, I was glad to know the news shattered her world just as much as mine. "Nobody has any say in it, unfortunately. The Army can do whatever they want to me."

"Then I'll come with you," she said resolutely. "I have no idea how I'll make that happen, but goddamn it, Zeke, I don't want this to be over already! We only just started dating! It isn't fair!"

"Maggie, you can't come with me. You wouldn't have anywhere to live." I hated to refuse her, especially when her determination for us to continue dating sounded like music to my ears. Maggie truly was invested in us. Whatever happened with Spencer really didn't mean anything to her.

"I'd just live with you, dummy!" She rolled her eyes as if it were obvious.

I snorted. "You can't live in the barracks with me. Not unless we were married, and even then they would make us stay in some kind of house or apartment set up."

Maggie's eyes widened as she stood up. "That's the answer, Zeke. Let's do it. Let's get married."

"Married?" I repeated like an idiotic parrot. I couldn't tell if my heart stopped out of alarm, anxiety, or bliss. That animalistic beast inside roared at the idea of making Maggie my wife, having that permanent bond and claim over her.

But I also didn't want Maggie and I to be another Army statistic. It was as common as grass for a young, foolish couple to dive headfirst into marriage when one of them was in the Army. Usually it came before or after a deployment when the soldier grappled the possibility of death or the relief of living. If I married Maggie, I wanted it to be after years of getting to know her, and I wanted to do it the right way.

"Yes! Let's get married! Today! Right now!" She bounced on the balls of her feet as if she were thrilled at the prospect.

I stood up to grab both her hands, squeezing them just enough to wake her up from whatever delusion she was having. "Maggie, you are talking about marrying me and moving to the other side of the world. That's not a decision you make on the fly."

"Then how else are we gonna see each other, Zeke?" Maggie challenged me. "You said yourself that you threw up yesterday because you didn't know when you'd get to see me again. How are you gonna go to *Korea* not knowing?" One of her carefully sculpted eyebrows rose in defiance, and she crossed her arms over her chest as if daring me to contradict her.

But I couldn't shake the vision of seeing Maggie walk down the aisle towards me in a white ballgown, something shiny with sparkles like the first time I saw her. That was how this was supposed to happen, a good five or six years from now.

"If you marry me, Maggie Eaton, I'm never divorcing you. We do this, and we do it for life. Is that a gamble you really wanna take on the spur of the moment because I'm leaving?"

I thought for sure I stumped her. The way her eyes rounded and she took a half step back, I could sense the defeat in the air.

Then Maggie shocked me as she steeled herself, clenching her hands into fists at her side, and nodded firmly. She threw my own words right back at me. "Count me in."

CHAPTER 26
THE PAPERWORK
MAGGIE

This is insane.

That thought played on replay over and over again as I fluffed up my hair and fixed my makeup while Zeke called down to the courthouse to find out what we needed to do. I, Maggie Eaton, was getting married. Today. To probably the world's sexiest man alive.

Except that wasn't why I wanted to marry Zeke. Sure, his good looks added to the overall package, but it was something more than that. Life was cruel to take him from me so soon after we decided to make a real go at this, so if I needed a piece of paper from the state of Georgia to ensure we got to keep making a go at it, that's what I'd do.

Besides, as romantic as Zeke's declaration was, I didn't believe he wouldn't divorce me if it really came down to it. Every couple gets married thinking that they're going to be together forever. Then life happens, people show their true colors—like Diana did to my father—or some strange twist of fate drives them apart. Hell, look at what Fate had done to Wes and Celeste. I had to grab this chance with Zeke with everything I had or else I'd have to live the rest of my life wondering if he would have been the one.

Celeste would try to talk me out of it. It probably would sound like we were rushing things to the rest of the world. I couldn't blame anyone for thinking it. But I also knew I wanted to keep getting to know Zeke, no matter what hurdles were thrown our way.

There was nothing left for me in River's Run. I hadn't found a job yet and Diana would never even know if I left. Leaving Marla, Celeste, and Iris sucked, but Zeke and I would come back to visit. They weren't as much of a reason to stay as Zeke was a reason to go.

"Do you have a passport, birth certificate, and social security card?" Zeke asked from the doorway. He looked pale, like the idea of marriage made him queasy, but he never said he didn't want to go through with it.

Thankfully, I had planned a senior girls' trip in high school where we thought we were going to visit the Carribbean on a cruise. Most of us would be over eighteen by the time spring break hit, so we all applied for passports over winter break only to realize that none of us had enough money to go on that kind of vacation. We settled for driving down to Daytona Beach instead.

I nodded at him, biting on my lower lip. "Are you okay with this?"

Zeke paused before answering. "I just never pictured getting married this way. I feel like I'm cheating you out of something. Don't you want a big, fancy wedding with a dress and a veil and all that stuff?"

I shrugged. As much as I enjoyed makeup and glamour, a wedding was the one thing I never really planned. "Why envision a wedding when you can't envision the groom?" The joke fell flat as Zeke's eyes tightened.

"And now that you've met me?" He moved further into the room, so close that the dresser knobs jutted into my back as I tried to back away. "Am I who you can see as the groom?"

Why was formidable Zeke so stupid hot? My nipples peaked and arousal pooled at my core from the dominance radiating off him.

"Yes." It was a simple answer, loaded with complicated tangles of feelings, needs, and desires. My voice sounded breathy, even to me, and I fixated on his mouth as Zeke's gaze dropped to mine. He licked his lips as he stared. Was he remembering the way he fit in my mouth yesterday in that dressing room? Did he know how badly I wanted to taste him again?

"Collect your things. We're heading to probate court to get the license, then we have to head on post to get you signed up for DEERS," Zeke said. Gravelly and low, his voice made everything sound so seductive.

I waited to see if he would kiss me, or better yet, explore more of my body than he'd been able to yesterday, but instead I was doused with cold air as he turned away from me and broke the spell. It took me a full minute before calling after his retreating back, "Wait—what does a deer have to do with this?"

DEERS, it turned out, was yet another Army acronym I needed to know. It stood for Defense Enrollment Eligibility Reporting System. Zeke explained it would give me a special identification card so that I could get onto any military base to utilize the services there. Apparently they had special shops and activities that only military personnel and their "dependents" (aka family members) could access. Plus, enrolling in DEERS was what gave me health insurance through the military. Zeke said it was important to have me in the system right away because I needed to be listed on his orders to Korea as an eligible spouse in order for the Army to pay for me to move to Korea with him.

First, though, we had to have the marriage certificate from the Georgia courthouse.

"Okay, Miss Eaton, I need to see your driver's license and birth certificate, please." The clerk behind the tempered glass at the Smithson County courthouse didn't bat an eye to my casual attire, the Army uniform Zeke had changed into, or our sudden need to get married. Zeke politely declined when she offered to schedule something further out so that we could plan for a small ceremony.

She did, however, flip her brown hair over her shoulder and try to flirtatiously catch his eye as she commented, "We don't often get soldiers like yourself in here."

I wanted to scratch her eyes out. Possessively, I wrapped an arm around Zeke's waist, and stared the woman down.

Zeke tried to hide his smirk. "I guess other soldiers aren't as lucky as I am." He leaned down and planted a kiss onto the top of my hair.

Take that, bitch!

The clerk jerked as if coming to attention. "Of course. Congratulations. If I could just see your driver's license and birth certificate as well, sir, I'm going to have Miss Eaton fill out some paperwork." She handed me a clipboard after accepting Zeke's documents. "And if you're taking your husband's last name, you'll need to fill this out as well."

I glanced at Zeke in suprise. His eyes softened and he flashed me a small smile that reminded me of Celeste.

"You don't have to if you don't want to," he whispered. "Your name is entirely your choice."

The clerk melted in her chair. "Oh, isn't that sweet. I've got a good feeling about you two. Now, here's your paperwork, Mr. Hayes. Just bring it all back to me when you're done."

Zeke and I took seats in the waiting area. The name change form on top stared at me, and I wiped the sweat off the palm of my hand as I steadied my breath. Changing my last name didn't really matter to me; I didn't feel like an Eaton anymore than I felt like a Rockefeller. The act of changing it, however, brought the weight of my current situation into stark clarity.

We were getting *married*. I was going to be somebody's *wife*. I couldn't even manage to make toast without burning it—didn't you have to have more qualifications than that to be a wife?

"Having second thoughts?" Zeke looked at me pensively, chewing on his bottom lip. His form already had everything filled in, and he glanced at the blank papers on the clipboard.

"No." Thankfully, my voice sounded firm, even if my insides squirmed like worms in a tackle box. "I don't have any second thoughts about you." That much was true. I might not exactly be wife material or have my life together in any conceivable way, but I knew Zeke made me feel good enough, and that was worth pursuing.

With a flourish, I filled out the top line, requesting the courts change my name from Margaret Elizabeth Eaton to Margaret Elizabeth Hayes. Maggie Hayes had a nice ring to it.

I just hoped this new version of Maggie didn't screw up quite as much as the current version.

CHAPTER 27
THE VOW

ZEKE

As a kid, I thought weddings came from fairytales. They included lots of flowers, men in stiff tuxedos, and a woman wearing a dress wide enough for an entire classroom of children to hide under. I never attended a wedding before, but I never knew anyone who got married. I wouldn't have imagined that the first wedding I experienced would be my own. That I stood here now, in a courtroom, holding Maggie's hand in mine as she recited a vow to love, honor, and forsake me above all others seemed surreal.

I had tunnel vision as we had walked down that aisle. The justice of the peace's face blurred and I couldn't get a bearing on my surroundings. Only Maggie's face kept me grounded. I thought my heart was going to beat out of my chest.

Her hands felt warm in mine, but maybe that was because mine were so cold. Marriage meant forever. I had to provide for her, to give her the kind of life she deserved. Could I do that? I sure knew I wanted to try. Maggie would be my responsibility after this and it was up to me to make her dreams come true.

"Mr. Hayes, it's your turn," the justice said. "Please repeat after me. With this—"

"Actually, sir, I'd like to say my own vows, if I could," I interrupted. He nodded. "Maggie, I've always been on the outside of things. Never had a family. Never really had a friend. I just accepted that I was meant to live my life alone.

"But then I met you, and now I can't stand the thought of being alone. I wake up and look for you; I fall asleep at night and see your face. You've shown me more light and happiness in the past few days than most people know in a lifetime. Thank you for the honor of being my wife. For committing to share more of that light and happiness until I take my last breath. Knowing you, Trouble, it's gonna be one hell of a ride."

Tears leaked down Maggie's cheeks as she gave a watery chuckle. Even the justice of the peace coughed to cover a laugh.

"Then I guess, by the power vested in me from the great State of Georgia, I now pronounce you husband and wife. You may kiss your bride." He clapped a few times and beamed at us.

Maggie's smile lit up her whole face, even with the tears steadily falling.

Our first kiss as husband and wife was soft. Gentle. Full of promise. I might've only known her less than a week, but I vowed to love Maggie Eaton—now Maggie Hayes—until the end of forever.

We returned to the clerk's window to pick up our temporary certificate, providing Marla's address as the physical location to send the official license. Maggie would have Marla forward it to us in South Korea.

"I wish I had time to take you somewhere special to celebrate," I told her as we walked hand in hand out to my truck. "But we've gotta hurry up and get to post to enroll you in DEERS. I don't want to risk you not being included in my orders."

Maggie nodded and squeezed my hand in reassurance. She didn't say anything the entire drive back to Fort Stewart, listening intently as I called Bridges to give him a head's up.

"Sir, this is Hayes," I greeted him on speakerphone. "I am en route to the DEERS office to get my wife entered in the system. Please don't send the paperwork until you have confirmation."

Bridges' sharp intake of breath indicated how much I surprised him.

"Hayes, you son of a bitch. When I told you to go handle whatever you needed, I didn't mean to go get married."

"I know, sir, but this is exactly what I needed to do. Please make sure my wife, Margaret Hayes, is on my PCS orders. I'll text photos of our temporary marriage license over as soon as we get to DEERS."

That animal inside rippled in satisfaction over hearing me call Maggie my wife.

My staff sergeant sighed. "Roger that. I'll work on giving you an extra day. I don't wanna be the one who made you pack up all your stuff on your wedding night." He laughed to himself. "Send me that picture as soon as possible."

With a click, the line disconnected.

We drove in silence for several more miles before I finally exclaimed, "Say something, Maggie. Jesus, you're freaking me out over here."

One shoulder raised in a shrug. "I'm just trying to wrap my head around everything," Maggie said. "I'm your wife. We actually got *married*."

The hair on the back of my neck bristled as panic set in. Did she already regret the decision? Should I have told her no? I promised her the world, yet I couldn't even make her happy enough to stay married to me for an hour.

"Maggie, this was your idea…" I trailed off in uncertainty, unsure of what to say.

"I know that. I'm not saying I regret it. I'm just saying that it didn't really hit me until we left the courthouse. I mean, I barely know you. What if you're secretly an axe murderer?"

I raised an eyebrow at her. "A secret axe murderer with a government security clearance?"

She snorted. "Okay, yeah, I know that sounded stupid. But you get what I mean."

"I do and I don't. You said you wanted to get married, that you didn't want to give up on us right as we were beginning. Do you not mean that anymore?"

"No." Maggie mulled it over, twisting a curl around one of her fingers as she tended to do whenever she felt anxious. "Can we just pretend like we're not married and instead just treat each other like we're still in the early stages of dating?"

That sounded like a dangerous option to take when I already knew I was completely smitten with her. Like she wanted an out in case our marriage didn't turn into what she expected. I meant it when I told her there would be no divorce. We were in this thing together, whether she liked it or not.

But I didn't want to scare her away by admitting that out loud.

"We'll just keep taking it one day at a time," I suggested. There, that didn't sound too threatening or overbearing.

We needed to talk about Spencer, though, and the money she supposedly owed him. Starting married life with a threat looming over her didn't seem like a good choice.

How would I bring it up without sounding accusatory?

"Is there anything you need to tell me?" I hedged. "Anything that I need to know about you before we move to another country?"

Maggie cocked her head to the side. "No? I don't have anything to hide."

A lump formed in my throat at her lie. "Nothing about that Spencer guy?"

Her face flushed and she visibly bristled as she recoiled from me. "How do you know his name? Have you been snooping around on me or something?"

"No, of course not! But I know that you owe him something and he thinks it means he has a claim on you!"

As soon as the words were out, I knew I said the wrong thing. Maggie's jaw dropped as if I'd slapped her. Her hands shook until they clenched into fists on her lap.

"You don't control me anymore than he does," she snarled. Venom dripped from her voice. "I don't want to talk about this anymore."

And with that, she turned to face the window, refusing to look at me again.

I pounded my hand on the steering wheel in frustration. "It's not about controlling you, Maggie. It's about making sure my wife is safe!"

Still, she wouldn't turn from the window. We drove the rest of the way in silence. When we approached the gate, I asked for her driver's license for the Military Policeman, otherwise known as an MP, granting entry. Rather than look at me, Maggie chucked hers on the dashboard in front of me.

My heart dropped into my chest. We were barely married and already fighting. How could I take her to the other side of the world if I made her so miserable?

I pulled into a spot at the DEERS office and cut the engine, turning in my seat to look at her. It hurt to see how stiffly she sat, how much she concentrated on ignoring me. It served as a startling reminder that I didn't know how to talk to people or what to say. Just because I had a slip of paper labeling me a husband didn't mean I could carry a conversation as one.

"Look, I know I don't say the right things. Most of the time I don't know what to say or how to understand people. If what I said came out wrong, I'm sorry. Do you still wanna be married to me? Are you still going to Korea with me? Because if so, we need to go set things in motion. If not, I need to take you back to River's Run and start packing my stuff."

Maggie swiveled to me, tears glinting in her eyes again. "I don't say the right things either. Celeste always says that I'm a drama queen. Please don't bring Spencer up again. There are…things in my past I don't want you knowing. Things you shouldn't be a part of. Okay?"

I nodded. "Then let's go inside and make you an official milspouse."

She crinkled her nose. "You make it sound like I'm joining a cult."

"It's not that kind of initiation."

Maggie snorted, though I had no idea why. I'd read a lot about cults a few years ago and military spouses as a group didn't meet any of the eligibility criteria to be considered a cult.

I got out and rounded the front of the truck so I could open the door for her. Lacing her fingers through mine, I added, "Last chance to back out. After this you'll officially be Mrs. Hayes, set for Korea."

Although she gulped, a smile tugged at her lips. "Count me in."

CHAPTER 28
THE GOODBYE
MAGGIE

THE REST of the day went by in a blur of introductions and explanations I would never remember. I had no idea there was so much paperwork involved to be a military wife. Zeke and I went to desk after desk, filling out forms and supplying our temporary marriage certificate along with the affidavit of my name change. At some point I had my picture taken and a laminated ID card pressed into my hand shortly afterwards.

"Don't ever lose that," the soldier warned me as he handed it off. "That's your access to everything on post."

Zeke also took me by his unit office to turn in copies of all the paperwork when we were done. He introduced me to another soldier, Staff Sergeant Bridges, and they exchanged a few heated words in a low voice while I waited awkwardly in the doorway.

Every time Zeke called me "his wife," a thrill shot through me. Call me a lovestruck fool, but I ate that shit *up*. He made no effort to hide the pride in his voice as he said it either, like he genuinely wanted everyone to know that he married *me*.

"Um, there's something I have to do, but you don't have to go with me. I'm gonna take you back home so that you can start packing your stuff. We'll need to move it all into my room so that the movers can take it, okay?" Zeke said.

I nodded faintly even though I didn't have the slightest idea what he was talking about.

"I'm sorry, Trouble, but I don't think we're gonna get that extra day. We'll be leaving tomorrow." His hand gently gripped my elbow while his thumb made soothing circles. "You'll wanna say goodbye to Celeste and Marla tonight."

Ice crystallized in my veins. In all my realizations today, it hadn't once crossed my mind that I would be leaving them. Marla, the mother I needed, and Celeste, the sister I should have had. How would I get used to days without them? How could I tell them what I'd done?

Zeke is worth it, I reminded myself. *He* sees *you*.

"Okay," I told him. I wasn't sure exactly what was okay, but I needed to say something. I need the brain fog to lift so that I felt like myself again and not a caricature of Maggie Hayes, Army wife.

Zeke apologized as he pulled up in front of Marla's bakery. He said there was something important he had to do, so he couldn't stay and share our good news with Celeste. I wouldn't want to hurt his feelings by admitting it, but I was suddenly very grateful that the Army kept him busy. Saying goodbye would hurt enough. This was something I simply needed to do alone.

Yet as soon as I saw his truck round the corner, I already missed him. Wistfully, I stared at his retreating taillights, uncertain but elated at what we had done. I didn't know how to be in a relationship, let alone be someone's wife, but I would figure it out for Zeke. He didn't realize how special he truly was.

Without turning around, I took a few steps backwards before ramming into something hard. Two hands clasped around my upper arms in a tight grip that made me wince.

"Well, well," a voice snarled in my ear, sending shivers down my spine. "Looks like I finally found you, Mags."

Fuck…

CHAPTER 29
THE FIGHT

ZEKE

SEEING Maggie grow smaller in my rearview mirror didn't sit well in my stomach. I immediately regretted leaving her, but given Bridges terse instructions to report to Leggett's office faster than the speed of light, I didn't have much of a choice. Rage would be his mildest reaction at this point, and the more I could spare Maggie, the better. I didn't want Leggett anywhere near her.

The lengths I already wanted to go to protect her should have been frightening, yet I only marveled at having someone to protect. I loved knowing I had someone waiting for me. The certainty of seeing Maggie as soon as I got home.

Home…that's exactly what she felt like.

A soldier at the DEERS office must have alerted the general as soon as Maggie and I arrived because by the time we reported to Bridges, I was in hot water. My staff sergeant pulled me aside as Maggie stepped away to tell me that he didn't appreciate Leggett getting his personal number. Apparently, Leggett threatened Bridges' pending promotion if he didn't comply with getting me in Leggett's office as soon as possible.

Now, as I braced myself outside his office, only the thought of seeing Maggie's smile again made me enter.

For once Leggett appeared to be lost in thought. He stared glumly out the window, unblinking and focused on something that I doubted existed in the here and now. It gave me time to notice how much his hair had grayed, the jowls that developed along his jawline, and just how many frown lines permanently etched themselves along his brow.

"You wished to see me, sir?" I asked hesitantly. Speaking first never ended well, but I wanted to bounce on the balls of my feet in my haste to return to River's Run.

Leggett jumped, startled out of his reverie. The frown lines deepened as he set his scowl upon me.

"I've been informed that you're now married."

Despite how much the emotional display would set him off, I grinned with pride. "Yes, sir, I am."

The general leaned menacingly over his desk. "This isn't funny, boy. You know the saying—if the Army wanted you to have a wife, they would have issued you one. You're about to throw your whole life away with this stunt you pulled."

"With all due respect, sir, is that what your marriage did for you?" My hands clenched into fists behind my back as I tried to calm the fury boiling beneath the surface. Leggett had no right to talk about Maggie like this.

A cold calm swept across the room at my accusation. He stalked around the desk, keeping his eyes on me like a snake that finally entrapped a field mouse. I knew what happened next and kept my gaze trained on a point over his shoulder. Striking back could land me in the brig.

"I think we both know I paid dearly for the damage my wife caused," Leggett said icily. "Think of how much further I would be in my career if she didn't make me take in snot-nosed, worthless bastards."

Tension clenched my jaw shut so tightly that my gums burned. I concentrated on that pain, which may have been why I didn't notice Leggett's fist until it made contact with my face. It was a good hit since he caught me off guard, one that would leave a shiner, but not enough to result in a fractured cheekbone. No medical attention. That was always Leggett's rule.

"You are the biggest mistake I ever made," Leggett spat. "I never should've let you stay." Disdain dripped from his every word as a muscle feathered in his jaw.

My anger flared as I tried to rein in my temper. It would be the general's word against mine, and since we were in his office while he stood in his uniform, a court martial could ruin my entire future. That's what Leggett wanted. If he kept pushing, he might make me snap and then he could take away the one thing I cared about—Maggie.

I barely dared to breathe. When Leggett got like this, he was ruthless. Any small reaction on my part could set him off. As much as it pained me to do it, I straightened to my full height and returned to attention, maintaining my gaze on the wall over his shoulder.

After more than a minute of my silent compliance, Leggett deflated. "Get out of my sight, you piece of shit. Enjoy Korea—and everything that comes with it."

I spun on my heel at his dismissal. Pain throbbed in my cheek from where he hit me, but it was his sinister threat about my new duty station that had me in a panic. Even on the other side of the world, Leggett had the power and influence to make my life a living hell.

CHAPTER 30
THE ANNOUNCEMENT
MAGGIE

"Get your filthy hands off me, Spencer!" I shoved him as hard as I could, which wasn't much given my small frame in comparison to his. "Don't ever touch me again!"

Spencer towered over me, a glassy-eyed leer playing across his face. He reeked of alcohol and I crinkled my nose in disgust.

"That wasn't what you said the other night, was it, doll face?" Spencer smirked. Reaching for me again, he gripped my biceps tightly enough to bruise and yanked me forward, throwing me off balance. Using my equilibrium against me, Spencer whipped me around and shoved me into the brick wall in the alleyway of the building. I tried not to cry out as my head smacked stone.

I gritted my teeth so I wouldn't cry out. Bullies thrived on seeing your fear, and Spencer was the worst bully Smithson County High had ever seen.

"What do you want, Spencer?"

He grinned sinisterly, bending down so that he could look me square between the eyes. "I want all the money you owe me. Plus twenty percent interest."

"I don't owe you shit! It was a fucking accident!" I growled.

Spencer's nostrils flared. He tightened his hold on my arms, pushing me harder against the wall behind me. There was no way I could fight him off. I didn't have that kind of body strength.

"Yeah, well your little 'accident' cost me five grand!" Flecks of his spit landed on my face, making my stomach turn over.

I frantically glanced down both sides of the alleyway. It was completely abandoned, not uncommon for this time of day in River's Run. Everyone was at work and none of the major businesses were on this block. Even if I grew a spine to yell for help, nobody would be around to hear me. I was utterly alone.

"There's one way you can work off what you owe," Spencer offered with a lecherous grin. He leaned down and ran his tongue along the side of my face. "My boys and I could use an easy cunt like yours to pass around."

I snapped my head back in disgust. "Get off me!"

Instantly I knew that was the wrong thing to say. Spencer's bloodshot eyes darkened and he slapped me hard across the face before a hand cupped my jaw to hold me still.

"You think you're better than that?" he sneered. "Are you gonna start quoting Bible verses and claiming you're reformed like every other dumb bitch in this town? You're a whore! A pitiful, ugly whore who'll never get a guy beyond a few pumps in the back of his car. Like mother, like daughter, right?"

Tears clouded my vision as I tried to stop my legs from giving out beneath me. His words were like blazing arrows straight to my heart. Except I couldn't deny that everything he said was true. Diana had been caught multiple times in the back of men's cars here in River's Run. That was why none of the other women her age would talk to her. She'd ruined more than one marriage since we moved here.

And now I would do the same thing. My own marriage would suffer this time, because like Spencer said, I was ugly and pitiful. A good man like Zeke wouldn't want me. Especially not when I owed so much money and had no way of paying it back.

As if he could sense the conclusion I'd drawn, Spencer loosened his hold and smirked at me. "Get down on your knees for me like a good little slut." He started undoing his belt buckle, gleaming as he saw the defeat and despair take over my face. I lowered myself down on autopilot. Shame made me numb.

"My god, Maggie, haven't I taught you to be more discreet than this?!"

Never in my life did I think I would be grateful to hear my mother's voice. Diana stood in the opening of the alley, a hand on her hip, in a too short miniskirt and a low cut tank top she stole from me. She didn't look shocked or upset by my predicament, though.

Spencer snatched my bicep again, jerking me to my feet and turning his leer to Diana. "Sometimes the mood just strikes you, Ms. Eaton."

Diana glanced between us as if unsure how to proceed. If there weren't tears streaming down my face, I knew she'd be flirting right back, but my overall unhappy demeanor must have clued her in that something was wrong.

"I guess the mood will need to strike you with someone else, Spencer. Looks like I need to get our Maggie here back to the house." Diana gave him a small smile and wound an arm around my shoulders, steering me towards the sidewalk. "See you later!"

We only made it a block, with my mother checking back over her shoulder to make sure Spencer didn't follow us, before she threw her hands up in disgust. "Maggie, if you need a place to entertain a man, at least have the decency to take them out to Randy's!"

Randy's Motel sat just off the highway on the edge of Smithson County. It had a reputation for lot lizards and drifters because they charged by the hour rather than by the night. A lot of shady things happened there. Diana was a frequent customer.

Her response made me want to vomit. "Do you seriously think I'd do something like that outside Marla's apartment?" I seethed.

Diana rolled her eyes and shrugged. "Lord only knows with you, Maggie. I wouldn't think you'd be wearing jeans two sizes too small, but you're standing right in front of me in them, so it must be true!"

My jeans are not *two sizes too small!*

"Then I guess it's a good thing that I won't be standing in front of you again any time soon!"

"Oh really? And why is that?" She crossed her arms over her chest expectantly.

"Because I'm moving out of the country tomorrow!" I snapped.

Up until that moment, I had no intention of telling Diana anything about Zeke, our marriage, or our upcoming move. But if it meant wiping the smug look off her face then all the secrets were coming out.

She snorted. "Out of the country, huh? Why not off the planet, too? Maybe then you could get far enough away from me."

"Oh my god, this isn't ABOUT you!" I thundered. "I got married! And my new husband has orders to South Korea!"

I wish I had a camera to relive the moment over and over again. Diana's jaw dropped and she staggered back a few steps, clutching her heart. "Margaret Eaton, you lie!"

"It's Margaret Hayes, now." A smile broke free, in spite of the fear still racing through my veins. "You remember Zeke, right? You met him outside of Marla's the other day."

Now I could knock my mother over with a leaf. "Oh my god, are you PREGNANT? You can't make me a grandma yet! I'm too young for that!"

Of course, because it always came back to her. She couldn't even congratulate me, just worry about what it meant for her.

"I'm not pregnant, but I do need to get packing. I'll see you around, Diana."

I had just made it across the street when I heard her call out, "Don't do anything stupid, Maggie! A man like that has needs that you'll never be able to meet. Make him happy, whatever it takes. Stay on your back, or let him stay on his."

The insinuation made my hackles rise. My own mother all but echoing Spencer's sentiments. I was unworthy; always had been, always would be. Nobody could ever see me as anything other than an ugly girl who knew how to spread her legs. And according to Diana, that seemed to be the only thing capable of making a man like Zeke happy.

I didn't bother to look back at her as I hurried away. Only after I saw the lights of The Comfy Cushion ahead did I finally let the tears fall.

CHAPTER 31
THE TEARS
MAGGIE

THERE HAD BEEN many times that I walked into The Comfy Cushion crying over a boy, but the fact that this might be my last made me cry even harder. Even after Zeke received orders to leave Korea, we probably wouldn't be moving back to this area. I didn't know much about the military or how they decided where we would go, but it seemed unlikely that we would come right back to where we stared. Although what had Celeste told me her mom used to say? Something about life coming full circle or some shit. Maybe ours would, too.

Still, it was with a heavy heart that I spied my best friend and soul sister behind the counter of her beloved diner. She stood with her profile to me, talking to Jesse on the grill line while she filled the napkin dispensers at the counter. Her frizzy brown hair sat in a tangled knot atop her head that I immediately wanted to brush out and plait.

How the hell could I handle an international move without my best friend?

Jesse noticed me first, doing that weird head nod that all guys did rather than communicate in a way that anybody else could understand. Celeste turned and immediately rushed over.

"Maggie, honey, what's wrong?" She pulled out a chair for me at the closest table and gently pushed me into it.

The tears returned, leaking out of the corners of my eyes like a broken faucet. I couldn't tell her about Spencer and I didn't want to admit out loud how vile Diana had become. Doing so would only make it that much more real. Plus, if this would be my last time seeing Celeste for a while, I didn't want to spend my remaining little time whining about my egg donor.

"I got married," I whispered. Even with all the sadness in my heart, I couldn't stop the smile that broke across my face at any mention of Zeke.

Celeste's mouth formed the perfect O in disbelief. "Excuse me, you did what, now?"

I hiccupped out a laugh as the tears came faster. "It's true. I'm now Mrs. Maggie Hayes."

She slowly sank into the chair across from me. "I knew you liked him, but doesn't that seem a bit drastic? You only just met the guy last week, Maggie."

Nodding, I grabbed her hands, twining our fingers together on the table. Her nails still held the chipped polish from my last manicure attempt. I had to repress another laugh. Celeste probably didn't even notice her nails had polish on them.

"I really like him, Cee," I whispered. "There's something special about him, I can feel it."

Her response solidified why she was my best friend and would remain so until the end of time. "I like him, too. Hayes is a good man."

I shot her a grateful, watery smile. "That's not the big news I have to share," I admitted.

Celeste chuckled. "Well it's too soon for you to be pregnant!"

My best friend joking about babies didn't hurt the way my mother's accusations did. Celeste would never hold a pregnancy against me, the same way I never held her pregnancy against her.

"He has orders to Korea. We leave tomorrow," I explained sadly.

Her shoulders drooped and her hands left mine as she drew them back into her lap. "You're leaving?" she whimpered.

I felt like I slapped a homeless person. Her voice sounded so small and fragile, which only made me cry harder.

"Yeah. But we can video chat every day! I won't have any friends over there, and I don't know about getting a job anymore, so...it'll be exactly as it is right now." I laughed halfheartedly, though there was nothing funny about it.

"Except you'll be in a different time zone," reasoned Celeste. "And we don't know when I'll ever see you in person again."

My bottom lip quivered. I didn't want to bust out the full on sobs, but I couldn't exactly stop it if she kept saying things like that.

"You'll see me again," I promised. "It's not like you could ever get rid of me."

Celeste cocked her head to the side as she considered me and the situation at hand. "Do you love him?" she asked.

That got the tears to quit. Where the hell had that come from?

"Cee, we're still in the 'infatuation' stage and things don't happen overnight."

"Just marriages," she deadpanned. It was so reminiscent of Wesley that I nearly turned around to look for him.

I sighed. There was no way to explain this where she wouldn't think I sounded crazy. Although as far as I knew, Celeste didn't have any special pull with the local looney bin. "He got orders to Korea and neither one of us were ready for this to be over before it really began."

A knowing smirk crossed her face. "Perfectly logical."

"I mean it!" I argued, rolling my eyes.

"I mean it, too."

"Celeste!"

"Mrs. Hayes!"

Hearing that made me blush. I didn't want to examine the way my heart fluttered at my new name. "We had no choice," I insisted.

Celeste's smirk grew wider. "You could've dated long distance."

"But then we'd never see each other!"

"An utter travesty."

I sighed. "I can't talk to you if you can't take this seriously."

She let out a dramatic sigh, mocking mine. "I can't talk to you if you can't admit the truth."

Stubbornly, I clamped my mouth shut and refused to say another word. She grinned at me like the Chesire Cat finding Alice in another conundrum. After several minutes where I wouldn't budge, Celeste sighed for real.

"Maggie, I don't know why you're so afraid of falling in love, but listen to me when I say that it doesn't take a genius to recognize there's something between you and Hayes. Maybe you're just not ready to call it like everybody sees it, but I promise you, that's what this is. You *love* him. And he loves you, too, so it's not like you're doing this alone."

"He doesn't love me." I rolled my eyes again at her ridiculous speculations. "We just don't want to be away from each other."

Celeste nodded thoughtfully for a moment before standing to go back to work. "Kind of like how Wes and I never wanted to be away from each other, hmm?" Her green eyes dulled, as they always did whenever she mentioned her ex, but her words had the desired effect. They were the only couple I had ever seen who were well and truly in love. Nobody could deny it.

That didn't mean Zeke and I were the same. No, it couldn't be love. Not even close.

Could it?

CHAPTER 32
THE ALARM
ZEKE

I ALWAYS ASSUMED when the time came and I received orders to my next duty station, I would be methodical and organized while packing my belongings. I didn't have much anyway since I still lived in the barracks and all my furniture had been provided by the Army. Unlike other soldiers, I didn't want to clutter the space with stuff I knew I'd have to move eventually so I made do with whatever had been provided. Organizing all my gear took the most amount of time, a grand total of two and a half hours.

With it being Maggie's last night in River's Run, I didn't want to bother her. Saying goodbye to Marla and Celeste would probably be really emotional and I didn't need to get in the way of that. I still missed her, though. I could imagine the way her nose would crinkle at the stack of library books I needed to take back, or how she would laugh at the knowledge that I didn't even own a television. She probably expected me to own a lot more clothing than just the three boxes stacked in the corner. I'd be surprised if all her clothes even fit on the plane to Korea.

Life was a blank, beige canvas until Maggie streaked through in all her technicolor glitter. And I wouldn't have it any other way.

A knock at the door interrupted my thoughts. Other than a room inspection, I couldn't recall a single time I had a visitor. Maybe Maggie missed me as much as I missed her and she decided to join me. I certainly wouldn't mind the alone time with her.

One of the soldiers from my unit who I'd barely ever spoken to stood at my door, Specialist Brandon Sparks. Everyone called him Sparky. If he and I lived outside of the Army, we wouldn't have a single reason to interact. Whereas I considered myself to be rather quiet and reserved, Sparks was all flash and attention. We frequently saw each other at the gym, and I knew he could bench more than I could, but he had a much leaner physique than I did. To my knowledge, he hadn't renewed his contract and would be getting out of the Army soon to return to his home state of California. His tan skin and bright blue eyes made him the perfect SoCal stereotype—and definitely a Sparky.

"Hi, Sergeant," he said, glancing around the room behind me. "I heard congratulations are in order."

I frowned. "Can I help you with something?"

Sparks shrugged nonchalantly. "Just wanted to lay eyes on the girl everyone's talking about."

"Everyone's talking about a girl? You mean Maggie?" She was the only woman I really knew, after all.

"Is that your wife?"

I nodded, trying not to puff out my chest as I'd been wanting to do all afternoon.

"Then yeah, that's who everyone's talking about." He leaned against the doorframe and crossed his arms, eyes twinkling like he found the whole exchange funny. Based on the little I knew about the guy, he probably did. "Is that how you got that shiner?"

"What?" Yeah, I wouldn't be taking headshots any time soon, but my face didn't look that bad. Just a little red and tender. I'd looked worse after a long day in the field.

Sparks held up his hands in surrender. "I'm just saying. If people were talking about my wife like that, I'd have to shut them up."

"I don't want anybody talking about Maggie. Tell them to stop." My frown grew deeper.

Sparks shrugged again. "You have a hot wife, you give the guys something to talk about. I don't make the rules."

"There aren't any rules about this, Specialist," I scoffed. This guy could fuck right off. "Go back to your room. And tell all the soldiers you're reporting to that I have every right to make them do pushups until their arms break."

The twinkle in Sparks' eye grew brighter, as if my challenge excited him. "Will do, sir. Congratulations again. Give my best to the missus." He sauntered off down the hall, hands casually in his jean pockets like he didn't have a care in the world. Which, I reminded myself, he didn't since I would be gone by tomorrow and his contract was about to end with Army.

Fucking prick.

Now that the image was in my head, I couldn't get rid of it. Creepy men ogling Maggie like Peeping Toms. Stupid, immature soldiers catcalling her as she walked around post...like those men at the party where we first met.

Or that jackass who claimed she owed him money. The jackass who was currently in River's Run with her while I holed up in my room.

Screw her space. Maggie needed to stay by my side. Even an arm's length was a step too far.

Sighing, I grabbed my truck keys and prayed my cave man act didn't piss her off.

CHAPTER 33
THE PACKING
MAGGIE

"I CAN'T BELIEVE you're really leaving," Celeste said again. She sat on the floor while Marla stood near the bed, helping me sort through what stayed and what I needed to pack. Zeke told me to keep it light because the movers the Army used weren't very reliable. I wanted to put all of my favorite clothes in my suitcase to guarantee their arrival, but that proved difficult when I had so many hair care and makeup products. I already had another full suitcase just for shoes. A girl could never part with all her shoes.

"Maggie, the internet says that Asian countries have some of the best beauty stuff in the world," Marla started, "so please explain to me why you need to take all that."

"Because!" I wailed, stomping my foot. "I might need it!"

Celeste rolled her eyes. "You will *not*."

Practical, level-headed Celeste made the call that I could only take one suitcase full of clothes. She dutifully folded everything that remained and put it inside a box that Marla promised to keep in the closet for whenever we came back. She was also the one who insisted I didn't need to take all three of my hair dryers, five straighteners, and the four different sized curling wands. "You'll make do!" she'd insisted.

I tried not to sulk. Sort of.

"Next time one of you gets married, can I please be a part of the big day?" Marla asked snidely. She flashed me a small smile that let me know she didn't hold it against me.

"Don't worry. For husbands two and three, you can stuff me into a dress of your choosing and conduct the festivities wherever you like," I promised.

Marla and I both tried to ignore the way Celeste flinched. "Not all of us will get married," she said quietly.

"Oh, just ignore me," Marla finally offered. "I'm a bitter, old spinster."

"You could be a crazy cat lady if you'd just buy some cats," I offered sweetly.

"Except I don't like cats!" Marla argued.

Our exchange brought enough of a smile to Celeste's face that Marla and I both sighed in relief, keeping the subject on much safer topics as we worked through our designated sections.

"God, didn't we just pack up everything at Diana's?" I finally exclaimed. "How the hell did I accumulate so much stuff already?"

"Because you're a hoarder," Celeste commented while stuffing one of my many mannequin heads down into a box.

"Am not!"

Marla snorted. "Maggie, no woman has that many pairs of shoes unless she's a hoarder. You're lucky the store had two of the oversized suitcases."

"I—"

"My wife, the hoarder," came a voice from behind. "Can't imagine that."

For the second time today I had a man at my back, speaking low in my ear. Only this one sent tingles down my spine. Zeke placed a light kiss on my cheek as he rubbed my biceps in a gesture I found comforting rather than terrifying.

"Hey, Trouble," he whispered. I turned to look at him over my shoulder, my breath catching again over just how gorgeous he was. Only...

"What happened to your eye?!" I yelped. "Marla, go get some ice!"

She rushed out of the room immediately.

Zeke brushed my hand away so that I couldn't touch it. "Don't worry about me. Who did this to your arm?" He gently tugged at my elbow so that the light better illuminated the bruise from where Spencer grabbed me.

I gulped. "Nobody." I kept my voice as low as possible, praying that Celeste wouldn't hear.

Zeke frowned. He pulled me into a tight embrace, his hold on my waist tight and grounding. "I won't push in front of Celeste, but this isn't over," he warned in my ear.

A shiver ran down my spine, from the threat in his words or the sudden ache of arousal in my core at his savior complex, I had no idea.

"Here, Hayes, put this on." Marla handed him a bag of ice with a thin cloth wrapped around it.

"What are you even doing here?" I asked. "I thought you needed to pack up all of your stuff."

"I did," he nodded.

"Everything?"

"Everything."

"All of your stuff? Packed?" I questioned. I had three people working on mine and I was no where near ready.

Zeke laughed. "Yep. Guess I'm not a hoarder like my wife."

I wondered if the others could notice the way he glowed when used the words "my wife."

"So when are you getting Maggie a ring?" Celeste asked.

I tried to glare at her because I didn't want Zeke to think of me as some magpie out to add to her collection. But I also kind of wanted to know myself.

"A ring?" he repeated.

"Well, yeah. A wedding ring is kind of a big deal." She laughed, but I could see the growing panic in Zeke's eyes.

"I didn't want a ring," I declared. "Look at all this stuff. I'd just lose it anyway!"

Celeste and Marla both laughed and went back to their prospective piles. I leaned in closer to Zeke, wrapping both my arms around his waist.

"Why are you really here?" I whispered. "Is everything okay?"

"Now it is." Zeke kissed me on the forehead, and I all but melted into a puddle. Forehead kisses counted as foreplay in my eyes.

"When is your flight?" Marla inquired as she gathered up all of the notebooks, yearbooks, and loose leaf paper I shoved into the nightstand drawer.

"We'll fly up to Atlanta at 0600," Zeke replied, "then head out to Los Angeles. We'll have about a four hour layover in L.A. before we fly out to Humphreys."

Celeste shook her head wistfully. "I can*not* believe you're married, Maggie! And heading to live in another frickin country! That's some powerful serendipity."

"Sounds like y'all better get to bed soon," Marla added.

Heat flamed my cheeks, and I pulled away from Zeke's embrace. "Oh, um, we didn't really think we'd get much sleep tonight. Once everything is packed, we'll have to take all of this to the barracks so the movers can pick it up.

"Well we've got all the big stuff done," my best friend pointed out. "Just load up the boxes you're actually taking and your suitcases and head out."

"I'm not gonna leave you here to pack up this mess!" I argued.

"Maggie, it's your wedding night." Celeste shot me a look that told me she wouldn't budge on this, no matter what I said. "Take your stuff, get some rest, and enjoy your time together."

When I looked to Marla for support, she nodded along with Celeste. "We're gonna miss you, darlin'." She held out her arms for a hug, first me, then Zeke. "Gonna miss you too, Hayes, truth be told. You ain't half bad."

Zeke chuckled, despite how stiff he remained from Marla's hug. He seemed to be weird with anyone touching him other than me, I'd noticed. "It's been an honor to meet you both. I'll take care of her."

Celeste pointed a finger at him, giving Zeke the Mom Glare normally reserved for Iris. "You better, or else!"

He nodded, giving me a look that said he knew the girls and I needed privacy before he grabbed one of the boxes to take downstairs.

"Don't look back," Marla insisted. "You focus on building the life you want, not on where you came from, you hear me? You got one of the good ones." She pressed what I would consider to be a tearful kiss to my hair and swept from the room. Marla rarely showed that kind of emotion, and a lump formed in my throat. I already missed her.

"You're still my best friend," Celeste vowed.

"And you'll always be mine," I agreed. She enveloped me in a hug that had me second-guessing my decision. River's Run was all I knew. How could I leave any of this behind? Especially when Diana and Spencer's taunts ran fresh through my mind. I had nothing to offer Zeke other than a body to warm his beds. I never even had a real job. Now I legally became his burden.

You're not a burden, you're a gift.

"Call me when you get there," she added, breaking up my thoughts.

"Yes, Mom," I teased her. Celeste flashed me a small smile.

Zeke came back in to grab another box, making Celeste and I jump, then laugh at ourselves.

"Trouble, grab that box there and I'll get these. They aren't that heavy." Zeke stacked three boxes on top of one another and disappeared down the hallway, leaving one for me. What a showoff.

"Enjoy your new life, Mrs. Hayes!" My best friend tried to keep the heartbreak from her voice and failed miserably. The past six years of our lives stretched between us. One way or another, Celeste Hendricks had been present in every single one of those days, and I hated that I didn't know when I'd see her again.

But Marla was right. It was high time I focused on the life I wanted, not the one I left behind.

CHAPTER 34

THE NIGHT

ZEKE

THE CAB of my truck suddenly felt stifling as we headed back to Fort Stewart to drop off Maggie's boxes. All the air stopped circulating at some point because I could hardly breathe. Spending forever with Maggie never seemed more real than in the moment when it was just the two of us and forever stretched ahead. Now that I had her back at my side, all the stuff Sparks said sounded like a lot of bullshit.

"So…" I trailed off, uncertain where I wanted the conversation to go.

"So…" she echoed. "Now what?"

"We can't really stay in the barracks," I explained. "There's not a whole lot of room with all the boxes and there's only a twin bed."

"Where do you want to go?" Maggie asked.

I swallowed thickly. "We can get a hotel room next to the airport. That way you can sleep in until the last possible second." I meant it to sound like a joke, but it came out as more of a criticism.

Maggie's mouth opened and closed. "Is that what you wanna do? Sleep?"

Nope. Right about now I wanted to drive off a pier into the bottom of the Atlantic.

"We can do whatever you want," I amended. "I just want to make you happy."

We drove in silence all the way to the barracks, though I sensed a tension rolling off her. She fidgeted, twisting the ends of her hair around her finger. Occasionally she snuck a glance that I tried to ignore. I didn't know what to say.

Together we managed to load all the boxes into my room in record time. Maggie waited in the truck while I turned the key to my room into the soldier on staff duty for the night. He would let the movers inside to pick up our belongings.

Thankfully there was no sign of Sparks or any other soldier from my unit either. With how high my anxiety spiked from the awkward tension crackling in the air, if someone looked at Maggie the wrong way, I was liable to go nuclear.

Shortly thereafter, I pulled into a small hotel across from the Savannah airport and still hadn't managed to say a word to Maggie. Every time I tried my tongue got stuck to the roof of my mouth. Books always discussed the significance of a wedding night, and for once I didn't think I misunderstood, given my wife's own unease. I didn't want to do anything more than what made her comfortable.

That was why I requested two rooms when the line in the hotel lobby cleared and we made it to the concierge desk.

"Excuse me?!" Maggie sputtered. "It's our wedding day and you want to sleep in separate rooms?"

My body went stiff as several pairs of eyes throughout the lobby turned to glare at me. "I don't want to pressure you," I mumbled as low as I could.

The concierge smiled, clearly trying to alleviate the tension. "Aw, newlyweds! Let me upgrade you to our honeymoon suite. It's on the house," she added with a roguish wink. She slid a card across the counter to me and gestured to a hall on my left. "Just follow it all the way 'til the end."

To my surprise, Maggie beamed at her. "Thank you! That's real nice of you!"

We were not the kind of newlyweds the hotel envisioned when designing the honeymoon suite. Large mirrors lined every wall, and an obnoxious garden tub separated the bathroom from the sleeping area.

The only walls to block off any space were for the water closet, leaving everything open and exposed. Maggie and I couldn't even brush our teeth without the other one watching. A king size bed sat on the far wall with rose petals strewn in the shape of a heart on the duvet.

"Aww! Isn't this sweet?" Maggie cried. She ran over to bed and jumped in the middle of the rose petals. "Ooh, this is really bouncy!"

"B-but where sh-should I sleep?" Sounds weren't coming out right and I didn't know how to fix it. Although the way my heart stopped might have been the bigger medical emergency.

Maggie's skin flushed from her hairline to her neckline. Only I tried not to stare at her neckline because noticing the way her tank top curved around her breasts made my brain go fuzzy and my cock take charge. Expecting anything from her just because it was our wedding night was a recipe for disaster…right? Or was that what she expected from me?

I didn't have a fucking clue how to do this.

"Um…don't you want to sleep next to me?" Her voice seemed smaller somehow.

I gulped. "Is that what you want?"

She nodded slowly. "That's what married couples do."

"I thought you wanted us to act like we weren't married?"

The question came out before I considered the implications, and I knew instantly it was the wrong thing to say. Maggie leapt from the bed, staggering backward like I hit her.

"Why don't you tell me how you really feel?" Her arms folded across her chest like Maggie needed a shield from me. "Don't hold back now."

"I didn't mean it like that. I just don't want to do anything wrong. I don't know how to act!"

Frustration bubbled in my chest, and I started pacing to work it out of my system. Maybe I wasn't meant to be married. So far marriage seemed a lot harder than I originally thought. Nothing I said or did went right.

Leggett's face flashed through my mind, his fury from earlier that morning, and the sinking disappointment I used to feel from letting him down. That's what I was good at—disappointing those around me. Maybe it was better before I met Maggie. Being alone was easier.

Maybe I needed to call this whole thing off.

Maybe love made me a fool and this was my last chance to do right by Maggie.

Maybe—

Soft, cold hands cupped my face as I collided with a tender body. Maggie's hazel eyes held mine as she went through exaggerated motions of breathing in through her nose and out with her mouth. I mimicked her actions, and the panic started to loosen around my chest. My heartbeat raced like I'd just finished a sprint, a cold sweat lining my brow.

"Sweetie, I think you're having another panic attack," Maggie whispered. "Come sit down, okay? Stay with me." Slowly, she guided us to the edge of the bed, keeping her hands on my face and her eyes on mine. The solidity of her touch grounded me.

We sat there for several minutes until my breathing returned to normal. A shudder rippled through me as I finally felt the last dregs of anxiety leave.

"What triggered it?" she asked quietly. Moonlight flooded in through the window, the clock now reading midnight, and I decided this was now my favorite time of day. White light filtered along the column of her throat, making me want to trace its path with my tongue.

Until I glanced down at the bruises on her arm.

"I'm not sure, but I think we need to talk about this first." I brushed my thumb along her arm over the marks and realized they roughly matched the size of my fingertips. "Who did this to you?"

I knew enough of my wife's tells already to know that she was about to try and change the subject. She stood up in a huff, refusing to meet my eye, and grabbed the handle of a suitcase. "It's getting late. We should try to get some sleep."

"No, we should talk about how you got those bruises," I countered. Angrily, I snatched the handle of the suitcase and shoved it behind me. Maggie still wouldn't look at me, sinking back onto the bed instead. Only she sat as far away from me as possible.

"Just let this go, Zeke. I'm begging you." Her voice sounded hoarse, like she choked back tears as she tried to get the words out. "Once we leave in the morning, it won't happen again."

I nodded. "Yeah, because I'm about to go kill whoever touched you." If she didn't want to tell me, that was fine. I had a sneaking suspicion I could figure it out with a single conversation with that Spencer guy. Jumping up, I headed for the door and only stopped when I felt a hand tug at my wrist.

"Stop, please!" Maggie whimpered.

"Then give me a fucking name!" I snapped and immediately regretted it with the way I saw her flinch.

A tear trickled down her cheek. "Seems like we're both a little messed up," she whispered sadly.

All the fight drained out of me. Making her cry on our wedding night didn't bode well.

"You're not messed up," I assured her. "But the thought of anyone hurting you makes me want to throw some C4 in their bed. I have to protect you, Maggie. At all costs."

For several tense moments, Maggie didn't say anything. Wisps of her long brown hair fell out of her bun, a few of them framing her face in a way that made me want to reach out and brush them aside. But her thoughtful gaze held me captive and I couldn't move. An emotion I didn't recognize shone in her eyes, bright from the glow of the moon, and zeroed in on me like she too struggled with what was right in front of her.

Slowly, like she might spook a deer, Maggie took a step closer so that her body barely stood a heartbeat from mine. She leaned up on her tiptoes and kissed me gently—tentatively—on the mouth.

Every tortured, confusing emotion from the long day faded away until I could only exist in that moment. Her touch felt welcoming. Calming. Like the ray of sunshine after a chaotic storm. I left a turbulent war zone after more than a year of deployment and never felt the same kind of aching relief as I did in that kiss. The sense of surety that everything now would be alright.

I twisted a hand around the back of her neck, pulling her close and deepening the kiss. My acceptance must've made her relax because I felt her body go pliant and mold into mine. Her tongue demanded access, and I let her take control, wanting to offer some kind of sign that this night, and whatever took place, would be entirely up to her.

She broke away with a muffled cry, kissing down my throat and pushing my shirt up so she could run her fingers along my abdomen. The feel of her skin on mine sent an electric pulse straight to my dick. Somewhere in the back of my mind was delight and gratitude that the circumstances from the fitting room at Madden Markets weren't a one time thing, but my unease over the night pushed to the forefront.

"Maggie, wait." I stepped back and tried to force my brain to do the talking. "We don't have to do this if you're not ready."

With her head slightly cocked to the side, she eyed me wistfully. I could practically feel the gears turning as she processed some sort of internal dilemma, sizing me and the situation up, before letting out a breathless sigh.

"You truly mean that, don't you?" asked Maggie. "You aren't gonna demand sex from me just because you're my husband."

I scowled. "Uh, that's called rape, and in no way shape or form will that ever occur! Is that what you think of me?"

She shook her head. "I just know that's what guys in the past always wanted from me. Now that we're married, isn't that what you want too?"

A fissure cracked its way through my heart at how tiny her voice sounded. She looked so unsure, so vulnerable, that I almost found it amusing when I noted how her fingers drifted up to twist on the ends of a stray piece of hair. Without even trying, Maggie told me how much she worried over my answer.

"I'm so, so sorry, baby, that someone taught you sex is the only way to a guy's heart. That's not what I want from you at all. Maybe I'm not really a guy," I joked, earning a breathy giggle from her. "I meant what I said in our vows. Every day with you here is enough for me. I married you, Margaret Elizabeth Hayes, because I want every single second of your forever. All the good, bad, ugly, and everything in between."

Maggie inhaled sharply. "I—I believe you." She whispered it like she couldn't believe she revealed that thought out loud. A half-hiccup, half-sob escaped and before I knew it, she launched herself into my arms, wrapping her legs around my waist and her arms around my neck.

I clutched her to me, reveling in how good she felt in my arms. Hot tears soaked my neck, and although I didn't fully understand what Maggie was going through, I was so glad to be there for her. I walked us over to the bed and sat down, keeping her on my lap and stroking her back in what I hoped to be a soothing gesture.

It took a long time before Maggie quieted down. She pulled away just enough to look me in the eye, her cheeks blotchy and red from crying. "Zeke, I'm scared. What if I fall for you?"

"Then I'll finally relax," I replied.

"What? Why?"

"Because we'll both be falling together, and if I'm doing it with you, nothing scares me anymore."

CHAPTER 35
THE FLIGHTS

MAGGIE

WHEN I WOKE up the next morning, my surroundings left me momentarily disoriented. Two strong arms kept me in a vice grip against a firm chest. Mirrors surrounded us on all sides, giving me an unobstructed view of Zeke's body wrapped around mine. Even his leg pinned my body to his.

We must have fallen asleep in each other's arms. Our wrinkled clothes from the day before were still on.

I zeroed in on the streaky mascara lines and smudged eyeliner decorating my face. Trash pandas would claim me as their queen. I fell asleep last night before I had the chance to brush out my hair or put on my silk cap. My hair would be a disaster all day.

The Rapture would come before I'd let Zeke wake up to see me like this. As cute and romantic as the room seemed last night, I hated it now that I realized there wasn't a bathroom for me to perform my ritual in. I couldn't even wash my face and reapply my makeup without running the risk of rousing Zeke.

Hardly daring to breathe, I crept out from between his arms as slowly as I could. My muscles screamed in protest as my locked up limbs fought the movement. I tiptoed like a cartoon villain towards the door, toiletry bag in hand, and escaped into the hall. Thankfully there was no one else in sight to witness my shame.

A single hotel employee, a girl about my age with a face full of pimples and square-framed glasses, stood behind the counter. Her eyebrows rose in panic as I scampered up to her.

"Please, I'm desperate!" I cried. "Let me use the bathroom in another room. Any room!"

"Are you a guest here? Is there something wrong with your bathroom, ma'am?" the employee asked.

I huffed in annoyance. What happened to sister solidarity? "No, I'm in the honeymoon suite and I can't have my husband see me like this!"

"Does the water work in your room?" she inquired. At least she started typing into the keyboard. Maybe she would give me some kind of help.

"Look, I know I seem like a nutcase, but I am begging you! If you have any ounce of compassion, or empathy, or I don't know—human decency, *please* let me use another bathroom. This face is NOT what my husband needs to see first thing in the morning!" I winced at the image, picturing Zeke's look of abject horror.

The girl hesitated. "I'm really not supposed to…"

I recognized a lifeline when I saw it. "I know you're not, and although I have nothing to offer, karma always takes notice when women help women."

Another long pause followed before her shoulders finally caved.

Sighing, she typed something into the computer and slid a hotel key card over the counter. "It's the first door there on the right. You have to be in and out as quickly as possible, though! Shift change is coming up and my boss can't know that I did this."

Relief flooded my system. "You are an angel! I could kiss you!"

The woman's cheeks reddened. "Please don't."

"Ha!" I didn't bother to wait, snatching the key card and racing to the door she indicated. This had to be the world's fastest shower. I wouldn't have time to mark my reflection with all the imperfections, but thankfully I hadn't eaten anything in over a day. My stomach remained gloriously empty.

There wasn't enough time to wash my hair, but I managed to take a decent shower and put on fresh clothes. Since we had a long day of travel ahead of us, I kept the makeup light and fresh, foregoing lashes and sparkly eye shadow. Hair was a lost cause. I twirled it into a knot at the base of my neck and hoped for the best.

I slipped back inside the honeymoon suite twenty minutes later, glancing at the clock. We had only thirty minutes to make it to the airport in time. Zeke looked so peaceful in bed, his limbs still in place from where he once held me, that I hated to wake him. From what I gathered, he didn't sleep much so nights like this were rare.

Gently, I slid onto the bed next to him. The little bit of length he had in his hair swept across his forehead, and unbidden, my hand brushed it off. A featherlight touch was all it took to wake him. He blinked a few times until his gaze focused on me. The resulting smile warmed me from the inside out.

"Good morning, Mrs. Hayes," he said.

I grinned. "You slept in, Sergeant. Must've been a good night."

"The best I've ever had," Zeke agreed. "Although waking up to this view is my favorite part."

"You didn't even look outside!" I snorted.

A slight blush crept along his cheeks. "That wasn't the view I meant."

Now it was my turn to blush. I chose to ignore his flirtation because I didn't know how to respond. Guys didn't usually flirt with me, and those who did never made butterflies explode in my stomach like he did. This was dangerous territory for a girl like me.

Thankfully, Zeke didn't push it further. He flung off the covers and started to get himself ready. We both paused awkwardly in the uncomfortable space where you don't know your partner's routine.

"I'm gonna go grab a coffee from the lobby," I offered. "I'll see you out there." I had almost reached the door, my hand on the doorknob when Zeke murmured my name.

"You're not gonna leave, right? You'll be waiting out there for me?"

A lost little boy. That's what Zeke reminded me of in that moment. A lost little boy desperately seeking a hand to hold in the dark.

"You can count on it." I winked and left him to get ready.

* * *

Flying across the country turned out to be exhausting. I hadn't been on a plane since Wesley flew Celeste and me to Atlanta for her birthday celebration. That had been a private jet and a much shorter flight. The Los Angeles airport was a nightmare to navigate. Despite a four hour layover, we barely made our flight in time because we stopped to eat and couldn't figure out how to get to the next terminal.

Thankfully I had the convenient excuse of being a nervous flyer to get out of eating anything. Zeke bought my excuse of having an upset stomach and didn't push.

The flight to South Korea took everything out of both of us. Zeke and I stretched out as much as we were able, lifting the armrest up between our seats so that I could curl up against his chest. My head tucked perfectly under his chin, like our bodies were designed to line up like Lego pieces, and we both slept fitfully, jostled by air turbulence and the strange sounds of other passengers.

It took over thirteen hours to get to Seoul, then another hour to collect our bags and board the Army shuttle that took us to Camp Humphreys. With the time difference, it was now close to five in the morning in Seoul. We technically lost an entire day in transit between the time zones.

I was far too tired to look outside or pay much attention to our surroundings. The blue haze of twilight cast everything in dark shadows anyway. Somehow Zeke managed to sign us in and provide all the documentation we needed to get us squared away with the Army. Someone took us to what Zeke called "temporary lodgings" until the next day when we would meet with someone from the housing office to get keys to an apartment. I couldn't have described the lodgings if someone held me at gunpoint.

Korea. I now live in Korea.

"Tomorrow," I muttered. "Tell me again tomorrow." That was the last thing I managed to say before my head hit the pillow and the world faded away.

CHAPTER 36
THE ADJUSTMENT

MAGGIE

ZEKE WOKE me up by gently shaking my shoulder. The sun had set further in the sky by then, but according to the clock on my cell, it was only three o'clock in the afternoon.

"Sorry, sleepyhead," he said, "but the lady from the housing office called and said there's a bigger place available if we want it. We need to go meet her now if we're going to take it."

I blinked at him slowly. My ears still felt like they needed to pop and somehow that translated into my brain processing things in slow motion.

Suddenly, it dawned on me that Zeke got up before me. Makeup caked my face and my hair resembled a rat's nest more than a bun because once again I went straight to bed without the cap. The crypt keeper probably looked better. I tried to muffle the squeal as I leapt to my feet and raced to the bathroom, but I caught a brief glimpse of the shock written on Zeke's face first.

A few minutes later, a gentle tapping came through the door. "Maggie? What's wrong?"

Stifling the tears, I managed to choke out, "I'm sorry, I'm just not feeling well. Bad jet lag. Can you go without me?"

After a fleeting pause Zeke asked, "You don't want to pick out our apartment? I don't want to get a place you won't like."

"It's fine," I insisted, sinking to the floor and leaning against the door. "I trust you."

A longer pause followed. I almost thought Zeke left before he said, "You know that you don't need to always look perfect around me, right? I don't care what you look like."

Tears forced their way out at the sincerity in his words. I knew Zeke meant it, and so far he hadn't given me a single reason to doubt him. In his heart of hearts he genuinely didn't know there was a difference between me with makeup and me without. But I couldn't stop hearing Diana's warning about keeping a man like Zeke satisfied. Her cries of horror whenever I went out in public without my hair curled and my face done up. Perfect was acceptable. Perfect was *safe*.

"I'm sorry," I whispered through the door.

My voice was so low that even I barely heard it, but only a moment later came Zeke's reply.

"Me too."

* * *

Several hours later, after I showered, shaved my entire body, dried and curled my hair along with applying a little bold glam makeup to match the sparkly top I threw on, I sat on the balcony overlooking a parking lot at Camp Humphreys. The mirror in the bathroom wasn't quite long enough for me to examine my entire body, but the release from at least going through the motions and marking the nasty spots I witnessed in my reflection had me practically panting in relief. Although there were a few basic snack items on the counter of the kitchenette, I couldn't bring myself to eat any of them. I felt lightheaded from the lack of food.

I had no idea what buildings were close by and all of the signs were too far away to read from the balcony on which I stood. Our room must've sat on the back of the property because I never saw any vehicles coming or going, but doors could be heard echoing from the hallway.

The air smelled different here. Somehow crisper and sharper than what we had in Georgia. Frost lightly coated everything; in relocating to the other side of the world, we left summer behind and transplanted directly into winter. The landscape reminded me of the States and the buildings were reminiscent of the buildings I saw at Fort Stewart.

Thinking of Fort Stewart brought a whole new wave of homesickness. I texted Marla and Celeste as soon as we arrived at baggage claim, but they hadn't answered yet. We all probably needed a few days to adjust to the time difference anyway.

A thud came from inside the room as Zeke returned. "Maggie?" he called out.

"Out here!"

Zeke didn't look a bit ruffled after all the hours spent traveling. How he managed to function on such little sleep, I would never understand. He did, however, look visibly concerned.

"I got us a place, Trouble, but you kinda freaked me out earlier. I get that you like to look a certain way, but aren't we passed that by now? You're my wife—why can't I look at you in the mornings?"

A simple question with the most complicated answer. When I originally proposed the idea of marriage, I didn't consider how I would hide my eating and grooming habits from Zeke. And he was observant, too. Way more than most guys. I wouldn't be able to hide it from him for long.

"You can look at me," I replied. I tried to keep my voice sweet and light, hoping to convey a sense of innocence. "I was just out of it from all the traveling and lack of sleep. It won't happen again."

The words managed to pacify him enough that he broke out into a grin. "Good. Grab your bags, Trouble, and let's go move into our new place."

Despite it only being the two of us, Zeke's rank meant the Army offered him a three bedroom apartment that came fully furnished. "It's not great furniture," he warned me, but I only felt grateful that we wouldn't have to scrape together money to buy anything. Living frugally wasn't new to me, so I didn't care if the furniture looked out of date. There wouldn't be anyone else to see it anyway. Celeste and Marla could never afford to come all the way out here.

The apartment building stood relatively close to the shopping center and Zeke promised we could make a list and go there for everything we needed after we walked through the apartment. Our unit sat on the fifth floor, and although the hallways reminded me a bit of a prison, everything was clean, well lit, and safe. We were lucky to have an extra window since it was a corner apartment, he explained. This would be our home for the next two years.

Zeke handed me a set of keys before he paused outside the door. "Well, Mrs. Hayes, welcome home."

CHAPTER 37

THE SCARE

ZEKE

Two weeks passed in the blink of an eye before I had to report to my new unit. Hands down, the best two weeks of my life. Maggie and I spent every moment together. We explored all of Camp Humphreys, then ventured out for a couple days in Seoul. The language barrier wasn't as difficult as we expected since so many South Koreans knew English from the American presence in the area. We managed to go to the top of the North Seoul Tower, tour the Gyeongbokgung Palace, and visit several street markets loaded with food, clothing, and jewelry unlike anything we'd ever seen.

Every night turned into date night, whether we went out to one of the post-sponsored activities or stayed in. We laughed until tears ran down our cheeks watching Korean television where we each made up the dialogue. Our versions grew more and more ridiculous as the shows went on, and at one point I had Maggie laughing so hard that water came out of her nose.

The only thing that confused me were the sleeping arrangements. All three of the bedrooms had a bed, dresser, and end table, but the first night there, Maggie asked to sleep in the primary bedroom by herself. The last thing I wanted to do was pressure her, especially for something I wasn't entirely sure I wanted myself, yet I went to bed every night feeling empty and bereft. Our marriage seemed so fun and easy that I simply figured going to bed at night would be like a slumber party with a friend. Maggie, I guess, didn't feel the same way.

I ignored it in favor of focusing on the positive. And life with Maggie had an overabundance of positive. I couldn't remember another time in life where I smiled as much as I had over the past two weeks.

Now everything would change again. Work resumed and we had to find our new normal with it. I assured Maggie that she didn't need to find a job if she didn't want to because I'd overheard a lot of other soldiers before grumbling about how difficult it was for their spouse to find work. There were only so many options available when stationed in a foreign country. I earned enough to cover our expenses, so I didn't want Maggie to feel pressured to contribute when she didn't need to be.

She still hadn't mentioned anything about the money she owed Spencer, though.

Leaving her that first morning was both exhilarating and sad. I hated not spending the entire day with her, but I loved looking forward to seeing her smiling face when I came home. My new unit seemed fairly standard; Staff Sergeant Whittenburg would be my immediate superior, and his welcome speech included a promise to get me before the promotion board as soon as possible. He insisted on all of his soldiers excelling in leadership.

I sensed something was wrong as soon as I opened the door to the apartment later that evening. The faint sound of water running surprised me. My office was only a few blocks away from the apartment, and I texted Maggie shortly before I left. Why would she wait to take a shower now?

"Trouble?" I called, knocking on her bedroom door. The force of my knuckles was enough to open it, the water sounds growing louder. I paused, waiting for a response, before I poked my head in through the gap. "Maggie?"

Clothes exploded across every surface as though Maggie tossed them around rather than hang them up. The door to the bathroom stood ajar, but I couldn't see anything or anyone inside.

"Maggie, answer me!" My heart began to pound. Danger became

second nature to assess in my line of work and warning bells now rang out in my head. "I'm coming in!"

I shoved open the bathroom door hard enough to leave a dent in the drywall behind it, but I couldn't focus on anything other than Maggie's naked, crumpled body on the floor in front of a full length mirror. Only the mirror had markings all over—circles, lines, even an exclamation point in a cipher I didn't understand. Tears streamed down Maggie's face as she stared off into nothing.

A whimper escaped her mouth, stirring me to action.

"Maggie! Baby, what happened?" I dropped to the floor and pulled her into my lap. Leaning my back against the tub and hauling Maggie's shivering frame against my chest, I could hear her teeth chatter as she whimpered again.

"Zeke, I can't—I can't—" Maggie stuttered. Words turned into a blubbering cry and she pressed her face into my chest to muffle the sobs.

"Baby, you're scaring me right now! What happened? What's wrong?" I yelled. All composure left my body. Maggie was hurt, in one way or another, and I would turn the earth inside out before I let it continue.

She sniffled and mumbled into my jacket, something that sounded like "ten pounds."

"What's ten pounds, Maggie?" I screamed. "What?!"

"I gained almost ten pounds!" A wail, full of the worst kind of pain, followed.

"Huh?" My brain spun in circles trying to make sense of what Maggie said versus the scene in front of me, but I couldn't connect the dots. "What does that have to do with this?"

She sobbed again and the noise shot straight through my heart. "I can't do it, Zeke! I can't live like this! I can't gain weight here with you!" The blubbering took over again, muffled as she returned to the hiding spot on my chest.

"Maggie, baby, we've been out having fun! It's fine that you gained weight! That's okay! You're beautiful!" I didn't know what to do or say, and I hated feeling so helpless. I didn't understand what she tried to tell me.

Her whole body wracked with sobs as she shook her head into my jacket. "No, I'm not!" she wailed again. "I'm ugly! I'm so ugly! Zeke, help me! I'm so ugly!" Maggie succumbed to more sobs, these even harder than before. She started to jerk as though seizing from the hyperventilation.

I grabbed her firmly by both biceps, holding her an arm's length away so that I could see her face. I needed her to focus on me and breathe or she would pass out. It was then I noticed that she still held a thick black eyeliner pencil in her hand, and the marks on the mirror imitated marks on her body.

Realization clicked. Maggie had drawn these on herself...*because she loathed her own body*. Scanning in abject horror, my mouth fell open as I saw where she wrote things like FAT and GROSS over her stomach and thighs. This was the first time I'd ever seen her nude body, and I doubted I'd ever get the image out of my head. How could my stunning, gorgeous wife see herself like *this*?!

"Baby, I have to get you help," I said, my voice coming out a hoarse whisper. "We—we have to get you help. Just hold on, okay?"

Either she was so far gone in her misery or she simply didn't realize what I was doing, but I managed to pull my cell phone out of my pocket and call the emergency number I programmed in upon our arrival at the registration office. Basically a Camp Humphreys version of 911.

"Emergency Services," a calm female voice answered, "how can I help you?"

"Hi," I croaked out, "I need paramedics for my wife immediately."

"Yes, sir," the woman replied. "Can you tell me what's wrong?"

Tears streamed down my own face as Maggie gasped for air against my chest, her cries intermittently broke up with mumblings about weight and ugliness.

"I think she has an eating disorder," I explained, "and I think something finally snapped."

CHAPTER 38
THE AFTERMATH
MAGGIE

Three Months Later

"Maggie, you know we don't make any progress in these sessions when you don't talk to me," Barb reminded me. Barb, my hopeful therapist who still believed we would make progress despite never really talking about anything important. Although I had faithfully maintained our twice weekly sessions for the past three months, we still had yet to discuss anything to do with my so-called disordered eating habits.

Body dysmorphia. Anorexia nervosa. That's what the hospital on post diagnosed me with after Zeke called emergency services and they transported me via ambulance to be assessed. The Army doctor initially wanted to send us back to the United States as an overseas medical center was not equipped to handle this kind of treatment. But I didn't want Zeke to be punished for my failures. He already had an ugly wife who apparently needed psychiatric intervention—there was no need to send his career down the shitter, too.

So Zeke and I compromised. I agreed to go to therapy and follow a new diet program with a certified nutritionist as long as he did the same. "We'll tackle it together," Zeke had promised. "Married couples are supposed to share their problems with each other."

Even if I lived a thousand lifetimes, I would never deserve that man.

And as much as I despised going to therapy, I couldn't deny that Zeke kept his end of the bargain. Somehow, he managed to maintain his own appointments and cook us the specific foods that the nutritionist outlined. Every morning, he left a balanced breakfast in the microwave for me, with an equally nutritious lunch in the refrigerator. He never uttered a word of reproach on days when he came home to find the meals untouched. Zeke's therapist could only meet with him once every other week, but he didn't have the pressing concerns I did. He always managed to come to my doctor's appointments, though, even if it was simply to hold my hand in the waiting room.

Barb made sure to always point that out, too. "You're so lucky," she assured me, "to have a partner who supports you the way Zeke does."

Lucky or not, therapy grated on my nerves.

I wanted to keep my promise to Zeke. I wanted to be better *for* him. But there was something so aggravating about opening up to Barb. So far she wanted to know a lot about my parents and my life back in River's Run, not about my self esteem or body insecurities. And wouldn't it make sense to start there since all the hospital paperwork diagnosed me with extreme body dysmorphia and anorexia nervosa—purging subtype? I already knew my wackjob of a mom and absentee father gave me problems. I didn't need to go to Barb for that.

"Maggie?" she prompted me again.

I sighed. "Sorry. What was the question?"

Barb frowned, her corkscrew curls wild around her wrinkled face. Rectangular glasses sat perched on the edge of her nose so that she could easily see to jot down notes in the notebook opened on her lap, but I hadn't given her much to write today. She lived here in Seoul as a government employee along with her retired Army husband, who now worked as a director for the sanitation liaison program. Based on the reviews I found for her online, I had no doubt she was an excellent therapist. I just didn't know that she was right for me.

"I want to talk about your mother," repeated Barb. "Tell me about her."

That was the last person I wanted to talk about. "Diana is irrelevant. I barely have a relationship with her. I've told you this. We don't need to talk about her."

Barb hummed. "I see. And why do you think that is?"

I huffed in annoyance. "Because there's no point! All she cares about are how many men she can con things out of. She's probably had ten different boyfriends since I moved here."

"Sounds like that makes you angry," my therapist commented.

"I'm used to it by now," I scoffed. "She's been like that my whole life."

"And you hate her for it," Barb continued.

"Wouldn't you?" I countered. It irritated me that Barb always seemed willing to defend Diana, especially without knowing the kind of person she was.

The older woman shrugged. "Hate is too strong an emotion for me. I'd be more concerned with making peace with her so that her actions didn't affect me."

"Her actions don't affect me," I automatically contradicted. But even I could hear how hollow the statement sounded.

"They don't? I must be misunderstanding, then. Maybe we should start over—tell me about Diana."

I ground my teeth. Her trick worked on me this time. "Fine," I huffed. "My mom's comments sometimes get to me. Happy now?"

Barb grinned without any amusement behind it. "What kind of comments?"

"She always had something to say. You never knew what she would criticize next. Sometimes my hair didn't look right, or sometimes I wore a color that looked bad on me. She didn't like it when I grew up and started getting more attention than she did. It's—"

"It's almost like she became the voice in your head," Barb finished for me. Although that wasn't at all what I was about to say.

"No—" response died in my throat as I considered Barb's insinuation. She wasn't exactly *wrong*…

After a long pause, Barb tried again. "Do you think your mom's dating history has anything to do with your own marriage?"

I glared at her. "Leave Zeke out of this."

The therapist shrugged. "I can't exactly do that when you're telling me he's the only family you have."

Shrinks really thought they knew everything, didn't they? Or at least Barb did. She might have been smarter than me and have a bunch of framed degrees on the wall behind her, but that didn't mean she knew what I was going through. It definitely didn't give her permission to bring Zeke into the mix either.

"I just don't see why you would jump from one topic to another. Why would all Diana's boyfriends have anything to do with my marriage? It's not like she slept with Zeke or something!"

"True, but didn't you tell me that you and Zeke got married after only knowing each other less than a week?" Barb glanced down at her notes before returning her attention to me. "Doesn't seem like much time to get to know someone, let alone fall in love with them."

"Marriages don't have to be about love," I pointed out. Lord knew my parents' divorce proved that.

"You're right, they don't. Something your own mother probably taught you, wouldn't you say?"

I folded my arms across my chest in annoyance. She totally set me up for that one.

"Zeke is different. We just couldn't be away from each other. Diana never had a relationship like that."

Barb nodded sagely as she considered my answer. "So, you're confident that you're different than your mother? You're not repeating her mistakes?"

All the psychobabble bullshit drove me insane. I hated feeling like I was under a microscope for Barb to examine. It came across as judgmental, whether she meant it that way or not. Keeping my promise to Zeke was important, but how much could a poor girl take? Especially when we weren't talking about the actual reason I needed therapy in the first place.

I squirmed in my seat, uncomfortable with the line of questioning.

"I don't think she sees any of it as a mistake," I finally offered.

"But you think it is?"

"Yeah, I think repeatedly cheating on your husband and then sleeping your way through half the town is a *bit* of a mistake," I countered gruffly. "But none of that has anything to do with me!"

This time Barb's smile contained a hint of triumph. "I think we found where we're going to start today."

CHAPTER 39

THE REQUEST

ZEKE

WHITTENBURG SCOWLED as he looked out into what was affectionately known as the Sink Bowl, or rather the open office area where soldiers in my unit gathered and tried to be productive. After Maggie's incident a few months ago and the resulting doctor's appointments that followed, I'd been remanded to desk duty, essentially working in a role similar to that of an administrative assistant for the entire chain of command. It was dull work, mostly busybody stuff to keep me doing something, but I didn't mind. Taking care of Maggie mattered more than the Army's mission.

I already knew from Whittenburg's face as he searched through the motley crew assorted in the office that he wanted to see me. Emails from General Leggett became more and more frequent as time went on, and the more I steadfastly ignored them, the more he directed them to Whittenburg rather than myself. It was only a matter of time before Leggett took things one step further.

"Hayes!" the staff sergeant snapped. "Where the hell are you?"

It would only get worse the longer I held off. I popped up from my makeshift desk in the corner and waved. "Right here, sir."

"My office-NOW!"

"Yes, sir!"

I scurried into his office and automatically shut the door behind me, keeping my head down. So far I'd been more focused on Maggie than anything else and I barely knew the soldiers in my unit. Learning that I had a one star general back Stateside who dictated my entire career wouldn't exactly earn their respect, and it was unlikely that Whittenburg had anything positive to say. I finally had Army leadership who wanted to move me along in my career simply because they believed in professional development, yet I sat at a desk and barely did any work. Leggett would hardly let that go unnoticed.

"Care to tell me why I received a phone call at four o'clock this morning from General Leggett, Sergeant?" Whittenburg leaned back and bobbed in his office chair, gazing at me sternly from behind his desk.

"I will reply to the general's inquiries in due time," I replied, trying to keep my voice even. The last thing I needed was a permanent counseling on my record about insubordination because Whittenburg thought I yelled at him.

"No, Hayes, you will reply to them right now!" barked the staff sergeant. "I haven't had the honor of meeting General Leggett, but I'll be damned if this is the impression I give him! You're making our entire unit look bad."

I nodded. My back stayed ramrod straight and I kept my gaze focused on the bookshelf above his left shoulder. "Yes, sir. I'll go out to my desk now."

Whittenburg grunted his dismissal.

All of Leggett's emails contained chastisements that let me know as soon as I accepted accountability for my actions, he would authorize another reassignment back to the United States. Leggett anticipated his own orders to come soon for Washington, D.C. and he wanted me to follow. He seemed to think I would jump at the opportunity to work so closely with him.

The truth was I hadn't answered because I found the anonymity to be refreshing. This was the first time I had any real distance from him and his influence, and I kind of liked being in charge of my own fate. Yes, the Army still owned me and determined what I did and when, but I no longer felt like I had to run interference between Leggett's orders and my chain of command's. I could simply be another cog in the machine without a spotlight to keep me in line. The Army wasn't so bad like this.

Plus, I had no desire to move now that Maggie finally received the treatment she needed. Ever since that night I'd beaten myself up over all the signs that I now saw clear as day about her eating disorder. I should've helped her sooner. I should've made her see herself the way I did, with all the beauty and laughter and goodness she had to offer. It was like I let her down at the first real test of our marriage, and I wasn't the kind of guy who accepted failure so easily. Maggie would get better or I would die trying to make her.

My therapist, an older veteran named Chuck, frequently told me that I had obsessive-compulsive tendencies when it came to Maggie. That was about as much progress as we had made since our first session.

Dear General,

Everything is fine here at Humphreys. My wife and I have assimilated well into the unit and the community at large. Good luck with your relocation to the Capitol.

Sincerely,

Sgt. Hayes

Short and simple. Direct, leaving little room for interpretation. Nothing Leggett could manipulate into holding against me, yet respectfully removed enough to maintain distance. I sent it off before I could second guess the decision and returned to my work.

Ever since Maggie left the hospital, I had worked through my lunch hour so that I could leave earlier in the day. I tried to text her periodically, keeping the messages light and fun, but also checking in. That was the only way to maintain my own sanity.

Watching the doctors in the emergency room assess her, discussing the possibility of hospitalizing her at a treatment facility, broke something inside of me. I hadn't felt well since then. Any time I closed my eyes, I re-lived the moment I found Maggie on the floor in the bathroom, and all the panic came rushing back.

We both carefully danced around the subject when we were at home. Maggie tried to eat something every night when I cooked dinner, but it was fairly obvious that she found my hovering afterwards to be an annoyance. After learning how she forced herself to throw up, I didn't trust Maggie to keep food down, though. We would then spend the rest of the evening in some sort of silent standoff where we each pretended the other didn't spy on our every move. Maggie looked for any opportunity to escape to the bathroom unencumbered and I tried to stop from so much as blinking in case she hurt herself again by purging.

By early afternoon I managed to exhaust everything on the to-do list from my superiors and Whittenburg said I could head out for the day. I stopped at the commissary to grab Maggie a bouquet of flowers. She probably saw it as a bribe, but I only meant to thank her for committing to therapy. I made sure that there was a fresh bouquet after every session.

Maggie sat on the couch with a laptop balanced on her lap. She flashed me a wane smile when she spotted the lilies in my hand.

"You don't have to keep doing that, Zeke," she said. "I promised you I'd go to therapy and I meant it."

"I believe you." It came out as a reflex, though I meant it wholeheartedly. But I longed for us to return to the happiness we had before. Everything between us felt strained now.

Maggie stood and took the flowers from my hand, heading into the kitchen to replace the slightly wilted bouquet of daisies from a few days prior. "I'm serious. I know I scared you and I'm really sorry."

I nodded, unsure of what to do. This was always the point of the conversation where one of us would suggest a mundane activity like watching a movie or working on a puzzle until dinner time. "So...how did therapy go?"

"Good, I guess. Barb says we're making progress, whatever that means." Maggie offered me a cautious smile. "And I managed to eat everything you left me for lunch today. It's the first time I've done that."

Beaming, I pulled her to my chest for a hug. "That's so great! I'm proud of you!"

"Yeah. Me, too," Maggie said sadly.

We stood like that, chest to chest, arms entwined around each other's waists for several breaths. Hope filtered through the cracks of my heart. This almost seemed like the old version of us and I didn't want to jinx it.

"So Barb made a request," Maggie finally whispered. She didn't look at me, but I could feel the tension in her body as she held her breath. "She wants to do a few couple's sessions with us."

"Oh." I hadn't considered couple's therapy since we still didn't seem like much of a married couple. We maintained our separate bedrooms and our distance. This was the most I'd touched her since the day Maggie came home from the hospital. The beast that used to roar at claiming my Shiny Girl had long since hibernated.

After several long moments, Maggie peeked up at me. "What do you think? Are you willing to go?"

"I'll do anything for you, Trouble." It took all my effort to keep my voice light and carefree. I didn't want to admit that I barely thought of her as my wife now. Somehow in the course of the past three months I turned into Maggie's keeper rather than spouse. And she gave me no indication that I should hope for it to change. "Whatever you need."

CHAPTER 40
THE SESSION
MAGGIE

STOPPING myself from throwing up or marking up my reflection took all of my energy. I meant it when I promised Zeke I would try to get better, but I didn't admit how much my own brain terrified me.

Most of that night seemed fuzzy when I tried to remember it. The doctors at the hospital told me that memory issues were common with anorexia nervosa. When people experienced a breakdown like I had, sometimes our minds tried to protect us by blocking out trauma. The only thing I could remember was the thought on repeat right before Zeke found me—how much the extra weight made me want to die.

Shame kept me silent. I hadn't even admitted that truth to Barb. Rationally I knew that gaining weight shouldn't make someone contemplate ending their life, but having a mental illness didn't have to be rational. The suicidal ideation was the only reason I committed myself to getting better. I refused to hurt Zeke, Celeste, or Marla that way.

A chasm grew wider between Zeke and I as the days went by. Although he agreed to go see Barb with me the following week, he remained as distant as ever throughout the weekend. I stayed in my room most of the time. Everything tasted like chalk, but I swallowed enough food that Zeke didn't hover.

Loneliness became my best friend.

By the time we entered Barb's waiting room on Monday afternoon, I wanted to scream. Zeke and I barely looked at one another.

"Well, Sergeant Hayes, thank you for joining us. I'm glad you came," Barb began. "I recommended some joint sessions because Maggie and I are on the verge of a breakthrough. As her husband, you can be instrumental in achieving that next level."

Zeke smiled wryly. "Happy to help. So where do we start?"

By the time our hour drew to a close, I panted like I ran a marathon. If I thought talking to Barb before made me vulnerable, a therapy session with Zeke was the equivalent of getting a pap smear in the middle of Disney World while buck naked. There were still facets of our personalities that we never got to know since we jumped so quickly into marriage and then immediately became more like roommates. Half the time the things that came out of his mouth shocked me, like when he declined to describe his plans for the Army. "Maggie and I are two halves of a whole," Zeke told Barb, "so I no longer have any goals until we decide on them together."

Barb, however, wore a pleased expression. "Great work today, you two. I'm exceptionally proud of you, Zeke. I know how hard you struggle with social cues, but you were right on target for Maggie."

Zeke and I exchanged matching puzzled expressions. "How do you know he struggles with social cues?" I asked. Up until Barb suggested a couple's counseling session, we didn't talk much about Zeke.

The therapist shrugged nonchalantly. "I mean, I can hardly diagnose him after one session, but I've done this long enough to recognize someone with autism when I encounter them."

My jaw dropped. From the corner of my eye, I saw Zeke go rigid in his seat.

"Haven't you ever been diagnosed?" Barb asked in surprise.

My husband shook his head. "I-I—I don't know," he stuttered.

"Well there's certainly nothing wrong with it," Barb replied. "I'll have you both back next Monday, okay? Maggie, I expect you here on Thursday."

Neither of us said a word as we walked out towards the shuttle stop together. Zeke's truck still hadn't arrived from the U.S. so we resorted to utilizing the public transportation available on post any time we needed to travel more than a few blocks. For once I was glad because I was still at a loss for words. The other passengers served as buffer for a conversation I didn't know how to have.

Zeke's unofficial diagnosis made so much sense from the little I knew about autism. One of my classmates at Smithson County High had it. I'd seen firsthand how much Zeke struggled with eye contact with anyone other than me, just like Marshall Weatherbee back home. I wondered how no one else had noticed it about Zeke before. He still hadn't opened up to me about his childhood—didn't he ever go to the doctor as a kid? What did it mean for him in the military?

The silence stretched between us as the apartment door closed. How do you offer comfort for something like this?

"If you don't mind, I'm gonna go lay down," Zeke said, his voice low. "This is kind of a lot to process."

As he stepped away, my hand shot out on its own, clutching his wrist. He paused at the edge of the hallway, angling his head towards me to indicate he would listen, but refusing to look at me. I no longer knew if that was from autism or his indifference towards me.

"Hey," I whispered. "You're not alone in this, Zeke."

Large blue eyes found mine. All the warmth had drained from their depths. "That's the thing, Maggie. I'm always alone," he murmured.

CHAPTER 41
THE SHOCK
ZEKE

MAGGIE'S crestfallen face was hard to ignore as I closed myself in what had become my bedroom. I knew she wanted to be there for me, but I couldn't accept her comfort right now. There was a phone call I needed to make.

Although roughly 0600 Georgia time, I knew Leggett would answer the phone. He wouldn't lose an opportunity to yell at me.

"It's about time you came to your senses," Leggett greeted me.

Anger rippled through me. This entire thing was his fault. "Did you know?" I snarled. "Did they tell you I'm on the autism spectrum?"

For once, Leggett remained uncharacteristically silent. But that was honestly an answer in and of itself.

"How could you keep that from me?" I hated how weak and faint my voice sounded. I hated even more that he still had this power over me. "You're a goddamn bastard," I ground out. Rather than hang up, I chucked my phone at the wall, where it shattered on impact.

It wasn't enough of a release. I punched the wall behind the door. That crunch didn't satisfy me either, so I did it again.

And again.

Then again.

Cool hands clutched my arm. Blood coated the skin all the way down to my elbow. Maggie slowly pulled me back, guiding me towards the en suite bathroom. Bright red splotches dripped down to the floor. Somewhere in the back of my mind I cringed at how difficult cleaning up the blood spatter would be, but I couldn't bring myself to care.

I had an out of body experience as Maggie helped me strip out of my clothes. She turned the shower on, and though the icy water should have shocked me, I barely felt it when I stepped under the spray. Leggett's silence on that phone call echoed louder than any words ever would. It all but confirmed what I suspected—my original diagnosis came during childhood.

"Patty is the woman who adopted me when I was three years old. Patty Leggett, and her husband, James." There was no logical reason for me to tell Maggie any of this, yet I didn't stop. It all came out like a confession that I couldn't control. "After Patty died unexpectedly a few months later, Leggett raised me on his own. He's an officer in the Army. He never wanted kids."

Maggie tenderly scrubbed my arm with a washcloth. The blue fabric slowly dyed to purple as the blood saturated the cloth. "Is that how you got the scars on your back?" she asked quietly.

Nodding, I agreed. "He raised me to be a soldier, not a human being. If I didn't follow orders, punishments were severe. Leggett's controlled me since Patty died. He controls me now. That's why we're here."

"What?!" In her shock, Maggie dropped the soaking wet washcloth, splattering bloody water everywhere.

"I took sick for the first time ever after I met you. He didn't like that, so he gave me orders to Camp Humphreys, expecting me to apologize. 'Nothing comes before the mission' he always used to say. I was never allowed to be sick."

"*Allowed* to be sick?" she repeated, her voice high. "Zeke, nobody has to give you *permission* to be sick!"

I snorted. "Not in the Leggett household."

Water ran in rivulets down my abdomen as Maggie resumed washing the blood off, though her brow remained furrowed in thought. I inhaled sharply as I realized this was the first time our skin made contact in months. The soap couldn't compete with the strong scent of vanilla wafting from Maggie's hair. She wore it down today in thick, heavy waves.

I wondered if Maggie realized how long it had been since we touched, if she missed it as much as I did. Did her heart skip a beat now? Did her breathing slow down in case she ruined the moment? Mine did.

Judging by the way her eyes sought mine, though, I suspected we might be in sync. We both froze in wait. As cautiously as a deer hunter, I leaned towards her, the magnetic urge to touch her—be closer to her in any way possible—just as strong as the day we met. She swallowed thickly before her gaze darted to my lips.

I wanted to kiss her, probably more than I wanted to wring Leggett's neck for keeping such an important diagnosis from me. Maggie would never judge me or look at me any differently, I knew that, but having her support right now made me feel marginally better. Our roles reversed, her the caretaker and I the invalid, and I understood why Maggie tried so hard to be better for me. Having your well being matter to someone after a lifetime of being invisible created another inseparable bond between us.

Without thinking of it, I leaned my head down, bracing myself against the wall as I zeroed in on her mouth. I wondered if it tasted as good as it had the first time.

Maggie took an involuntary step forward into the water of the walk in shower. The slick floor sent her flying and we both fell. I managed to catch her right before she landed on her knees.

The magic of the moment shattered. A flush crept across Maggie's features as we both realized she came dangerously close to my dick. She extracted herself and scampered across the room to the door.

"I'll get you some clean clothes," whispered Maggie.

I didn't have a chance to answer before she swept from the room.

CHAPTER 42
THE FACTS
MAGGIE

Zeke didn't cook anything for dinner and stayed shut in his room, laying on his side and staring out the window. I made a sandwich for him and set it on the nightstand, but he didn't acknowledge me, so I backed out of the room and closed the door. As much as I wanted to help, no words of wisdom came to mind. What do you say after hearing your husband grew up in an abusive, neglectful household? And that he had autism the entire time?

Actually, I didn't even know what that meant.

I pulled out my laptop and typed "autism" into a search engine. A dozen medical sites came up first to describe the autism spectrum. I learned that there are different levels of severity with autism; Zeke clearly fell on the lower end of the spectrum because extreme cases typically didn't speak and had rage-filled outbursts.

Yeah, maybe Zeke's not that far off on that one. The bedroom wall didn't destroy itself ,after all.

The lack of understanding with social cues stuck out the most on the list of symptoms. Zeke always talked about being isolated, especially as a child. While it couldn't have been easy to grow up with James Leggett, having untreated autism certainly didn't help him make friends. My heart broke for little boy Zeke who just wanted someone to talk to.

I spent the rest of the night reading about autism, its symptoms, and the treatments for it. While an autism diagnosis wasn't a worst case scenario, I recognized how hard it had to be for Zeke to learn this about himself. It also made sense why Zeke thrived in the military. All the structures and routines were good for him.

Maybe I couldn't comfort Zeke with words, but I could offer him the one thing I knew—my body.

The clock read two A.M. by the time I crawled into Zeke's bed. He laid in the same position as before, on his side facing the window. Shadows danced along the wall from the moonlight flooding in; Zeke never closed the blackout curtains. I curled up against his back and wrapped my arm around his chest, causing him to jerk up. He held my hand in a vice grip painful enough for me to whimper.

"Zeke, it's me," I murmured. "It's just Maggie."

"You're not 'just' anything, Trouble," he whispered back. The hold on my hand loosened. Turning over, he faced me without trying to hide the tear falling down his cheek. "Thank you for being here."

I pushed closer so that our bodies pressed against one another from the chest down. Zeke drew an arm around my waist to hold me in place. Even our noses brushed against one another. His eyes were so round and pure that they broke my heart.

I didn't let myself think, I simply acted. Closing the distance, my lips met his with everything I had. I needed him to know how supportive I planned to be, how much I was on his side. He didn't have to be alone anymore.

And as the tension in his body melted away and he sank into the kiss, I realized I didn't either.

Zeke helped me when I hit my lowest point. Hell, he still helped me every time he cooked dinner or met me for a doctor's appointment. He asked about every therapy session. I didn't know for sure, but from what I gathered, Zeke didn't work his normal job anymore so that he had more time available for me. Always for me.

Everything Zeke did was for me.

"I'll always be here for you, Zeke. You never have to worry about being alone again," I promised.

Yielding to him, I flattened onto my back so he could straddle my hips. Kisses peppered my jaw and down my throat. Need ignited like an inferno low in my belly. Zeke's weight on top of me felt divine, so much so that I moaned before I could stop myself.

"Maggie," Zeke whispered in a husky voice that sent a new wave of arousal to my core, "I love you."

I froze beneath him. Even my lungs stopped functioning.

"Maggie?"

He pushed up higher on his forearms and stared down at me with concern. My husband—someone I *should* be able to love.

But nothing came out. An invisible hand gripped my throat, preventing me from speaking. Icy tension filled the room between us.

Zeke's blue eyes filled momentarily with pain, but it was there and gone in the blink of an eye. He scrambled off the bed to the other side of the room.

"Zeke, I—" Only I didn't know how to finish the statement.

"It's fine," he replied, but he wouldn't look at me. His eyes stayed trained to the floor. "We should both be getting to bed. Good night."

Rather than waiting for me to move, Zeke entered the en suite bathroom and shut the door with a firm snap. Metal scraped against wood as the lock shifted into place.

My footsteps sounded soft as I pattered across the floor on tiptoe. I raised my hand to knock, but stopped halfway. "I'm sorry," I murmured against the bathroom door.

CHAPTER 43
THE FALLOUT

ZEKE

After I heard the soft thud of the door closing when Maggie left the room, I returned to bed and laid back down on my side. Now something entirely new bothered me. It was the first time I'd ever told Maggie how I felt and the results made the Hindenburg look like a warmup. I never meant to say it, let alone in the heat of the moment, but it slipped out before I could think it through.

Sleep never came that night. As soon as I could get away with it, I dressed in the physical fitness uniform and headed over to the post gym. It was a cowardly thing to do, but I wasn't ready to see Maggie just yet. Vulnerability felt shitty. Emotions usually eluded me and on the very first attempt to label them with her, I ruined it. She clammed up tighter than a Venus flytrap.

I managed to get in a semi-decent workout by the time the rest of the unit showed up for training. Staff Sergeant Whittenburg approached me with both his eyebrows raised.

"Did I miss the memo about reporting at the ass crack of dawn?" he asked.

"Sorry, sir. Just have a lot on my mind."

Whittenburg sighed. "Go home, Hayes. We don't need you here if your attention is elsewhere."

"But, sir, I—"

"NOW, Hayes!" the staff sergeant barked.

The coppery tang of blood coated my tongue as I bit down on the inside of my cheek. Arguing with him would only lead to more problems. "Thank you, Staff Sergeant," I ground out.

Only once I made it outside, I turned in the direction of the medical clinic instead. The soldier at the receptionist desk called after me as I stormed past and headed straight for Chuck's office. He sat in front of his computer, typing notes from the journal that lay open on the desk, but jumped up in surprise when the door slammed open behind me.

"Did you know I'm autistic?" I demanded.

Chuck clutched his chest, the faded KISS shirt he wore wrinkling in his hands. "Geez, all you had to do was knock!"

I glared at him, fists clenched at my sides.

"Yeah, man, I know you're autistic. It's in your medical file." Chuck plopped down hard in his desk chair. What had once been a body cultivated to Army fitness standards now sported a protruding belly, long hair, and a goatee that was more salt than pepper. He looked every inch his age as he scrubbed a hand down his face before readjusting his glasses. "Why are you bursting in here for that?"

"Because *I* didn't know that I'm autistic!" I bellowed. "No one's ever told me that before!"

Understanding dawned and Chuck winced in sympathy. "I can't imagine how hard that's gotta be for you, man. I had a cancellation this morning—do you wanna talk about it?"

Talking about the diagnosis sounded about as appealing as talking to Maggie after the disaster of last night. But my options were one or the other at the moment, and at least when I talked to Chuck my heart wouldn't shatter.

"Yeah," I agreed, "let's talk about it. We'll start with everything you can see in my medical file."

* * *

A good therapy session really helped put my diagnosis into perspective. So many aspects of my personality clicked into place as Chuck and I discussed the symptoms of autism and what signs had always been there. He also disclosed that in recent years the Army started allowing medical waivers for people with autism disorders. Given that I had General Leggett as my mentor, Chuck seemed pretty confident my enlistment came under a waiver that Leggett himself cleared. My service so far had been exemplary, and there was nothing in my personnel records that Chuck could find that made him question the continuation of my service.

Relief lifted my spirits. My career in the military wasn't set in stone by any means, but if Maggie didn't mind our frequent moves and separations, I saw no reason not to renew my contract within the next eighteen months when the window opened. We could discuss it…whenever I decided talking to her didn't make me want to dive headfirst into a pool of battery acid.

"I'm glad we were able to work through this," Chuck said. He clapped me jovially on the shoulder as he guided me towards the door. "I'll see you for our regular time next week, alright?"

"Thank you, sir," I replied.

He twitched, like a shiver ran down his spine. "Don't call me that! It's like you think I'm old or something!" Chuck's eyes twinkled at his own joke. "Now go home and talk to Maggie."

I blanched. *How the hell did he know about the issue with my wife?*

"Kid, you practically pissed yourself every time I brought her up today," Chuck laughed. "I might be old, but I'm not blind! Go talk to your wife!"

"It's not always that simple." Even my ears blazed with how hard embarrassment flooded me.

"It's not always that hard, either." Chuck shrugged good naturedly before shutting the door in my face.

My anxiety diminished slightly when I entered our apartment and found Maggie sleeping. Only she slept in my bed, with my pillow squashed against her face. Long hair fanned out around her like a halo.

Exhaustion slammed into me with the power of a freight train. As quickly and silently as I could, I slipped on a clean pair of underwear and sweatpants so that I could slide into bed behind her.

This was my room and my wife, after all. I had every right to sleep in one with my arms wrapped tightly around the other…even if I didn't have the balls to talk to her. Maggie's hair accosted my face when she snuggled in closer, needing me in sleep far more than she needed me while awake.

Minutes or hours may have gone by before she jostled the bed to turn and face me. I slowly blinked my eyes open to gaze at her. If I moved too quickly, it might break the spell and she might bolt. I wanted her to stay in my arms. Even with the terror of conversation, having her close enough to smell her warm vanilla shampoo eased my anxiety. This felt like home.

"Hey, Trouble," I finally whispered.

"Hey, baby," she mumbled back, making my heart soar. She never used a pet name with me before. "We need to talk about last night."

I shook my head and rolled onto my back so that I didn't have to look at her. "No, we don't," I replied firmly.

Maggie scooted closer so that she could lay her head on my chest. Instinctively, my arm encircled her waist. "What you said just caught me off guard," she explained. "I've never said it to anyone before. Not even Celeste. It's a big deal."

Swallowing hurt with the lump in my throat. "Yeah. It's a very big deal. I've never said it before either."

She sighed and drew featherlight touches along my chest. "I don't know what I feel about anything right now, Zeke. Ever since getting out of the hospital, it's like I don't even know myself anymore. I'm trying so damn hard to do better for you. The thought of hurting you, or scaring you again like I did, drives me crazy! How can I tell you I love you when I don't even know who I am?" Maggie's voice cracked.

Hot tears streamed down my ribcage, but that was nothing compared to the way my heart imploded. I recognized the fear and devastation in her words because they mirrored my own.

"Our promises to each other are still the same." I spitballed out loud, just saying whatever came to mind. "Clearly now we both have things we need to work on. Neither of us really know who we are. Maybe it would be easier just to start over."

Maggie sat up, a tentative smile on her face. "Hi there, I'm Maggie Hayes. Pleased to meet you." She held out her hand—an olive branch as we created our new way forward.

This was the Maggie I remembered. Full of light and love, who made me feel like everything was possible. It didn't go unnoticed that she called herself by her married name either. Hope shimmered on the horizon.

"Hi, Maggie," I grinned. "My name is Zeke Hayes, and wouldn't you know it, I think I might be your husband."

Taking her proffered hand, we shook on it before her gaze traveled down the length of my naked torso. "My husband, huh? Lucky me!"

CHAPTER 44
THE TRIAL
MAGGIE

OVER THE COURSE of the next month, Zeke and I created our new normal under the guise of re-discovering ourselves. We both learned more about each other's diagnoses in order to better support one another. For instance, I never realized how much order and structure Zeke needed. Weekends weren't just a time to lay around. He needed a set expectation, established by a routine, that needed to include a designated time to wake, workout, and an exact plan for the day. We decided to plan Saturdays for adventures, either in South Korea itself or simply with designated activities offered on post, and plan Sundays for cleaning, meal prepping, and laundry. He breathed easier if we assigned specific household chores rather than simply doing things willy-nilly as they came up, so we worked out a system for what I would tackle and what he would tackle.

He continued to cook and monitor the signs of my eating disorder. The bathroom scale had disappeared before I returned from the hospital after my breakdown, but when I mentioned in passing how bad I felt about myself every time I looked in the mirror, the next day I woke up to find all the mirrors gone, even in the bathrooms. When I pointed out that Zeke still needed a mirror to shave and tend to his own hair, he merely shrugged. "I can shave after I shower at the gym. And why worry about my hair when you can do it for me and it will look ten times better?"

I nearly glowed from that compliment.

Zeke noticed, though, in a way that only he could. From then on, I found small notes with sweet sayings on them all the time. On the lamp next to my bed, stuck to the gallon of milk in the refrigerator, tucked inside my jeans pocket. They never repeated the same statement either. Sometimes there were famous quotes on love, beauty, or marriage. Others came directly from Zeke's own mind.

Your smile reminds me of a sunset.

I love the way your nose crinkles when you concentrate.

Thank you for going to the library with me. It made me feel special and important.

The notes served as a reminder of why I married Zeke in the first place. He treasured me in a way that no one else had before, and while I wasn't yet ready to call it love, every note gave me hope that love could happen down the road.

Zeke and I kept up with couple's therapy sessions. Barb helped tremendously as we discovered more about each other and our respective illnesses. We both agreed it was far easier to navigate disagreements or misunderstandings with Barb in the room. Especially Zeke, who struggled a lot with finding the right words or reading my signals. He frequently took notes in a small notebook that he kept in the breast pocket of his Army uniform.

One of the exercises Barb liked to end sessions with included revealing one truth about us that we never told anyone before. She said it helped Zeke and I connect on a deeper level as husband and wife.

"I never considered doing anything other than being a soldier," Zeke admitted at the end of one particularly grueling session. "It was the only option ever talked about, and now that Maggie is in my life, I don't know if the Army is really what I want to do."

My eyebrows rose in surprise. We had never discussed the possibility of Zeke getting out of the military. I never considered it.

"Good, Zeke. I'm really proud of you for admitting that. Marriage is all about compromise, and it sounds like you recognize how much you need to compromise to be considerate of Maggie's needs, too. Excellent! Now Maggie, your turn!" Barb smiled fondly at me.

I wanted to give just as much of myself as he had. We would match bravery for bravery.

"Diana never let me cut my hair," I confessed. "At least, nothing more than a trim. I've always wanted to try a really short style. Maybe even a pixie cut."

After I said the words out loud, I realized how stupid they sounded. Here Zeke was, pouring his heart out about his future—our future—and all I could do was complain about my hair.

Barb, however, beamed at me. "That's real growth, Maggie! You finally recognized that you've been altering your own desires to earn your mother's approval. Well done!"

I smiled, despite myself. Earning my therapist's praise grew to be nearly as addictive as Zeke's. And she always knew the right thing to say to make it encouraging. Maybe Barb was a cheerleader back in the day. I could totally picture her cheering with school pride.

"I'll see you both next week. Until Thursday, Maggie!" Barb waved jovially to us as we exited her office.

The seasons were on the verge of changing, making the air outside crisper. Long shadows leaped behind us, and I blushed under the intensity of Zeke's gaze as we emerged out on the street.

"What?" I finally asked.

"You have no idea how much you take my breath away," he murmured.

A fevered blush crept up my face, making my skin hot. The way Zeke looked at me in that moment set my soul on fire.

This was how loved formed, I realized. The milliseconds in between everything where love and joy filtered in. It hung tantalizingly close, just out of reach. Why couldn't I reach up and take it? What made me so afraid?

"Zeke, I…I…" Words failed me as he continued to stare at me as if the very stars thanked me for their existence.

He laced his fingers through mine, giving them a gentle squeeze. "C'mon," he said, "there's something we need to do."

* * *

"Zeke, you can't be serious!" Delight wormed its way into my chest, but old instincts convinced me that it was too good to be true.

"Of course I'm serious. Why would I lie?" My husband poked the tip of his tongue out through the side of his teeth, and I'd never seen him look so playful or sexy. Although that might have been the excitement talking.

We stood on the threshold of a salon just off post that advertised walk-in appointments. Several of the stylists I could see from the doorway looked to be American, based on their clothing. Zeke wanted to make my dreams come true by taking me to get a major haircut.

I giggled. "Fine, but then you have to wait out here. You don't get to see it until the big reveal at the end!"

"Deal!" Zeke pulled me in for a quick kiss to the forehead. As if I could melt any more over this man.

We went up to the receptionist and my husband slapped a credit card down on the table. "Give my wife whatever she wants," instructed Zeke. "I just want her happy."

The South Korean woman behind the counter beamed like she won the lottery. "Absolutely, sir!" she cooed in accented English. "Your wife will be beautiful when we're done!"

He only had eyes for me, however. "She already is."

CHAPTER 45
THE MOMENT

ZEKE

Maggie's appointment took a little over an hour, and I sat in the waiting area with a library book. The way she looked didn't matter to me. I only wanted her to feel happy with herself. If a shorter haircut would help, then that was the least I could do for her.

Only I didn't consider how much Maggie's new look might send me into cardiac arrest. When she emerged with what she called a "fiery pixie cut" I resembled a cartoon in how my jaw dropped and my tongue lolled out. Her shorter hair allowed me to see the slope of her delicate neck, the angle of her jawline, the perfect arch of her dainty ears. That had to mean it was true love, right? Why would I notice Maggie's ears if I didn't love her?

"What do you think?" A rich, pink blush worked its way across Maggie's cheeks. Her hands moved automatically to curl around the ends of her hair, only now there weren't any strands dangling down far enough.

"I think you're stunning, but it doesn't matter what I think. How do you feel?" It was a struggle to take my eyes off her. Rather than looking at the receptionist to pay, I kept my focus on Maggie, not even bothering to look as I scribbled something that barely resembled a signature. There was something different about her face, too. I couldn't identify what the difference was, but I liked it just the same.

Maggie's blush grew deeper. "I feel amazing! Kaitlin did such a good job!" She babbled the rest of the way through our evening, including dinner, about how well her stylist knew the color palette and how much she enjoyed that salon. I didn't understand two thirds of what she said, but I loved how excited she looked while saying it. Maggie hadn't been this happy in months.

"Actually, Kaitlin said they may have an opening soon." My wife's smile fell at the corners as she waited for my response with bated breath. "What do you think?"

I shrugged. "I think the Americans there are all military spouses, so the salon likely has a high turnover rate."

She rolled her eyes, but the wide smile returned. Leaning against the wall, Maggie waited for me to unlock our apartment door. We were finally home for the evening after having dinner at a restaurant near the salon and picking up a few things at the market. I didn't want the night to ever end; this was the best day we'd had together in months.

"I really do have to spell things out for you, don't I?" she mused once we were inside.

"What do you mean?"

Maggie rolled her eyes again and then laughed to herself. "A job, Zeke. I'm talking about getting a job. At the salon."

"Oh." I blinked a few times to process what she meant. That was something both Chuck and Barb encouraged me to do so that I only said things after considering all of the implications. "We don't need you to work, you know. I'm happy to pay for everything you want or need."

My wife nodded. "It's not about money. I just worked really hard to get through cosmetology school and I want to have something to show for it."

"If working at that salon is what you want, then I say go for it. We're making a new normal, right? Will you keep your appointments with Barb? Your wellbeing has to come first."

"Of course!" Maggie positively glowed, clapping her hands gleefully as she jumped on the balls of her feet. "I could just kiss you!" She grabbed my head with both hands and yanked my face to hers, then planted her lips firmly on mine.

I hadn't done more than kiss her forehead since the night of my autism diagnosis. Kissing my wife made the world finally stop spinning as it reoriented itself to her axis. Maggie was the center of my everything; the only person worth living and breathing for.

I loved her. Whether she ever returned the feeling or not, Maggie Hayes was the love of my life.

"Can I sleep in your room tonight?" Her hopeful voice broke through my intrusive thoughts. She bit her bottom lip as she waited for my response. "We don't have to do anything! I just…want to be near you."

Slowly, a smile spread across my face as the hope from the kiss blossomed deeper in my chest. "You never have to ask, Trouble," I assured her. "Wherever you are is exactly where I wanna be."

CHAPTER 46
THE REMINDER
MAGGIE

I LOVED MY NEW HAIRCUT. Kaitlin foiled in several shades of coppery red and light blonde to complement the rich brown tone we settled on as a base. Losing all the hair took so much more than the weight of the length off my shoulders. It freed me—I truly let go of Maggie Eaton, which made it that much simpler to embrace Maggie Hayes. Maybe she was someone I could actually like.

The only difficult part proved to be ignoring the mirror during my appointment. Kaitlin accommodated my request to have my chair turned away from her station, but due to the layout of the salon and the other hairstylists' stations, I could still see angular reflections of myself. I tried not to fidget as I forced myself to stare at my knees. The brief glimpses I caught made me want to throw up.

When Kaitlin finished, I allowed myself one critical gaze at my reflection. The haircut and color suited my face. Somehow, I had developed a rosier complexion since moving to South Korea.

But I couldn't pretend that my face didn't appear fuller or that my shirt didn't strain against my body where it had once been much looser. My brain lashed out at the image. It took both hands for me to grip the chair hard enough to stop myself from bolting to their bathroom in the back of the salon. I could go in there and complete a quick ritual, and Zeke would never know.

Thinking about Zeke and how much he wanted to make me happy—how much he was willing to do and sacrifice to make me feel beautiful—sobered the compulsion, though. I couldn't do that to him. I couldn't break his heart by slipping up when he made such an effort.

Once Kaitlin mentioned a job opening, it was easier to avoid the mirror and its dismal reflection. She genuinely liked working there and said the owner was very understanding of Army wives' schedules. They would help me build up a clientele of my own so that I could work as much or as little as I wanted.

Another week went by with my days getting substantially brighter. The salon manager, a robust woman named Seo-yeon who married an American soldier as a young woman and moved back to South Korea when he retired from Active Duty, hired me on the spot. I would only work two or three shifts per week, but that meant I could easily maintain my therapy appointments.

Life never looked better. Until I managed my first Skype session with Celeste and Marla.

"Oh my word, look at you!" Marla gushed. "You're as pretty as a picture!"

Celeste grinned from the seat next to her, a sleeping Iris on her lap. "Holy crap, do I miss you! Tell us everything."

It was late at night back in River's Run, meaning I had the apartment to myself while Zeke went to physical training with his unit. Neither Marla nor Celeste had a computer, so we had to wait for a video call until Marla bought one for the bakery. Seeing them, even little Iris, made me homesick in a way that turned my stomach in knots. I felt like such a different person from the Maggie they knew. Everything had changed.

I laughed at Celeste's giddiness. "I love it here. Our apartment is way bigger than anything we'd ever need. It's too bad y'all can't come visit. I just got a job at a salon, too! I start next week."

"Congratulations, honey! That's great." Marla's approval meant the world to me. As the only real mother figure I had, I wanted to make her proud. She and Barb would've gotten along well.

"How's married life?" Celeste wiggled her eyebrows suggestively, making me roll my eyes in response.

"It's great. Zeke and I are having a lot of fun exploring Seoul. We talked about maybe taking a trip to Japan over the winter holidays. Travel isn't too expensive here and it's actually not far from us."

They both oohed and aahed theatrically. I was the first person from River's Run to travel any farther than Florida, unless you counted Wesley. Taking a trip to Japan probably sounded as unbelievable to them as traveling back in time.

"How's the bakery coming along, Marla?" I asked. "Zeke is so bummed he ain't there to help!"

Celeste and Marla exchanged a loaded glance, and Celeste adjusted Iris guiltily on her lap.

"We might have hit a snag or two," Marla finally confessed.

"What do you mean?" Another exchanged look made me huff in exasperation. "Just tell me!"

My best friend sighed in resignation. "What she means to say is there's been some trouble getting everything done. Supplies keep disappearing, someone broke in and spray painted on the walls. Just stupid teens playing pranks!" Celeste waved her hand to dismiss the actions while my stomach sank.

Spencer.

He still thought I owed him money for the drugs I ruined. Since he couldn't find me, he probably turned on Marla. It was just a matter of time before he started going after Celeste, too.

"I'm so sorry, Marla. How far did that set you back?" Guilt nibbled at my conscience as I debated whether or not to come clean.

She waved it off. "Don't you worry about it. I wouldn't set out to do something just to give it up over a little paint! Tell us all about Seoul. Don't leave out a single detail! I have to live through you."

We talked for close to an hour and although I participated in the conversation, I couldn't focus on anything they said. Spencer never did anything seriously violent against someone—that I knew of—but I also wouldn't put it past him. If he hurt either of them, I would never forgive myself. My mind ran through reel after reel of possibilities, each one more gruesome than the last, all the way up to a horrific image of sweet, little Iris bleeding out on the floor of The Comfy Cushion.

That was how Zeke found me when he returned home to check on me before heading into work for the day. The laptop still sat open on the kitchen table in front of me as I stared into space.

"Trouble? Maggie, baby, what's wrong?" Zeke kneeled on the floor in front of me, a look of concern maiming his beautiful face.

I blinked away the tears that threatened to fall and swept past him into my bedroom. "It's nothing. Don't worry about it."

Zeke stayed hot on my heels. "I don't think so. The last time I came home and found you like this, I thought I might lose you. I'm not going through that again!" He grabbed ahold of my bicep to keep me in place.

"This isn't the same thing," I promised, "but it's not something I'm ready to tell you yet, okay? I need you to respect me on this, Zeke. Please."

His face fell at my plea and the guilt worsened. Slowly, his fingers loosened and he stepped backward. "I always respect you, Maggie. I just wish you would do the same for me."

A sharp inhale of surprise escaped, but I made no effort to contradict him. There were simply some things I had to protect him from. Spencer Church happened to be one of them.

My mouth remained closed in a resolute line as the silence stretched between us. Giving in, he sighed and turned away, leaving me with a quivering bottom lip. I watched Zeke's shape disappear down the hall, vision clouded with tears, until he walked out of sight.

CHAPTER 47
THE HOMEWORK
MAGGIE

THINGS REMAINED strained between Zeke and I up until our next couple's session with Barb. I didn't want him to worry over me, especially when I had been trying so hard to eat the food he made me, but I couldn't bring myself to admit the truth about Spencer. I knew Zeke would want to help. He would likely hand over the money instantly if I asked, which made me all the more resistant to doing so. Knocking over that baggie had been a stupid accident; he didn't need to drain his savings because of me. Now that I had a job, I would find a way to get Spencer the damn money and put the entire thing to rest.

Barb sensed the tension between us the moment we stepped into her office. We took our designated spaces on the sofa across from her as she pursed her lips and shrewdly eyed us over her glasses.

"What happened?" she asked.

I shot a nervous glance to Zeke, who kept his posture rigid and his face blank. "What do you mean?"

She pursed her lips even tighter, so that her top lip was barely visible. "I mean I've seen soldiers holding live grenades with less anxiety than you two. Something happened since I saw you last."

"There are still some things that Maggie isn't ready to share with me," Zeke explained, "and that hurts because I want her to share the things that matter with me."

Barb nodded before jotting something down in the notebook on the table next to her. "And Maggie, how does it feel when Zeke says that?"

"It kills me because the last thing I want to do is hurt him," I admitted. "But there will always be some things I can't share with him. We're two separate people, after all."

Zeke sighed in frustration. "I know that. I'm not asking for everything. But if something bothers you to the point where you can't focus on anything, I deserve to know *something*. I'm your husband, after all."

His goddamn labels! Zeke's preconceived ideas about marriage mostly came from books, I'd learned. He read faster than anyone I ever met, but after devouring all of the classics as a child, he now primarily read non-fiction. All he knew of husbands and wives could be gleaned from Dickens, Steinbeck, Poe...nobody relevant in the current century.

"Why does that mean so much to you? It's *just* a slip of paper!" Irritation made the words come out harsher than I meant, but I didn't apologize.

"Because I know there are expectations involved and I'm afraid I'm not meeting them because I don't understand them!" Zeke confessed angrily.

Our therapist nodded sagely, like the wise old owl I imagined her to be. "Then let's start there, Zeke. What do you think the expectations are?"

Barb's calm demeanor helped settle both of us down. Zeke's shoulders sagged a little as some of the fight left. "Husbands are supposed to be the providers. They work hard so that their wives don't have to. The good ones make their wives happy. I can't seem to do that."

"But Zeke, you *do* make me happy," I argued. "Happier than I've ever been. That's why I wanted to marry you in the first place!"

To my utter shock, a tear slid down his cheek as he growled, "Then why did you break down right in front of me?!"

My jaw opened and closed several times as I fought over what to say. Barb stayed uncharacteristically quiet, her eyes volleying between the two of us as if she simply needed to referee the match.

"That had nothing to do with *you*, and everything to do with *me*. Don't you see? The only reason I want to get better is for *you*!"

Zeke shook his head fiercely. "No. No, that's wrong. You have to get better for you, Maggie. At the end of the day, no matter how much I want to keep you, you always have the option of leaving me. You can never escape yourself!"

A truth bomb ignited between us. Now I really didn't know what to say. He was absolutely right. My health journey didn't affect him the way it did me, and using him as a motivator would only lead to resentment. That was far too much pressure for anyone to handle.

This whole time I'd been unwittingly placing my recovery on his shoulders. Zeke didn't have an eating disorder, I did. Zeke didn't struggle with self-loathing, or anxiously check the sizes on his clothing, or count every single calorie he consumed. Those were my vices.

None of which had anything to do with his expectations as far as our marriage went. The paranoia of coming home again to find his wife in the midst of another depressive episode made him question what he knew marriage to be. Zeke needed answers. Having something so important remain so uncertain must have been eating him alive.

"We agreed to make our own version of normal, right? That we would find a way to be healthy and happy as we learned about ourselves? Shouldn't that be true for our marriage, too?" Tentative hope cracked in my voice, but Zeke's eyes latched onto mine just the same. "It can be whatever we want it to be, baby."

We both offered small smiles, signs of truce, to one another. Lost in the moment, I jumped in my seat when Barb suddenly cleared her throat. I forgot she was even in the room.

"How are things intimately?" the therapist asked.

This time Zeke jerked in his seat. We exchanged guilt-ridden glances, two kids sitting in the principal's office unwilling to rat the other out.

After a tense pause, I finally spoke for us. "We haven't really been intimate. Not since we got married, at least."

"I don't know if I can," Zeke suddenly admitted. My eyebrows rose in alarm. He had *zero* problems with his equipment way back in Savannah when we stopped at Madden Market.

"And why is that?" Barb asked.

Zeke's hands started fidgeting, a clear sign that the topic made him uncomfortable. After several long minutes he confessed, "I told Maggie that I loved her, and she didn't say it back. I'm glad she didn't, because I don't want her to say it if she doesn't mean it, but I feel wrong being intimate with someone who doesn't feel the same way."

"It's just sex!" I snorted.

The emotion pooling in his eyes would haunt me for the rest of my life as Zeke turned to me and said, "It's never just sex when it's you, Maggie." I wanted to crawl under a rock and hide until the shame swallowed me whole.

Barb, however, nodded in understanding. "You know what that means, don't you, Zeke?" she asked. "That means you're likely a demisexual."

Both of us frowned in confusion at her. "A demisexual?" I repeated blankly.

Our therapist nodded again. "Demisexuals are individuals who only experience sexual attraction after creating a strong, emotional connection to another person. The gender doesn't matter as much as the feelings do."

Zeke let out a long breath, like he had been holding it while waiting for bad news. "I guess that does kind of make sense. I've only had sex with two other people before that I didn't really know. Both experiences were awful."

"That doesn't surprise me," mused Barb. She wrote down another few notes in her journal before slamming it shut and leaning towards us. "I just have to give you both homework. By the time you come back to my office next week, I want you two to be intimate. Be physical. Learn to identify the other's needs. Touch is an important part of a marriage, and if you're going to really give this thing a try, you have to engage in all aspects of it. Maggie, don't worry about our Thursday session. Just enjoy some special time with your husband! Now scoot!"

Walking out onto the street after a couple's session like that felt oddly the same as walking out of the justice of the peace's office. The realization that I was married came crashing down, just like it had then, and I didn't entirely know how to function in real time. I kept glancing over at Zeke out of the corner of my eye, desperate to know if he was just as confused and lost as me.

"So…that went well," Zeke joked. It lightened the moment enough for us to both laugh as we stupidly stood staring at one another in the middle of the sidewalk.

"I've never had a homework assignment quite like this one," I added. I meant it as another lighthearted joke, but I noticed how Zeke winced. "I didn't mean—"

"It's fine, Trouble." Zeke cut me off with the wave of a hand. "We're both learning."

"Maybe we should schedule it?" I suggested. He thrived on structures and routine. "That way we both have time to prepare?"

"Okay. Saturday night," he agreed. "We'll spend the day together, do something fun, and then go home to…" his voice trailed off in unease as we both mentally filled in the blank.

Saturday arrived by warped speed. Zeke and I remained distantly polite throughout the week, operating like strangers sharing a hostel, as we counted down to D-Day. My nerves were raw by the time I finally gave up on sleep the morning of. I already heard Zeke in the kitchen making breakfast, so I decided to rip it off like a band-aid when I joined him.

Usually on Saturday mornings, Zeke opted for a simple run instead of a full blown workout, then he came home and cooked breakfast before I even woke up. He would be in the shower, his own breakfast long gone, by the time I staggered out to the kitchen in search of coffee. Seeing him now, nylon shorts slung low on his hips, back muscles rippling in their naked glory, while he minded the turkey bacon frying on the stove made it really easy for me to imagine sex with him. I wanted it. I wanted *him*.

But wanting him wasn't enough. Barb said Zeke needed to feel an emotional connection. So if we were going to do anything, I had to open up a little bit and let Zeke feel something.

Gently, I came up behind him and slid my arms around his waist, leaning my face against his spine. Although he jolted initially, Zeke didn't push me away or become tense from our proximity. Had he ever done so before? Or was I simply looking for signs now that I knew how he felt?

He rubbed his hand along my arms, letting me relax further into his back. "Do you still want to go to that underground mall today?"

Today's adventure consisted of visiting Myeong-dong, a shopping district in Seoul that also featured an underground mall. According to some of the people Zeke worked with, it had all kinds of bizarre shops along with some of the best clothing stores. We didn't really need anything, but exploring the city always provided a lot of entertainment and laughter.

I doubted there were enough shops in Seoul for us to be entertained right now.

An hour later, Zeke and I wandered down the crowded street near the mall. There were so many shops and restaurants to see that we agreed to walk a bit first before descending below. A throng of people cut along the sidewalks, pointing animatedly to their destinations. Broken pieces of Korean, English, and what I had learned to recognize as Japanese interrupted the noisy traffic on the road. Coming from a small town like River's Run, Seoul never ceased to shock me with the sheer volume of its inhabitants.

"Come on," Zeke directed, grabbing my hand. "Let's go down here for a minute. I don't like being in such a big crowd." He pulled us down a small side street with fewer people, and I instantly spotted a storefront that made me gasp in delighted surprise.

"Zeke, look! There's a giant penis in that window!"

His mouth formed a perfectly round O as I dragged us inside.

The store turned out to be a sex shop. A male clerk sat behind the counter, flicking through a magazine, and barely looked up at us in greeting. There weren't any other customers, but displays of toys, lingerie, and even furniture made it difficult to move through the space. Dildos in all shapes, sizes, and colors sat on plastic shelves along the wall to our left, and I stared in fascinated amusement.

Judging by the look on Zeke's face, he wanted the floor to open up and swallow him.

"Let's pick some things out to help us!" I suggested excitedly. "Toys and things might make tonight easier for us!"

"Really?" He sounded skeptical as he picked up a dildo spiraled like a unicorn's horn, complete with rainbow colors and glitter. It was easily longer than my forearm. "You think something like this will help us?"

"We're finding a new normal, right? Why not include sexual preferences on that list?" I challenged, one brow quirking up.

Zeke didn't look entirely convinced, but he nodded in agreement. "I'm willing to try if you are."

I made us go through each and every display in the store before settling on our purchases. Most of them only had directions in Korean, so I couldn't explain all of them to Zeke. What I did know, I only read about from dirty magazines that some of the kids in high school used to share around. Zeke knew even less than I did. What started out as very serious conversations quickly gave way to snarky laughter as we made up names and uses for the devices we didn't recognize or understand.

Despite being so uncomfortable with the store, Zeke made every effort to listen to my fantasies. It was almost freeing to bare my desires in front of him. He asked questions about my previous partners not out of jealousy, but because he genuinely wanted to know my past. He didn't make me feel dirty or "boy crazy."

I selected two kinds of vibrators, a basic set of nipple clamps, and a few bottles of flavored lube. After carefully considering all the toys we talked about, Zeke's choices both surprised and intrigued me: a set of handcuffs, a blindfold, and dildo with an attached penis ring. Arousal swirled low in my belly as I imagined him using any of them on me.

On our way to the register, he stopped next to a lacy green teddy. "Would you ever wear something like this?" Zeke asked, gesturing towards the hanger.

Crimson flamed across my cheeks. "I don't have the right body for something like that. It wouldn't look right on me."

Zeke contemplated the teddy for another minute before plucking it off the rack. "I'm going to prove you wrong."

The clerk didn't speak a word of English, which somehow made the transaction less nerve-wracking. Both of us automatically headed towards the bus stop that would take us back to Camp Humphreys.

I didn't want to lose the little bit of ground we gained by doing something so bold and intimate, so I laced our fingers together as soon as we took our seats on the bus. Leaning into him, looking deep into Zeke's eyes, I felt a connection so tangible that I swore I could reach out and touch it. He needed to feel it, too.

"You make me so happy," I breathed into his ear.

A gleam of intrigue hit his eye, the resulting smirk sending a quiet thrill to my pussy.

Lying wouldn't be fair to either of us, and I wasn't ready to say those terrifying three little words, so I opted for something that was just as much of a truth as it was emotional. "I'm honored to be your wife, Zeke Hayes. Honored."

There was definitely a spark of something in his eyes now. Zeke flashed me a small smile before brushing his lips against my ear and taking a deep inhale of my hair.

"I know what you're doing, Trouble," he murmured low enough that I could barely hear.

"Is it working?" I teased.

Another flash of a smile. "You damn bet."

My feet never moved faster than when I tried to get off the bus. Zeke and I both tried our best to be patient, but the moment the last person stepped out of our way, we took off like a rocket, hands still interlaced. We each clutched a bag in one hand as we ran all the way to our apartment.

The click of the door shutting behind us echoed loudly throughout the apartment once we made it inside. Shyness suddenly made me blush, my body hyper-aware of being alone with Zeke. He looked at me expectantly, an expression of joy and longing crossing his face, before handing me the paper bag with his items inside.

"Will you try on the outfit for me? Please?" he added, his voice husky. My blush grew deeper.

"What if I look bad in it?" I asked. Emotions clogged my throat—the desire to please him, arousal, and unadulterated fear of disgusting both of us with my ugliness.

Zeke stepped into me and tenderly rubbed his thumb across my check. He angled my chin up, forcing me to look at him. "Maggie Hayes, that's not possible. You're a not a burden, you're a gift."

His affirmation from all those months ago in River's Run.

"Now go change," he ordered in his sergeant's voice. "I'll meet you in the bedroom in a minute. I'm gonna shower first."

"I will, too!" My anxious mind started running through a rolodex of beauty regimens. Should I find a way to put makeup on? What if the lighting wasn't right and I looked washed out? My hair might need to be fixed. Or if I—

"I can see those wheels spinning, Trouble," Zeke interrupted. "Shower, but no makeup. No hair stuff. Just you in that pretty green getup, okay? I want to see my wife as she is, not how she thinks she should be. You have ten minutes."

Ten minutes was barely enough time to shower, but I managed to wash the important places. The teddy slipped on easily, with a plunging neckline down to my belly button. Since there were no mirrors anywhere, I couldn't tell if it looked ridiculous with my small boobs or flat butt. I only hoped that it would be enough for Zeke.

A soft thud echoed as I heard him enter the bedroom and pad across the floor. Taking another minute to calm my heart's ferocious beating, I steeled myself before stepping out to join my husband.

It was time to pop this cherry.

CHAPTER 48
THE CURVE

ZEKE

I MEANT for the shower to buy me some time to calm my nerves, but the prospect of sleeping with Maggie made me panic. Racing thoughts and insecurities plagued me. What if I wasn't good enough? What if I truly didn't know what I was doing?

But this was Maggie. My Shiny Girl. Trouble with a capital T. I'd do anything for this woman, including rearrange my entire future, a future that she somehow still seemed to want to be part of.

Barb identified me as a demisexual. The word fit, and I trusted the therapist's assessment. According to her, that meant I needed an emotional bond with a person before I could fully experience sex. Mechanically, my body might be capable of responding to the right stimuli, but I wouldn't feel the experience like others would.

Everything with Maggie felt like an emotional connection, though. I could tell the moment she entered a room even with my eyes closed, ears plugged, and the lights off. I didn't know if there was a word for that kind of bond. I only knew that it was stronger than anything else on Earth.

I lit a few candles that I placed on the dresser before pulling the blackout curtains closed. It wasn't that I minded the light seeping through, but Maggie probably would. Both of us needed to be comfortable for this to work.

Before I could say anything, my wife slipped out in that dark green strip of lace. Something about the color caught my eye in that store and I practically salivated from the image it procured in my head. That image couldn't hold a candle to the sight of Maggie wearing it in the flesh. A deep V divided her torso in half, the lace basically see-through. The dusty pink circles of her nipples caught my eye as I remembered the nipple clamps she bought at the shop. I didn't even know those were a thing until she mentioned how sensitive her nipples tended to be during sex. Their rosy hue taunted me now, begging me to find out.

A wary expression froze on Maggie's face as her eyes darted around the room. Anywhere but on me.

"I know you need me to say something, Trouble, but I'm having a hard time forming words right now," I told her. That earned me a small smile along with her attention. We both visibly relaxed.

Until her gaze perused my entire body and her eyes threatened to pop out.

"I wasn't sure what I was supposed to wear," I admitted sheepishly. My hands hung awkwardly near my groin as I fought the urge to cover my naked shaft.

"I just can't believe you're mine," she finally whispered.

Her claim did me in. My cock lengthened in need, and two strides I crossed the room to her, cradling her face in my hands. "We don't have to do anything you don't want to do," I reminded her.

A brush of her lips along mine and she whispered, "The same goes for you. We're in this together."

I grinned against her lips. "Count me in."

A promise we both needed. I sat down on the edge of the bed, drawing her between my legs, and simply let my hands wander. Due to the height difference, my face lined up perfectly with her breasts, and kissed the exposed skin in between them. A tiny gasp escaped her mouth. Maggie's hands slid through the wet strands of my hair to hold me in place as I languidly feathered kisses along the curve of one breast, then the other. My nose gently lifted the lace off a nipple, and I sucked the whole breast greedily into my mouth.

Maggie's whimpers reverberated throughout the room and my cock became a titanium rod. I wanted to play that sound on repeat until my dying breath. As I continued to lave my tongue over the nipple, I allowed my hand to graze over the length of her sex. What had once been an erotic outfit now became a lace prison. I tugged at the offensive fabric, making her laugh.

She took a step backward and held my gaze as she slipped one strap over her shoulder, then the other. The teddy slid to the floor as Maggie stood bare before me and let me get my fill. Although I didn't know which places exactly like she did, I could see that her body looked fuller. Healthier.

Exquisite. That was the only thing that came to mind as I tortured myself by staring at her like a love-drunk dumbass.

This was my wife? I got to come home every single day to *her*? What kind of gilded lottery did I win in Heaven to deserve that?

Scooting backwards, I laid down on my back, arching my hands behind my head. I wanted Maggie to take control so that I knew what pace to take things. I recognized enough of her tells that I trusted myself to follow her lead.

She crawled up the bed on all fours until she straddled my hips. "Get out of your own head, Zeke," Maggie whispered. "You're allowed to enjoy this, too."

I winced at how accurate her assessment was. "What if I'm bad at it?"

Maggie shrugged. "And what if you blow my mind? Now. Brain off. Heart on. Got it?"

CHAPTER 49
THE NIGHT
MAGGIE

I DESERVED an Olympic medal for how well I managed to hold myself back. Zeke's sculpted body was enough to make the most chaste person alive weep. And when he looked at me like he wanted to kiss the very ground I stood on, I stopped caring about what I looked like in the lingerie. No one could fake an expression like that.

Zeke wanted me, flabby skin, scars, and all.

Once he laid back down on the bed, I could see him start to retreat into his own head. Sex didn't necessarily involve a routine, and even if it did, Zeke wouldn't know it in his innocence. He focused too much on how to please me rather than experiencing the moment as we pleased each other. I needed to take charge or else we wouldn't make it through the night.

Tilting forward, I kissed Zeke forcefully, thrusting my tongue in his mouth to claim what was mine. My hips rocked upward so that my wet folds parted around the rigid cock straining against his abdomen. One of my hands snaked down to work my clit, letting my arousal coat his shaft. Zeke groaned.

I broke away from his mouth so that he could get a full view when I inserted two fingers inside my pussy. I was sopping wet by that point, my arousal making his cock slick to the touch. My middle finger barely grazed the tip of my thumb as I wrapped my hand around his shaft and started to pump.

Zeke's pupils blew out until only blackness remained.

"I can't decide how I want to take you first," I admitted coyly. "In my mouth, my pussy, or my ass."

Surprisingly, Zeke growled in response. His hand came up around my throat and squeezed, shoving me onto my back. Zeke's body hovered over mine, my knees bent near his waist. "You're not doing anything just yet."

And my innocent, sweet husband transformed into an animalistic sex god right before my very eyes.

The stilted hum of a vibrator clicked on. Zeke used the Romp Rosebud on my clit while he inserted a single finger inside. Only he didn't start the vibrator on a low setting, he went straight for gold. I panted as I lost all sense of self to the vibrations. His finger matched the rhythm, curving up inside me to reach that elusive spot that most men never find. Another finger soon joined, then a third, but it was too much sensation all at once.

My own hands twisted my nipples as my body tried to split into a thousand different directions at once. I didn't know how I could take anything more until Zeke replaced his fingers with his tongue. Stars exploded across my vision as the world faded to black. All I could hear were the gurgling sounds of Zeke guzzling my cum like it was the elixir of life.

I barely came to before he had me flipped over on my stomach with my ass in the air. "Are you okay?" Zeke whispered in my ear, his chest pressed against my back. "I just wanted to do it, so I—"

"Don't you dare start overthinking this," I warned him faintly. My soul still circled the air above us, waiting for a safe opening to return to my body. "That was the best orgasm I've ever hand in my life!"

I felt more than saw his satisfied smirk as he pulled away to kneel behind my exposed backside. "I really like this thing," he offered before dropping the clit vibrator down next to me. "It's like I have a toolbox just for the bedroom."

"*Our* bedroom," I reminded him. A sudden, savage need to possess him, to claim him, to keep Zeke away from every other woman on the planet, gripped me.

"Yes, baby, our bedroom." His voice came out as a satisfied purr.

One knuckle slid tantalizingly slow back and forth between my pussy lips. I angled my head to look at him over my shoulder, catching sight of the concentration he gave to my lower half as he did so.

I hadn't noticed before we started, but Zeke had a stack of condoms and all our new sex toys lined up on the nightstand next to the bed. He absentmindedly snagged a condom packet now as he continued light strokes along my pussy.

The buildup started to get to me.

"Zeeeeeke!" I whined, arching my back into his touch. "Please don't tease me."

"Be quiet, Mrs. Hayes, or I'll stop right now."

The use of my married name sent new waves of arousal through me. There was something so primitive about the way he claimed me. I loved being his Mrs. Hayes, especially when he sounded so authoritative like this.

"Yes, sir," I moaned. I continued to arch into his touch, letting his knuckle spread my lips further and further until I finally managed to grind my clit on his knuckle. "Please fuck me!"

"'Sir.' I like that," mused Zeke. The sound of ripping plastic drew my attention and I watched from underneath my body as he rolled the condom onto his thick cock. A lesser woman might have gawked at the prospect of something like that impaling them. I merely salivated with desire.

With a jerk, Zeke yanked my hips backwards. The brutal head of his cock poked at my opening, but didn't move any further. I started to turn around and check, but with a harsh "HEY!" from Zeke, I returned my focus to the room in front of me.

After several agonizing moments, I tried again. "What's going on?" My heartbeat thundered in my ears.

"Just admiring the view, Trouble. Are you ready? There's no going back from this."

Despite the heat of the moment, I smiled to myself. Nothing could obscure Zeke's soft side that wanted my consent down to the very last second.

"I want you, Zeke. Only you," I promised. Maybe it didn't convey enough of an emotional attachment, but it was the only truth I trusted myself to say. After an orgasm that rocked my world in this life and the next, I was liable to say anything. Even something as crazy as *I love you.*

A soft, tender kiss graced the middle of my back, and then Zeke and I gasped in unison as he finally thrust inside. While mine sounded more like relief and longing, my husband sounded awestruck as though he couldn't believe what he managed to do.

Zeke sheathed himself all the way to the hilt before we both froze in place, each of us adjusting to new sensation. My body felt full in the most delicious way; a switch flipped internally so that every neuron fired at hyper speed.

"What do you think, Mrs. Hayes? I'm really liking this version of normal." Zeke's voice sounded raspy, an octave lower than normal, as if something finally broke through his tin man chest to the real heart underneath. He pulled back slightly and paused again for my answer.

I glared at him over my shoulder. "I think you better fuck your wife before she snaps and no one ever finds your body!"

He merely preened like a peacock. Gripping one of my breasts in each hand, Zeke started pumping into me, working his way up to a new rhythm. He pinched my nipples so hard that I cried out. "Finger yourself, baby. Don't make me do all the work!"

With a half-exasperated, half-floundering laugh, I reached an arm between my legs and began massaging my clit. A moan escaped unbidden and Zeke thrusted faster. The smacking of skin on skin echoed throughout the room as he worked himself into a frenzy. His arms slid from my breasts to the tops of my thighs, holding me in place as he lifted my knees off the bed to wrap around his torso. I could already feel the bruises forming along with another orgasm.

"Come with me, Mrs. Hayes! I need you to come!"

Sweat tricked down between my breasts at the same time I felt drops fall on my ass from Zeke's face. Having abandoned my clit to help support my torso in the lift, I let my face fall into the mattress as I returned my fingers to that important little bud. All it took was a single, hard pinch and I came with a strangled scream.

Zeke joined me, roaring like a mighty dragon behind me. He immediately pulled out from my pussy to fall on his back. Although the resulting position left my legs strewn across his groin, one of which latched onto the sticky condom still on his shaft, neither of us moved for a long time.

There wasn't enough air in my lungs for me *to* move.

I hovered in that lush limbo between fully sated sleep and the urge to go another round for a long time before I felt Zeke rouse enough to remove the condom. Warm hands gripped my underarms, lifting me like a child's rag doll so that I laid flush against Zeke's chest. His semi-hard cock nestled against my lower back.

"We should go wash up," I mumbled without any conviction.

"Just sleep, baby. We'll clean up later."

Too tired to argue, I gave in and let sleep overtake me.

CHAPTER 50
THE BLISS

ZEKE

Something woke me up as abruptly as a drill sergeant screaming in my ear. Flames flickered across the ceiling from the candles still burning across the room, but it was the supple body in my arms that grounded me. With the curtains drawn I had no idea what time of day it was, nor could I tell how long we'd been asleep, only that my muscles stiffened when I tried to move them.

I gave up and instead settled against Maggie's back. Her head tucked under my chin perfectly so that I only smelled her strong shampoo. We were in her bedroom, which the housing office designated as the primary bedroom, meaning the one we were meant to share as husband and wife.

If the labels meant a lot to me before, they meant everything now. I craved to relive that kind of intimacy with Maggie again. Sex was utterly meaningless; making love with your wife, however, was far more reverent and holy than any religious experience I'd yet heard of. In that moment when we joined together, moving and breathing and living as one body, I transcended. That was the only way I knew how to describe it.

My cock grew harder between us the more I remembered, until it strained against the bulge of her ass. The need to be inside her, to feel her warmth surround me again, grew too strong to ignore.

I tentatively slid my fingers down to the soft, downy curls at the apex of her thighs, then gently drew my fingers along her slit. Even in sleep Maggie's legs parted for me and a happy sigh escaped her lips. With just a few strokes, I already had her wet enough that I slid my cock back inside her folds all the way up to my hip bone. Somewhere in the back of my mind, the possessive beast rumbled in satisfaction that Maggie fit so well around me.

I didn't want to wake her, but sheathing myself inside her wet heat brought all kinds of new sensations. Pumping my hips ever so slightly to take the edge off, I heaved a sigh of relief. This had to be what everyone meant when they talked about sex. There was no greater high. I didn't need drugs or adrenaline, I just needed Maggie.

For once in my life, I felt normal. Understood. Connected. Ours was a bond so airtight that even our bodies aligned.

With that comforting thought in mind, I fell back asleep.

* * *

"Mmm...Zeke, baby, what's going on?" Maggie's husky morning voice woke me up. She shimmied her hips, making my semi-hard penis that was still inside her move to a standing ovation. "Oh my god, are you...?!"

Maggie shot up and out of bed, flicking on the bedside lamp. She gaped at me in horror as she pointed an accusing finger to my groin. "Did you have your dick in me? *Without a condom?!*"

Without a brain firing on all cylinders, I sat up and drowsily wiped my eyes. "Uh...I think so? Why?"

She let out a strangled snarl and stomped into the bathroom. "Pre-cum, that's why!"

"What?"

A second later I heard the sounds of the shower turning on. I still didn't completely understand the fight we seemed to be having after what I would have described as the perfect breakthrough night for us, so I scrambled out of bed and into the bathroom after her.

I found Maggie inside the glass shower, scowling as she lathered up a pink loofa. "Zeke, I'm *naked*!" she screamed. Her hands shot out in a vain attempt to cover herself.

"Seriously? After last night? I know what your cum tastes like!" I reminded her.

"Cum is why I'm so pissed at you right now!" she screamed back. "Didn't anybody ever teach you how babies are made?!"

I rolled my eyes. "Yes, Maggie, I know how babies are made. I also know what the odds are that a baby could be made just because my penis entered you one time without a condom!"

"Once is all it takes! You've probably got some sort of hot guy super sperm and now I'm doomed!" Maggie hissed at me.

"'Hot guy super sperm?' Do you even hear yourself right now?" I folded my arms across my chest and waited, but after several seconds of her furiously scrubbing her nether regions, I had enough. Flinging the glass door open, I punched down on the lever to cut the water off.

"Hey! I'm not done!"

"Oh yes you are!" I hollered back. There was barely an inch between our faces. "You're ruining my breakfast with all your dumb scrubbing, so you better stop that right now!"

Feisty Maggie appeared, and she tried to pull my hand off the spigot to turn the water back on. We fought like stray cats, me holding onto the shower lever for dear life while she yanked on individual fingers to pull them off. Our free hands slapped at the other without ever meeting their mark.

"What's so bad about getting pregnant anyway?" I ground out. It hurt like a bitch when she managed to pull two of my fingers off at once.

"ZEKE!" my wife shrieked when I wrapped my hand around the lever again.

The feistiness drained out of her in an instant as she wailed plaintively, "I can't handle the thought of my body changing. I can't do it. I would rather die than see the numbers on the scale go up from pregnancy."

She slumped against the tiled wall, so I let go of the spigot. We both panted like we ran a mile. "I know that makes me a horrible person,"

Maggie continued, more to herself than to me. "And I hate myself for it. But I can't do it, Zeke. I can't look down at my stomach and see it bloated and stretched like that."

"Okay," I agreed. "Then I'll just go get snipped. Problem solved."

"What?" Maggie looked up at me blankly, as if she couldn't process the statement.

"You don't want to ever be pregnant. So I'll make sure we can't get pregnant," I summarized.

"But...but what if you want kids...someday?" she hedged. A tiny flicker of hope bloomed in her eyes.

"Maggie." I crossed the shower to her, taking both of her hands in mine. "I want *you*. Hypothetical kids don't mean shit to me when I have you living and breathing right here in front of me."

Her jaw fell open as she gaped. "You really mean that, don't you? You'll actually go and get a vasectomy if I asked you to."

"I'll schedule it first thing Monday morning." I didn't understand why she looked at me like I offered to wrangle the moon for her. She was the only reason I had anyone in my life now. And I'd let myself be skinned alive before I'd ever be so selfish as to make her carry a child, knowing how that made her feel about herself. That wasn't love.

"Brace yourself, Zeke. I'm about to climb you like a tree," was all the warning I got before she sprung herself at me.

Turned out I could eat my "breakfast" just fine from the bathroom floor.

CHAPTER 51
THE RETALIATION
MAGGIE

Zeke and I struggled to keep our hands off one another after that. Our Sunday chores took twice as long because of the frequent interruptions. When Zeke left shortly after lunch and came back with a Plan B that he retrieved from the emergency pharmacy on post, I dropped to my knees and gave him a blow job right there in the apartment foyer.

"Can we…uh…go back to the bedroom and try…something?" Zeke panted as I worked him in my mouth.

I grinned around the head of his cock, fluttering my lashes as I looked up at him.

"Yeah, like, right now!" There wasn't a moment for me to react before he looped an arm around my waist and hauled me over his shoulder, caveman-style. I giggled and playfully kicked my feet. He smacked me hard on the ass in response.

Dumping me on the bed, Zeke proceeded to rip off the simple t-shirt and yoga pants I wore. He growled in approval upon discovering I didn't have on a bra or panties underneath.

His mouth descended on my clit, his tongue creating lazy circles around the swollen bud. All of my nerve endings fired at once. I wanted to jump out of my very skin from the pleasure building. In one quick move, Zeke removed his own shirt before returning his tongue to my pussy, hastily using one arm to fully remove his pants that were still bunched around his knees from my hallway blow job.

"You're so wet for me, Trouble," he moaned. Pausing to softly blow air on my clit, Zeke glanced up at me in wonder. "Is it always like this? Does it always feel like the world's on fire and the only way to keep myself together is to be with you?"

All the lust gave way to that gooey, melting feeling Zeke always gave me. "No, baby, it only feels like that because what we have is so special."

Zeke gave a satisfied nod, pleased by my explanation. "That's what I thought.'

Without warning, he inserted three fingers inside, stretching my walls for a few quick pumps before he slid the same fingers back to my asshole. Drenched with my arousal, Zeke circled the fingers around until my body relaxed enough to let one finger, then a second enter. I was no stranger to anal sex, and actually found it quite enjoyable when the guy knew what he was doing, which seemed to intrigue Zeke when we looked at toys. His tongue continued to flick across my clit while the two fingers gently thrust in and out of my ass.

The orgasm built at the base of my spine, causing my knees to quake. I gripped the duvet cover with both hands as I cried out, "Yes, baby, just like that!"

His tongue moved faster with the encouragement and my body finally gave in, the climax tearing through me so my teeth chattered. I was barely coherent enough to register the sound of plastic tearing as Zeke ripped open a condom and slipped it on his length. An awkward pause followed, making me lift my head to check on him.

Zeke stood at the edge of the bed and guided the cock ring dildo down as far as it would go on his shaft. The ring didn't widen enough to meet the base of his cock, and I recognized the apprehension on his face as he glanced up at me for reassurance.

The sight alone made me want to cum.

"It's okay, baby, it's still going to feel good," I promised.

Zeke nodded and climbed over me, letting the dildo slide against my lower abdomen as he hovered on his elbows. "You are absolutely perfect, Maggie," he murmured. "Thank you for being with me."

I didn't know if he meant being with him physically or being his wife, but in that moment, I only felt grateful for all of it. *I am so damned lucky!*

Smiling, I arched my head up to tenderly kiss him. "There's no one else I'd rather be with." I stretched an arm up to grab one of the bottles of flavored lube from the nightstand before jokingly holding it up. "You need to use a lot of this if we're doing what I think we're doing."

"Yeah?" Zeke took the bottle and sat up on his knees, slathering the dildo that bobbed underneath his rigid cock.

He did a doubletake between the bottle and my bum, indicating when he realized adding more lube to my back door would be beneficial, too. Slathering it on and using the same two fingers to massage the rim, the strong scent of strawberries filled the room.

"I'll never look at berries the same after this," Zeke chuckled as he returned to hover over me. "I much prefer your vanilla smell to this!"

A stunted giggle broke free, cut off when the head of the dildo notched at the entrance to my asshole. Zeke guided the head of his cock up and down the slit of my now soaking wet pussy. I willed my body to relax so that it would accept the double penetration. It wasn't every day your husband made one of your sex fantasies come true!

"I don't want to do this if it hurts you," Zeke hedged.

"You would never hurt me, Zeke."

With his mouth hanging open in ecstasy, my husband gradually inserted both his cock and the dildo into their prospective entrances. Both of our eyes rolled in the back of our heads as we collectively panted in desire. The exquisite sensation of his cock pressing against the walls of my pussy and hitting the toy sent waves of pleasure through me. He moved with painstaking precision, pausing every few seconds to ensure I adjusted to the double intrusion and didn't voice any pain or discomfort.

It was the enraptured way Zeke watched me, however, that might send me over the edge. So much love shone through his eyes...I didn't even care what I looked like. My cellulite and freckles didn't make him love me any less. The size of my boobs or the way my hip bones jutted out weren't taking anything away from our connection in that moment. Because they truly didn't matter. The way we felt about each other mattered so much more than anything as trivial as my weight. My weight didn't define my worth.

The dildo bottomed out sooner than Zeke's abnormally large dick, so he settled into a rhythm with both before leaning down to capture a nipple in his mouth. I reached down to work my own clit. He moaned around my breast, the sound laced with sin and sex appeal. Another orgasm crescendoed as the passion between us skyrocketed.

Passion blazed in his eyes as we came together, something so pure and honest, that I knew came from a molecular level. Our souls merged. We both smiled in unison.

I had never felt so loved.

Something changed between us that day. I finally saw us as a real couple, recognizing that I was now half of a whole. I could visualize our future together as a tangible thing whereas I used to see it more in the abstract way of "seeing where things went." I didn't need to see, I already knew. Zeke was The One.

Without discussing it, we both knew that we would sleep in the same bed that night, and another bloodcurdling orgasm helped me sleep like a rock. At some point in the middle of the night, I rolled into Zeke's naked body and woke him up, so the whole thing started all over again.

I woke up the next morning happier than ever.

This is it. This is love, Margaret Hayes.

Except I was too scared to tell him.

All that joy had to go somewhere, however. Even though I didn't hold much in stock by social media, I created a Facebook account just to see the goings on back in River's Run. Maybe I could offer to run the accounts for Marla's bakery and help get her a broader range of customers. Every legitimate business had some kind of social following now.

After a couple hours of surfing through the profiles of the girls I hated in high school, a message popped up with a name that chilled me to the bone.

Wesley Madden.

HI, MAGGIE. I HOPE YOU'RE DOING WELL. DO YOU STILL LIVE IN RIVER'S RUN? I TRIED TO CALL CELESTE A FEW TIMES, BUT MY NUMBER COULDN'T GO THROUGH.

I paced the kitchen as I contemplated what to do. Celeste cried herself to sleep for weeks after her daddy died, in part because Wes, the only other boy she ever needed, disappeared that same afternoon. Then I held her hand as she sobbed all over again for months when she discovered that Iris was on the way. Nobody deserved that kind of trauma, yet my best friend lived through it and became all the stronger for it. Wes didn't have the right to waltz back into her life like nothing happened.

While he *did* deserve to know about Iris, it wasn't my place to intervene. Everything could implode for Celeste and that was the last thing I wanted to happen.

As much as it hurt, I knew what my response had to be.

HI, WESLEY. IF YOUR CALL DIDN'T WORK, THAT SHOULD TELL YOU EVERYTHING YOU NEED TO KNOW. CELESTE IS A BIG GIRL NOW AND CAN DECIDE WHO SHE WANTS TO SPEAK TO. CLEARLY YOU AIN'T IT. PROBABLY BEST THAT YOU LEAVE HER ALONE.

I blocked him afterwards for good measure.

I automatically reached for my phone to text Celeste and warn her about Wesley's message. If he kept trying to call her, it was only a matter of time until he managed to get through. But then I imagined how I would feel if Zeke reached out to Celeste behind my back, how hurt I would feel if I knew. Celeste decided on her own that Wes no longer had a place in her life. That was her decision to make, not mine.

Setting the phone down, I sighed heavily. Growing up kind of sucked sometimes.

The front door opened and closed, and soon Zeke joined me in the kitchen. "Hey, Trouble," he greeted me with a smile and a kiss on the forehead. "Are you ready to head to counseling?"

"Yeah, baby, get changed and I'll meet you in a few minutes." I smiled back at him before he disappeared down the hallway.

Right as another message popped up, this one making it hard to stifle the scream that followed.

SPENCER CHURCH: LISTEN, CUNT, YOU BETTER HAVE MY MONEY SOON OR NEXT TIME I'LL BLOW THE PLACE UP.

With it followed a photograph of the front of Marla's bakery. Construction was much further along now, with a sign etched into the glass window and everything, so I knew it had to be recent. Marla herself stepped out of the doorway in the candid shot.

Spencer could be ruthless, but he'd never been so reckless. Desperation must've made people do really crazy things.

Which was why I needed to come clean with Zeke. Things with Spencer had to end.

* * *

Zeke noticed my detached attention during our counseling session, but I managed to rally enough to make it through. Barb congratulated us several times on our "successful" homework assignment and said that she felt comfortable with stopping the joint sessions.

"But why?" my husband asked incredulously.

"Because we managed to bring you two closer than ever, and now Maggie has someone in her corner that she can rely on. She knows you have her back, Zeke, and sometimes that can make all the difference in the world!" Barb grinned at us triumphantly before nodding in my direction. "That also means there's no more hiding from the truth, Maggie."

Not this again…

"Barb, I told you, I don't need to talk about my mother. She's crazy, and she's not in my life."

"But she's in your head," countered Barb, "and that's what we have to make peace with. Your anorexia will never be cured until we cut it off at the roots. Diana is your root."

Maybe it was the threat looming over Spencer's message. Maybe all the mixed feelings over contact with Wesley again after so long got to me. Maybe I simply wanted to go back to the happy bubble of that morning, waking up to Zeke pushing his way inside me. Everything seemed so much simpler then.

No matter which way you sliced it, I had too much bottled inside that had to come out.

"I will NEVER be cured from anorexia!" I shouted, jumping to my feet. "This is who I am, Barb! So what if it started with Diana? Who cares? It's going to end with me! I am going to beat it because I want to, not because I've 'made peace' with my goddamn mother!"

Zeke reached forward to hold my hand, just a simple touch to anchor me. I wasn't alone anymore. I never had to be alone again.

To my surprise, Barb began to clap. "Bravo, my girl! What a breakthrough! This is exactly what I needed to hear from you!"

Tears began streaming down my face as exhaustion hit. All of the emotions collided and suddenly I couldn't bear to stand in that room for another minute. I needed to get home, with Zeke, so we could have the dreaded "talk" and figure out what to do next.

"Can we please go?" I pleaded. "I…I've had enough. For one day."

"Absolutely, my dear. I'll see you on Thursday at our usual time. Have a good night, you two!" She waved us out of the room without further ado.

I slumped against Zeke as we made our way up the street to the shuttle stop. He remained quiet and simply steered us in the right direction. We managed to make it all the way into the apartment and through our nightly bedtime routines, settling into what had become our marriage bed, before I finally broke the ice.

"Look, Zeke, I need to tell you something important, and I need you to really listen before you react, okay?"

"Sure, Trouble. What is it?" Forever the White Knight, Zeke scooted closer and brushed the hair from my face, hanging on my every word.

"Right before we got married, I got into…some trouble. Real trouble. Not the kind you think of when you call me that." He nodded in encouragement for me to continue. "I owe someone money. Like, a lot of money. More money than we have just lying around."

Zeke paused for a moment. "You mean Spencer, right? You owe Spencer this money."

A lump welled in my throat, but I fought back the tears. I had to be accountable for my actions and that included confessing to the act. "Yes."

"And why couldn't you tell me before?" he asked thoughtfully.

The question I feared he'd ask, that might very well end our marriage. The lump in my throat grew bigger.

"Because," I sniffled, "I was afraid to tell you why I owe him the money. I don't want to lose you, Zeke. You mean everything to me."

For the first time ever, he pulled away from me, putting as much distance between us as the bed would allow. "Do you love me?" Zeke's voice had that authoritative tone to it, his Army voice that made soldiers fall in line. When he used it with this line of questioning, the tone made me tremble in fear.

I wanted to answer him. I really did. But as hard as I tried, the words wouldn't come out.

"Then I guess it doesn't matter why you owe him the money, does it? At the end of the day, you still won't put me first. That's all I need to know." Without a further glance in my direction, Zeke swept from the room and slammed the door behind him.

CHAPTER 52

THE REQUEST

I**T DIDN'T MATTER** what time of day it was back in the States when I called Leggett. I knew he would answer as soon as he saw my name on the caller ID.

"Finally come to your senses?" he greeted on the first ring.

I swallowed thickly and idly wondered if it always tasted so bitter to eat crow. "Yes, sir. I'm sorry for my actions. I'd like to come back."

Leggett grunted, the closest thing I would receive as far as acceptance went. "You'll have to come back to Stewart for the time being. My promotion is still being negotiated. Don't worry, I'll have you in front of the promotion board in no time, too."

"Thank you, sir."

"Are you going to divorce her?"

"What?" Panic set in as Leggett asked the one question that would get through to me.

"Now that you've realized your mistake. Are you gonna cut her loose so that you can stay focused on the mission? The Army doesn't need anymore married pansies. We need human weapons with the ability to kill at a moment's notice. Get rid of her."

"General, I ca—"

"Don't worry, I'll take care of it when you get back," Leggett interrupted me. "I'll have the paperwork pushed through within twenty-four hours. Stand by."

I gritted my teeth as I slipped back into my old self, the obedient servant who never questioned or fought back. A snake reverting back to its shed skin. So much for a new normal. "Yes, sir. I'll be ready."

Sleeping alone in my room felt wrong. How had I been so happy for such a short period of time? Is that what love usually felt like, rare highs in a sea of extreme lows? I hated the way I still kept an ear out for Maggie. So much so that I heard her tiptoe into my room hours later. A hoarse whisper cut across the room.

"Zeke?"

I remained frozen in my position, keeping my breathing slow and my eyes shut. Yeah, looking at her would signify I was awake, but it would also sever the remains of my heart in two, and I didn't have that in me just yet. I needed time to slowly sink back into my old habits to keep everyone at bay. Feelings hurt too damn much.

When I didn't respond, she slowly crept out, taking a small part of me with her.

Leggett must have called in special favors to get the paperwork pushed through in record time because Whittenburg barked for me to report to his office before we were done with first formation.

"Heading back to Stewart, I see," the staff sergeant read from the paper on his desk. "We were told this is an emergency transfer. That you're to be on a plane, ready to report back to General Leggett himself by Friday."

Rather than respond, I stared straight ahead at the spot over his shoulder, keeping my stance rigid. The old me barely spoke, right? There was never anything to say.

"Clear out, soldier!" Whittenburg snapped.

I just reached the doorway when he added, "And good luck to you and your wife. I hope things get better for you back home."

Home. Yeah, right.

By the time Maggie arrived back at the apartment after her first shift at the salon, I had most of my bedroom packed in boxes. The furniture all came as temporary pieces anyway. I listed all the household items we purchased on arrival on one of the housing websites military families frequently used. Several people were on their way to pick things up.

"What's going on?" Maggie asked. A tremor made her voice shake, but I refused to look up.

"I'm being transferred back to Fort Stewart. We have to clear out of here within a day so I'd get packing if I were you. I put some boxes and tape in your room."

"What? We just got here! I thought you said we'd be here for at least a year or two!"

I shrugged as if it didn't matter. "The Army can do what it wants with me. You're free to go wherever you'd like."

"Zeke, c'mon," she said tearfully. A thin hand grabbed mine before I could pull away. "Don't be like this."

As much as I knew it would sting, I had to pick at the freshly formed scab. "Do you love me?" Like the good soldier I was, I focused on something just over her shoulder rather than look her in the eye.

A sob broke free as she answered. "That isn't fair!"

I shrugged again. "Sometimes life isn't. Now if you'll excuse me, I'm gonna go pack up the stuff from the kitchen. A few people are stopping by to look through it."

The hollow feeling in my chest from before, the days that I now called B.M.—Before Maggie—returned as I strode past her.

CHAPTER 53
THE RETURN
MAGGIE

BECAUSE ZEKE REMAINED SO diligent in selling our belongings, he ended up sleeping on the sofa while I slept with a blanket and cheap pillow on the empty mattress in my room. There were too many people coming and going throughout the evening for us to have a chance to talk again. But I knew it wouldn't do any good to try anyway. I broke everything when I couldn't admit the truth.

And I still didn't understand why I struggled to say it. I felt it, with my whole heart. I loved Zeke. That was as natural as drawing my next breath.

Saying it out loud, however, didn't feel natural. Every time I thought of telling him, I went through the same emotions as I did with my purging obsessions. There was some kind of mental block preventing me from admitting my feelings to him.

Going through the motions the following day seemed like more of regression than a relocation. We signed with the movers who arrived to load up our stuff, then Zeke headed into the housing office to sign us out of the apartment.

I called Seo-yeun to apologize for not returning to work. She didn't seem to mind, having worked with so many Army wives before. She wished us well on the move and the ended the call with a click. I only worked there for one day, after all.

The finality of what I lost hit me hard with that click. We had a *life* here at Humphreys. A life I didn't want to lose.

There wasn't even enough time for me to say goodbye to Barb.

Zeke returned so we could head out to the airport. From the outside looking in, he acted like a typical attentive husband. He carried both our bags, kept track of our tickets, boarding passes, and passports, and always waved me in front.

We made it all the way onto the plane before he spoke to me. "Once we get back to Savannah, I'll drop you off in River's Run."

I waited for the rest of his statement. When it never came, I clarified, "And you'll be…?"

His jaw clenched. "I'll go on post so I can get a room."

"Another apartment for us?"

Finally, he turned to me. "Maggie, you won't be going with me after this."

Horror rooted me to the seat. There was an emptiness to his gaze that I didn't recognize. With all the people on the plane around us, I would cause a scene if I started crying the way I wanted to. That fact probably served as a prime motivator for Zeke to tell me the news right then.

Instead, I turned to the window and let the tears fall freely.

The layover this time landed in Dallas. Zeke offered to get us food, but I ignored him and powerwalked to the next gate. We had close to six hours to kill; I would spend every single minute of those six hours with my headphones in if I had to.

A decision that immediately exasperated Zeke. "Don't be like this, Maggie. You know this is for the best."

Nobody else waited near our gate, so I whirled on him with a vengeance. "Don't tell me what I know, Zeke Hayes! None of this makes a lick of sense!"

He slammed his carryon down before kicking backwards into the seat. The impact left a small dent. "Goddamn, Maggie, just tell me that you love me! There's no way that you don't feel this, too! I don't get why this is so hard!"

More tears filled my eyes, but I blinked them away. "I don't either," I whispered.

* * *

The Savannah Airport looked cold and gray when we landed. I managed to get a few hours' sleep on the plane while still keeping my distance from Zeke, but I felt haggard and weary beyond my years.

Zeke picked up a rental truck and we silently headed back to River's Run. His own truck was lost in transit somewhere, never arriving in Korea, but no longer parked on post here.

Seven times I tried opening my mouth to say something. To yell at him for being foolish. To declare my love for him. To cry over what he wanted us to give up. But each time, I remembered Barb's advice on not letting my emotions do the talking. "Not every thought in your head has to come out your mouth!" she always told me.

I missed Barb something fierce. She would tell me exactly how to handle things with Zeke.

As we passed the sign for River's Run late in the afternoon, panic really started to set in. This couldn't be good-bye. I didn't want this to be the last time I saw Zeke.

We were almost to Main Street when I finally burst out, "Spencer says I owe him five thousand dollars. He threatened to blow up Marla's bakery if I didn't pay him."

Zeke's head whipped around in my direction before he pulled off on the side of the road. He put the truck in park before turning his whole body to face me.

"Why does he think you owe him so much money? And what does Marla have to do with it?"

There was no sense hiding it anymore if I already lost Zeke anyway. "Because the last time I went to his place, I accidentally knocked over some drugs he had on a table. I think it might've been cocaine. The shit went everywhere. Spencer's always been a bit of a dealer, but usually it was small potatoes—weed, maybe a little X here and there. Something harder would've been a step up for him."

My husband pinched the bridge of his nose in frustration. "So let me get this straight. You accidentally ruined a drug dealer's stash, so now he's threatening to kill Marla? Where does she fit into this?"

Chin wobbling, I sniffled back my tears. "He's using her as a way to get to me. Because I left and he couldn't find me. If he knows we're back in the States, he'll probably try to come after you, too." That thought sent a shiver down my spine.

"I'd like to see him try." Zeke sighed from the weight of the world on his shoulders. "Do you have a means of contacting him?"

"I can message him through Facebook. I deleted his number as soon as we got married."

The statement earned me a small smile that I couldn't return.

"Tell him to meet you someplace out in the open, someplace discreet, okay? This guy sounds like a lunatic and I don't want to run the risk of anyone nearby getting hurt." Zeke put the truck back in drive, pulling back out onto the road.

"Like the old canning factory?" I suggested. "The company built a fancy new building closer to the highway a while ago, but left the original building. Teens use it as a place to meet up and smoke on the weekends. No one will be there now."

Zeke nodded. "That's perfect. Tell him to meet us there at ten o'clock tonight, and I'll have his money."

I gasped. "We're gonna pay him?"

"We're gonna end this," came Zeke's cryptic reply.

Another shudder made the hair on my arms stand up, so I didn't question him any further. Until it dawned on me right as we pulled into Marla's parking area.

"Why are you doing this? You don't have to help me if we're…if we're not…"

"Because no one gets to threaten you, Maggie. Whether we're together or not. You're not a burden, you're a gift, remember?" Zeke's voice sounded as cold and detached as it had our entire journey back, but I couldn't stop the hope that bloomed in my chest. He still loved me. I had a chance to fix this.

And I knew exactly how to do it.

CHAPTER 54
THE MEETING

AFTER DROPPING Maggie off at Marla's, I drove straight over to the sheriff's station. I only met Sheriff Hillsborough the one time, but he seemed like the kind of man who had a lot of respect for someone in uniform. Spencer's reputation in the community aside, I figured I could get the sheriff to at least listen to what I had to say.

"What can I do for you, boy?" Hillsborough said when I entered his office.

I held out my hand for a firm handshake. Men like him thrived on respect. "It's Sergeant Hayes, sir. We met several months ago when Marla Doyle had that rock thrown in her shop window."

Hillsborough returned the gesture. "Oh, yeah. Nice to see you again, son. What can I do ya for?" He sat back down behind his desk and waved me towards one of the seats across from him.

"Do you know anyone in town by the name of Spencer? He's young, around twenty years old."

The sheriff nodded. "Sure, Spencer Church. Been a thorn in my side his whole damn life. Why do you ask?"

"Well, sir, I'm pretty sure he's the one who damaged Marla's window. He's been threatening my wife and Marla for several months now." Small towns usually cared about violence against women, right? The sheriff had to take something like this seriously.

"Who's your wife?"

"Oh, Maggie Hayes—well, I guess you know her as Maggie Eaton." Saying her old name was akin to saying a slur. It left a nasty taste in my mouth that I immediately wanted to rinse out with strong mouth wash. What if Maggie decided to go back to her old name after this? It would be like our time together never happened.

"Yeah, I definitely know Maggie!" Sheriff Hillsborough sounded surprised by my wife's name. "Never thought I'd see the day that she got hitched. And to a decent fella, too! Didn't you say 'sergeant?'"

I frowned at his commentary. "I'm not sure how to take your statement, Sheriff."

He shrugged as if what he meant was harmless. I considered it anything but. "Only that Maggie had a bit of a reputation herself around here. Just like her mother. Wouldn't imagine either one of 'em sticking with one guy very long. It's not their way."

"You're wrong!" I fired back, much louder than I intended. "My wife is *nothing* like Diana. She is loyal, and sweet, and everything good in this world, so I highly suggest you talk about her as such. She's also being threatened by this Spencer guy. So I'm asking you, man to man, uniform to uniform, what are you gonna do about it? Because I'll serve you Spencer's head on a plate before I'll let him hurt a hair on her head!"

Both of us sat in shock at my sudden outburst for a moment. Hillsborough looked dumbstruck. Maybe nobody ever talked to him like that before, or maybe I truly overstepped my bounds, but desperation made the speech for me. I needed to know Maggie was safe.

"Alright. Tell me exactly what's going on," Hillsborough finally said. He grabbed a pen and a fresh sheet of paper, pausing for my answer.

"I'll do you one better, sir," I offered. "Do you know the old canning factory?"

For the next thirty minutes, the sheriff listened to my story before he pulled out the old blueprints of the building. We established the best places for cover and high ground and then dispatched units. Maggie texted me somewhere over the course of the meeting that Spencer agreed to the time and place.

I held out my hand again when we finished. "Pleasure doing business with you, sir."

"I'll see you soon, Sergeant," he agreed.

Once I returned to Fort Stewart, there would be no going back. I understood now why Maggie had been too afraid to tell me what happened with Spencer. And while I still didn't know exactly why she went to his house to sleep with him, I knew the actual details didn't matter when I loved her as much as I did. That was why I still had to do everything in my power to protect her.

Could I give that up? Could I walk away from the love of my life because she didn't love me back?

Barb once told us during a couple's session that love isn't a feeling, it's a verb. It requires constant action and reiteration. We had to make the choice to love one another every day or our marriage would never work.

I always chose Maggie. Across all sense of time and space, I'd choose Maggie. But if she didn't make the same choice, we were dead in the water.

At least when I left, she would be safe. That could be my final gift to her.

Marla and Celeste both sat next to Maggie on the couch when I returned to Marla's apartment. All three women were teary-eyed, clutching one another and catching up on everything that happened during their time apart. Although her friends both greeted me when I arrived, Maggie kept her eyes trained on me as I continued down the hall to change in the bathroom. Even through the walls I felt her gaze waiting for me to emerge.

After quickly donning plain jeans and a slightly rumpled blue t-shirt, I returned to the living room where the ladies still cried as they swapped stories from the past five months. If Maggie mentioned that we were splitting up, none of them showed it.

"Hayes, you're a sight for sore eyes!" Marla said. She broke away from their huddle to stand up and give me fierce hug. I stiffened, surprised by the contact, though it wasn't altogether unpleasant.

"Yeah, thanks for bringing our girl back looking so pretty and new,"

Celeste chimed in from the couch. Maggie leaned her head on the woman's shoulder in thanks. "I just can't get over how much I love your new hair! And there's definitely something different about you, Maggie. What's the secret? Some fancy Korean lotion?" She chuckled lightly over her own joke.

Maggie glanced at me before replying, "A happily married life will do that to ya, I guess!"

"She's eating again," I cut in.

All three women turned to me. Marla and Celeste appeared startled while Maggie shot bolts of lightning from her eyes.

Marla snorted. "Sounds like you're implying that Maggie here doesn't know how to put food away! This child packs in more sugar than sweet tea!"

So she hadn't told them yet. About her eating disorder, the way I found her in the bathroom that night, or all the hard work that came after. An entire portion of her life and only I knew it existed.

Maggie pleaded with her eyes for me to stop talking.

"Yeah, well, it's normal for people to struggle when they move overseas. They don't make food there like they do at The Comfy Cushion," I offered instead.

She mouthed the words "thank you" that neither of them caught. Celeste and Marla both seem to accept that answer because they immediately started chattering about something else instead.

I turned to leave so I could meet up with Sheriff Hillsborough, but a hand stopped me.

"Are you going to meet Spencer?" Maggie asked in a hushed whisper.

I didn't say anything. The silence spoke for itself.

"Zeke, no! He'll hurt you! Maybe even kill you!" She blanched at the thought.

She definitely didn't expect me to snort in response. "Maggie, I hate to break it to you, but I signed my life away on a dotted line when I enlisted. My sole purpose on this planet is to keep people like you safe. I'm just doing my job."

"Then I'm coming with you!" she insisted. The hand wrapped around my wrist tightened in challenge. Maggie wouldn't let me break that hold.

There came all the fire and sass Maggie always had. It wouldn't do me any good to argue with her.

"Fine, but you'll have to stay by my side, with a hand on my belt loop the entire time. If you see a weapon, you get behind me immediately, understand?"

"You…care?" It came out as the ghost of a whimper.

By now we had Marla and Celeste's attention. They eyed us curiously over Maggie's shoulder. If they didn't know where things stood with Maggie and me yet, I wasn't going to enlighten them.

That faint flicker of longing grew stronger, no matter how much I tried to ignore it. Even with her standing right in front of me, I missed my wife and wanted things to be different.

"I never stopped caring, Trouble. All you have to do is say what you feel and things can be different."

Maggie visibly deflated.

"I thought so. Let's go."

CHAPTER 55

THE RECKONING

We arrived with plenty of time to get Hillsborough and a few other deputies set up to hear the exchange. The sheriff side-eyed me before congratulating Maggie on getting married. I nodded my approval. That counted as an amends in my book.

The old canning factory sat on a few abandoned acres of land on the edge of River's Run municipality limits. Most of the windows were busted, a few doors were missing, and a skylight formed in the roof where the ceiling caved in. Shadows cloaked everything in darkness except for the battery-powered lanterns Maggie and I placed at our feet. Just enough light for Spencer to recognize us, but not enough to see farther than a foot or two behind us.

Law enforcement got into position as Maggie and I stood in the center of the parking lot. Their cruisers parked a few hundred yards away, behind the edge of the tree line, where Spencer wouldn't be able to see.

All I had to do was get him talking.

Tires screeched as Spencer spun out in front of us. Maggie backed up several feet in fear, but I stood my ground. I faced worse enemies than this before.

"Well, well, well," drawled Spencer as he folded himself out of the dark sedan. "If it ain't the town bicycle coming back for a ride." His long hair hung limp around his face, looking as unwashed and greasy as the stained tank top he wore. I couldn't make out the shape of a weapon, but that didn't mean he was safe. The wretched stench of whiskey and weed emanating off him made my nostrils burn.

He just wants a reaction. Don't give it to him.

As hard as it was, I kept my face impassive, not even clenching my fists in response. I'd known bullies like Spencer my whole life. They looked for micro-actions to vilify their dominance. He wouldn't see a single thing from me.

Spencer cast a cursory glance at me before smirking at Maggie. "Really, babe? What, d'you need a guard dog with me now?"

"I'm her husband," I snapped back. "And I've come to end whatever you think this is."

He barked out a bitter laugh. "What I *think* this is? Didn't your little wifey tell you? She knocked over my ticket out of this fucking town as soon as she got done fucking me. That's what I *know* this is."

The same possessive beast from the party where I met Maggie and Spencer roared in pure rage. I wanted to snap the bastard's neck with my bare hands.

"Five thousand dollars seems a bit steep for a simple ticket," I remarked casually.

Even in the dim light, I saw Spencer's face contort in anger.

"Don't be a dumbass. I had a bag of pure White Boy that would have set me up just fine down in Miami. That's where you can get the good shit anyway. And that fucking slut of yours ruined it. Now, either pay up or make your peace with God!"

With that, Spencer pulled a handgun out of the back waistband of his jeans. Maggie whimpered behind me. Without breaking eye contact with Spencer, I managed to pull her so that my entire body shielded hers. Spencer smirked like he found the act amusing.

"Aw, think you're gonna protect the dumb hoe? Think she's something special? She's gonna be the reason you die tonight!" He held the gun higher in his left hand.

I couldn't help but laugh. Maggie's audible gasp faintly registered, although Spencer only focused on me now.

"You think you're gonna kill me? With that?" I mocked. "You're not even holding it right. You're a righty, aiming as a lefty, with absolutely zero training. Go ahead, Spencer, take your best shot. It's only a six foot distance—any idiot could hit me from close range!"

"EZEKIEL HAYES!" came Maggie's fierce whisper over my shoulder.

My laughter turned maniacal now as confusion distorted his features. The hand holding the gun trembled, and I noted how his eyes darted back and forth between the gun and me. A frantic glance back at my wife really set me off, however.

"Do it, Spencer! Take your shot! You're such a badass with a gun, right? I'm totally unarmed. Make your move!"

Slowly, with my hands level with my head, I walked towards him. I continued to goad him the entire way.

"What's the problem? Aren't you man enough? Can't even take down an unarmed dude in the middle of a dark parking lot? GO FOR IT. TAKE YOUR FUCKING SHOT, SPENCER!"

Spencer trembled like the junkie he was as my chest met the barrel of his gun. He closed both eyes and turned his head away to pull the trigger.

CHAPTER 56
THE EMERGENCY
MAGGIE

ALL THE THINGS you see and hear about death usually talk about when you know you're going to die. Sometimes after watching a slasher flick or reading about a freak accident, you might stop to consider your own death, but most people I knew didn't openly contemplate their last moments. And those who did only worried about the ones they'd leave behind.

Nobody ever talked to me about what it might be like to see the person you love die right in front of you. Even with all the time I spent consoling Celeste, I secretly thanked whoever was upstairs that she didn't actually have to witness Mr. Hendricks leaving this world. The last thing I ever thought I would do is watch my husband die right in front of me from a gunshot wound directly into his heart.

My scream probably woke the living and the dead in the tri-state area. Heart flatlining, eyes bulging, I lunged forward only to…

Watch Zeke sneer at Spencer in disgust. With a move worthy of James Bond himself, Zeke broke Spencer's hold on the handgun and spun it around so that he held it firmly in the palm of his own hand.

"And next time you wanna kill someone, genius, make sure you put the gun together with ammo inside." In two swift hand motions, Zeke had the handgun in three separate pieces on the ground. The echo of the metal clanked loudly in my ears.

"Oh, by the way, I never properly introduced myself. I'm Sergeant Ezekiel Hayes, weapons expert in the United States Army, and husband to the unforgettable Maggie Hayes. I suggest you remember both of those names as you rot away in prison." His fist reared back before clocking Spencer square in the nose. The crunch of the cartilage breaking echoed through the night, and blood spurted everywhere.

Sheriff Hillsborough and the other sheriff deputies slowly approached with their guns drawn. Spencer sighed before holding his hands up above his head, letting the blood run down his face. Zeke backed towards me, keeping his eyes trained on Spencer until the sheriffs had him in handcuffs, before turning to kiss my forehead.

This was beyond anything a forehead kiss could solve.

"Zeke Hayes, as I live and breathe, I will NEVER forgive you for scaring me like that, and if I have to come back and haunt you as a ghost for the rest of your life just to remind you of what you put me through, then I'll do it! I will!" Great ugly sobs broke free as I clung to him, letting his strong arms wrap around me like a security blanket.

"I'm sorry, Trouble, but I had to give Spencer enough rope to hang himself. Think of how much longer he'll be locked up now that they can charge him with attempted murder." Zeke swiped his thumbs across my cheeks to dry the tears.

"THAT IS NOT A REASON!" I shouted.

Zeke's response was cut short when Sheriff Hillsborough joined us. "You're either the dumbest kid I've ever met or the luckiest son of a bitch to ever cross the Mason-Dixon Line. How the hell did you know the gun would misfire?"

My husband snorted. "There was no magazine and he had the chamber open. I took a wild guess that he hadn't thought to load that up either."

The sheriff shook his head. "Yep, one lucky son of a bitch alright! I'll be in touch. Y'all go home now."

Neither of us could tell if I laughed or cried when Zeke turned around to look at me again. Probably a mixture of both. All the adrenaline-infused emotions flooding my system made me a tad bit batty.

A cruiser pulled away with Spencer in the back before Zeke led me back to his rental truck.

"I'm sorry if I scared you," he said, "but I'm not sorry that I made you safe. Spencer's gonna go away for a long time. You never have to worry about him again."

Crying won out over laughter now. "I shouldn't have to worry about him because I should be with you wherever the Army sends us."

Zeke put the truck back in park so he could turn to face me. I knew what he meant to ask even before he opened his mouth.

"Do you love me?"

That goddamn question!

"I can't live without you," I replied tearfully. And truthfully.

"That's not the same thing, Trouble, and you know it." Zeke sighed before putting the truck back in drive and heading back into River's Run. Silent tears streamed down my face the entire ride. I made no effort to stop them. Let him get a good, hard look at the misery he created.

He pulled up in front of Marla's apartment, but didn't park the truck to signify he would come in with me. "Tell Marla I said good night. I'll be in touch."

"When?" I demanded.

Rather than answer, Zeke got out and came around to open the passenger door for me. Reluctantly, I accepted his hand to climb down. Even with the threat of Spencer gone, Zeke walked me to the door. Only now he kept at least three feet of distance between us the entire way.

"Good night, Maggie."

I watched him walk away until he reached the door of his truck.

"Zeke!" I called out.

He paused, watching me warily.

"You're not a burden either. Not to me. You've been the greatest gift a girl like me could ever have."

Before he could reject me again, I raced up the stairs to Marla's apartment.

Celeste had to get home to Iris and Marla needed to wake up early so a contractor could come in to install the marble countertops for the front part of the bakery, meaning both were already gone or in bed by the time I got back. There were only a few more final touches and then Marla's Sweets would be open for business. Thankfully, that meant I didn't have to answer a million questions when I walked inside because the adrenaline crash made me start shaking. It would take me a hundred sessions with Barb to process what just happened.

I tossed and turned for hours. I loved Zeke. Who he was, everything he did for me, the way he made me feel. My life had done a total one eighty since we met, and when I reflected back on that infamous night where I stepped on the scale and lost myself...Zeke was the only reason I picked myself back up. I was no longer the same person, thanks to him.

My clothes fit differently now. I no longer spent hours a day putting on makeup. It was kind of hard to put any on without a mirror to see the finished effect. After I finally took the plunge and chopped off all my hair, my morning routine took me only a quarter of the time it used to.

But I also received compliments far more than I ever had. Marla and Celeste both accused me of "glowing" when I first walked through the door. Even a haggard day of travel halfway around the world hadn't dimmed it. Barb frequently commented on how healthier I looked. I even had people stop me on the street in Seoul to tell me they liked my hair or how pretty my eyes were. People noticed me for entirely different reasons now.

It wasn't just the outward appearance, though. I *felt* better. The days when I managed to eat some of the food on my plate for all three meals made Zeke burst with pride, making me grin from ear to ear. I carried myself differently, with my shoulders back and my head held high, and Barb's lessons in the background to remind me that I had everything I needed to overcome my eating disorder.

Strength didn't come from taking the road with every obstacle. Strength came from recognizing your own limits and adjusting your course. Zeke was my navigator from the beginning. I got stronger because of him.

I loved him. He deserved to hear that from me. He deserved to *know*. Barb, of course, had been right about everything. Love really was a verb, action constantly in motion. And I had to act fast if I wanted to keep the man I loved before he did something crazy like divorce me.

Nope, we were in it for the long haul now, poor guy. He'd have to deal with my sassiness for a good long while.

"I love him," I said aloud to the room. Just to prove I could. Visualizing Zeke's face, I tried again. "I love *you*."

Righting wrongs needed to start at the source, I realized. Zeke needed to hear the words out loud because the one person who should have said them to him never did.

By the time I finished getting ready, streaks of an orange sunrise peaked over the horizon. I selected an outfit that I bought recently from a street vendor in a Seoul marketplace. They had a small "changing room" that was really a narrow tent, but the way Zeke's eyes lit up when he saw me still sent a thrill of pleasure to my belly. It was a simple shift dress that flared out a bit right before it hit my knees. The rich plum-like color somehow made a perfect backdrop to all the colors in my hair. I liked an outfit that let my looks do the talking for me. I needed that kind of confidence boost for what I was about to do.

I hoped Marla wouldn't mind if I borrowed her car, but since I didn't hear her stirring yet, I didn't want to wake her if I didn't have to. Silently slipping the keys from the hook by the door, I headed out.

Thankfully by now I was an old pro at using military gates. I stopped next to the military policeman with my Army dependent ID already in hand.

"Do you know where I can find General Leggett's office, by any chance?" I smiled in a way that I hoped conveyed coy innocence.

The MP smiled back. "Why yes, ma'am. You're going to head down this main road here for a few miles until it curves around a bend. Take a left before you hit the commissary."

If Zeke hadn't explained what things on post looked like, those directions would have been worthless. Navigating the roads carefully because of the soldiers running in physical training formations, I managed to find what I assumed were the General's offices fifteen minutes later. There were already several cars in the parking lot. That was a good sign.

A young female soldier sat at a secretary's desk and greeted me when I entered.

"I need to see General Leggett," I demanded.

"Do you have an appointment, miss?"

"No, but I need to see him anyway."

The girl blinked a few times as though she questioned my mental faculties. "I'm sorry, miss, but that's not how things are done. What is the nature of your business and I'll see if I can set you up with an appointment."

I shook my head. "Sorry, toots, but that's not gonna work for me!" I swept past her and entered the first door to my right, which turned out to be a utility closet. "This will go a lot faster if you just tell me where I'm going!"

"Ma'am, I'm gonna have to call security! You can't just—"

"I NEED TO SEE GENERAL LEGGETT!" I screamed at her.

A door to the left burst open and an officer with the coldest eyes I'd ever seen stomped out. The patch on his chest read *LEGGETT*. Bingo!

"Sir, I'm so sorry, I have no idea who this woman is, and she—" the young soldier started to sputter. Leggett held up a hand to stop her.

"It's alright, Malkin, I'll see her in my office now." The general turned a reproachful look on me. "This way."

I followed him into a large office. An oversized desk, sans computer, sat on the far side of the room. A large world map had been tacked onto the wall to my left and a bunch of pins stuck out of various places. There were no photographs anywhere, nothing that made the space personal in any way. It was just as cold as the man who moved to sit behind the desk.

"What can I do for you, ma'am?" Leggett stared me down as I stood awkwardly near the door.

"Well, for starters, you can apologize to your son, Zeke!" My hands fisted on my hips as I let the full Southern girl out.

Leggett scowled, leaning back further in the desk chair so he could fold his hands over his abdomen. "All right, you have my attention, Miss...?"

"It's 'missus,' actually!" I snapped. "And let me just tell you something, I know exactly the kind of man you are! You're a coward! A cold-blooded coward!"

"Listen here, I don't know who you think you are, but I don't generally let people storm into my office and accuse me of nonsense that is none of their concern."

I bristled like a mama bear catching a hunter with her cub. "This is ALL of my concern! You abused Zeke! Hit him! Hated him! Made him think he's worthless!"

"So you're the wife." Leggett cut me off before I could say another word. "You're the reason he can't follow orders anymore."

"He doesn't need to follow your orders!" I seethed. "My Zeke is kind, and sweet, and loving. God, he's so damn loving! No thanks to you."

The general shook his head with a smirk. Like the whole thing amused him. "You can leave now. I don't have to listen to this."

Rippling anger seared through my chest at his callousness. Leggett truly didn't care. He didn't know how.

As much as I hated letting him see the weakness, a single tear trailed down my cheek. "You're not even worth it. Zeke is so much better off without you."

"Hayes only matters if he is significant on the battlefield!" General Leggett barked. "I have no time for sissy men who might get everyone around them killed! If Hayes is going to be the weak link now, he has no business being in my Army!"

"Zeke matters *to me*! I don't give a flying fart in Finland about your Army! How can you be like this about your *son*?"

The general leaned back in his office chair, a cold, calculating look on his face. "That boy is no son of mine. Now leave my office."

More tears leaked out, but I jutted out my chin defiantly. I pitied this man who would never know more than the sterile walls of this office. "That *man*," I growled, "is my husband and the only real family I have. We have no use for you in our lives anymore. If that means Zeke has to get out of the military, then so be it. As long as we're together we'll be just fine."

"Hayes isn't equipped to do anything other than be a soldier," Leggett sneered.

"Yep. No thanks to you. But that's not what makes a house a home. Zeke and I will figure it out. And we'll do it together because you stand by the people you love."

I didn't bother wiping the tears from my cheeks as I slowly backed towards the door. Only two steps in, I hit something solid and two familiar hands grabbed my biceps to keep me from falling.

"Maggie?" Zeke croaked over my shoulder.

Spinning on my heel, I found his warm blue eyes swimming with hope. Zeke barely moved as his very being waited for an explanation. All the air in the room seemed to still.

"Hayes, I suggest you get a leash on this woman until I can push through the annulment paperwork," Leggett called out angrily. "Get her out of my sight!"

"No." Zeke didn't so much as blink as he kept his gaze trained on me. A small smile tugged at my lips, eliciting a tiny smirk from him. "My wife and I will be leaving now, and I will not be reporting to your office again."

General Leggett shot to his feet, making the desk rattle and my trance end as I jumped in alarm. "Are you gonna throw your career away for a piece of ass, boy?!"

Zeke straightened to his full height, pulling me behind him to shield me from any more of Leggett's vitriol. "I'm gonna go find my own version of a happy ever after…with my wife, Maggie. Anything less than that just won't cut it."

He whirled around and grabbed my hand, leading us out together as the general continued to shout threats of ending Zeke's military career at our backs. We made it all the way to the parking lot before he stopped abruptly to face me.

"Can he really kick you out of the Army?" I asked. I didn't want to be the reason Zeke got a dishonorable discharge.

Shrugging, Zeke replied, "It's not against the military code of conduct to have a wife. I'll probably get the ass chewing of my life when I report to my new unit because I mouthed off to a general, but I have a feeling I can take it." He chuckled before sobering. "Thank you for defending me back there, Maggie. You didn't have to do that."

"Yes, I did. He's so out of line, treating you that way and acting like he gets to call the shots on our marriage! I couldn't let him drive a wedge between us, and—"

"Maggie?" interrupted Zeke. "Do you love me?"

A slow, wide smile crept across my face. Golden light from the early morning sun highlighted the angular set of his jaw, a shiver trailing through his body as I wrapped my hands around his neck and pressed my body against his. Whether it was a reflex or happiness, Zeke's arms entwined around my waist to hold me close, Army regulations be damned. He looked so handsome in his uniform, a knowing twinkle in his eye.

"Zeke Hayes, I love you more than life itself."

CHAPTER 57
THE FUTURE
MAGGIE

"And we even went to a penis park!" I giggled to Celeste. "I swear to you, I have the pictures, there is an honest to God park you can visit there that has these penis statues everywhere!"

My best friend's jaw fell open as my husband snorted into his coffee mug beside me. We sat at the counter of The Comfy Cushion, regaling Celeste with more tales of our brief time overseas. Celeste had never traveled further than Atlanta and found our stories as wild as dragon fantasies. She kept wiping down the same forks as she hung onto our every word.

I may have embellished a bit in response to such a captive audience.

"Yeah, it's all for a fertility god or something, like we have to worship the penis to get lots of babies!"

"Babies, huh?" Celeste prompted with a grin. "And when are we gonna talk about babies for the Hayes family?"

Her jest may have been playful, but a wave of distress washed over me. I still couldn't bring myself to come clean about my eating disorder with her. She was my best friend, and I knew she wouldn't judge me, yet somehow telling her about what I had been doing all these years made me too ashamed to admit the truth. Barb always encouraged me to take the time I needed. She said it was up to me to decide when I was ready to come clean.

"Actually, Maggie and I decided we aren't going to have kids," Zeke supplied. "And at the end of the day, that's a choice only the two of us can make, so it's really no one's business but ours."

Gratitude surged through me. Zeke didn't want me to disclose my body dysmorphia if I wasn't ready. He gave me an out while politely reminding Celeste that our family making decisions weren't up for debate.

God, I loved this man.

Celeste appeared momentarily stunned before nodding. "Of course. Being a parent is a serious job. No one should do it if they don't want to."

I could tell that she wanted to pry more, though. We never actually talked about our futures since Celeste's had sort of been decided for her and I was too chicken shit to actually think about mine. Most people in River's Run just assumed women wanted to be mothers. It was more of an expectation than an outright desire. Not a lot of critical thinking involved.

"I love being Iris' godmother and if you ever bless me with any more honorary nieces and nephews, I promise to spoil the shit out of them," I vowed. "Motherhood just isn't something I want for myself. I don't think I could handle a pregnancy."

Her signature small smile made an appearance, then vanished. "Iris might be all I have."

Should I tell her about Wes reaching out to me?

Guilt swirled in my gut as a mental war raged between the two sides of my conscience. If telling Celeste about Wesley's message did more harm than good, what would be the point of saying anything?

Yet she deserved to know. I would want her to speak up if Zeke tried to reach out. Not that I would let him go after this.

As if he could read my thoughts, Zeke smiled and placed a comforting hand on my thigh. He leaned in close to my ear to whisper, "I'm so proud of you."

"For what?"

I glanced down at my plate, assuming it had something to do with how much I managed to eat. Half a slice of wheat toast and most of the fruit on the plate were gone, which didn't seem like much to some people, but Zeke knew my eating habits better than I did by now.

"For admitting something so hard to Celeste. That takes guts." Zeke placed a gentle kiss to my temple and I warmed at his praise.

"Ugh, get a room, you two!" Celeste griped. She stuck her fingers in my water glass and flicked the droplets at us, making all of us laugh.

The temperature of the room fell by several degrees as Desiree, Celeste's stepmother, entered the diner behind us. My best friend's joy instantly evaporated and Zeke immediately threw a couple twenty dollar bills down on the counter when he sensed me bristling with rage. I had already told off one parental figure that morning. Why not continue down the list?

Zeke wrapped a firm arm around my shoulders to steer me towards the exit, nodding to Desiree as we swept past. I waited until we crossed the street before shaking him off.

"I had a right to tell her where to shove it!" I argued.

"Always getting in to trouble," he teased. "I have no doubt you could've insulted that woman from here to Doomsday, but Celeste didn't look like she needed that right then."

My shoulders slumped as I accepted the truth of that statement. Desiree still pulled all the strings when it came to Celeste.

Zeke took my hand in his, trying to distract the depressing thoughts. "I love you, Mrs. Hayes."

It worked, damn him.

"I love you more, Mr. Hayes."

Since Zeke still didn't have an assigned unit to report to after the disastrous meeting with General Leggett, we had nothing but time until someone from his new chain of command notified him. We continued down the street, hand in hand, while I pointed out all the local businesses and their corresponding town gossip.

"That over there is Mike Greenwald's sporting goods store. He actually played football for Georgia State, and if you give him enough of your time, he'll recount every single play he ever made while on the team. Some of the hunters in the area are *still* trapped inside, waiting for him to shut up!

"And that little boutique up ahead? Sandra McCleary owns it. She makes her daughter, Willa Jo, model all the clothing, even though none of it fits right. Willa Jo hates it so much that she threatened to burn the whole shop down! All the kids at school made fun of her because her clothes were so damn ugly.

"Now, across the street you can see—"

"My word, Maggie, what happened to you?" Diana's voice cut me off, and I instantly felt as if I was sinking into a pit of quicksand. Her calculating eyes assessed me, starting with my feet in what I realized were scuffed up flats all the way up to my sheared hair. A hand came to her chest as if Diana was so stricken with the changes in my appearance that she had to catch her breath.

Everything might have changed in my world over the past several months, but time stood still for Diana Eaton. Her long brown hair still hung in stringy curls along the side of her face, and I could tell just from sight that she had to use way too much hairspray to get them to hold. Thick makeup coated her face that either she didn't know how to blend in at her neck or did not match well to her skin tone. I recognized one of my old dresses, one that I discarded for being too tight and itchy, on her lanky frame. For once, she was without a male presence of any kind, and I couldn't help but wonder if she was just leaving a man's house or on her way to one.

Rather than say anything, I merely nodded, and pulled Zeke around her. I had no desire to engage in conversation with this woman.

"You really don't have anything to say to me?" There was a hint of surprise and intrigue to Diana's voice that I've never heard her use with me before.

Sighing, I turned to face her so she could see the honesty in my expression. "No, I don't."

"But I'm your mother!" Her harsh whisper was followed by a quick glance up and down the street. Couldn't have a potential boyfriend know her real age.

"Don't even use that excuse with her!" Zeke balled up his fists as he stepped towards her, ready to defend me like I did for him earlier in Leggett's office.

I reached out to grab his wrist, minutely shaking my head. No, this was something I needed to do. In fact, I had needed to do it for a long time.

As I cautiously approached her, Diana's cold assessment began again. "Not sure what possessed you to cut off all your hair like that, but then again, looking like a man is all the rage these days. Good luck keeping that man's attention when he can't separate you from all the soldiers around him!" She giggled like she just made a witty joke.

"I don't care about your opinion," I said simply. And as the words slipped out, I could practically feel the shackles freeing from my wrists. "I love my new haircut. I love the way it makes me feel. Make whatever comments you want, but they don't matter to me anymore."

"Honey, I'm only trying to help you! What is a good looking man like that gonna want with a girl who doesn't take care of herself? You look like you've gained weight since I saw you, too. Honestly, Maggie, what has gotten into you? I taught you better than this!" Diana gestured to Zeke behind me before sadly shaking her head with another perusal of my body.

In the past, comments like these would have led me on a self-hatred spiral. I would have immediately gone to the bathroom to perform my ritual, marking up all the areas in the mirror that she pointed out to me before forcing myself to purge everything I just ate down at The Comfy Cushion. I would have cried in the shower as I washed myself, letting her criticisms drown out all the other noise as I repeatedly told myself that I was ugly. For the rest of the day, I would've refused to eat, probably even foregoing water in case it led to any bloating. I would have jumped on the scale at least a dozen times until I saw the numbers drop.

The allure of that spiral hung in the air like a phantom. It beckoned me to follow, to return to my old patterns. To fix all the things that made me such an ugly duckling. I didn't deserve a gorgeous husband like Zeke Hayes. Not when every word she said was true.

Except…none of it *was* true. Having short hair didn't make me look like a man, and even if it did, why did that mean I was any less worthy of love? Love had no sight, no scales of judgement, no sense of merit. Zeke showed me time and time again that he loved every single thing about me.

You're not a burden, you're a gift.

And in that moment, I didn't really care about Zeke's love for me as much as I cared about my love for myself. I had such a long road ahead of me. I still couldn't eat a full meal. Desserts sent me into a panic attack. Mirrors made it too easy for me to fall back into old patterns. But I wanted to get better more than I wanted to keep letting Diana's comments control me.

"I hope that someday you find out what love truly is. Maybe then you'll be lucky enough to meet a man like Zeke, who sees everything on the inside, beauty and ugly alike, and loves you anyway. Until then, I want nothing to do with you. Good-bye…Mom."

Somewhere in my heart of hearts, the little girl desperate for love smiled, taking the phantom and shackles with her as she disappeared. Barb would be so happy with my progress.

Grabbing Zeke's hand again, I led him down the street toward Marla's bakery, leaving Diana sputtering in confusion behind me. He didn't say anything, but the resulting squeeze and gleam in his eye let me know that my declaration meant the world to him.

Marla herself stood outside in the middle of the road, shouting out instructions to two men on a forklift installing the new sign on the outside of the building. Shielding her eyes from the sun with one hand, she ordered the guy on the left to raise the sign a quarter of an inch.

"No, a quarter! A QUARTER! I swear, don't they teach fractions at school anymore!" lamented Marla.

Zeke and I exchanged a grin as we walk up to stand beside her.

"It looks real good!" I smiled at the cute sign that she had custom made for her bakery.

"It'll look better when these two nimrods figure out how to make things level!" Something about our appearance caught her eye enough for her to drop her hand and look at us dead on. "Y'all look like you're about to head out on an adventure. What's going on?"

"Oh, we'll find some kind of trouble," I agreed cheerfully. I shot Zeke a conspiratorial wink.

Marla's attention shot back to the sign. "C'mon, did they send a couple of idiots to do this?! Newborn babies have better eyesight than that, fellas!" Without another word, she stormed towards the lift.

Zeke pulled me flush against his chest, one hand sneaking up to cup my cheek while the other held me in place at the hip. Instinctively, my own hands followed, pinning him to me, a slap-happy grin on my face.

"See, Trouble, even Marla knows what to expect from you!" he teased.

"Um, I believe she said *we* look like we're going on an adventure!"

There was no doubt about the love that flooded his eyes as he gazed at me. "Then what do you say, Mrs. Hayes? Care to go on an adventure with me, every day, for the rest of our lives?"

I pursed my lips as I pretended to contemplate the question. He grinned in response, his mouth drawing closer to mine.

"Alright," I agreed. "You can count me in."

EPILOGUE

Zeke

Seven Years Later

"STAFF SERGEANT, there's a phone call for you!" The private's hands trembled as he waited for dismissal in the doorway to the conference room. Several other members of the chain of command sat around the table as we wrapped up our final briefing before the holiday break. Piss poor reception in the building meant we all resorted to using the landlines, but the only person who had the number was my wife, making me jump to my feet in fear.

"Thanks, Baldwin," I replied before skirting around him. I pointed to the desk phone that lay on the paperwork, clearly where Private Baldwin answered, and instructed him to transfer the call into my office. Being a staff sergeant now meant I had my own designated workspace as one of the perks.

"Maggie," I breathed into the phone as soon as the line clicked over, "what's wrong? Are you okay?"

"Everything's fine! I just wanted to double check that you're absolutely certain you don't want me to pack another swimsuit for you." My wife's voice sounded an octave higher than usual with giddiness. I could hear thuds and bangs echoing through the line, making me wince at the mess I knew would be waiting for me when I got home. Maggie didn't know how to pack a suitcase without leaving our bedroom a disaster zone.

"Baby, I'm pretty sure three sets of swim trunks are plenty for a cruise. I don't even own another pair."

She snorted. "Yeah, because I only got you three when I went shopping for this trip. Sometimes it's like you don't even know me at all."

I couldn't help but laugh. Maggie still earned her nickname. Trouble with a capital T.

"We're just finishing up here, so I'll be done soon."

"I know. I made that Baldwin guy tell me before he went in to get you. He's terrified of you, in case you were wondering." Maggie sounded far too gleeful at the idea that one of the people in my unit was afraid of me.

"Just pick me up in about a half hour," I replied, unsuccessfully stifling a laugh. "I love you, Trouble."

My wife's smile beamed through the phone. "I love you more! See you soon!"

We would soon be en route to the Phoenix airport so we could fly out to Miami and meet Celeste, Wesley, and their family for an eight day cruise to Turks and Caicos. It would be our first time seeing them since they got back together and they insisted that they wanted a real "family" vacation with Maggie and me. Marla would be there along with Celeste's grandmother. Maggie had been obsessively counting down the days on our calendar for months.

I hadn't spent much time with Wes, but he already seemed like someone I could count as a true friend. Even after all the time adjusting to my diagnosis and learning more about social expectations, friendships were hard for me to form. Wesley didn't have the best people skills either, so Maggie said we got along like two peas in a pod. Whatever that meant.

After my fall out with Leggett, Maggie and I only stayed at Fort Stewart for another couple months before I received orders to Fort Lewis, followed by almost immediate deployment orders to Afghanistan. That deployment was a real testament to Maggie's and my love for one another. We grew so much stronger as a couple when we relied on infrequent video calls, emails, and care packages.

Despite my fear that Maggie would start to purge again, she made it through the deployment without a single incident. She found another great therapist and fully committed to her program. The time apart let her focus on really developing her sense of self outside of our marriage. I had never been more impressed or proud to call her mine.

After three years in Lewis, eighteen months of which I spent on deployment, I came home and we moved again to our current duty station at Fort Huachuca. We managed to get a year in here before I had to deploy again. By that time, Maggie established a pretty steady clientele as a hairstylist. She used all her free time to go to the community college and earn an associate's degree in business management so that she could open her own spa and salon. We agreed that once I hit retirement eligibility for the military, I would get out and she got to pick where we settled permanently. I had a strong feeling we would return to River's Run, though.

Diana tentatively reached out to Maggie about a year into my first deployment. Their relationship wasn't great, from what she shared with me, but it was a work in progress. As long as Diana kept her opinions of Maggie's features to herself, I found a way to tolerate her. She even came out for a visit once we moved to Arizona.

Maggie had warned me that this cruise would be a special occasion. For some reason, I had to pack my dress uniform for the occasion and she packed one of the gowns she wore to a military ball. As long as I got to experience it all with her, I didn't care what we did. Maggie was where my world began and ended.

"Look at that sexy, Mr. Hayes!" She leaned out the window of my truck as she pulled to a stop in the parking lot outside my office. "I bet he's got some hot wife back home!"

A few of the guys heading to their cars laughed. One even gave a wolf whistle in response as I climbed into the cab of the truck beside her. The grin on my face grew wide enough to hurt as I murmured, "Oh, she's a total smoke show!" before kissing her fiercely. We broke apart to beam at each other like the lovestruck fools we still were, then Maggie headed for the highway.

I read once that couples experienced something called "the honeymoon phase" which lasted about a year after first getting married. Supposedly, that was the stage where everything still seemed blissful and exciting until the realities of marriage set in.

That phase had yet to end for me. Everyday I woke up with my head on Maggie's chest, hearing her heartbeat steadily in my ear, felt like the most twisted sense of reality. Her beauty still took my breath away while her sassiness always made me laugh. I didn't see a single sign of that changing.

I now had a family, thanks to her. Marla treated me like I was her own son and Celeste regarded me as the equivalent of a brother. There was nothing I wouldn't do for Iris, who made me nearly tear up when she called me "Uncle Zeke" for the first time. I loved them all. Me—the kid who never even knew what love was until that Shiny Girl struck me dumb at a party.

Any adventure she wanted us to take, she could count me in. We found our new normal, after all.

* * *

Maggie

I bounced on the balls of my feet, looking through the crowd for Wesley's mop of blonde hair. As the tallest person in our family, he would be the easiest to spot so we could get on the ship together. Zeke's hand squeezed mine tightly to keep me in place, and without looking at him, I knew the crowd of people around us made him anxious. My bouncing only worried him that somehow I would get hurt.

"Easy now, Mrs. Hayes, or I'll have to restrain you," he warned.

"Oh no! I forgot the handcuffs!"

An older couple walking past us along the dock gave a scandalous grunt. They hurried away with genuine shock on their faces.

Zeke snorted. "I can't believe you just said that in public."

"Well, your toolbox isn't really complete without them!" I shrugged, flashing him a deceptively sweet smile.

The "toolbox" as Zeke still liked to call it, had evolved a lot since our days in South Korea. We both enjoyed incorporating new toys in the bedroom, and I'd worn out my fair share of dildos copied from a mold of Zeke's dick while facing deployment alone. Since this was our first real vacation in several years, I packed everything to ensure we had plenty of options to celebrate in our room the whole time.

"I'm sure we'll make do." Zeke nodded towards the crowd. "There they are."

Celeste and Wes appeared and Iris raced over to envelope us in a hug. "Aunt Maggie! Uncle Zeke!" Marla and Nana came up in the rear, and I had to bite my tongue so I didn't laugh at Nana's shirt. As yellow as a highlighter, the shirt's neon pink letters declared SUNS UP, TITS OUT.

Only someone as bold as Celeste's nana could pull off a look like that. My feistiness would never match hers.

After a slew of greetings and hugs, some tears and laughs, the seven of us made our way up through the line and onto the ship. Wesley insisted on paying for suites for all of us in honor of the occasion and a complementary concierge led us to our rooms. Iris bunked with Marla and Nana, and Zeke and I had our own. I swore up and down that we didn't need an ocean view or private deck, but Wesley wanted to splurge.

I think he liked blowing his dad's money after everything his dad put him through.

"Okay, we have to be up on the deck by six, so don't be late," Wes called out to everyone before we entered our assigned rooms.

"That means I'll be down to your room at five on the dot, Cee, so you better be dressed!" I warned. "I will literally pull you two apart, if I have to!"

Iris looked up at Marla in confusion. "Why wouldn't Mama and Daddy be dressed?" she asked quizzically.

Zeke, Nana, and Wes all tried to cover their laughs with coughs.

"Thanks for that." Celeste shot me a Mom Glare. I stuck out my tongue in response.

The door closed softly behind us, shutting out all the sounds of the ship. Our suite had a dining table with four chairs next to a kitchenette along with a living area that included a sectional couch and oversized television. Sliding glass doors led out onto our private deck that had a small hot tub.

Zeke opened a door to the right to reveal a tiled bathroom. Bright lights turned on as soon as the door opened, revealing a shower big enough for a bench seat. A vanity mirror and a full length mirror showed our reflections, and I noted how Zeke flinched at the sight.

"I'll have those covered in no time," he offered.

But I waved it off. Mirrors no longer had the power to scare me, even if they did have overly harsh lighting like this bathroom. They held neither truth nor worth.

"Let's go see the bedroom," I suggested. Another door divided the space between the dining and the living room, which we entered to find a king sized bed and another set of glass doors leading out to the private deck. Zeke deposited our suitcases in the walk in closet while I jumped on the bed like a little kid. I whooped with delight.

"I feel like I'm missing something," Zeke said as he joined me on the bed, electing to sit politely on the edge rather than jump with me. "What's going on at six tonight?"

I plopped down beside him, slightly winded but no less giddy with excitement. "Um, they're getting married? I told you this!"

His eyes widened. "You definitely did not tell me that! We don't even have a gift! Is there a dress code? What is the proper etiquette for a wedding on a ship?"

Zeke's autism meant he tended to hyper fixate on things he didn't understand. If I would have told him ahead of time about the wedding, he would have spent every free moment in the library to research weddings, their history, cultural significance, and the ways in which a cruise wedding differed from a traditional wedding. Plus, he would have started panicking over a comparison between this kind of lavish affair to the simple courthouse wedding Zeke and I had, which wouldn't have been fair to any of us.

Sure enough, within seconds, Zeke turned to me and asked, "Is this the kind of wedding you wanted? Did we need to have something more formal like this? I want you to be happy, Maggie."

Therapy could only do so much with Zeke's obsessive thoughts. Learning about our diagnoses meant adjusting our lifestyle, communication, and behaviors so that they didn't overwhelm our partners. In Zeke's case, I knew to always allow extra time for him to process a change in his routine or an unexpected circumstance because he needed reassurance and patience.

"I *am* happy. More than happy. It's kind of ridiculous how happy I feel," I giggled. "We're going to be there as I watch my best friends get married—best friends who have loved each other since we were kids. And I get to share it with the love of my life. I'm pretty sure it doesn't get any better than this."

Zeke paused. "I think I know one way."

Like a lightning strike, my husband clamped a hand around my throat and shoved me onto my back. Instant goosebumps broke out along my arms as he pushed his way between my legs. He leaned down to my ear, still clutching my throat to whisper, "Take off your shorts, Mrs. Hayes."

Arousal pooled between my legs. My toes curled in anticipation. I used both hands to shimmy out of my jean shorts, revealing the bright turquoise bikini bottoms I had on underneath. A wicked grin crossed Zeke face, and he let go of my throat to lean back on his heels and tug on the strings on both sides of my hips. Like opening a present, Zeke gleefully folded the tiny strip of fabric down to reveal my pussy. Cool air hit my bare skin and my husband's groan sent another wave of arousal through me.

"Did you shave all the hair off?" He bit down on his fist to muffle the sound of another groan. His fingers tested the totally nude folds with featherlight touches.

"I got a bikini wax." My first in years, and Lord above, did it *hurt*. Why the hell had I done that to myself for so long? The obsessive way I used to alter my appearance felt like another lifetime.

His mouth descended on mine in a frenzy as his fingers parted my seam. The slick sounds of my arousal met my ears as Zeke trailed two fingers through before pumping them inside. He sucked my tongue like a lollipop and used his thumb to rub small circles against my clit.

Breaking off abruptly, Zeke rolled us so that I straddled him. "Get on my face," he commanded.

Back when Zeke and I first met, an order like that would have sent me into a panic. I would have hesitated, hemming and hawing over the possibility of being too heavy, making the entire encounter uncomfortable for both of us. Not that Zeke would've had the confidence to make such a demand.

Now that we both came into our own, I loved that he knew how to order me around the bedroom. My husband knew exactly how rough I liked it, and he had studied all of my cues and expressions enough that the moment I so much as raised an eyebrow, he changed positions or grabbed something from the toolbox to pique my interest all over again. And I learned that he worshipped every square inch of my body. There wasn't a freckle, wrinkle, scar, or stretch mark that Zeke hasn't traced with his fingers or tongue. He would put me on his face until I passed out from the orgasm.

It made it so much easier to love myself when I saw myself through Zeke's eyes. I liked his view better.

That was why I didn't bother arguing. I climbed up his torso and lowered myself so that I was fully seated with my pussy on his face, knees braced on the bed next to his ears. His tongue immediately speared me. I rocked my hips forward, leaning back on one arm so that I used my free hand to rub my clit. Zeke nodded enthusiastically. Both of his arms circled my thighs to help give me more leverage as my hip rotations became wilder. Cataclysmic power built at my core as I rode his tongue to chase my own release.

When it erupted, my eyes rolled to the back of my head and I fell back onto Zeke's torso. He was up and over me in seconds. Throwing my knees over his shoulders, he sheathed himself inside me in one powerful thrust. I slipped in and out of consciousness as he pistoned faster and faster, hips slapping hard against my ass cheeks, my body basically folded like a lawn chair. He came with a guttural groan and my pussy clenched around him automatically, like Pavlov's dog recognizing the war cry.

Falling into a heap next to me, Zeke kissed my temple and cuddled me while we both came down from our high.

"I love you, Mrs. Hayes," he murmured.

"I love you more, Mr. Hayes," I countered, a sleepy, sated smile playing on my lips. "C'mon, we've gotta hurry up and shower so I can get ready before I have to help Celeste."

I clambered off the bed and headed into the closet to grab my toiletry bag. As soon as I turned the water on in the shower, Zeke joined me under the spray.

"What am I supposed to do? I want to help, too." He took the loofa from my hands and massaged it down my back, making it nearly impossible for me not to purr like a cat in satisfaction.

"You're going to hang out with Wes and keep him calm," I explained. "He's gonna be a basket case."

Zeke nodded. "Yeah, this has been a long time coming, hasn't it?" By now, I'd told him everything about their twisted love story. He knew the kind of hoops they had to jump through to get to this moment.

"Now Celeste and I both get our happy endings," I grinned, leaning up on my tiptoes to place a light kiss on his lips.

* * *

A crystal blue ocean stretched as far as the eye could see, kissing the horizon all around us. The sun set at Celeste's back, bathing her in a pink effervescent glow as Iris escorted her down the aisle. I couldn't stop crying as I clutched the bouquet of silk flowers in my hand, waiting for her up at the alter as her matron of honor. Nana and Marla both had wads of tissues clutched in their hands. Just like I predicted, Wes had been pacing like a lunatic right up until the moment that Iris and Celeste stepped out onto the deck. The moment he spotted them, though, his lips puckered as he fought back his own stream of tears. Zeke kept a hand on Wes' shoulder as if grounding him, standing stoically beside him as his best man.

The moment my best friends had wanted since they were thirteen years old finally arrived. Iris, the world's most perfect god daughter, stood between them, holding both of their hands in hers. And as they recited their vows to one another, an eternal promise to love and cherish one another until death parted them, I locked eyes with Zeke, a proud smile on both our faces. It might not have been our wedding, but I renewed my promise to love that man until the end of time right along with Celeste.

We all cheered when they took their first kiss as husband and wife, even the ship captain who married them. Wes looked mesmerized the whole time, like taking his eyes off Celeste might make the whole thing disappear.

We trailed down the stairs to the public deck below where there was already a party in full swing. A DJ played pop music poolside. Zeke, Marla, and I danced with Iris while Celeste and Wes slow danced in each other's arms, lost to their own music. The party continued well into the night until Nana and Iris both fell asleep on chaises.

Our turn to dance as a couple finally arrived later in the night. Zeke spun me out before pulling me back into a dancer's hold as a slower ballad came on. My cheeks would likely hurt by morning because I couldn't remember the last time I'd smiled so much.

This was my family. Celeste and I might not have been born sisters, but we were sisters in all the ways that counted. Marla might as well have been a mother to me. Iris—and any other kids Wes and Celeste deigned to bless us with—was the perfect substitute for children of my own.

And of course, there was Zeke. The exact person I needed, who still proved every day just how right Barb was. Love was a verb. Love meant choosing that person, day in and day out, even when they struggled, even when you fell to your lowest point.

Zeke saved me in more ways than I could count. He gave love a definition, and that definition set me free. I no longer cringed when I looked in the mirror. I no longer died a little inside when Celeste or Marla assumed I wanted something sugary to eat. Nobody knew me as "boy crazy Maggie" anymore; now I was respected as the wife of a soldier. We would celebrate seven years of marriage in a few months, and there wasn't a single thing I would change about our life.

A shooting star streaked across the sky above our heads. It happened so fast I almost thought I imagined it until Zeke gasped, too.

"I could get used to family vacations like this, Trouble," Zeke whispered.

"Sounds like our new normal to me," I agreed. "Count me in."

THE END

ACKNOWLEDGMENTS

Wow, this book took a lot of my blood and sweat, and all of my tears. For a while I didn't even think I would manage to publish this story. Maggie's experiences are some of the most autobiographical scenes I've ever put to paper. I struggled with an eating disorder for most of my life, and I hope everyone who reads this book recognizes how debilitating they can be. As hard as it was to put myself back in that headspace and relive those feelings, I know I'm not the only person out there who has suffered with body dysmorphia and purging, and it was important for me to let others know they are not alone. Better days are coming, I promise.

Thank you to my core group of book club friends-Toni, Lisa, Ky, Renee, Heather, and Brooke. You kept me sane throughout this process. Additionally, Staci Leupp and Sarah Pace, having you as a sounding board for everything in the bookish community gave me the strength to keep writing. From the bottom of my heart, thank you.

To my wonderful editor, Lea, please know that this book is just as much your accomplishment as it is mine. Quite simply, you make me a wonderful writer. The fact that people continue to enjoy my books is a testament to how well you guide my pages. Thank you for sharing your talent with me.

To Kate, my cover designer, friend, and cheerleader-please never stop creating gorgeous covers. This book literally would not exist without the inspiration from your design.

A giant thanks to my sensitivity readers, Lisa and Travis. Your input was invaluable and I appreciate the time you gave to help me keep this as truthful and realistic as possible.

Toni Baker, the world's best proofreader and number one fan, thank you for being by my side and supporting me through all the ups and downs Count Me In has to offer. Our friendship means the world to me. You are simply the best!

For all the military wives who put their own dreams on hold for the love of their spouse and their families, I am eternally grateful for your sacrifice. It's not easy being a milspouse and you aren't given nearly enough credit for all the work you put in behind the scenes to keep your military members functioning.

Jack, Tristan, and Cael, my beautiful boys, I am so grateful to be your mom. I hope someday you live a love story like the one between Zeke and Maggie. Fairytales really do come true.

-SG

ABOUT THE AUTHOR

Samantha Gail is a former Probation Parole Officer who supervised sex offenders before deciding she needed more happily ever after's and decided to write books instead. Her work falls in multiple genres, primarily thrillers, romances, and fantasies. She currently resides in Ohio with her three children and three fur babies.

ALSO BY SAMANTHA GAIL

Behind My Hazel Eyes

Full Circle